WORD ON TI

BILLIBUB BADDINGS

Let me share a piece of wisdom I've picked up being the reviewer for the Dragon Page. You simply cannot go wrong reading anything Tee Morris writes. You won't find a better blend of action, humor, suspense, and romance anywhere else. Many genre authors like to mix the genres together to create a new flavor to their stories. This is the first time I've seen fantasy and mystery blended quite in this fashion. It makes for fantastic dialogue and laugh-out-loud funny narrative.

— Joe Murphy, The Dragon Page Radio Talk Show

Cynics will say that Glen Cook has already mined that concept about as deep as it can go with his Garrett P.I. stories but Morris has struck on a rich vein here. Morris cleverly plays the clichés of fantasy, detective, and gangster stories off of each other in a carefully plotted, subtly witty, action-packed thriller. I haven't enjoyed a cross-genre detective story this much since *Who Framed Roger Rabbit?*

— Michael Pederson, *Nth Degree*

Billibub Baddings is the latest from Tee Morris, who turns his attention from the swashbuckling Renaissance to Gangland Chicago. Morris is a fine storyteller, and he's done his homework in this entertaining tale that moves quickly (like a good Mickey Spillane) and keeps the reader turning pages all the way through. Personally, I can't wait for Billi to take on his next case.

— Walter H. Hunt, author of *The Dark Wing,*
The Dark Path and *The Dark Ascent*

BILLIBUB BADDINGS

AND

THE CASE OF

THE SINGING SWORD

BY

TEE MORRIS

Dragon
Moon

WWW.DRAGONMOONPRESS.COM

WWW.TEEMORRIS.COM

Billibub Baddings and the Case of the Singing Sword

ISBN 1-896944-18-3

CIP Data on file with the National Library of Canada

Dragon Moon Press
PO Box 64312
Calgary, Alberta, Canada
T2K 6J7
www.dragonmoonpress.com

Printed and bound in Canada

Acknowledgments

When I put together my Acknowledgements (the UK dictionary spelling) for my first novel, MOREVI: *The Chronicles of Rafe & Askana*, I caught a bit of heat for thanking everyone in the world and their second cousins (twice removed). But there were a lot of people that Lisa Lee and I had to thank. And with this novel I am reminded that writing a novel is many things, but it is not a solo effort. In fact, being a writer is a lot like being an actor—I'm only as good as the cast I'm a part of, and the cast behind *Billibub Baddings* is nothing short of incredible.

I've been putting her through the motions since signing that first contract, and it is my history with Gwen Gades of Dragon Moon Press that makes me appreciate her support all the more. Another one surviving the paces with me is editor Adrienne deNoyelles (a/k/a Number Two) who took me in so many unexpected directions with this dwarf detective. While she never needed to unleash the rovers on me, she kept me honest in double-checking my resources and my history.

And speaking of keeping me honest, a huge set of thanks to *The Dark Wing's* Walter H. Hunt, *Team of Darkness'* Tony Ruggiero, and *Dragon's Fire, Wizard's Flame's* Michael R. Mennenga for making a few catches that were particular to their know-how. Thanks, guys. Both Billi and I appreciate the time and attention.

Finally, there is the support team at home. VickieMom and Natalie, the two women in my life who listen to me rant, hear me noodle out idea after idea, and refuse to hold back on their feedback and opinions. The newest member of the crew, Serena Aeryn, I can't thank enough for keeping me grounded. It never ceases to amaze me how changing diapers, 3am feedings and scoring a burp brings a sense of perspective. Thank you for all the joy, love, and encouragement.

This title has been one incredible trip for me. Now, it's your turn…

DEDICATION

To Alexandria R. McGrath,
English and Humanities Teacher
Monacan High School
Richmond, Virginia

A good teacher teaches,
but a great teacher *inspires*.

Table of Contents

TROUBLE IS A PRINCESS IN HIGH HEELS

Chicago, 1929. There are a thousand stories in the naked city. And when you're a dwarf at four-foot-one, they all look that much taller.

The name's Billibub Baddings. I'm a private eye. I know you're probably scratching your noggin right now, wondering how the hell did a dwarf of the Highlands of Gryfennos get to be a detective walking the asphalt jungles of the Windy City? It's an easy story to tell, but not one I enjoy telling again and again...and again. I won't lie to you—being a four-foot-one detective in a world of six-foot thugs, creeps, and low-lifes is tough, but I manage. Just as I manage, every time, to tell the tale of how I ended up in this crazy, mixed-up world called Chicago.

Let me take you back in time, and then to the left a nudge, to the world of Acryonis. With valleys and groves greener than Hyde Park in springtime, it wasn't a bad place to hang your axe and shield at the end of a day. Where there wasn't green, there were mountainous arctic regions, rolling moors, and clear, vast lake districts. Yeah, Acryonis had it all. It could've been paradise if the noisy neighbors upstairs—Black Orcs from the North, who weren't that happy with being cold all the time—hadn't gone stirring up trouble.

The Great War of the Races began as a series of more-than-occasional village burnings along the borders of Stone Guardian Valley and the Shri-Mela Plains, and then grew hair over time...and as it was orcs who started this mess, this war grew hair in places that you wouldn't think to look for hair. This Great War (and to this day, I still don't know why they call it that, as there was nothing great about it), which started back before my great-grandfather's day, now started to pick up steam in mine. It fell upon me to uphold the great estate of Baddings—to carve out a name for myself, my future offspring, and my ancestors on the Holy Tablets of Yearnese.

Yeah, big deal. My family name and a nickel might get me a cup of java or a taste of foam from a freshly tapped keg. The "great estate of Baddings" I was charged to uphold consisted of a couple of rickety chairs, a wobbly table, and a thatch roof that leaked on rainy days. Since I really didn't have much to lose, I figured I would find my fortune in the heat of battle…thirst for glory, rattling sabers and all that.

Unlike my ancestors, I did all right for myself. Managed to make Captain of my unit. We dwarves were the best in the Allied Races, our sterling reputation with infiltration and search-and-destroy missions preceding us to the point that other races were willing to pay or barter only the finest goods for our services. We never disappointed. The 25th Dwarf Warriors Company went so far as to adopt the motto, "Don't let 'em know you're comin', but let 'em know when you're leavin.'" At least, that's a rough translation in Chicago's native tongue.

It was this particular talent of getting in unannounced and leaving with a bang (and a boom, for good measure) that got the "Stormin' Scrappies" noticed by The Council of Light. It appeared that the Black Orcs, who had fought this Great War for decades only to find themselves on the losing side, were cooking up this cockamamie scheme of taking over Acryonis by calling on the Darkness of Ish'tyis: an all-supreme evil that could make the most crooked politician look straighter than a flagpole.

I know I should be pissed beyond reason at the arrogance the orcs displayed in dabbling in dark magic, but it's more of a pity I feel. Truth be told, orcs ain't the brightest bulbs on the moviehouse marquee. They had their eyes on the prize, but hadn't considered how they would control this Darkness once it was unleashed. Instead, they kept their plan to the basics: collect the ancient talismans of Acryonis and open the Portal of Kraketia, unleashing the Eternal Night of Ish'tyis in the process.

You think these names are hard to read? Try living there.

Anyway, our counterplan was to get this crossbreed blacksmith, Sirus Hawthorne, up to Death Mountain's summit so he could drive his handcrafted toothpick into the heart of the Black Orc Barbarians' top dog. Along with Sirus and his tagalong cleric came me and my boys, leading a team of representatives from every race in the Allied Forces.

We were trying to sneak in undetected, but humans are a loud and clumsy bunch. But even with the Black Orcs closing in on us, we managed to reach the Central Chamber, where the Talisman Ritual had already begun. Sirus took on the Black Orcs' Big Cheese while we fended off his thugs. I broke free of the melee and got over to the Portal of Kraketia, and from the sounds coming out of there as it opened, I had to think fast. Otherwise, a bunch of grumpy orcs would have been the least of our troubles.

I figured the best way to separate the talismans would be to toss them into the Portal, condemning them to Oblivion in the process. As I threw the last talisman into the portal and watched the rip in front of me slowly close in on itself, it looked like the plan was working.

The only problem was that I didn't know how close "*too close*" to the portal was. As the rip became smaller, I found myself getting closer to the gaping chasm without necessarily wanting to get closer. Ahead, I could see slips of dark-blue mist quickly disappearing into a black void darker than goblin's blood; the void was growing larger, but only because I kept sliding forward towards this closing maw. No doubt about it: It looked like I was to be a final dessert for this portal's nine-course dinner.

The kind of fear I was feeling at that moment can motivate you—no matter how desperate that last act may appear—to make a final stand in order to live to see another day. To that end, I turned around and shot out a hand for this cute elf in our party, just out of arm's reach. She was a pretty little creation with finely-honed muscles, the end result of disciplined training and a few too many tours of duty in that friggin' war. There was just a touch of the wild child left in her, what with the V-cut shirts and leather armor that worked like a barmaid's bodice to push her tiny breasts up and together, giving this hardened Elvish warrior enough cleavage for a dwarf to enjoy. I looked deep into her brilliant green peepers—a pair of emeralds set in a hard, intense face framed by long, thick locks of silky fire billowing in the strong currents that pulled me ever closer to Oblivion.

Yeah, she was a cutie. Always had a soft spot for the redheads. Still do.

I remember feeling her fingertips just brushing mine...and with that, everything I knew and accepted as my world slipped away like dirty bathwater taking its time running down a slow drain. But at least

I knew that pretty little thing and the rest of Acryonis would be all right. I had done my part to uphold the all-important Baddings name. I had sacrificed my life for the tranquility of my kinsmen, and of the kinsmen I would never know.

I remember the chamber disappearing from me in a blur. I remember falling. I remember seeing all kinds of stars, like on a winter night where you can see the edge of the universe and just a yard past it. I remember the wind growing louder the longer I fell.

Then everything stopped…and I mean *stopped.* I was surrounded by that silence you hear (and to an extent, feel) after you've been thrown against the nearest wall in the middle of a tavern brawl.

So, I guessed I was done. This was it. The big sleep, and it felt like being thrown against a wall in the middle of a barfight. Damn, this was going to be one hell of an eternity!

Now, here's the funny thing about Oblivion: Everyone knows *what* it is, but no one knows *where* it is. You can consult those All-Mighty Oracles, and they will describe the same thing I've just gotten through telling you about. The stars. The wind. Flashes of light. Okay, they might skip the "being thrown against the tavern wall" analogy, as the average Oracle doesn't drink, smoke, or enjoy a good woman. (If that's the price for clairvoyance, let me forever wallow in the bliss of ignorance!)

Ask the Oracles what happens *after* the silence, and suddenly the planets are out of alignment, or the cards are refusing to yield their knowledge. If ever an Oracle answered with a simple *"Gee, I don't know…"* it would probably trigger some bizarre spell and make their heads explode or something. No, instead of 'fessing up that they're about as enlightened as the darkest part of a goblin's butt, they spew this bizarre rhetoric that makes Irving Berlin lyrics sound like Shakespeare. *"The Winds of the Future are brewing into a storm I cannot see through…"* is always an old standby of theirs.

Oblivion, as I discovered, is not the part you see, but the part where you end up. Makes sense, right? And since no one has ever come back from Oblivion, no one—not even the wizard with the biggest hat of the nine realms—knows where Oblivion is.

But now I'm here to tell you exactly where Oblivion is and where it ends. The portals of Oblivion, at least the ones I fell through, end at the Chicago Public Library on 78 East Washington Street in Chicago, Illinois, USA.

When I finally came to, my head was pounding harder than a wardrum firing up the troops before the great push. I picked myself up to make a fire and brew up a good home remedy for headaches like this one. That was when I realized I wasn't in the Everlasting Fields of Yernase. I wasn't in a forest. I wasn't even outdoors. Books. I was surrounded by shelves upon shelves of books.

I'll be the first one to tell you that I was never a bookworm. I always preferred a good battle-axe and a bad attitude over protocol and diplomacy any day. *"A good book is worth more than any treasure of a king,"* our village's elder told me once. I was forty-two then. Thought I knew everything, so I didn't really take that one to heart.

Once I found myself in this library, I knew I was standing in a vault of gold, platinum, rubies, and sapphires.

I understood enough to find my way through the simple books in the Children's section, but quickly figured out I would have to wrap my brain around human tongue (the dialect of Ro'hema in particular) because it was the prominent language here. The hard part wasn't learning the lingo (which, I found out later, was called English) so much as staying out of everyone's way during the day before coming out at night for my education.

All my previous training in getting in and out of keeps, dungeons, and fortresses without setting off traps or alerting any guards was now paying off with an intellectual interest. Here, the only thing I left in my wake were a few books out of order and some perplexed librarians wondering where their lunches had disappeared to on certain days. I noticed from the shadows that these humans were, on a whole, a bit thick in the head. I managed to work up to what they called a sixth-grade level while others continued to struggle with "See Spot Run."

Once I was done with the Children's wing of the library, I began to search for books on world culture, hoping to come across groups who practiced magic. But the only documented "magic" was hardly worth talking about. I read about something called "voodoo" that was practiced in a city called New Orleans, and newspapers often advertised traveling carnivals that featured fortunetellers and their all-knowing crystal balls alongside entertainment greats like "Alligator Boy" and "The World's Fattest Lady." And I even overheard a couple of librarians offering to read one another's tea leaves to forecast the future. These gimmicks were no better than the hocus-pocus scams in my world, pulled by failed apprentices for the out-of-towners. Not what I call magic.

The papers also kept me up to speed on the dates and daily news, teeming with stories about the Prohibition Act, the Gangland Wars, and the war waged by the Treasury Department on Organized Crime. This was where I got my bearings on the concept of time—at least, how time is measured in this world. By the time I learned what a year was and that I'd arrived in the year 1927, I'd been here for roughly four months.

And just my luck—I finally figure out the year, and according to the *Tribune*, Chicago was ready to ring in the *new* year. 1927, I barely knew ye.

As I put it all together in that moment, it felt like some invisible squire had thrown a suit of armor equal to the weight of a pregnant Cerberus on top of me. The truth finally sunk in: I had been here four months, and there was no way back home.

I felt my legs give way underneath me along with the impulse to relieve the unbearable tightness in my throat with a good, old-fashioned howl. That wasn't an option, unless I wanted to be discovered by anyone working late in the stacks. So I covered my face and let it all go, sobbing into my calloused palms every emotion, regret, and memory that had been bottled up inside of me.

You would cry too if you had the same epiphany I did: my family, a collection of dwarves that could fill a small banquet hall; my friends, comrades-in-arms of both Dwarven and Human races, and maybe the odd crossbreed here and there; my home, not a great castle by any stretch, but still mine. Gone. There were issues I hadn't resolved, a few wrongs I wanted to right. I still had a lot more to do in Gryfennos, be it as Captain Baddings of the Stormin' Scrappies, or simply as landowner and faithful subject, Billibub Baddings.

Everything—*everything* I had known—was lost. I had just spent four months in a library, and the only magic in this realm existed in works of fiction. While there were some distinct advantages to a world void of necromancers, wizards, and soothsayers, it looked like I was never going to see Acryonis again unless I had the right spell and the right mage calling it. Here, in Chicago, that wasn't going to happen.

So yeah, I cried. You got a problem with that?

When I finally removed my hands from my face, the first thing my eyes focused on through their watery haze was another librarian's lunch I'd helped myself to earlier that day. *No,* I thought, *there ain't no way I'm living like some second-rate street urchin!* I couldn't, and wouldn't, spend the rest of my life hiding in the stacks and pilfering bag lunches. My Mama Baddings had brought me up better than that. So, I gave the bootstraps a yank and committed myself to finding a place in this new world.

When I wasn't searching for something I could do to make an honest living, I turned to the fiction shelves for something light. Here, I was drawn to those mysteries of Hercule Poirot and Sherlock Holmes. Now, there was a vocation I could see myself excelling at. A detective. Why not? I could see the application of my military skills put to a daily test and kept sharp. It was, of all the different jobs I had read about, the one that I found most appealing. I remember smiling wide, content that I could find a place for myself here after all.

Then, I caught a glimpse of my transparent reflection in a window. This wasn't going to be easy.

The first thing I needed to do was to step out into this real world and get to know it better. Sure, you can learn a lot from hitting the books, but nothing beats walking your battlefield before facing the cavalry, truly knowing where you would be making your stand.

When I finally made it back to the library after that first night, I honestly considered applying for a job stacking and sorting books for the rest of my days. I'd seen a lot in Acryonis, but when you see your first skyscraper, which easily towers over the tallest keep you've seen in all your years above ground, you tend to feel a little intimidated.

Then, there were the cars. Whenever I'd overheard these humans calling this age the "Roaring Twenties," I thought in my early ignorance that this was an oblique reference to twenty-ton dragons nesting somewhere in town. No doubt, the number of these horseless coaches added to the roar of the times. Okay, so they were efficient, but they were also loud, and belched out fumes that made troll farts smell like a dozen roses! And I was going to call *this* place home?

From the shadows where I watched the humans of this world, I silently ran down the list of the Fates and tried to figure out which one I'd crossed.

I soon learned that the "Roaring Twenties" referred to the lifestyle: late-night parties at the supposedly hard-to-find speakeasies, flappers dancing the Charleston, guys trying too hard to act like Rudolph Valentino's "Sheik," and what have you. At the same time, it was also an accurate description of this city being nothing more than a cement jungle with a pack of noisy lions, all trying to be the king. The rules of the game were "survival of the fittest"—not too different from the Acryonis days.

Accepting the fact I stood out from a crowd like a desert sphinx in a pedigree dog show, I continued to slip out of the library in my most plain clothes: a simple shirt and breeches with deerskin boots. I walked the city at night, sticking to shadows and alleyways, not only getting familiar with the mean streets but also gaining some confidence. Little by little, I started to find a common ground between some parts of Chicago and a few cursed realms I'd crossed back home.

The next step was to get a bit of the green. I cased pawnshops and antique dealers, keeping an eye out for merchants who dealt in "the unique and unusual." If I found the right trader, I figured that some of my gear would sell. I also checked out local talent agencies. There was this book called *The Wizard of Oz* that everyone was raving about. (I read it in the library because I caught the word "Wizard" in the title, and I held a glimmer of hope there really was a place in this realm called Oz and maybe there was a wizard there.)

Between its popularity and Semon and Hardy's moving picture from 1925, really short people were in demand for high-priced birthday parties and special events. So I showed up on the front doorstep of the Harvey Showenstein Talent Agency one morning and became their golden boy for a couple of months. While I'm sure my ancestors weren't entirely happy with my antics as "Waldorf, the Protector of Munchkinland," it did get me those first Hamiltons and Franklins. I'm still on Harv's calling list, as a matter of fact. When business is slow, I do an occasional job for him, provided the pay is good and I'm allowed a lot of stage make-up to keep my identity in the anonymous category.

In between my numerous "Waldorf" appearances, I started looking around for two things every detective needs to begin a career in the city: office space and suits. Before too long, I found a perfect corner office overlooking the library, where it had all begun for me. When I added up the cash to see what I could start, I was more than impressed by what a novelty act could make in less than six months' time. It also helped that I wasn't already paying for a flop, thanks to the library's boiler room.

After putting cash down for the office space, furnishings, and even a secretary, I still had a nice bundle left over. While being four-foot-one meant wearing custom-made suits, at least I didn't have to worry about paying for a lot of material. I kept it simple, with pinstripes being my only luxury. According to the library's newspapers and from what I saw on my nights on the town, brown and navy blue seemed to be the fashion.

Hey, just because I'm a dwarf doesn't mean I can't take steps to look good.

So, I bit the bullet and hocked a few tools of the soldier's trade, along with the deerskin boots and leather armor. It wasn't like I was parting with any treasured heirlooms. This was who I was back in Acryonis. Wearing the suits and paying the landlord for the first month's rent was my big goodbye to the past. So began the career of Billibub Baddings, private eye.

I still had, mounted proudly on the walls of my office, my "survival gear." There was a charmed battle-axe and war hammer crisscrossed over a two-handed broadsword that, if you stood it on its tip, nearly matched me in height. I also had a reliable mace and a ball-and-chain that countered the display on the opposite wall. I'm not the sentimental type, but I did want to hang on a couple of things, just to remind me of the good times. And let's face it—these were reminders that still mattered. In a pinch, I could dust off the axe and hammer and do damage, if need be. I hadn't found a use for these weapons in this world. Yet. For now, I defended myself just fine with my modest collection of boom daggers.

"Boom daggers." Yeah, I remember calling "guns" that in my first few weeks in town. Looking back on it now, I can't help but laugh, but now and again I still like to remind myself of my origins to keep me right with this world.

Now, you might think throwing daggers and axes in battles involves nothing more than muttering a quick prayer to the Fates, closing your eyes, and throwing a blade in the general direction of a bloodlust-filled scream. I don't *think* so. You got to know how to throw, how hard to throw, and how to *aim*. Without aiming properly, throwing your weapon is just plain stupid. It leaves you unarmed, for one thing.

I was really good when it came to accuracy. (Won a couple of axe-throws in my Gryfennos days.) Turns out that my natural ability also extended to boom daggers. Not too long after I bought my first gun, I set aside cash to pay some country bumpkin for a few pointers on how to shoot. By the end of the day, I was teaching old Farmer Brown how to draw a better bead on moving targets.

In one desk drawer was a spare Roscoe, and in another drawer, a hogleg with a .38 that only came out to play if I expected too much trouble for Beatrice. Beatrice was my first gun, a. 45 automatic in its shoulder holster, draped on the coat rack. The weapons of this time were pretty impressive, and if you knew how to use them, they could be lethal. Even if you didn't, you could still do enough damage to make a guy think twice about looking at your wench in an ungentlemanly way.

Ever since Chicago was dubbed "Gangland" by some bureaucrats far off in Washington, D.C. who wouldn't know bathtub gin from seltzer water, everyone needed something done on the Q.T. Cops were either on the take, or too busy playing it safe so as not to turn their wives into widows. I took all this to mean that I had chosen wisely to pursue the career of a private investigator.

Once I got my name on the door, the clients were steady. This month, though, had been slow. I could hear Miranda outside my office door, filing her nails. Obviously finished with the paper-pushing and bill-paying duties, she was now counting the minutes to the weekend.

She was a cute, bosomy brunette from Leonard, Missouri, who had stepped off the bus with a meager life savings and a smile, determined to make it big in modeling. Her plan was to make connections here and follow the catwalk all the way to New York. The kid had potential, with legs that went up to her neck, a waist that an elf would kill for, and a good, healthy chest blessed with God-gifted buoyancy. She was almost the perfect woman in her five-foot-eight stature, but she was a bird who had brains, and that made her a dangerous combination.

I still thank the Fates that she answered my ad in the *Chicago Chronicle*. She was the fourth applicant who was easy on the eyes, but Miranda's predecessors lacked something that she had in abundance: a command of basic grammar. She not only had a way with a Smith & Corona, but could also write with a flair that would make Fitzgerald green with envy. I hired her right away. She immediately put the office to order, keeping my books balanced and the place looking tidy and nice. Even brought in a few plants to liven up the surroundings, although the modest rubber tree by my desk was silently turning a depressing shade of brown and black. Guess my thumb wasn't green enough for its liking.

When Miranda and I first laid eyes on each other, it wasn't the best of beginnings because we both couldn't stop staring. She was staring at me because—well, hell—look at me! I'm a dwarf! A four-foot-one Casanova with a thirty-something-inch waist, long red beard and braided hair in a custom-made blue pinstripe is going to catch your attention! As for me, I kept staring at her chest on account of the low-cut blouse that provided a sneak peek at what the Good Lord had graced her with. Now, I'd seen my fair share of racks strapped in chain mail, leather armor, and a wide assortment of fashion that gives the term "breast plate" a whole new spin, but there was just something about the clothing of this realm and what it left to the imagination.

Miranda finally quipped, *"Take a picture and the memory's yours forever..."* to which I replied, *"Yeah, well, not only am I a private dick, I'm also a great footstool in a pinch!"*

We had a good laugh, and the interview finally made it to Mick's, where we enjoyed java and chili together. (You got to love a girl who appreciates fine cuisine.) There, I fed her a story about parents who didn't love me, my days with the circus, and finally jumping ship to find myself a home here in Chicago. (The circus idea worked really well because I would sometimes get the odd phone call from the agent asking for the "Waldorf" routine.) She never knew the real story because, quite honestly, I didn't think she needed to know. Even though being my right arm for these many moons now (and coming up on a year…damn, I'd better think of something special to do for her!), I just don't think she needed that kind of a burden. Some secrets are best kept to yourself.

The rapid *scritch-scritch-scritch* of Miranda's nail-sculpting broke the stillness in the air. A stillness like that before a storm conjured by a necromancer's hand. My eyes stared at the words spelling out "Baddings Investigations" in reverse, gracefully arched across the smoky glass of the doorway's pane. The frosted glass caught the glow of the hallway lights, but no silhouettes of approaching customers.

The quiet times were when I grew the most anxious. I hopped down from my chair and paced the office floor, slowly stroking my long, red beard. It had been a really dry month, and my brain started to ponder, plan, and worry. I picked up my mitt and bounced a worn-in baseball against a blank spot on the wall between the baseball pictures I'd hung in my office for personality.

Of all the things in this strange world, I found a natural attraction to baseball. Don't know if it was just the spirit of competition nurtured in the sport, or the carefree attitudes of the pastime's finest. I suppose you could say that the sport had a magic all its own, and I fell victim to its spell.

I couldn't help but smile whenever I cast a glance on my prized possession: an autographed picture of Babe Ruth, posing with yours truly. It was one of those "right places at the right times" kind of photographs. Me being a dwarf, he thought I was a bit of a laugh. Imagine his surprise when this dwarf gave the attitude right back at him. That gave way to the picture of Babe, enjoying a big guffaw while shaking my little hand. He respected attitude. I like that.

The ball I now tossed was a pop fly I'd caught while in the cheap seats at a Cubs-Phillies game. Sometimes it pays to be the "odd man out."

"Billi!" Miranda snapped while continuing to file her nails. "You keep that up, and you're going to knock a hole in the wall. Landlord will have your ass on a plate."

"Eh, come on, Miranda, you know I do this when I get restless."

"I know that. *You* know that." Miranda paused in her chiding to pop her chewing gum. "The landlord looks at it as property damage, not therapy."

She had a point, but I couldn't shake this restless feeling. It was that same uneasiness I always knew before a charge against enemy ranks, battle-axe in my grasp with my fingers splaying slowly around the handle. If I were pacing the office with my axe in hand, it would have probably made Miranda's chestnut-brown mane turn white. I figured the pitching practice was a nicer alternative.

The ball bounced back from the plaster wall and returned to the form-fitting mitt with a satisfying *snap*.

"Fine, then," Miranda shrugged. "Just don't take it out of my paycheck."

"You got nothing to worry about, sweets. If anything, you deserve a raise."

I could hear the creak of Miranda's chair as she stood up and crossed the room to my own office. A second later, she was leaning against the open door frame and smiling, lightly blowing her nails clean. In the blouse she wore, her voluptuous beauties presented themselves proudly. Yeah, that's what I really love about Miranda. She knows what she's got, and isn't shy about showing it off. To that end, I did take her under my wing (a short wing to say the least) and gave her a few quick pointers on how to protect herself if any mook wanted to give her a reason. She's a good girl.

"What's that about a raise?" she pressed.

"Now, come on, Miranda." I smiled, defiantly throwing the ball back against the wall. "You know as well as anybody the book's been a little tight lately. What we need is a case that'll set us up better than some of these nickel-and-dime divorce jobs. Then, I can finally give you that raise I've been promising. The Fates know you've earned it, keeping a dwarf like me in line."

Miranda gave a heavy sigh. "You're just like all the other men in my life."

I raised a bushy eyebrow. "Four-foot-one with scraggly beards, fiery-red hair, and devilishly handsome good looks?"

"No, just telling me what I deserve but not delivering," she smiled with a mischievous wink.

"Miranda, honey." I snapped the glove tight around the ball and turned to face her. "Now, you know I don't want to mix the business life with the personal one. I wouldn't want to hurt you emotionally…" I returned her the same kind of wink. "…or physically."

She rolled her eyes and popped her gum again. "If I were given a buck every time a guy told me *that*, I wouldn't *need* a raise." Miranda measured with her thumb and index finger a space in the air about the length of a yeoman's arrowhead as I wound up on my imaginary pitcher's mound, with the Sultan of Swat threatening to send my next pitch into the Acryonis Highlands. "I ask you, Billi, since when is *this* eight inches?"

And this is yet another charming aspect of Miranda's personality. She is every inch of a woman—sultry and hot as a dragon's den, where the humid air collects against rock walls and coats the floor with a silvery sheen, one drop at a time. She also has the edge of an enchanted blade, an attitude absent from the stereotypical "small-town girl" found in the farmlands of El Hanor Durea or in Norman Rockwell's *Saturday Evening Post* covers. Miranda can talk like one of the guys, smoke a stogie with a twinkle in her eye, kick back a shot of Jack Daniels, and still keep her elegance while sinking an eight ball in the corner pocket. It is something I do love about her, and something about her that continuously catches me off guard.

I gave my next pitch to Babe a bit too much pepper. The ball impacted at a high speed, sending a few chips of paint behind the file cabinets and covering my mitt in plaster powder with a leather-kissed *snap*.

"I'm not gonna say it, Billi," Miranda said with a shrug.

"That's good, since I know you're already thinking it," I scoffed. "How about you take the rest of the day off? It's Friday. Find a nice book or bachelor to curl up with tonight, why don't ya?"

She smiled. "Sounds like a plan, Billi."

It was Friday and the clock was at three-thirty. I couldn't justify keeping Miranda in the office simply out of spite. She *had* warned me about the wall, and I'd chosen not to listen. The phone rarely jingled between now and five o'clock, anyway. Far be it from me to keep the little minx imprisoned in this cage of stone, paint, and office supplies.

She was out the door faster than her shadow could keep up.

I always enjoyed this time alone in my office—even now, with my anxiety hitting unusual levels—because this was when I sorted out the thoughts of the week. My usual ritual between five and six: across the street to Mickey's for a chili dinner special, and then a couple of blocks home to a modest one-bedroom flop. I was starting the weekend a little early myself, albeit not an exciting one by the looks of things. Eh, I never hit the town unless the mood suited me, and even then, I needed the right company. Seeing as I didn't have either, I was looking at a quiet weekend, and that suited me just fine. Maybe a couple days on my own was just what the apothecary ordered.

The tink of the bottle's lip sounded like it hit the glass hard, but it was merely the quiet of the room. It was a city kind of quiet, peppered with the soft rumble of traffic, the occasional car horn or siren, and the newsboy shouting out the headline of the *Chicago Defender* or the *Tribune*. I poured a healthy dose of Canadian whiskey and raised the glass to my lips. That warm nectar blessed my body like an old friend, sending a shudder that ale, mead, or my family's home recipe couldn't match.

Yeah, another love of mine in this world—the alcohol. Sweet Ambrosia. Sure, we were in the middle of the Prohibition, but in Chicago, it wasn't a question of how you got the alcohol, but *where*. This little vice's hiding place was a small compartment behind the team picture of the '28 Cubs. (My first season with the guys! What an arm on that Sheriff Blade!) I couldn't take the chance of any surprise visits from the local precinct. Nowadays, you needed the talents of a seer to tell who in the police was crooked and who was straight. Besides, I needed a drink. I didn't particularly like the financial alternatives facing me. Calling up Harv and dusting off the "Waldorf" routine kept reappearing as the only solution. If I had to tell one more high-society dink the way to the can was to *"Follow the Yellow Brick Road…"*

But a dwarf's got to do what a dwarf's got to do. I got responsibilities to Miranda, the business, and myself. My fingers gripped the receiver, and even the slight chill of its surface didn't sober me up enough to stop me from placing this call. I dialed the number and waited. One ring. Two rings.

Her voice made my blood go ice-cold. "Showenstein Talent Agency." It was Mabel. It was always Mabel. The woman was older than some mountains in my valley.

My mouth moved to say, *"Hello, Mabel, it's Billi Baddings…"* but I paused.

"Hello? Hel-*lo?!*" the voice crackled angrily. "I know someone's there. I can hear you breathing!"

The doorknob was turning. At first I thought Miranda had forgotten her compact, or something. Then I saw the silhouette through the window, and that was when I hung up on Mabel.

The silhouette wasn't Miranda. The silhouette was an opportunity.

She was a tall, cool woman, and through her veil I could still see, set in a pale canvas of smooth, supple skin, eyes as dark as a man's intentions on that first meeting. The perfume she wore carried a bouquet of lilacs, rose, musk, and a touch of sandalwood. In a single word: expensive. She wore her hat at a tilt to block out the slanting rays of the early-evening sun, giving her angular face an even more exotic look. Her body held every curve in just the right place, giving her frame a profile that would make a Highland Elf long for the rolling hills and valleys of home. She was tall to begin with, but the designer heels she wore made her a six-foot mountain I would take delight in climbing sometime. The dying sunlight streaming through my office window caught the cascade of hair spilling from her wide-brimmed hat for only a moment, a blanket of raven-dark hair falling to the small of her back. Her lips matched the hue of a fine Italian red wine, and in that moment, I couldn't help but feel a bit parched.

Oh yeah, the weekend was off to a good start.

"Excuse me." It was a voice that spoke to me in a dream once. She had a polished, refined tone, sounding close to the "British" dialect of this world. "I'm looking for Mr. Billy Baddings of Baddings Investigations."

"That's me."

"*You're* Billy Baddings?"

And you just asked the prize-winning question—give this girl a Cupie doll! The question never came as a shock to me, because I knew a dwarf in this realm tended to turn a few heads wherever he went. Face it: Would *you* really expect a Scrappie like me as a private dick? Ringling Brothers, sure. Party entertainer, absolutely. But a gumshoe? So yeah, this was a familiar routine to me. Familiar, and annoying as hell, but I always have to handle this routine like a pro. All I need to do is get a client in the door, and the rest is up to me to sell them on my talents in discretion.

But first, the floor show. "Yeah, I know I don't look like a Billy. I'm more of a Todd, or maybe a Brian."

Ten minutes. Ten minutes is the average time a client's shock at seeing that Billy Baddings is a dwarf glues their feet to my office floor. If I could keep her on my side of the threshold, I knew the case was mine.

"It's all right, ma'am. I know I'm probably not what you expected. You probably expected someone less handsome, less dashing, and not so much in the facial hair department. I can only say this: It ain't easy being this good-looking."

When I got the laugh, I knew we were getting somewhere. Humor was the best way to get over the whole dwarf issue. Now, it came down to the credentials.

"I know you may think a dwarf stands out in a crowd, and perhaps I do. But I can also get in and out of many places without being noticed. My specialty. It's this specialty that has built me a reputation for being discreet. I'd love to give you a list of references, but how 'private' of a private investigator would that make me? And, being a dwarf, I tend to be left alone, and being left alone tends to keep my investigations all the more private. The proof of the pudding with me is my work, and let me tell you something: I make *great* pudding."

I got the impression she was impressed.

"I'm impressed, Mr. Baddings," she nodded.

Back in Acryonis, no dwarf read the dames better than me. Yeah, I still got the magic.

"You appear to have overcome your—" And her voice ceased abruptly.

"Shortcomings?" I smirked.

She grinned with a reluctant nod. Obviously, that had been the next word on her lips. "There's more to you than meets the eye, Mr. Baddings."

"You can keep it formal if you like." I gave her that million-dollar smile that made all the barmaids of Acryonis swoon. "You can also call me 'Billi' with an 'i.' Short for Billibub."

"I hope my instinct was right in choosing you to handle this delicate matter. I need someone unshakable, someone who is a master of discretion. I cannot afford to go to the police concerning this matter. My family earns enough attention as it is."

"Do they, now? Mind if I ask who your family is?"

As her head tipped back lightly, the scarlet sunset creeping through a forest of buildings created a delicate lace-checker pattern across her face. Her posture wasn't revealing anything to me (although her blouse had a tough time concealing a tavern wench's bounty of a chest! If I weren't smiling, I would probably be staring!), and I still couldn't make out what she was thinking from either her eyes or her scent.

Part of being a dwarf involves having an uncanny ability to understand scent. It isn't magic, just a discipline that you develop the older you get. We dwarves trained ourselves to "sniff out" metals, ores, and minerals, because the more precious ones were in caverns that never knew daylight of any kind. Imagine our surprise when we found out that our heightened olfactories worked on people as well as rock. A nervous disposition gives off a bitter, harsh scent. If someone's in a happy, pleasant mood, it's sweet, like cinnamon. If someone's in that *particular* mood when the lights are dim and the skin warm to the touch…well, you get the picture.

Problem with this dame's scent was the designer perfume she wore, so expensive it cost you a buck just to utter its name out loud. Because her bottled fragrance masked her scent, I couldn't tell if she was upset, nervous, or all of the above.

Her voice didn't help matters much. "I thought you were a discreet private investigator, Mr. Baddings." As calm and even as a millpond on a cold winter's morning. Whoever she was, she was very good at this game.

"Now hold on a minute there, sweets," I said, hopping up into my office chair and positioning myself on the elevated cushion so I could appear as normal as a dwarf could behind a second-hand, human-sized desk. "Just because the door says '*Private* Investigator' doesn't mean '*Blind to Trust* Investigator.' There are always need-to-know facts between investigator and client, and those facts *stay* between investigator and client. It's a matter of protection for you, protection for me, and assurance of trust for both."

She paused, her eyes studying me through the veil. If this princess was coming in here in search of some bizarre entertainment from the commoners, she was starting to wear thin with me. I was about to tell her to buzz off when she finally spoke.

"I'm Julia Lesinger, the youngest daughter of Henry and Wilma Lesinger."

While she waited for my response, I tried not to suddenly break into a Sornomian jig. A job for the Lesinger family would not only make up for a slow week, but also set the office up for a few months and even score Miranda that raise she was fishing for! The Lesingers were the established money of the town; if it existed in Chicago, there was a good chance they owned it. Why one of the Lesingers wanted a two-bit private investigator instead of the cops was beyond me.

Then again, when you're only four-foot-one, a lot of things tend to go flying over your head.

By the time I managed to find my voice, Miss Lesinger continued. "It's my boyfriend, Anthony DeMayo."

"Wait a minute. 'Pretty Boy' DeMayo is your *boyfriend?!?*"

"*Was* my boyfriend. He was killed in the hit on Sal's Diner."

Although the hit happened earlier in the week, the news story was as fresh in my head as this morning's headlines. According to the *Defender*, only a few chunks of Sal's still remained standing after the bomb detonated. That was a real pity, too. If I was ever working in that part of town, Sal's was the best place for a coffee and a danish. Maybe the company there was not to my liking, but you couldn't beat his coffee.

"Miss Lesinger, that was no hit. What happened at Sal's Diner makes a wizard's maelstrom look like a spring drizzle."

"I know," she replied, as if commenting on the weather. For someone who lost her knight in shining armor, she didn't seem all choked up about it.

Speaking of which, I never understood why humans—even the ones in my realm—believed in this overly melodramatic image of a "knight in shining armor." The average squire couldn't polish shoes properly, and the average "knight" was usually some noble who couldn't fight his way out of a thumb-wrestle. And the way those clumsy dolts fought when wearing *full* armor, it was impossible for a squire to keep armor in pristine condition, anyway. They're a sentimental lot, humans. Eh, you got to love 'em, though.

"Mr. Baddings, I want to know why—"

"Now wait a minute there!" My hands went up as if Miss Lesinger were holding me up at gunpoint. She would have to if she wanted me to do what I thought she wanted. "Everyone knows who ordered that hit. If you want some kind of proof…"

"Mr. Baddings, you know who was behind it. I know who was behind it. All of Chicago knows who was behind it. I want to know *why*."

I could count on one hand how many murder cases I had been asked to investigate and still have digits left over for stirring the milk in my cup of java, sampling whipped cream off my ice-cream sundae, and flipping off some punk who is eyeing me up as an easy score. In that murder case, I was asked to find out "who." Once I found out the "who," the "why" would inevitably follow. But this was something different: The "who" was already understood and accepted, and I wasn't being asked to finger the man behind this hit. Good thing, too. Simply point a finger at Alphonse "Scarface" Capone in a way he didn't like (as in, "That's the guy I saw whack my cousin!") and you could not only lose that finger, but suddenly end up with the rest of you misplaced as well.

That was the way Al Capone ran the Organization. He loved telling the papers that he was simply a "businessman" answering to the needs of the people. His business, though, was something you were in for life, and in Capone's business, "early retirement" never led to a gold watch and a place in sunny Florida to enjoy the sunsets. With Capone, whether it was a double-cross or an *"I want out,"* it always led to the same end: a one-bedroom flop, six feet under.

"Just find out why?" I asked, breaking the unnerving silence we were swapping. "Seems harmless enough, but Miss Lesinger, can we agree there's nothing harmless with anything involving *La Cosa Nostra?*"

"Mr. Baddings, do you wish to have me tell you that I was daddy's little girl, never getting into trouble?" She cocked an eyebrow at me and tilted her head. "I enjoyed living dangerously, but Tony was...special. In his own way. I only ask a simple question concerning his death."

I wouldn't deny that. It was *who* I had to ask that gave me pause. "And since we're being so honest with one another, why hire me, a streetwise dwarf? Hell, everybody knows the Lesingers have their own legal team, including detectives."

"My father is hardly pleased with my public image at the moment. I wish to hire you for your talents of discretion," she continued, "keeping this professional relationship of ours out of the papers."

And no doubt, away from Daddy Dearest's attention. Blunt. And to the point. When called to the mat, it appeared that the girl wasn't shy in showing a little moxie.

"This job is gonna cost you triple." I leapt from the chair and landed firmly on the floor with a hard thud. "Hazard pay."

"Hazard pay?" she asked incredulously. "Are you sure 'costing me triple' isn't because I'm a Lesinger?"

"Miss Lesinger, you could be heir to the Throne of Zelir and promise me a dukedom, and I would still charge you triple. This case involves Capone. You follow me?"

She didn't know what to say then. She was probably trying to figure out the hometown reference. This is a tactic I use whenever I want to close a discussion or get in a last word with someone. Whip out the Acryonis allusions, and I'm guaranteed to end any conversation. It's also a lot of fun to watch humans try and noodle through whatever I've just thrown at them. I can almost hear them thinking, *"What did he just say?!?"*

"Very well, Mr. Baddings." She reached into her purse and produced five clean, crisp C-notes. "This should be an adequate down payment for three days' work at triple your normal fee. I'll return later with another payment. I will expect a progress report at that time, if you please."

Time to test the waters. "Is there anyone else I should answer to?"

"Talk to anyone other than me, I will not only deny knowing you, but I will make your life very uncomfortable."

No surprise that kitty has claws.

"That's why it says '*Private* Investigations' on the door, sweetheart. I'll talk to ya in a couple of days."

The door closed, but I didn't watch her leave. My eyes remained on the five greenbacks fanned out on my desk.

Suddenly, the neon lights outside were casting shades of pink, light blue, and green into the dim lighting of my office. It was getting late. I had lost track of time because my mind was trying to grasp my new client and my new job. Julia Lesinger of the Lesinger estate had hired me to ask Big Al '*Why?*' concerning one of his hits. It's not like he needed to explain to anyone why he did anything. He was, and still is, the Boss of Chicago. Capone's business is Capone's business.

Now, these five C-notes in front of me made it my business.

This was a serious score for a private eye, no doubt. But did the payment make the risk worthwhile? Maybe I didn't have to ask Capone outright. Maybe I could check a few sources, ask around in that subtle Baddings style I was building a reputation on. I couldn't deny this was going to be a risky job, but I also couldn't say no to the green. No, sir. There was that nagging voice in my gut telling me I was stepping into a world of hurt. But it was either this or playing "Waldorf" again.

So, Billibub, what's it gonna be?

I hadn't even finished asking myself that question before reaching for the down payment and stuffing it in my pocket. Who would have known my Lady Trouble was going to be a princess in high heels?

CHAPTER TWO
SCENE OF THE GRIME

A quiet weekend is a private eye's best friend. There were no special parades or galas planned, the ball team was out of town, and other forms of revel and raucous were either enjoying their current run or getting ready to shut down. Since nothing special was happening in the Windy City, there would be the same number of cops on the streets as usual—and those cops tended to take it slow on the weekends. No one likes to be working on a Saturday when you can be at home with the wife and kids, enjoying a picnic, or huddled around a radio enjoying a morning with the Philharmonic or an afternoon of theater. So while the cops were taking their time walking the beat and the Chicago nightlife types were catching their breath, a dwarf could expect to enjoy a day of honest work without too much hassle.

"You work too hard," I could hear Miranda saying just before popping her gum. *"Even a guy like you needs to take a break."* She never liked it when I worked weekends, and I wouldn't argue with that. I *did* work hard, even with things as slow as they had been at our office lately. But I needed to turn things around for Baddings Investigations, so my weekend began with the biggest case this little guy ever had cross his desk.

Two's a crowd when you're snooping where you're not wanted, so I got this morning started before the early bird sounded its battle cry. The trolley dropped me a few blocks shy of the corner of Kingston and D Street, where Sal's stood—excuse me, where it had once stood. Rounding the corner of a brownstone, I couldn't help but just stand there for a moment, taking in the epic scale of this mob hit. All that was left were a few stone pillars and wooden beams, charred by the heat of the fire but defying the urge to collapse into dust and soot. Maybe it was the ghost of Sal himself keeping the last shreds of his place standing. I don't know if he had paid protection money or not, but whatever his deal was with Capone, it certainly didn't protect him or the few innocents in his place when the bomb went off.

So far, my only company this morning were bakers, butchers, and various other tradesmen, sweeping their porches free of the soot and debris that had wandered over from Sal's the night before. They paid no mind to this pile of rubble that had singed the buildings surrounding it, nor did they seem to care about the lives lost. As far as they were concerned, it was a week-old *Tribune* headline that would soon be replaced by another gang-related incident. Life had to go on.

Casting a final glance over my shoulder at the merchants still busy opening their shops, I crossed the street and stepped across the threshold of scorched tile work. I was on my own for the time being, at least until the more-adventurous tourists showed up.

The locals here were smart enough to respect Sal's for two things: First, that it was a crime scene, and you only wandered through it if you wanted to announce that you were involved; second, that they considered this place a gravesite. Disturbing a grave, even in this magic-free realm, was considered an invitation to curses and bad luck. Still, there were those "mob fans" who wanted a piece of the action—a little memento of a true gangland crime.

In Acryonis, we had a name for trophy-hunting dinks like this: Lycanthrope's Lunch.

Suddenly, my eye caught sight of a tiny crater in the floor next to the remnants of a bar. This must've been where an inconspicuous, Italian-pinstriped goblin left the bomb. With nothing like a storeroom underneath to take part of the blast, whomever sat around here got the full taste of Capone's wrath. Ouch. This bomb took most of the bar and the surrounding tables with it. Good bet that ol' Pretty Boy was somewhere in this vicinity.

Yeah, Capone didn't care for anything on a small scale. He liked his hits like he liked his operas and his picture in the papers—big and brash. I think his smile irked the Feds more than anything else. It was one of those genuine "F.O." smiles, letting them know they had nothing on him but speculation, circumstantial evidence, and J. Edgar Hoover breathing down their necks demanding results. Even if I were human-sized, I wouldn't have wanted to trade places with a Fed at this point. Too much overtime, with very little hazard pay.

I placed a hand into the hole created by the explosives, rubbing the dust and soot between my fingertips and giving the mix a few whiffs. Nothing new or out of the ordinary here: It was a standard, Capone-style bomb, triggered by a timer that gave his man a chance to casually walk out the establishment and then double-time it across the street. The bagman probably looked like an innocent jaywalker trying to avoid the traffic, so no one would notice him running from the scene—especially when the bomb blew.

The stench of burnt wood still clung to the place, even after a week. From the faint traces of burnt flesh I was also picking up, it wouldn't have surprised me in the least if the coroners had overlooked a finger or toe in here somewhere. The sight of this place reminded me of orc raids that me and my boys would clean up after. Orcs didn't think a village was properly raided until everything—houses, barns, and the villagers themselves—weren't level with the ground. They called it efficiency. I call it a serious lack of self-control.

I stepped over a small pile of timbers that had collapsed to make what resembled the skeleton of a tent. Just the glimpse of it brought back campaign memories. I smiled at the chance happening, but the smile quickly faded when I caught what was hidden behind it. Shooting another quick look around to make sure I was enjoying the private time at a dead man's party, I bent down to sample the second crater. Sure enough, my fingers felt the unmistakable grit of black powder; and the sharp scent assailing my nostrils confirmed my conclusion.

Like a broadsword into a troll's gut, it now started to sink in why this crime scene had struck me as particularly eerie. Usually in a mob hit involving a bomb, the building's front gets obliterated in the blast, leaving behind a gutted-out shell that serves as Capone's reminder to everyone—be it those closest to him or not yet part of the Organization—that things are done his way. Period. It's important to have that reminder to the good people of Chicago, so lessons are not only learned, but *stay* learned. Teaching those lessons requires only one bomb.

So, this second crater was way out the ordinary. Two bombs for one hit? Capone liked his hits big, sure, but a few pounds of dynamite and a timer would have sent DeMayo the message. A second bomb, even for Alphonse, was too much of an orc's approach to things. Even the St. Valentine's Day Massacre had a *panache* to it, brutal as it was.

Unless…this was something more than the standard hit. Had "Pretty Boy" been planning some kind of *coup d'état* (I just love those French words, but they're a bitch to learn when working your way through a library!), and Capone caught wind of it? Or was he pledging his allegiance elsewhere? Had "Pretty Boy" been thinking of changing his nickname to "Stool Pigeon" and turning state's evidence? Had he reached the decision that a retirement and old age suited him better than a dirt nap at the prime of his life? What could Capone's second-in-command, sitting pretty in the right hand of the Big Boss himself, have been up to that would merit this kind of drastic retaliation?

Why? That is what my client wanted to know. Why was Capone's confidant in all matters suddenly and unceremoniously removed from his court via methods of extreme prejudice? This hit clearly wasn't intended to send a message or a warning—Capone had intended this hit to be the final solution to a problem. From the looks of this hit, the problem must've been a big one.

Hearing the unwelcome sound of other shoes against soot, I crouched lower behind the rubble and peered through cracks between blackened timbers to see exactly how many cops I was had to contend with this morning.

Well now, yet another surprise this morning for ol' Billi Baddings. The two guys belonging to the shoes contaminating the crime scene along with mine were not cops. One of them was a real behemoth, chiseled jaw and all that. The other one was his doppelganger, but shorter, definitely the runt between the two of them.

I couldn't hear a word they were saying, but guessed they weren't working for the Mob because they weren't communicating with grunts, whistles, and clicks. The drab, off-the-rack suits that probably weighed as much as your basic leather armor were the second clue.

When I noticed the duo making a beeline for the site of the first crater, my eyebrows went up. These guys knew exactly where to look for the location of that bomb, and they studied the soot and ash found there very closely, even giving it a few whiffs themselves. It didn't take an extraordinary honker like mine to get a hint of the kind of bomb used, but for humans, it took someone with the training and the talent.

"Now, wha' d'ya think yer doin'?" came a brogue thick as potato soup from behind the two newcomers to my investigation. "This is wha' we here in Chicago call a *crrrime seen*,' an' unless yer warin' a badge, yer either a corpse or a con ta be mullin' about 'ere! Bett'r thin's in Chicago ta do than disraspect tha dead, don'cha think?"

Slower than keep slime, the two guys stood up from the crater, opened their coats with one hand, and withdrew their wallets with the other.

As the suits opened their billfolds and did the ID routine, I took an opportunity to make my exit. Keeping low (which was easy for me), I stayed close to anything that would conceal my presence: overturned tables, razed foundations, burned-out booths, and so on. The cover that remained was enough for me to slip out of the ruins and into the now wide-open alleyway.

From my new vantage point, it looked like the two bombs had done little surrounding damage. When I vigorously rubbed my fingers against the worn, blackened blocks of Sal's next-door neighbor and gave my stained skin a few whiffs, I picked up those signature scents that I knew Chicago for. Engine exhaust. Coal soot. Standard city smells.

After a good, strong exhale, I took a slightly deeper whiff. Yeah, I could detect minute traces of the blast, but I couldn't convince myself that this building had been even impolitely nudged by the two bombs. The new blast scent I was picking up was a lot stronger…but it wasn't coming from the alleyway.

I returned to Sal's through what was left of the men's bathroom, daring to get caught. And there it was, just as my gut had told me it would be, where the ladies' loo had once been: A *third* crater.

The crunching of debris underfoot, much closer than it was before, reminded me my borrowed time was now gaining serious interest. It was that moment when a bard knows he's hit his final note for the evening, or when a jester drops that joke that kills. Know when to make your exit. If I didn't get out of there, and get out of there now, the cop would probably use something a lot nastier than a hook to haul my ass off of this stage!

"*That was no hit. What happened at Sal's Diner makes a wizard's maelstrom look like a Spring drizzle.*" Hey, I was just joking when I said that in my office to Miss Lesinger. Still, my own words kept echoing in my head as I wiped my fingers with a hankie, making sure I was clean of any evidence.

Now I was back in the alleyway and coming around the corner to Sal's nonexistent storefront, where the cop and two suits were continuing their Saturday-morning tea. Keeping my head down, my face concealed under the Stetson I was wearing, I took advantage of the angle to study Sal's sidewalk. While there were no real scorch marks projecting outward to indicate a blast, this sidewalk had not fared as well as that of Sal's neighbors. The damage implied this job was far from perfect. From the placement of the third crater—and if my hunch was right about possible other craters—Capone never intended to blow this place up. The Big Boss wanted to blow the diner *down*, effectively and efficiently burying whomever happened to be there that morning.

I lingered at the street corner, pretending to see if there was any oncoming traffic. It was still early in the morning, so traffic could barely be described as light. While the flatfoot continued to act like a cheerful tour guide, the suits knew this for the tactic that it was, and their hushed conversation went dead on me.

I crossed the street, then once again to the opposite corner, turning back to face the diner-in-ruins. This time, I was playing the part of a dwarf looking to hail a cab. By now, the cop's crusty demeanor had left for the Emerald Isle, and he couldn't have been more pleasant. Yeah, I guess the suits were cops after all, probably from another precinct. Chicago's Finest were working together to put on a show for the commoners, but still nowhere closer in riding the city of Public Enemy Number One.

Cute little show, but I enjoy the vaudeville at the State Theatre a lot more.

Halfway to the office, I slipped the cabbie a Lincoln and changed directions for the opposite side of town, toward Chicago City Hall and the courthouse. One of the big news stories of late was the commission for a new statue of Lady Justice to stand proudly in the center of the courthouse foyer, life-sized and elevated on a grand marble pedestal. Its completion had been slated for January, but January had come and gone. So had February. Now, it looked liked Ms. Justice, along with some of the other improvements happening throughout City Hall and the courthouse, would be unveiled sometime in the late spring. No later than the early summer, the sculptor assured *The Chicago Daily* recently.

The screws were beginning to tighten on the contractors, and no doubt a rack waited in the wings for Justice's artist. I guess those lawmakers were growing tired of the tarps and stepladders between their offices and the courtrooms. Can't say I blamed the suits too much on this one. Miranda had impressed on me the selling value of an image, and it's tough to sell the public through press conferences and photo opportunities when Chicago's legal hub appears to be a work in progress.

With all these steps leading to a set of massive doors with ornate carvings, you would think Chicago's downtown courthouse housed the finest and most prestigious of this realm. In fact, the lowest of lowlifes— low enough to make a nest of trolls look like the Rockefellers—spent enough time in these hallowed halls to call it home, if but a second one. Of course, as it was the weekend, the courthouse was quiet as well as locked up. Crime didn't take Saturday and Sunday off, mind you, but those who made the laws that got broken did.

Peeking through the crack between the doors, I could make out the scaffolding, tarps covering the commemorative plaques and busts of judges and men of history, and other signs of work crews who were either off for the day or sleeping in late only to come in and continue work later. And I could make out a few pair of coveralls lying to one side of a ladder. It was easy to imagine those guys wearing their pinstripes underneath their coveralls, painting right up to quitting time and leaping out of their work clothes before the last stroke was dry.

This was my stage. Let the play begin.

Out of a fine leather pouch, I slid out a set of favorite tools from my realm. The small pick and its longer brother had been forged from a charmed metal that would not break under any stress, even if a marsh dragon tried to use one as a toothpick.

When I "acquired" this little kit off a mercenary fighting on the wrong side of my battle-axe, the other officers thought I'd come up on the short end of the quarterstaff. Then again, I didn't travel in the same circles as those privileged dinks. The buddies I traveled with from tavern to tavern took one glance at the pouch and knew I had struck a mother lode of ore! Sure enough, a wizard passing through my village appraised the metal in the tools as being "of magical origin." Three words that a dwarf loves to hear.

The first pick fit easily into the top notch of the lock, and searched for a latch to catch. Once I struck it, the second pick slid inside the lock until it hit the bolt.

I casually walked away from the door for a moment, making certain I was in the clear. There was some weekend traffic on the street, but it was still too early for the tourists to be paying a visit. No beat cops in sight either, so I was all set to work my magic.

The last tool was a larger, U-shaped piece of metal forged into the top of a small metal rod. I rapped it hard against the door, producing a small hum from the fork—a perfect pitch.

The picks in the lock remained still until I placed the fork tongs on either side of them. The two slim rods now vibrated in a blanket of sound, and soon the picks moved on their own accord, searching for the grooves and bolts that a key would trigger. Suddenly, the top pick slipped forward while the lower turned slightly to an angle, and I heard the bolt in the courthouse's front door slide back with a loud *thunk*.

I'm not crazy about magic, but it does come in handy now and then, especially when your specialty is infiltration and reconnaissance. My bread and butter in Acryonis...and now, Chicago.

"One-Hanselthrop...two-Hanselthrop...three-Hanselthrop..." I whispered as I slipped through the massive doors. The alarm was sounding, and soon the weekend detail would wake up and find out who or what triggered the bells clanging in the main hallway. The only thing that could screw up this little plan of mine would be an eager beaver in his first day on the job.

"Ten Hanselthrop...eleven Hanselthrop...twelve Hanselthrop..." I now had my coat off and was drowning in the smallest of the coveralls I found by a covered paint bucket and a set of wide brushes and rollers. Regardless of humans' height, everything was big on me, but nothing that I couldn't solve by rolling up sleeves and pant legs.

"Seventeen Hanselthrop...eighteen Hanselthrop..."

Clop-clop-clop-clop. Yeah, here comes the infantry.

I jammed a painter's cap on the back of my head and tossed my own fedora on top of my coat, now folded up next to the nearest stepladder. I even added the final touch of paint can and brush in my hands by the time courthouse security—an older cop who was looking to make retirement by taking a job like this one instead of risking the beat walks—came tearing around the corner. I suppressed a smile on noticing the top buttons of his uniform and dress shirt were left open. Poor guy had been deep in the Fairy's Realm when the alarm went off.

"What the hell, bub?" I barked. It was always good to come out of the box strong. Adds to the disorientation of the initial sight of me.

"I was gonna—" he shouted, but then shook his head as he cast a wary glance to the alarm bell. "I was gonna ask you the same thing, Shorty!"

"Weekend detail!" I shouted back. I don't know if it was just me, but I had to wonder if those damn bells were getting louder. "I was told to be here this morning 'cause we were going to finish up the second floor today! Door was unlocked, so I figured everyone was here! Guess I got here early!"

"What?!? You got to hurry?"

And now, the vaudeville routine. "Guess—I—got—here—early!"

"Kinda small for a painter, ain't ya?" the cop shouted at me.

"Save the wall for later?!? Okay, but there's gonna be hell to pay when we start on the ceilings without finishing—"

"No, I said you're SHORT for a PAINTER!"

I shook my head, "Nah, we won't be short! There will be a full crew on today! I'm just early!"

"NO!" he screamed in desperation. "YOU—SHORT!"

"Oh, yeah! I'm short. So are a lot of us on the Saturday crew. Why do ya think we got so damn many ladders?!?"

The security guard flung his hat on the ground and leaned in closer to me. "Have you got a work order?'"

"Fork over?!?" I asked, stretching up and turning my ear closer to him. I could hear him just fine, but I needed him to go away and stay away. No better way to be left alone than to establish oneself as a severe pain in the ass. "Fork over what?"

"A WORK ORDER!!!" The poor sap was shouting so loud now that his voice was cracking. "I need to see the work order!"

I placed a hand on his shoulder and leaned on him as I stood on my tippy-toes. "I think my boss has it!"

"What?!?"

"MY—BOSS!!!" Since I'm used to shouting orders over charging axemen, sounds of sword on shield, and goblin battle cries, my voice nearly knocked him off his feet. "My boss should have the work order on him!"

The bells were really starting to get to me now, so I know his patience had to be wearing thinner than a wraith's wardrobe. He just nodded and pointed to the wide staircase at the end of the hall. "Offices are that way! Next time—back entrance!"

He was probably swearing up a storm over why he hadn't checked the courthouse doors at the end of the previous day. As I watched him disappear to shut off the alarm, I set down the paint and brush for a moment so I could grab my memo pad and lock-picks. I was about halfway up the steps to the second floor when the sound of the bells ceased, replaced by the *scuff-scuff-scuff-scuff* of my own feet ascending the stairs.

Thank you, ladies and gentlemen. Hope you enjoyed the show. I'll be here all week!

I climbed up to the seventh floor, where I knew the more important lawyer-types congregated: District Attorneys, Assistant D.A.'s, and the rest of their lot. I figured these were the guys who were keeping tabs, or at least trying to, on thugs like "Pretty Boy" DeMayo. Apart from the Feds itching to prosecute Capone for his various criminal activities, the D.A's Office would love to score one up on the Treasury

Department. Locally, it would easily make anyone's career in politics if it were the local law enforcement that brought Capone down. On a national level, it would attract a lot of attention—and alongside that, commerce—to the Greater Chicago area. And hey, if you wanted to leave Chicago for greener moors and cleaner shires, you could write your own ticket if you could boast how instrumental you were in taking down the Big Boss.

My enchanted picks barely broke a sweat with the Assistant D.A.'s office. I slowly poked my head around the doorway, because you never knew if an Assistant D.A. would be burning twilight torches in order to come across that one all-important clue leading to Capone. This Saturday morning, no one was home. The office was kept immaculate— a *very* good sign that I was in for a quick visit. Setting down the paint can and brush, I set to work finding what I would need in this office: Height.

There are certain constants in this new realm to which I have grown accustomed, and now I'm reaching a point where I appreciate them. I can always rely on hot dogs in Wrigley Field tasting a lot better than the dogs I get in Grant Park. I can always count on the news in the *Herald Examiner* to be less biased than that of the *Defender*. I know that politicians, be they local or higher up in the Congressional pecking order, will promise to make everything better while they're actually trying to make things worse for their successors. And I also know that humans who work in offices believe themselves to be in such a hurry that they need wheels on their chairs to shave off those all-important seconds between sliding away from a desk and getting on their feet.

The whole concept of a chair with wheels on it initially struck me as not only hysterical, but just a hint pretentious. Come on, you can't just get a normal chair, scoot up to a table, and conduct your business like anyone else? Does one truly believe the time saved between gliding away from a desk and planting your feet on *terra firma* is that crucial in getting things done? It really took a lot for me to not laugh at these humans in their "wagon-thrones," as I had called them from my hiding places in the library.

Of course, when I had gone shopping for office furniture, there wasn't a lot of "dwarf-sized" furniture around…and it was pretty disappointing to find out *how* miniature "miniature furniture" truly was. That was when I realized that the carpenters of Acryonis who specialized in "Scrap Furniture" were pretty skilled at what they did, regardless if what they called their wares made dwarves flinch.

So I swallowed my pride and bought my own office chair. And I love it. I not only get height, but I get a lot of mobility.

This guy apparently liked his chair with a lot of swivel, so I had to adjust to its give. I climbed into the seat and pushed against the desk, rolling over to one of the file cabinets. I opened up the top drawer and started scanning through the "A's," hoping that the Assistant D.A.'s filing system was as neat and pristine as his office.

The top drawer was continuing into the "C's," so this was a strike out. I pushed back from the filing cabinet to give me enough room to go down into the "D's" one drawer down. Still nothing. And when I was in the "C's" there wasn't even a file on "Capone." Was I not looking in the right place? Should I be checking "M" for "Mafia" or "Mobster?" Would I need to check under "I" for "Italians?"

I removed the painter's cap and scratched my noggin, trying to itch the answer out of my brain. You don't walk into an office as clean and organized as this and have to struggle to find something. I could tell from the absence of an old newspaper and the lack of clutter on his desk that there was no room for anything out of order. The easier it was for him to find, the happier he was and the more he could accomplish. I knew whatever I was missing was staring me in the face.

Then I realized I was staring at the Assistant D.A.'s desk. Considering the current state of Chicago, would I really keep mafia files on the other side of my office, or within arm's reach?

I hopped down from the chair and waddled over to this fine mahogany keep, taking a closer look at how well this thing was put together. The obvious craftsmanship that went into creating this monstrosity, I had to wonder what the District Attorney's desk looked like. It must take up one wall and continue down another!

The top drawer opened with no effort and its contents were as neat as a new blade, back from the forge and sharpened to a fine edge. Pencils were grouped with pencils. Erasers were grouped with erasers. Yeah, this Assistant D.A. redefined the term "particular." There were three small drawers on the left hand, and two drawers on the right. The top-right drawer, which was smaller, kept memo pads of various sizes. It was the most cluttered area of this office, as smaller pads slid freely over the larger legal-sized notebooks. (It would have come as no shock to me if he had partitioned the top drawer to remedy this. Maybe that was his weekend project.)

The larger drawer was locked. Oh, the search-and-infiltration memories this drawer brought back! Journeying down stone corridor after stone corridor, all doors unlocked or open…and then there was that last one on at the end of the corridor, locked. Usually, there was something mighty fine waiting for us on the other side of that door. (Although there was that one time when the locked door was actually a nursery of new-bred orcs. Yeah, that was a rough night.)

Applying the picks to this smaller lock proved a challenge, but I managed to find the necessary grooves needed to trigger it. I rapped the fork against the floor (not wanting to take any chances in scratching the oak of the desk) and passed the tongs on either side of the picks. The silver instrument vibrated lightly, and then…

Nothing. The instruments stopped suddenly, and the drawer lock remained engaged.

I gave the fork a much harder knock against the floor. Once in the cradle of charmed sound, these picks were working overtime. Let me put it another way: These metallic locksmiths were either trying to solve this puzzle of latches and levers, or knitting a sweater inside that keyhole.

I rapped the fork on the floor again, evoking an even stronger sound from its prongs. As the tone grew, the picks began to vibrate violently, and then *glow*. The longer they shook in the lock, the more the picks' light-blue glow turned bright white. The glass panes of the office windows shuddered lightly, and the symphony of tinkling from the plaques, law degrees, and various other honors hanging on the walls and sitting on bookshelves swelled louder and louder, reaching a level of sound that I was sure would attract the attention of that overnight wonder of a guard.

I gritted my teeth hard to keep them from chattering as the magic I generated turned more ferocious. The picks were now bright as a pure-white, prolonged flash of sunlight catching polished silver—so bright that I could no longer look directly at it. I heard two of the Assistant D.A.'s honors shatter, along with a vase of wilting flowers at the right corner of the desk.

Then I heard a sharp *crack*, and the tone of my fork, shuddering of windowpanes, and dinging of glassware faded together, much like the tunes of court musicians ending with a decrescendo that leaves only a moment of silence before the nobles' applause. The concert of sorcery was over. I almost broke out into applause myself, but I was still too busy catching my breath, wiping away the cold sweat from my brow, dabbing my lips on the cuff of those baggy coveralls.

The only sound in the office now was a steady *drip-drip-drip* of foul-smelling water from the vase, now partially covering the desk. Wisps of thick, pearly smoke slipped off my picks. Placing a hand on the drawer handle and closing my peepers, I whispered a quick prayer to the Guardians as I gave a gentle pull.

The drawer slid closer to me, and I gave a heavy sigh of relief. *I dodged a throwing dagger on this one*, I thought as I looked on the treasure waiting for me.

They were all here. Alfonse "Scarface" Capone. Anthony "Pretty Boy" DeMayo. Frank "The Enforcer" Nitti. Rio. McGurn. It was dossier after dossier of the Organization, many of them incomplete and only a sacred few with red tabs marking their folders. No doubt, those marked folders indicated the ones who were somewhere in The Big House.

I pulled out the DeMayo folder and started flipping through the various clippings and pictures of Capone's showy second-in-command. It looked like DeMayo loved the ladies, and he loved the lifestyle. I paused at the sight of one picture where he had his arm around my client's waist as she offered up a polite smile for the camera. Tony was obviously captured in a moment of true hilarity, because his mouth was open so wide that a marsh bat could fly in, remove his tonsils, and fly out without catching the roof of his mouth. He had Julia Lesinger in one hand, and a smoldering stogie wedged between the index and middle finger of the other.

Surrounding him were a variety of mob types (including an inside contact of mine that I was needing to get hold of) and a few of Julie's types: rich, good girls sampling the wild life. Yeah, life was good to Tony. Damn shame life couldn't remain so kind to him.

Julia's expression gave me a slight chill because of its complete detachment from the raucous setting. The people around Tony were definitely putting on a better act than she was. Or maybe Tony was, in fact, that funny of a guy. Maybe he was the life of the party, and Julia preferred to put on the airs of high society for this moment captured by Eastman-Kodak. Or maybe she knew what he really was at his core.

In my world, the minor nobility ranks—Countesses, Viscountesses, Barons, and (especially) knights—really enjoyed the privileges and prestige of their titles, but they were *appointed* their titles. You can dress an ogre in the finest silks of the Hun-she Dynasty, adorn them with the finest jewels from the mines of Gryfennos, encase their feet in the softest, most supple leather of the Elvish tanneries and bestow upon it the title of "Lord Constable of the Realm," but that doesn't change what you've dressed up in your Sunday best. That ogre, bathed, dressed, and titled, is still an ogre, and will tear out your throat so it can gnaw on your trachea. Same thing can be said for minor nobility. A peckerwood with a title.

That was the look Julia Lesinger had in this photo: The look of a Princess in the company of Baron Peckerwood.

I continued through the file's contents. Not so much as a mark, check, or a star to hint that DeMayo was caught with his hand in the cookie jar and singing to the D.A.'s Office or Uncle Sam so he could keep feeding his late-night social habits.

I had to give the D.A.'s Office credit—they were trying to catch the same big tuna that kept eluding the Fed's lures, hoping for a moment when they would be there and the Feds would not. You would think that Capone would sweat being tailed by both the Feds and the local cops, and he *would* sweat it, too, if they were working together. Capone probably figured he could count on the "healthy competition" between state law enforcement and J. Edgar's boys. And as the G-men and cops tripped over one another trying to trip up Capone, Capone sidestepped the law and ran his business much to the chagrin of honest folks.

And that was the end of the file. Nothing. According to what was in my pudgy little hands, the D.A.'s Office knew DeMayo was part of

The Business, but lacked any hard evidence that could persuade him to turn on his Big Boss. Of course, finding a witness willing to step forward against anyone in Capone's organization was about as likely as finding a survivor from a Goblin bachelor party.

I returned the file to its rightful place among the lower dregs of Chicago society, removing the picks from the drawer's keyhole as it slid shut. The instruments were still warm, their heat just seeping through the leather pouch.

Suddenly, my hand whipped back on feeling a sharp sting of electricity from the drawer's keyhole. I must have brushed against it while keeping an eye on the door for any visitors curious about the earlier noise I was making. My hand tingled lightly and I gave a small, spiteful laugh as I rubbed it.

The lock's bolt sliding into place seemed a lot louder than it should have been, but I chalked that up to my nerves playing tricks on me. I carefully stepped through the puddle formed at the corner of the desk, wiping my shoes clean on the modest office rug before returning to the hallway.

I could hear a commotion downstairs growing. The weekend shift was arriving.

I came back down the steps at a quick pace, unheard by the workmen who were lining up lunchboxes. Two guys were trying to talk in hushed voices about being stuck on the Saturday shift, but I could hear every word. Safe to assume the supervisor hadn't arrived yet.

The chatter came to a halt at the sight of me, and I clearly heard, *"What the hell is that?"* and *"Is the circus in town?"* followed by a few chuckles from the other three in the crew.

"You know something, pal?" I began, pointing a finger at the "Circus Comment" clown. "If the circus *was* in town, I'd give you the sound advice to ask if there was a job opening for mucking out the elephant's car! You're going to find yourself shoveling shit if you don't make some progress on this lobby pronto!"

One of these Rembrant-flunkies, still buttoning up his coveralls, didn't bother to look at me as he asked, "And just who're you, Shorty, to be barking at us like some kinda mutt?"

"I'm the mutt that'll piss on your leg and tell you it's raining if you don't drop the attitude! Now, if you want to keep your job, send a crew upstairs to the seventh floor. Some dink left the Assistant D.A.'s office a mess."

"Seventh floor?" another worker, the "What the hell" guy, piped in. "We haven't even finished the second!"

"Doesn't matter who made the mess!" I snapped back. "You know how these bureaucrats are! They are elected royalty. If there is *anything* wrong in their offices, it'll be our fault. So clean it up! Now I want three people here and two on the second floor. I'm going to call in a second team."

"Jesus, are we *that* far behind?"

It's amazing how much bigger I look when I rest my fists on my hips. Letting out a heavy sigh, I looked up to the ceiling as if I was about to blow my top. This was my little one-man show, and I wasn't going to disappoint.

"All I know is I got the phone call this morning to be here, do the walk-through, and let you dinks know where we stood. Now it's our asses if we don't gain some ground with this job, so GET GOING!" I grabbed my coat and switched the painter's cap for my Fedora. "I'll be right back. Call in that second team."

Halfway down the steps, I saw a mousy excuse of a human pass me, casting a nervous glance at first but then staring at my coveralls. He was probably thinking, *"Those look like mine,"* but then dismissed the thought, figuring I was way too short to fit into anything of his. He must have missed the rolled-up cuffs or sleeves. Too bad I had to leave so soon. I would have loved to hear him say, *"Anyone seen my cover—hey, wait a minute…"*.

A few minutes later, the coveralls were bunched up in the floorboards of the cab that I'd caught a block away. I was back in the preferred fit of my coat, my hand still tingling a bit from what happened in the Assistant D.A.'s office.

The last time I saw something like that glass-shattering sideshow, it was deep in the musty darkness of a labyrinth back in Acryonis when I was working with a rather tricky lock. My boys and I watched as my charmed instruments took on a glow, vibrated inside the keyhole, and then came to a rest. When I rapped the fork harder against the stone wall of the maze, like I'd just done in the office, some of us shielded our eyes at the light generated from my picks.

That was when our mage-in-residence (it was always a good idea to travel with some kind of sorcerer when breaking into an enemy stronghold, especially if that enemy was suspected of allying themselves with necromancers) gave us the bad news that we were not going through this door anytime soon. There was some serious magic in place, broken only by equally powerful magic—magic we didn't possess.

The buildings of Chicago passed by me, but I was paying less attention to the city and more to the people now awake and roaming the sidewalks. Someone out there, someone working for the Chicago D.A.'s Office, was casting spells on office furniture. Not particularly powerful magic, but enough to discourage any humans from trying to pick the lock of a particular desk. Much like Acryonis, Chicago was a town of surprises and secrets, and this secret was a doozie. It had been a long time since I'd gotten this homesick.

Spellcasters in 1929 Chicago. Just when you think you've seen it all in this town...

CHAPTER THREE
GETTING ON MY BAD SIDE

Chicago has gone unsung for its hidden treasures for as long as I've known her. When it comes to culture, sports and just about everything else, people drone on and on about New York. Oh, if you want theater, go to *New York!* If you want the latest fashion, go to *New York!* If you want to see a real ball team, go and see the Brooklyn Dodgers in where? *New York!* (Eh, the Dodgers and the Yankees can go sit in my hat. They pretend to be a team wrapped around one or two *real* players. Don't get me started…)

While dinks continue to babble on and on about how great New York is, Chicago gets labeled as a den of crime and corruption. They tell us that New York, compared to a second-rate shire like Chicago, is a realm fit for kings, queens, and nobility—where the streets are paved with gold, everyone thrusts out a helping hand, and doors of opportunity and prosperity open wide around every corner.

Let me tell you something about New York: The Big Apple ain't that sweet. More like it's rotten to the core. The only gold on the streets is where bums relieve themselves. That "helping hand" is pointing the barrel of a Roscoe between your peepers. And those doors of opportunity are double-padlocked with bars over the windows.

I got all this after one visit, and that was one too many.

So, you can keep New York. My heart belongs to Chicago. And when it comes to restaurants, my heart, and on the exceptional nights, my heartburn, belong to Mick's. That's where I now found myself after divvying up my day between a crime scene, the Chicago courthouse, and my former haunt, the ol' public library on Washington Street, going through past newspapers to see if anything—a string of raids, an arrest, anything—could clue me in on DeMayo playing footsie with the Feds. I wish I could say the afternoon had yielded up plenty of leads, but hell, that would've been too easy. "Frustrated" was the best word to describe me at this point, and the only cure was Mick's chili special.

Thirty years ago, Mickey Nowinski's dad came to America with a name that was tough as nails to pronounce and a demeanor to match. Seeing how things were in New York—what with the boats dumping half of Europe on America's shores, the jobs becoming as scarce as a decent flop, and street gangs cropping up like Dunheim ogreweed—he and the family headed out west, eventually settling on Chicago because the cold winters reminded them of home. As Nowinski Senior worked his way up from dishwasher to cook, those cold winters inspired him to concoct an incredible delicacy that eventually made him owner of his own place.

Mickey Junior now ran the joint his dad started, a short-order diner boasting the best chili in town. Well, I say "boast," but it's not a boast so much as it is a promise. Nah, more like a pledge of honor that Mick's meets every day! While the diner's never short on seats, Mick's delivery boys keep in great shape running his chili from place to place. Whether it's the big shots of the financial hub, the politicians of City Hall, the guys down at the docks unloading barges or those construction daredevils high above the sidewalks on an I-beam and a prayer, everybody agrees on where to find the best chili in town. Sooner or later, everybody goes to Mick's.

Back in the here and now, Mick's place ain't a far cry from his dad's. The backdrop's a little noisier, though. The usual *ting-ting-ting* of the tiny brass bell above the door was drowned out by a less gentle *ha-hoo-ga* from a flivver outside, causing a few heads to turn my way as I walked through the door.

Which brings me to another pet peeve: Humans, either from Acryonis or right here, enjoy this great wizard's illusion of "discretion" whenever they happen across an unusual-looking person (or dwarf). While they whisper to one another or try not to stare, the reality is that their voices carry in the wind like a battle cry and their eyes bore through you like a fireblade through butter. My ability to pick up their comments has nothing to do with dwarves possessing some sort of exceptional hearing, or anything like that. As a matter of fact, we've got a hearing range similar to that of humans, but God forbid humans should have anything in common with a dwarf! At least, that's the impression I get.

When people notice a dwarf like me walking into a place like Mick's, the resulting lull in their conversation reminds me of when me and the boys would open one of those thick tavern doors in a human-heavy village. Everybody shuts up for a moment, then goes back to their routine. Or one of those Western shoot-'em-up movies, where the bad guy in the black hat who knows he's being talked about pats his pearl-handled six-shooter and moseys on up to the bar, relishing being talked about.

The only relish I like is the kind on my dog, out at Wrigley Field. I spent my life building up a thick exterior, but it doesn't make dealing with whispers and snickers any easier.

The guy who works as my shield against these naysayers is my pal Mickey, who's capable of shooting customers operating under that "discretion spell" a crossbow's bolt of a look—a good, hard Polish stare that could stop a Blue Dragon dead in its tracks.

It usually works on the average Joe and Josephine, but tonight, there was a table of dinks in custom-cut pinstripes that continued to make jokes at my expense. I could hear them. They knew it.

Sure enough, this was beginning to look like one of those Westerns, with me being the *good* guy walking into the saloon, gearing up to introduce these outlaws to my girl Beatrice, who remained snug against my left breast in her holster. (You see, that was always my problem with those moving-picture cowboys. They were showing everyone where they were packing heat.)

"Hey there, Billi, how ya doin'?" Mick hailed cheerfully as he poured out a bowl of the special for the guy next to me.

God bless this crazy Pollack! First, he had fixed a seat at the end of his bar deliberately higher than the others, especially for me. Then, there was that winner of a smile and his battle-horn bellow of a greeting, an obvious one-fingered salute to those mooks snickering in the booth behind me. Now he presented me a bowl of the "Baddings-sized" Chili Special while the customer next to me now eyed his own bowl, wondering why the short guy hopping up into the higher stool was getting an extra ladleful of Mick's best.

Yeah, he's looking at his own bowl. Now mine. He's thinking about letting it go. Now he's thinking about how good this chili is. Takes another spoonful while staring at my own. He's reconsidering. Give it a moment...

Three. Two. One.

"Excuse me, sir..." The sap waved to grab Mick's attention.

I stifled a good, hearty laugh; I could tell he wasn't a regular. He called Mick 'sir,' and that meant it was time for the dinner entertainment. Mick does love a comedy routine for the Saturday-night crowd, and I was always the headliner at his vaudeville revue.

"Why is he getting a bigger order of the special?" the sap protested.

"Well, *sir*," Mick said sharply, giving his 'sir' an extra sting, "being as we are a family-run place, I'd like to know who I'm talkin' to."

Any paler, and this guy could have been mistaken for a swamp wraith. "Um, my name's Kevin."

"Kevin." Mick nodded, cleaning his hands with a towel and slinging it over his shoulder. "Y'gotta understand a couple of things here, Kevin. First, this is my place, an' I can do whatevuh I want. That's why the name of the place is Mick's and not Kevin's."

He turned to the counter behind him for a moment and then placed four fresh green jalapeño peppers in front of me, evenly spaced and lined up as if they were fine slivers of Dunheimian jade displayed before me for approval. I gave him a very subtle nod.

"Second, this here is *Mister* Billi Baddings," Mick announced curtly. "Don't let his height fool you. He's got a *big* appetite."

That was my cue to pick up one of the peppers and pop it in my mouth, stem and all. While a four-foot-one redhead with a scraggly beard and a thirty-something-inch waist dressed in a navy pinstripe suit hardly strikes fear in the hearts of mortal men, the ability to polish off a couple of raw jalapeños tends to give people a moment s pause.

Especially if they don't see you sweat.

Each pepper's crunch could be heard clearly by this guy at the bar and the handful of customers enjoying their chili, sandwiches and sodas. Even those orcs cracking the jokes on me earlier paused for a second as I held pepper number three between my pudgy fingers and lifted it to the light, savoring its color and firmness with the appreciation of a true connoisseur, before plunging it into the murky abyss of a dwarf's stomach.

I took a solid bite out of the last pepper, the resulting crunch causing the little nipper having dinner with his mom and dad to whisper "*Wow!*" I smiled and polished it off in a second bite, still no trace of sweat forming on my brow. Not even when I took a sip of the piping hot coffee Mick served as a chaser.

"Nice appetizer, Mick," I coolly remarked, dabbing at the edges of my mouth in a truly Poirot-ian manner. No sigh of relief. No intense flush on my face, apart from the brilliant red in my beard. No troll's belch. (That would come later.)

"I think I'll take that chili now," I purred like a Saber-toothed mountain cat of the Black Hills. "You got any hot sauce I can put on it?"

"For you, pal? Sure."

To desecrate Mick's chili would normally be considered sacrilegious, but this was just part of the show. Every chili-eater in the joint knew that another drop of Tabasco would bring down the wrath of the El Hanor Durea Temple Gods.

While Mick searched for his bottle of hot sauce, I leaned in toward Kevin, his own special growing colder and colder while he stared at me like I was a freak of nature. I knew my breath had to reek of jalapeños a nice touch that always made my next line a fun way to end this bit of dinner theater.

"If I were you, bub, I would scoot down a few chairs. Fresh vegetables give me gas like you wouldn't believe."

Had he moved any faster, I think the barstool cover would have gone with him. His change on the counter was still settling with a jingle before the door slammed shut, the bell above the door pealing wildly as if trying to get the last word in this scene.

Mick roared with laughter as he plunked down the tiny bottle of Tabasco and a tall glass of water with a fresh slice of lemon floating between clumps of crushed ice. "Goddamn, Billi, I never gets tired doin' that," he said gleefully between gasps.

"Just count yourself lucky that I got this cast-iron stomach!" I scoffed while shaking the still-capped hot sauce over my dinner. (Preserving the illusion, you know?)

I took another look at the crowd. A quiet Saturday night. Not normal for Mick's place. I don't know if it was a twinge of guilt I felt, or if the jalapeños weren't layin' right, but I looked up at my friend apprehensively.

"Look, Mick, you didn't think that was too much? I don't wanna—"

"Now don' you get in a sweat, Baddings," Mick scolded, scooping up the poor sap's change and ringing up the sale. "A dingleberry like that, comin' into my place, tellin' me how to run things...I don' appreciate that. If I want to make your Saturday Chili Special a little Extra Special, then that's my call, not Kevin's. Don' get in a lather, Billi. Jus' eat ya dinnah!"

If you're wondering why I'm getting this special treatment from Mick, it's got a lot to do with being a dwarf. Mick was telling me one day over a glass of some particularly cheap Canadian booze that his whole family was running this uphill race simply because they were "of Polish descent," as those "discreet" humans would put it.

Now, I can understand the animosity toward me to an extent. I'm a dwarf. Four feet tall. Redhead. A walking mass of pleasant portliness. I'm different. Sure, I admit that. But to slight a guy, let alone an entire family, for having a last name that sounds like a High Elder during a sneezing fit? You're kidding me, right? I could care less about that stuff, so long as you hold a steady bow, have a good eye for distance, and you're drawing a bead on the mook shooting at me.

Guess that's why Mick and I hit it off. A Pollack and a Scrappie, drunk off bootleg whiskey and having a good laugh at how much we had in common.

When I was first starting out as a gumshoe back in '28, my clients were not as reputable as Miss Julia Lesinger. Many of those first clients were down on their luck, what Miranda would call "good heart" cases. The kind that you do because bad things are happening to good people, and you get paid when you get paid. (Yeah, I had to keep the "Waldorf" routine polished and ready at a moment's notice.)

Well, Mick was one of those "good heart" cases. Back then, he was having a problem with break-ins. Capone's boys were going easy on him concerning protection money, as that was now considered "old hat" for the Organization. (The real money was in running numbers, bootlegging, and the old reliable income that was a moneymaker across Acryonis, too: prostitution.) The talk on the street was that Capone ran things differently, although a couple of the generals continued to take protection payment simply out of habit.

Mick wasn't being pressured into paying protection money (yet), and the evidence I came across didn't appear like a sales pitch for Capone Insurance. No, these "break-ins" were way too subtle. It smacked of an inside job.

I did a bit of asking around, watched Mick's place, and eventually found out it was one of his waitresses who had gotten herself into trouble with some slick-talking mook. Instead of taking it to the cops or to Capone, we all had a sit-down. It turned out that this waitress, a sweet girl named Annabelle, was in a maternal way unexpectedly, and it looked like the boyfriend was going to be anything but helpful. This guy actually had Annabelle believing it was solely her fault that she had a loaf in the hearth.

Now, you would think that the boss she was stealing from would consider kicking her into the streets, heavy with child or not. Not the Nowinski clan. Mick took her into his own home. Where the Nowinskis lived was hardly a castle estate, but there was a guest room open for visiting relatives. His family did all but adopt Annabelle and her newborn baby. She still works at Mick's as a waitress while Mick's wife, Gladiss, watches her kid.

After that "good heart" case, Mick and I became friends. Good friends, although I still can't release all the spirits from my keep. Not yet. For now, all they know is that I'm a guy who faced some hardships on account of my height. When the time is right, I'll let them know about Acryonis, the portal, and all the rest. Regardless of how much they come to know, I can always count on them being there because their hearts are always open to me. They're my new family in this new realm.

And with my new family constantly trying to hook me up with their numerous friends and relatives, I'll never have a lonely night in my life.

And lately, Mick has been getting sneakier.

"Why don't you come by the place Tuesday night, Billi?" He was smiling warmly. Too warmly. "Gladiss is fixing your favorite Bratwurst recipe."

The spoon stopped before entering my mouth. I raised a skeptical eyebrow. "Who is it this time, Mick?"

He paused in wiping down the counter, and then, without looking me in the eye, he replied with one breath, "Her name is Bertha. She's my third cousin."

"Ah, for the Druids of Hadismill!" I took a bite of chili, savoring its flavor while I took in my friend's imploring eyes. My meal would probably taste better if I could duck all the matchmakers around me. "Was your family the *only* family on that boat from Poland? You sure you ain't Italian?"

"So, I got a big family. So shoot me!" Mickey shrugged as he began stacking a few of the empty plates at the opposite end of the bar. "You'll like her. She's a redhead, too!"

"So that makes her what? *Irish*-Polish?" I held up a chubby finger, trying to drive this point home as I had tried time and again in the past. "Mickey, you know I don't want to disappoint you! I mean, c'mon, why are you wantin' to hook me up with someone in your family?"

"She's a nice girl, Billi. *You're* a nice guy! You'll like her!"

It doesn't take a detective to know the words *"You'll like her"* can be the most dangerous words used when setting up a blind date.

"You don't know me *that* well, Mick!" I joked. "All I'm going to do is go out with her once and break her heart."

"Or trip her up when you open the door for her."

The voice came from behind me. In the chrome of the napkin dispenser, I caught a blurred reflection of those mooks sniggering in their booth like a bunch of goblins cornering a litter of kittens.

Instead of cutting the offenders to the quick with his signature death stare, Mick just finished stacking the plates in front of him and carried them over to the sink, where he started running the hot water.

I shook my head, returning to my meal. "You'll let anyone eat here, won't ya?"

"Well, Billi," Mick replied quietly, "sometimes you have to let the customers get in the last word...especially when they're part of the *working class*."

That was all I needed to know. These brainless ogres behind me were Capone's ogres. The fine-cut suits, plus the dim expressions that implied these mooks could change their socks easier than their minds, should have been a giveaway—but one thing you learn as a detective is never to take things at face value. This was one of those times where my gut instincts had been right.

"I say you give this Pollack a break," the ogre grunted. "Date his cousin. She's only distantly related. Couldn't be as butt-ugly as him!"

All right, nobody was allowed to call Mick a "Pollack" aside from me. And taking a swing at my friend's family? The family I considered to be *my* family? Not smart. Swing and a miss. Strike one.

I watched the formless image move closer in the napkin holder until he was looming over me like a gargoyle extending from a parapet of a cathedral. His expensive cologne and cheap Chesterfield he was smoking completely overpowered the sweet bouquet of Mick's work. Wherever he was in the Organization, he was nothing more than a foot soldier. Still, he could make my life uncomfortable if he wanted to.

"Besides, Short Stuff here ain't exactly beating the birds away, are ya?" he chuckled, taking a long drag from his cigarette.

He blew smoke in my face. I was okay with that.

Then he put his cigarette out in my chili. Did I not mention Mickey Nowinski's chili is *that* good? Strike two.

"Then again, I don't know. I could be wrong." Mr. Funny Man motioned to Annabelle, who was trying really hard to become invisible in taking care of her customers. "What do you think, sister? Could you love a mick-leprechaun with a mug like this?"

Strike three.

One great thing about being four-foot-one is that whenever you have a creep trying to get your goat, he has to bend down to look you in the eye. It throws him off-balance, which makes hitting his face with the back of your elbow so very easy.

Sure enough, Funny Man toppled back, hands covering his nose and howling like a wounded pack-beast. Neither he nor his sidekicks had expected me to make a move, but he was 2 and 0 at the plate before the leprechaun crack. If he wanted to walk, he needed to be nicer.

I love Mick's Diner for some of the simple touches, like his plates and bowls. They're so thick and heavy that when Annabelle is having that occasional day of clumsiness, she can drop ten of these plates and only two or three will chip or break. They are solid, American-made.

In the hands of a dwarf with military training, they become weapons.

The second ogre was reaching for his piece, but not before I got a firm hold of the wide-rimmed soup bowl in front of me. As I did, I caught a glimpse of the bent Chesterfield sticking out of what was, at one time, very good chili. What I was about to do would normally be considered a horrific waste, but I had my back against the counter, and besides, the chili was ruined anyway. I'd rather have Mick's hard work go out in a blaze of glory than on account of some asshole's cigarette.

I gave that bowl a good hurl. By the time the second ogre's piece saw daylight, the bowl-now-discus nailed him square on the bridge of his nose. I got a real satisfaction in hearing the pop of bone and cartilage when it hit him. The girlish squeal he let out was an added bonus. On striking its intended target, the remainder of my still-hot-from-the-kettle dinner went straight into the face of the third thug.

Funny Man was attempting to get back on his loafers, but a hard spin of my barstool brought my Buster Browns around to clock my wisecracking buddy in the jaw and send him back to the floor in the throw-rug position.

The third guy (kinda skinny for a gangster, but I guess it takes all kinds) had just cleared the bits of chili from his eyes, the red in them matching the burn on his skin. I doubt if he could see clearly through his watering peepers, but I'm sure he could at least make out the blob that was his buddy—all bloody nose and lack of balance—falling on top of him.

When I heard the sound of heaters hitting the floor, I brought Beatrice out to play. She was looking good after the tender loving care I had bestowed on her after the visit from Miss Lesinger. It was a sure bet that asking questions about Big Al's business would invite some socially challenged types, so I had made sure Beatrice was ready for any one-night stands.

Right now, her barrel was resting between Funny Man's nose and his cheek, her hammer pulling back with a *click-click* that rang through Mick's place like a body collector's bell in the eerie quiet of a village struck by plague.

The rest of Mick's patrons hit the dirt, the mother shielding her young son from any stray bullets. But I wasn't worried about bystanders. These dinks were smart in one respect: If they caused any problems in their boss' territory, they wouldn't be seen around the neighborhood anymore. Hell, as pissed as Capone would get, it would be a stroke of luck if their own mothers took credit for them!

I looked up at the other stooges in their booth, both frozen in their clumsy stances. (They looked really uncomfortable. I liked that.) With the second ogre now sporting a crooked nose and a blood-and-chili-stained pinstripe suit and awkwardly leaning against his scrawny, red-faced sidekick, it could have been a laugh-riot for everyone at Mick's…but Beatrice had raised the tension just a hair. Maybe more like a hair-trigger.

My eyes darted from face to face, a nudge from my head motioning them to slide slug-like out of their cozy booth.

"Boys, boys, boys," I scolded, pressing Beatrice a little harder against the ring-leader's face. He was still disoriented from my kick, and probably also trying to work through his thick skull how a Scrappie had taken him down in a mostly-fair tavern brawl. "This could have been a friendly Saturday night at Mick's, but you had to go and spoil it for everyone. Now, if memory serves me right, I've heard your boss state pretty proudly that he's a simple businessman with his interests toward the people. I've also heard him deny that the *violence* in this city"—on the word "violence," I pushed Funny Man closer to the floor, with Beatrice just aching to give him a kiss—"doesn't come from him or any of his associates. Now when I arrange a little chat with the press about how the local mob muscle is getting out of hand, how well do you think that'll set with Mr. Capone?"

"Capone?" The scrawny one scoffed. "You t'ink we work for that greasy, jelly-belly dago?"

"Shaddup, Eddie!" barked Funny Man, his speech impaired somewhat by his face being pressed into Mick's floor. "Don't say nothin' no more until I tells ya, okay?"

These ogres didn't work for Capone and they were causing problems in his territory? Either these boys were particularly stupid, terribly lost, or had a *good* reason being in this part of town.

"All right then," I growled, "educate me. Who you mooks representing?"

I felt Funny Man, who was still getting cozy with Beatrice, quickly shake his head at his two dimwits, the looks on their faces silently begging him for an order. Why, oh why, did they have to play it the hard way?

I kept the big guy pinned to the floor with a knee to the back of his neck as I drew a bead on Scarecrow, who had made it through this scuffle so far with only a slight burn and a cleaning bill. Beatrice fired off a shot, knocking his fine felt *chapeau* off his elongated melon and knocking it several feet behind him.

As Scarecrow fumbled for his piece, Bloody Nose reeled for a moment and gripped the edges of the booth, his piece still underneath the table where he had dropped it. Meanwhile, my own heater was already back kissing Funny Man's cheek. I knew the barrel was still warm from the shot, reminding him I was worse than serious. I was downright nuts.

"Lemme whack this prick, Lou!" Scarecrow shouted, looking a little unhinged by my target practice. "He took a shot at me!"

I let out a chortle. "Who said I was aimin' for your noggin, Scarecrow?"

He followed my glance to the left of his shiny brown leather shoes, where there lay a tiny arrangement of quail feathers accented with a single bright yellow feather. Scarecrow quickly looked behind him to where his hat was still rolling unevenly, and then looked back to the adornment by his shoe—a terrific hat decoration just begging to be a sharpshooter's target.

"Now you know how good a shot I am." Beatrice's hammer pulled back once more as a muscle under my left eye twitched lightly. "I can promise you that with your boy here, I won't miss. We're going to try this again, boys. Who you packin' heat for?"

Neither Bloody Nose nor Scarecrow spoke up. They were being good little lapdogs, but Lou here apparently figured if he didn't speak up at this point, Beatrice would.

"Moran." And here I thought I was going to have to waste another bullet or three tonight. Lou was a lot smarter than he was funny. "We're workin' for Bugs Moran."

Beatrice doesn't usually make an appearance without hurting somebody. It has to be one serious exception to the rule to make her back down, and hearing that name in Capone's territory served as an exceptional exception. Beatrice's hammer slowly returned to a safe position as I stepped away from Lou, still keeping my girl in my grip in case any of them felt a sudden surge of idiotic bravery.

To say that George "Bugs" Moran and Alfonse "Scarface" Capone didn't care for one another would be like saying a Cleric of the Resh'ill Valley would "get religious" every now and then. Moran *hated* Capone. Capone *hated* Moran. They bickered so intensely that if they lived under the same roof, they would have been legally married by the Justice of the Peace. The only difference is that when married couples bickered, it usually involved a rolling pin, a few flatware projectiles, and maybe the odd pot or pan. When this Irish-Italian couple argued, it involved Tommy guns and switchblades.

Moran and his boys had been keeping clear of Chicago since Valentine's Day, and now these dinks were in Mick's kicking up a fuss. This couldn't be anything good.

"All right, boys." I nodded. "I know I don't want any trouble, and you don't want to be dead. So why don't we put our toys away and go back to our respective shires? I don't think either Capone or Moran would take too kindly to you orcs causing trouble in a protected establishment."

Yeah, yeah, I know I just said Mick's place wasn't officially a protected establishment, but Capone had a softer side for the working class who had come up from nothing and built up a legacy. Mick's legacy was the Chili Special—Capone's favorite indulgence, apparently, apart from the Italian food he enjoyed in Chicago's Little Italy. Either way, if something went down with Mick, Moran would be sure to feel a bit of payback in the morning.

Lou straightened his tie and removed the blood from the corner of his mouth; Scarecrow (who Lou was calling "Eddie") resheathed his boom dagger; and Bloody Nose (nameless, as well as brainless, so far), keeping his eye on me for as long as he could, returned to the booth and reached under the table for his own gun. While slipping it back into his shoulder holster, Bloody Nose flipped his once-white handkerchief to a clean side. The hankie was now a deep crimson, and I could only smile at the excuses he would give Moran about what had happened.

I slipped Beatrice back inside my jacket, giving Moran's muscle the grin of a *vermulth* after it devours a small hunting party. "Good boys. Now, how 'bout you three call it a night? Hell, I'll even pick up your bill."

Lou instinctively took a couple steps back as I passed him on the way back to the bar and hopped up on my barstool without so much as a second glance. "If we part on good terms, Capone and Moran won't know about this. So go home, and make sure your doc takes a look at Bloody Nose. I'd hate to have an infection on my conscience."

Yeah, I was enjoying this. I didn't think it could get any better until Lou the Leader leaned in, looking as if he were going to rip my head off and stuff it in his coat pocket.

"Anything else, leprechaun?"

I nodded, not looking at him. "Yeah, that reminds me…"

I grabbed his necktie and yanked him down to the bar, his chin slamming hard against its cool surface. I could hear Mick utter a sympathetic groan as Lou's teeth slammed hard against each other in his mouth.

"I am *not* a leprechaun. I am not an elf. And I definitely ain't no munchkin! I am a Highlands Dwarf! You hear me? A dwarf! *D-W-A-R-F!* Confuse me with anything else, and I will take great pleasure in teaching you the differences between dwarves, elves, and leprechauns." I leaned in closer and whispered, "And I'll let you in on one difference right now: dwarves *love* battle-axes."

I could hear his hands underneath the bar, trying to come up and rip the necktie out of my hand. Then I felt Lou grab my coat. (Guess he thought we were in Round Two. Bad guess.) I gave the necktie a bit of slack only to yank again, bringing his square jaw back to the bar. He let me go after that. "We understand each other?"

"Yeah," he grunted, struggling against my hold on his necktie. A few drops of blood dribbled out from between his gnashing teeth. Yep, he'd bit through his tongue. "I gotcha, dwarf."

"Good." Releasing the tie, I motioned to Mick, who already had a fresh bowl of the special waiting for me. "Now beat it. Your stink is killing the scent of my chili."

For a long minute, no one moved. Lou was holding all the cards in this game. I could tell the bleeding in his mouth was giving him a huge complex. But if Moran wanted him in Capone's territory, he probably wanted him to stay out of trouble. A death like mine in an establishment like Mick's would have been a bushel full of it.

"Let's go, boys," he muttered.

Mick watched wide-eyed as the rumpled, wrinkled pinstripes left his place. The family quickly ripped out a few bills, threw them on the table, and quickly hurried out, their little boy staring wide-eyed at me. That left only the young couple at a table in the corner, staring at me for a moment before nervously returning to their root-beer float and chitchat.

Annabelle frowned at the mess I had made with my chili discus, but she was soon smiling as she tidied up the family's table. In his haste, the father had tipped her fifty percent of the bill. Seemed like she and her kid were going to have a good weekend.

I adjusted my own hat and took a deep breath to clear my noggin as Mick presented me with the new bowl of chili. While I finally started to enjoy dinner, he wiped the old chili and Lou's blood off the bar, giving a high-pitched whistle and shaking his head as he did so.

"I tell you what, Billi: You either lead a charmed life, or you have a death wish."

"How so, Mick?"

His voice dropped to a sharp whisper. "Oh come off it, Billi, you *know* why! Those were Bugs Moran's boys!"

When the entrance bell jingled again, I thought Mick was going to jump out of his Polish-American skin. It was just his son Joshua, coming in from his last delivery of the day. He must have had a hot date lined up tonight, if the anxiousness in his eyes was anything to go by.

Ah, to be sixty and young again...

After heaving a sigh of relief, Mick continued whispering anyway, as if not to tempt the Fates and have Moran's boys return for another inning (although that they had just struck out in the bottom of the ninth and wouldn't risk another beating over Mick's name-dropping). Superstitious Pollack, but I love him like a brother!

"Good Lord, Billi, those are the kind of people you thank God every morning you don't know. If you do know them, you have to make sure to stay on their good side through the day so you can make it *through* the day!"

I shot him a grin. "Now, Mick, I know those boys could have made me disappear in an unforgettable kind of way, but this is where you have to look at the big picture. Last month. Valentine's Day. You remember that little party Capone threw?"

"Billi, come on." Mick was sweating, and it had nothing to do with how hard he was working. If I didn't calm him down, the poor guy was going to have a heart attack. "You got to watch what you—"

"Hey, you two! Romeo and Juliet!"

The couple halted their chat and looked at me with wide eyes as I addressed them. "Either of you work for Al Capone or George Moran?"

For a minute there, I thought that I had evoked the powers of a medusa. Those poor kids didn't move for so long that I was expecting to find the telltale veins of marble slowly appearing in their paling skin. With faces you would only find in a statue garden, they silently gave me a *"No"* with a simultaneous shaking of their heads.

"There you go. Some free detective work. So unless *you* are working with Moran, it is just you, me, and the star-crossed lovers over there."

He just laughed, shaking his head ruefully as I returned to the bouquet of spicy flavors in the bowl before me.

"Mick," I continued, "ol' Bugs knows that Capone has pissed all over this town like a possessive hunting hound. He's claimed his territory, and he intends to keep it."

He lifted a cautionary finger. "So what's your point, Billi? If I were anyone else, you'd be outta here without a second thought. I don't want any trouble in my place!"

"And you're not gonna get any, my friend." I smiled confidently, giving his shoulder a friendly nudge. "I don't start trouble that I can't finish. You know that. You and your customers were safe tonight."

"Eh, I knew they were, Billi," Mick replied, shaking his head in frustration, "but that's not what I mean. What I mean is, Capone leaves me alone so long as he likes my chili. But if Moran's boys mention what happened…"

"If Moran wanted to let Capone know he was back in his territory, or even if he wanted this to be a warning by starting up trouble, you think those ogres would have laid low for so long? You're gonna tell me they were waiting for some half-pint yahoo like me to walk in here so they could announce that Moran's back in town? It took a bullet to get them to spill the beans on their employer!"

"You mean they were here in *secret*?" Mick mused out loud. It's always fun watching him play detective. I had sung for my supper already—twice—and it was time I got a little entertainment with my meal. Whenever Mick assumes the role of my unofficial assistant in my casework, I can't help but smile.

"Then Moran would want 'em to stay that way," Mick added, continuing his train of thought. "Best way to blow a secret is to blow someone away, right? If they were made, that means Capone would know Moran is in town, making *two* bosses mad at 'em."

"I'll make a gumshoe of you yet, Mick," I winked, savoring another spoonful of chili.

"Doesn't take a gumshoe to read the papers, Billi," he replied with a chuckle, but I could see the gears starting to turn. "That ain't like Moran, being all secret-like."

Now, he was really getting caught up in it. This is usually the point where I have to remind him that I'm the detective, and he's the master of the chili.

"So what do you think Moran is up to?" he asked. "Checking to see if the coast is clear?"

I shrugged. "Well now, if I knew that, Mick, I wouldn't be that busy of a detective, now would I? Right now, I need to focus on only one problem at a time."

But then, I paused in my dinner. I don't know why it suddenly hit me on this particular spoonful, but then I popped the chili in my mouth and nodded. "There is a chance—and I'm thinking it's a pretty big one—it might have somethin' to do with my latest case," I sighed, producing a larger-than-usual amount of greenbacks from my wallet.

"Jesus, Mary, and Joseph! Who's your latest case? Joseph Rockefeller?!?"

"Now you know I can't go into that," I chided him as I paid for the dinner and the evening's excitement with a couple of Hamiltons. I had managed to get to the bank just in time before it closed for the weekend to deposit the down payment from Miss Lesinger and break one of her C-notes down to some smaller bills. Still, walking around with a few more Lincolns and Hamiltons than usual was a touch unsettling. I must've forgotten for a moment just how much cash I had on me. Some private investigator, huh? Well, I blame the night and the mixed company at Mick's. So I fell back on that client confidentiality clause that was my trade. "Remember? I'm a *private,* not public, investigator."

"Yeah okay, Billi. If you need anything, you just ask of me, okay?"

Ain't no way I would involve him or his home in anything this serious. Mick was the kind of guy you couldn't tell this to, though, because he would only work harder to get into the thick of things. I had to give him an assurance I'd call on him, even if I knew I had no intention of doing so.

"I hear you, pal. Thanks." I gave Annabelle a wink, hopped off the barstool, and straightened my hat. "Good night, ya crazy Polack."

"Sweet dreams, Scrappie," Mick shot back with a wink.

Yeah, I taught him that slur…and he's the *only* soul alive who is allowed to call me that. With the friendship we got, he's earned it.

The jingling of the bell was overpowered by the slam of the diner door closing behind me. I felt the slight March chill in the air as I looked around, savoring the sounds of Saturday night in Chicago. Car horns beeped, traffic started to pick up slightly, and I caught a riff of a trumpet solo coming from a jazz club a few blocks away. Yeah, this was the Windy City reveling in the apex of a weekend. My own weekend of rest and relaxation wouldn't start until I could close this case.

I was past that point where you reconsider a charge into battle, way past that moment when your battle-axe is firm in your grasp and you're matching the grunts and growls of a front line of orcs and ogres with your own regiment's cry. Still, I caught myself wondering if it had been such a smart idea accepting this job. Dealing with Capone was bad enough, but what was so important in Chicago that "Bugs" Moran would risk getting into Capone's business close on the heels of Valentine's Day? A hit Moran knew full well was intended for him personally?

Or was Moran just playing another one of his dangerous games with Capone? While Capone was a ruthless son of a bitch who left nothing to chance, Moran got this perverse joy in daring Capone through impromptu hits and other shows of disrespect, sometimes carried out on the same day a truce would be called between them. Capone just annoyed the hell out of me, but Moran gave me the willies.

Moran. Capone. Apart from the obvious, could there a connection that I wasn't seeing off the bat?

The obvious connection was, of course, my client, Julia Lesinger: a spoiled little rich girl with a taste for the wilder side of Chicago, mixed up with one of Capone's most trusted generals. And because no doubt "Pretty Boy" had served as a mouthpiece for Capone in certain social settings, Julia could have associations with Moran. Could she have known about the hit on DeMayo before it went down?

No, Lesinger wouldn't be that connected. She knew, like everyone in Chicago, that Capone was behind the hit. She wanted to know *why* the hit went down. I must admit, after my run-in with Moran's less-than-secret street spies, I now wanted to know why, too. Whatever Capone's business was, it was grabbing the attention of the well-to-do's and the ne'er-do-wells alike.

Feeling the rumbling of those four jalapeños in my gut, I decided it would be best to start fresh tomorrow. Tonight was going to be a quiet Saturday night of Pepto-Bismol and bed.

CHAPTER FOUR
My Boy, Benny

Sunday, I woke up exhausted. When your evening recreation includes roughing up a couple of Bugs Moran's boys at Mick's Diner, you tend not to sleep too well. All night long, I kept dreaming up possible outcomes from this case—all of them ending with me either taking a ride with Capone's boys, or finding myself on the wrong end of Moran's guns. Even though I vaguely remembered reassuring Mick that we had seen the last of those ogres, it didn't change the fact that being a dwarf in this city made you easy to find.

To that end, I spent Chicago's agreed day of worship in the office making sure that Beatrice, my hogleg, and any other weapons were all oiled, loaded, sharpened, and re-gripped. Even my old reliables from Acryonis would be ready for a fight. After last night, I wanted to leave nothing to chance.

As I was dragging a sharpening stone across a hunting dagger at my desk, I found real comfort in this thought: Regardless of whether I was dealing with Capone's or Moran's boys, all of them were cream puffs compared to what I'd dealt with before in Acryonis. I don't care how big Sammy "The Hammer" Garibaldi is, he ain't got nothin' on the scrappiest of orcs. This knowledge—partnered with the self-confidence one gains with a freshly sharpened battle-axe and a loaded automatic—was giving me just enough peace of mind to get a little sleep while working this case. That is, if you define "a good night's sleep" as sleeping with one eye open and a battle-axe under the pillow.

Yeah, yeah, I know. You probably think it would be smarter sleeping with a *gun* under the pillow. Well, I've heard talk about this fairy showing up when you leave a tooth there. Even though I knew the odds of coming across a *bona fide* fairy in this world were about as likely as the Boston Braves winning the World Series, the *last* thing I wanted to give a fairy an opportunity to get its mitts on was a loaded .45 automatic.

After another fitful night's sleep, it took a couple of chunks of ice in the sink and a few dozen splashes to the face to wake me up Monday morning. I called the office to let Miranda know I would be in later around lunchtime; the morning was going to be spent out on the town, hitting the sidewalks and streets for a little shakedown of my connection in the Al Capone machine.

Benny Riletto was your typical numbers runner, a high noble in a little corner of Al Capone's empire who loved to throw his weight around. Talking to Benny for too long would have you believing that when the major decisions were made, he was there to whisper the final word to Capone, who would then give Benny the nod and repeat verbatim what had been whispered into his ear.

In my world, Benny was no better than a tone-deaf bard whose stories continued to grow in height as he hopped from grove to grove. Thanks to some of those tall tales of his, Chicago's simple folk were terrified of his shadow and played Benny's lottery games without question. They had no clue that this dink consistently messed his trousers on the days Capone's boys collected from him. If his books were off even by the slightest, it would be a short-lived night on the town for Benny Riletto.

Ol' Benny was hardly a general, but he made enough to live well. Still, as I've said before, money doesn't grant a goblin manners, etiquette, or class. Although Benny loved to play the part of the big man on Mulberry Street, his reputation of being a cheap bastard preceded him wherever he went. But Benny's arrogance and his miserly habits weren't nearly as insulting as his smarmy *"Don't say Benny don't take care of his own..."* when leaving some sorry excuse for a tip. If there were any way he could have shined his own shoes without breaking a sweat, he would have.

What a prick.

Monday was Benny's primping day, when he begrudgingly surrendered some of his hard-earned gold to look the part of a big-time mobster. This usually meant he was hitting up dry cleaners, haggling for the cheapest rates to cover his even-cheaper suits. Then it was off to get a shoeshine...but not just any shoeshine. No, he was going to find the most desperate nipper with the widest eyes and most eager *"Shine your shoes, sir?"* offer, and then completely ruin that kid's morning by monopolizing it for a few coppers. And sure enough, that's exactly where I found this skinflint in nobleman's clothing, leaning hard on a kid who was buffing his leather shoes.

Benny saw me coming, but pretended not to as he turned his attention back to the shiner. "Aw, now c'mon, kid. Dese are da real t'ing! Dat's fine *eye*-talian leather y'got deah!"

I smiled, catching the boy's doubtful look. If anyone knew the real thing, it was this kid. And this kid knew there was nothing real about this mook's "t'ing."

"Yessir," the boy huffed, his brow starting to bead up as he worked.

"Benny!" I called out.

For a reply, he pulled out the newspaper from underneath his arm and opened it to the center. I wasn't fooled. Benny wasn't smart enough to read the funnies.

"Benny, a moment of your time."

"Dat's a mighty tall order, Short Stuff," Benny sighed with a shake of his head and a shift of the toothpick between his lips. He was already turning the page, but his face was still as dim and blank as ever. "Time is money. I dunno. I got places ta go an' t'ings ta do."

Looking down at his polished dogs, Benny nodded with approval (Yeah, like this kid who had sweated over these cheap shoes really lived for that!) and flipped the boy a dime. "Deah ya go, kid, an' hey, keep da change," he smiled with a wink. "An' don't say Benny don't take care of his own."

The shoeshine was nine cents.

"I need to talk to you about DeMayo..."

And that was as much as I managed to get out before he tucked the newspaper under his arm and started walking away... and by the sudden vigor in his step, he needed to be somewhere. "DeMayo...DeMayo... DeMayo?" he uttered over and over, as if he'd never heard it before.

"I'm proud of you, Benny. You can speak and walk at the same time. Now tell me what you've heard about Pretty Boy."

This dink knew that long strides were the best way to make me work for information. I was doing just that because I was now downwind of him, catching whiffs of his sorry excuse for a cologne: a scent best described as two-week-old dragon piss. By the Fates, did he bathe in the stuff this morning?

"Hey, look!" I puffed, my short legs moving as wide as my girth would let me. "I don't think I'll be keeping you from any important date you got, and I'd hate to have you sweat your scent off. So how about we stop and talk a bit about Tony DeMayo?"

On every mention of his cohort's name, Benny's long, lanky legs widened their stride. "Sorry, Short Stuff, can't help ya deah."

"Really?" I was now close to running in order to keep up with him. "Any reason why you're feeling tight-lipped today?"

Benny glanced over his shoulder, his eyes angled downward at me struggling to keep up. I could see the creases in the corners of his eyes and the slight rise in his cheeks. The son of a bitch was smiling. He was enjoying this, and he knew I probably couldn't keep this pace up for much longer. Sad thing is, he was probably right. If I had my familiar deerskin boots around my feet, he wouldn't have stood a prayer. But if I tried hoofing after Benny in these street loafers, I'd be looking at blisters larger than griffin eggs.

When you want to grab Benny's attention, you compliment his taste in clothes, dames, and the "finer things" in life. (Too bad he didn't know any of the "finer things" outside of an Ace comb.)

"Hey, Benny! Lemme see those shoes of yours."

That brought him to a halt. As I caught up to him, the idea of knocking that smug look off his face with a war hammer briefly took my mind off my aching feet. *Another time*, I thought to myself, *another time*.

Flashing me that salesman smile of his, Benny stuck out one of his loafers, proud as a peacock. I tell you, that shoeshine boy had a talent. He had given those imitations a gleam and polish that would have made the Chalice of Tyrian look tarnished.

I nodded approvingly. "Nice."

He still was still sporting that wide, self-aggrandizing grin when I gave him a sudden push back into the alleyway. The garbage detail hadn't made it to this corner yet, so Benny wound up accessorizing his pinstripes with banana peels, rotten lettuce, and other garbage when he landed hard on his scrawny ass.

While indulging in the more colorful vocab of this realm, Benny fumbled for something in his coat pocket. Maybe a switchblade, maybe a snub-nose. I didn't know, and I didn't plan to wait and find out. I pushed hard against his chest, pinning him back against the alley's brick wall, and gave him a hard slap across the face for a chaser.

"Pipe down, Benny, or the shoes get it next!"

Yeah, I made sure that he'd fall without junking up the shoes. It was my bargaining chip in this little chat we were having. His swearing now dulled to a pathetic whimper as I pressed my fist harder against his chest, just itching for a reason to give him a quick punch to his ribs.

"Now, I'm gonna ask you one more time—"

"Ya pissant! Goddamn runt! My suit!" Ah, Benny had found some new bolts for his verbal crossbow. At this rate, I figured it was only a few more minutes before he started crying like a baby. "I'm gonna—"

"What? Tell Capone? Now why you wanna do that, Benny?" I stepped back, giving my thick red beard a few long, thoughtful strokes. "If you did that, I guess I'd have to tell Big Al about your sticky fingers, wouldn't I? You think he'd be really concerned about a dwarf with a short temper when his numbers runner is skimming off the top?"

Now this was something a lot of people suspected of Benny Riletto, but no one could really prove. I, however, was the one exception. It was on a divorce case a few months back in which a local business mogul was suspecting his young, nubile wife of enjoying the nightlife a little too much. Naturally, he called on me and my talents of discretion to ferret out the truth.

So I began following the wench to some of the livelier nightspots of Chicago, where I discovered that one of her more frequent companions was Benny Riletto. He must've been quite the Don Juan (or Samirill Rubbiar for the Acryonis crowd), able to fix a permanent smile on a woman's face and keep her breaths in quick, raspy moans. Either that, or he was one hell of a conversationalist. (If the former was true, someone bury a short sword in my gut, *please*!) At any rate, Riletto never hesitated to pick up the tab on their nights together, which always ended in the finest hotel suites of Chicago.

Although my attention was still focused intensely on the princess and her casual trysts, I couldn't help but notice this numbers runner who was doing well for himself. Too well, the more I watched him. When I had collected enough dirty linen on the princess, I started watching

Benny on my own dime, even sneaking a peek his numbers book when he was schmoozing what I could only assume was his potential ticket to easy money.

My "personal quest" revealed two sets of numbers in Benny's book. One set of numbers, payoffs, and profits was given to Capone's boys, and these numbers always added up. Never a dime or a dollar missed. All the cash was presented in neat little piles with a smiling (and slightly sweaty) Benny Riletto behind the transfer.

Then there was the second set of numbers, the *actual* numbers pulled in by Benny. Now sure, he wasn't all that impressive when you met him (and especially when you got to know him). He sure could sell the numbers game, though. When I first came across Benny pitching the numbers racket, I had to wonder if he was in possession of some charm or subliminal influencing spell. I was soon convinced it was his own kind of magic—the con-artist's kind. If anyone could sell brimstone to a rock dragon, Benny could. I was in no doubt that he was pulling in the cash, probably a lot more than the other numbers runners in his neck of Chicago. The detail, length, and ingenuity to which this weasel went to hide this mismanagement of funds would have impressed Gryfennosian tax collectors.

Because his fudging of the numbers remained consistently subtle enough for Capone and his seconds to not notice, Benny had a nice little windfall from his creative bookkeeping that allowed him to attract and entertain the upper crust of Chicago society. Win a prize such as the dowry of a Chicago princess, and he could retire from the business and remain set for several lifetimes.

Yeah, Benny was still a dim-witted prick, but he was hardly stupid when it came to crunching the numbers and playing the con.

After collecting a goodly amount of evidence so clear you would think it was Illesria crystal, I joined Benny one night over a cozy Italian dinner, just the two of us. I knew I was going to catch him in a private moment because when I had dropped off some incriminating photos of the Missus to my client about an hour beforehand, I could see it in my client's face that he and his sweet little wife were going to have an immediate sit-down about their future relationship.

So instead of Benny's usual "party with the princess," it was "dinner with a dwarf" where we talked about *our* future relationship. He flipped the bill for this dwarf's lasagna and tiramisu (and even took care of the tip) while sweating up a storm at the evidence before him. Someone knew his dirty little secret, and it was going to cost him in detailed inside information about the Organization for a good, long while.

Lately, Benny had been getting cocky: calling me "Short Stuff," ignoring me from behind his newspaper, and otherwise not taking seriously the one dwarf who could guarantee him a permanent room at the "Six Feet Under" flophouse. Today was as good as any day to remind him why it was in his best interest to be good to me.

"You look mighty good in this brown pinstripe number of yours," I said with a grin while straightening his lapels. "Might wanna make a note of that to your undertaker."

"Screw you, Baddings!"

Oh yeah, Benny had definitely creamed his java with troll's piss this morning.

"Ya know," he continued, "someday, dat ain't gonna stop me from takin' ya head off. Ya just watch. Real soon, Big Al won't be da only boss people's gotta deal wit!"

"Really? You thinking about taking over, Benny? Making Chicago your own?"

Now *this* I wanted to hear. Sure, he loved talking like a big shot, but Benny was usually smart enough to keep a bridle on that stag. Idle threats toward Big Al really didn't do much to lengthen one's lifeline; the streets not only had ears, but a mouth bigger than a Sacred Oracle. Looked like Benny was feeling his oats, and there had to be a good reason.

"Ya nevah know, Short Stuff. Maybe one day, I'll be callin' da shots from downtown."

"You think you can take down Big Al?"

"Why not? He ain't so tough. Hides behind a lotta hired guns, but hey, he's not as tough as he t'inks. Maybe one day he was, when he was in da streets, but dat was den. We're talkin' 'bout da heah an' now, ain't we? And you're gonna see a lotta changes in da heah an' now, Baddings."

The smell of rotting vegetables and overripe banana peels was beginning to overpower his cologne, which was an improvement if you ask me. Standing again on his polished shoes, Benny kicked a freckled lettuce leaf in my direction. It landed just shy of me, but you would have thought it had slapped me in the face by his smirk. "You might just have ta find anudda sap ta get ya inside scoop."

"You sure talk like a man with a plan, Benny."

I reached into my inner pocket and pulled out my pipe, which was stuffed with a nice tobacco. (Well, nice tobacco for Chicago. Never could find anything close to the "good stuff" from home, but hey, you make do, y'know?) I scratched a match against the rough brick of the building behind him.

"I bet DeMayo had a plan, too," I continued. "I wonder if you've got better taste in dives than he does."

Benny gave a slight huff, his mouth tight in disapproval. "Too bad fa him he couldn't keep 'is yap shut. DeMayo was too busy impressin' th' dames. All he hadta do was keep quiet, an' den—"

That was when he caught himself.

"What?" I asked politely, taking a few drags from my pipe while eyeballing him.

Benny straightened his tie and scoffed. "What, are ya deaf, Small Fry? Maybe ya didn't heah me earlier, Baddings, so I'll put it in terms ya might undastan'. Fu—"

Before Benny could drop that four-letter bomb, I gave him a swift punch in the balls. (Who says there ain't advantages in being a dwarf in a human's world?) He was back on his knees, hands clutching his family jewels, face turning anger-red with just a hint of painful-pale as the wind I knocked out of him emerged in a surprised, raspy groan.

My mother would have been so proud of her Baby Billibub.

The safety was off and the hammer was back as I stuck the tip of Beatrice's barrel against Benny's forehead, pushing him back up to face me. He was still dazed as I reached into his coat and tossed his Saturday-night pistol back into the alley. The sound of the gun clanging against trash cans brought him back to the Land of the Living. Taking another deep drag from my pipe, I gave Benny the same winning smile that I used to flash to a goblin before taking his head.

"Now listen up, ya spineless twerp. You've been testing my waters today. I want to know why. This ain't like you, Benny. You've got the backbone of a Maktashian slug, and about as much motivation. So you tell me what you and Anthony were cooking up, and I won't let Beatrice get in the last word."

"Okay, okay, *okay!!!*" With each "okay" his voice rose in pitch, reaching a point that could crack glass. After he took a deep breath, still fighting back tears from my unexpected punch below his belt, his voice was back to his annoying nasality. "C'mon, Baddings, what's ya beef?"

"My beef"—I snapped, poking him in the chest with my finger—"is that you're wasting my time! I'm on the clock here, and I don't like settling my arguments with Beatrice. Blood is a real bitch to clean out of the barrel. I can always get a new suit if your brains splatter on it, but I can't find another Beatrice. So you're not winning me over, and you're definitely not improving my mood!"

"Look, look, *look, Baddings!*" His hands were up in the air and shaking like a couple of leaves while I resumed my pipe-puffing. Enjoying the weed kept me from laughing at the fact he was in no real danger. This cretin wasn't worth the price of a bullet.

"I wasn't suppos'ta know about da package. I was droppin' off some numbahs fa Capone, an' happened ta catch a coupla words between da Boss an' his generals."

I shook my head. "Benny, you dumb mook! You really do have a talent for being at the wrong place at the wrong time. Go on."

Benny stared at me for a moment, his jaw tightening. He really didn't liked being talked down by a dwarf (and that's saying something considering our height differences), but he liked it even less when I was right.

"So," he began again, "I heah dem talkin' 'bout dis package..."

"A package. What was it? Booze shipment from up north? Opium? What?"

"Nevah heard what da package was, 'zackly...just dat he was hell-bent on gettin' it first. His boys were suppos'ta do a simple grab-n'-run, but den da trinket disappeahed. It wasn' wheah da boss was told it would be. I don' know why, but Capone was really layin' into his boys."

"And let me guess…Pretty Boy was one of them?"

"Well, yeah, Pretty Boy was deah," Benny started, but then his head tipped to one side, as if his own memory of events confounded him. Wouldn't be the first time this dink confused himself with his own facts.

"See—heah's da t'ing I couldn' follow. Pretty Boy was in da cleah, standin' on da Boss' right side. Ya know, dat whole right hand-a God t'ing? It was like Pretty Boy was covahed." He nodded to me with a self-satisfied smile. "I could see past dat. I was starin' right at 'im. I could see it in his face dat he knew more den what he was tellin' Capone 'bout da package."

"Really? Well, ain't you the clever detective?" I scoffed, wiping the smile off his face. I knew the point had been made that I really didn't feel like playing the banter game with him today, so I returned Beatrice back to her holster as I continued.

"So you two saw one another? Exchanged loving looks? And what then?"

He shrugged. "Yeah, we seen each othah. I was on my way outta deah, an' Pretty Boy stops me outsidah Capone's place. He recognized me as one of his boys, y'know? Anyways, we go's for a walk, see? A *friendly* walk."

Benny's face was always like one of those magical tomes, left open to perhaps the worst spell one could accidentally read out loud. He probably had made it clear to DeMayo he was seeing through him and his game with Capone. I couldn't imagine how hard Benny was pissing his pants during that walk.

"Pretty Boy tells me deah's dis oppa-toonity fa a change in t'ings. He wants ta include me in dis change. I mean, he *knew* I was loyal to him. Dat I'd done good fa him."

"Yeah, and you thought if Capone were no longer running the show, you could have a clean slate, right? Retire the creative bookkeeping? Maybe enjoy a bigger piece of the pie with a new boss in charge? After all, I'm thinking you're tired of being the low man."

"I *am*!" he barked. And in one of those rare moments, Benny looked sincere. He was looking for a promotion in the ranks, and it wasn't going to happen as long as Capone remained on the throne. "I shouldn' be just a numbahs guy. Yeah, I'm good at it, but I deserve bettah. I deserve da respect dose captains and generals get. Goddammit, I can do what dey do—only bettah! I'm smaht! *I am!* If I can stick it ta Capone, dat shows I got da brains to be a general."

"It shows you like tempting the Fates, ya stupid troll!" I blew a puff of the rich, spicy tobacco into his face, narrowing my eyes on him. "They scraped Pretty Boy off the remains of Sal's Diner, and *he* was smart. Not smart enough to keep his plans low-key, though. I wonder if he was smart enough not to let your name slip."

Benny's swollen pride deflated quickly, and he started to turn pale again. Taking another slow drag, I heard the crackle of weed in my bowl as he contemplated this.

"So how was the New Order going to come about?" I continued.

"I dunno, but it had sumtin' ta do wit dis package Capone was screamin' 'bout. DeMayo knew wheah it was, an' it was me an' Two Times who knew DeMayo had it."

Pauley "Two Times" Bennetti was just another foot soldier in the service of King Scarface. My paths rarely crossed with Pauley's, but I'd heard of him. Two Times wasn't called Two Times because you couldn't trust him. It was some kind of nervous tic of his, a slight stammer that would make him repeat full names or sentences. I wouldn't have penciled in his name as one who would turn on Capone, but he did fit the mold of a follower.

"The plan was to keep it on da move," Benny continued, "havin' me an' Two Times passin' it from place ta place, an' den we'd recruit a coupla people ta help us out. Ya know, so as no one would know wheah it is? First Pauley would get it, pass it ta his people, den I'd get a holdah it, pass it along, an' den back ta Pauley. Nobody nevah knew who had it."

I raised a bushy eyebrow. "And DeMayo trusted his yeomen blindly?"

"Me an' Pauley were paid bettah den ya t'ink," Benny huffed. "Bettah den my special bookkeepin'."

"Pretty Boy" DeMayo could charm the chemise off a tavern wench with a wink and a smile. I already knew that. Listening to Benny, it sounded as if Pretty Boy could also rally a platoon of tired and downtrodden soldiers against several regiments of hungry, bloodthirsty orcs. It was not that far of a reach to think that Two Times, especially if he was the same kind of follower that Benny was, had fallen under DeMayo's spell.

Two Times had been found floating off the docks last week, dead from a severe case of lead poisoning to the back of his skull. At least a bullet is a faster death than an arrow.

So a major player in the Organization, and a couple of two-bit hoods who couldn't find the shortest distance between two leagues with an enchanted road map, had been planning to overthrow the Gangland Boss of Chicago. And this overthrow had centered about a smash-and-grab job that went south…at least, for Capone. Staying one step ahead of his lord and master, DeMayo kept this package on the move. Whatever this package was, DeMayo thought it was his ticket to the throne.

"You said Capone was raising a stench over this package, Benny. What can you tell me about it?"

"It don' matter." He shook his head resolutely. "I don' know wheah it is. Two Times was da last one ta have it!"

Did this moron have wax in his ears? "I didn't ask *where* it was, I asked what you *knew* about it. You ever see this trinket?"

"Nah, it was always in a long case." He didn't seem to particularly care anymore if he spilled his guts to me now. "Felt like I was carryin' a pool stick, or sumtin' like dat. Dis was a long case, but thin, y'know?"

"So Capone was all up in arms in losing track of this package. Got a clue where it was supposed to be?"

"Look, I don' make it a habit ta listen t'othah people's talk, y'know? Dat's rude. But Capone was yellin', so I couldn' help it. He kept yellin' on an' on 'bout some museum an' his connection deah, yellin' about how da whole pointah th' job was ta do it befoah some exhibit opens. Den he blew 'is stack dat someone else got da package befoah he did."

Benny suddenly realized that he was still kneeling in garbage. He picked himself up, looking relieved when I backed away from him, out of arm's reach.

"I dunno what DeMayo was up to, but he was casin' some oddball places. First, deah was dese museums dat Capone kept talkin' 'bout, so we were casin' dose places, but when I was suppos'ta meet DeMayo ta find out wheah da pick-up would be, I wind up meetin' him at a library. And dis was wheah da job was gonna happen. A goddamn library! I mean, what's so important in a library?"

I could have given him an earful on that comment, but I knew my case would have fallen on deaf ears because my boy Benny had the brains of a troll. What was the point? If he *did* have anything in that skull of his, he would have been able to follow the hunch now forming in my head. When it came to a museum that doubled as a library, the search for where this heist of DeMayo's took place just narrowed by leaps and bounds.

The momentary lull in the conversation brought us both back to Benny's imitation-leather shoes, and him praying to God that I stayed happy and informed.

"Are we done heah, dwarf?"

"Yeah, we're done here." I reached into my wallet and tossed a Lincoln at him. "Get yourself cleaned up, Benny. You stink."

DRIVING ON THE WRONG SIDE
OF MEMORY LANE

I think it would have done Benny's pixie-sized brain a good turn to spend an afternoon or two in a library. If he had even attempted to nurture a curious streak in that sorry excuse for a noggin, he might have then ventured to other libraries and begun to figure out why DeMayo was suddenly obsessing over them as meeting spots.

The Ryerson Library, an institution that doubled as both a library *and* a museum, was just a short cab ride from where I ended up having lunch. (It was a relief to have anything resembling an appetite after I left Benny Riletto still searching through garbage cans for his piece. The smell in that alley rivaled a female orc's perfume!) Although it had only been around for about thirty years, the Ryerson already boasted a growing collection of artifacts, literary works, and essays from the smartest minds of the country.

Although humans have the potential to be thorough and efficient information-gatherers, their attention spans just won't last without some kind of distraction, be it booze, sex, or crime…and that's in *both* realms. Still, I can't complain. These were the distractions pushing me through the massive doors leading into the rotunda of the Ryerson.

Benny had mentioned that DeMayo kept meeting him "at a library," which confused him because he had overheard Capone planning to pull a job "on a museum" instead. My resulting hunch was that DeMayo arranged to meet at the last place Capone or the cops expected to find him: the scene of his own private heist. Now, it was time to find out if I was unlocking the right chest, and if so, to reap the rewards.

Unlike the gloominess of the downtown circuit court, the Ryerson rotunda was covered in bright white marble, and accented by incredible columns reminiscent of Trysillian palaces. Mighty impressive and mighty pretentious.

As my steps echoed down the polished corridor toward the main desk, I found myself really hoping that the harpy sitting behind it was going to reveal her true beauty by the time I got there.

Hope springs eternal.

Her hair was a short-cropped field of brown, and I couldn't help wondering if the worry lines I saw were chiseled into the stone surface of her face. Her spectacles only magnified her cold, hard stare at what she was reading, as if she were intending to intimidate the words off the page for instant comprehension. If the corners of her mouth had been pulled back any tighter, they would have touched at the back of her head. In short, she looked as if she had been drinking a bad batch of homebrew bitter.

"*Now, come on, Billi, are you being fair?*" I chided myself. "*Calling her a harpy? Drawing assumptions? How do you feel when people do that to you? How about you give this girl a chance, eh?*"

As I drew closer to the receptionist, her features seemed to soften. There was a touch of light in her eyes. Maybe my guess about her had been wrong...

I softly cleared my throat.

"Can I help you..." She looked up from her daily paperwork, and then looked down at me. "...*sir?*"

I think I heard hunting dogs in both this realm and my realm yelp in pain. That was a voice that could make a siren flinch. Ouch!

Still, ever the optimist, I started off with a wink and a smile. "You could, toots, but I think we would get arrested for doing that in public."

No laugh. A stare worthy of a Scout. Yeah, even in my world, the academics were cold fish.

"The name's Baddings, ma'am," I continued discreetly as I showed her my credentials with a friendly grin, "and I understand you had an artifact get up and walk out without even saying 'Good night.' I'm currently involved in a case that could lead to its recovery, but first, I'd like to know a little more about it. Anybody here wanna talk?"

She still wasn't smiling, but I think she had found a moment of delight at the prospect of returning her attention to the work I had so rudely interrupted. "If you will just have a seat, Mr. Baddings, I will tell someone you're here."

Oh, this lady wasn't serious! I had to chuckle at the utter presumption of humans like this one. Somehow, it was thought that your height was equal to your comprehension skills, so there were those who assumed me short in both. And just a moment before, I had been giving this battle-axe the benefit of the doubt!

"Oh, that's fine, ma'am. I apologize if I was a little brazen earlier. I've been running around all morning. Guess I got a little light-headed."

As I delivered this, she continued to peer at me through her glasses, fighting that primal urge to go after me in much the same manner as her ancient ancestors would have hunted game.

"Really, it's fine if the Ryerson is too busy to talk to me," I added with a noncommittal shrug. "If you don't mind, I'm just going to take a moment and catch my breath before heading on to my appointment at the *Tribune*. I appreciate your time."

Her scowl receded a bit as I took off my fedora, fanned myself with it, and then waddled over to a nearby chair. Besides making me appear shorter than my actual height, that waddle was a warning to Ryerson's old war-horse that I had no intention of masking my appearance and blending in with the background. It also said that if I was going to carry myself with pride in this situation, then I had nothing to lose in talking to the press. Sure, the press could take a shot at me, but if I could buffet this old bat's blows, would I really be put off by a pack of reporters?

Probably not.

"Um, sir?" I winced as she managed a grin. I knew that had to hurt. "Sir, if you will just give me a moment, I'll get Dr. Hammil."

I replaced my hat, straightening it on my head as her footfalls faded out of earshot. In light of my comments and the frenzied pace she had taken down the corridor behind her, I would be surprised if Dr. Hammil weren't Ryerson's curator.

As I paced casually back and forth, I could just make out the paperwork on her desk—still out in the open, since she left in such a hurry. Looked like the Ryerson was planning to dedicate a new wing with an exclusive shindig, attended by only the most exclusive patrons of the arts. Quite the Who's Who of Chicago's Financial Elite. DeMont, Evans, Rothchild...

Funny thing, that—the Lesinger family was absent from the invitation list.

I was about to help myself to a closer look at this guest list when I heard the battle-axe's high heels returning, accompanied by another pair of footfalls. The shoes ahead of hers weren't expensive. They sounded more comfortable, practical. Academic.

He was taller than a High Oak and about as skinny as a Valley Pine, looking at me rather incredulously though wire-rimmed spectacles that were similar in make to the receptionist's. But unlike my helpful harpy, he was sweating. There were creatures of the undead I'd crossed (and had to kill again...damn, talk about redundant!) that looked healthier than he did.

From the look of his slight build, I surmised that this was about as much excitement and exercise as he could handle. His plain suit and unkempt hair told me he was not used to these kinds of sudden surprises. Assistants and tour guides usually dealt with people, while he usually dealt with further study. The prospect of an embarrassing state of affairs reaching the papers, though, was evidently enough to tear him away from his various parchments, scrolls, and testaments. This bookworm was trying his best to be the pillar of intellectual strength and control, but he only knew about "brave face" from tapestries and woodcuts. His smile seemed as painfully executed as his receptionist's.

He bent at the waist, extending a clammy hand to me. "Good morning. Welcome to the Ryerson Library." The bookworm adopted a bizarre, bird-like quality as he tipped his head slightly to one side, giving his long, angular beak the semblance of a hawk's. "I'm Dr. Samuel Hammil, curator of the Ryerson. How can I help you, Mister...?"

"Baddings. Billi Baddings. Well, Doc, you and I can go for a stroll...someplace a little more private?" I looked around us, hearing my own pipes bouncing off the walls. "Someplace a little more *quiet*," I added *sotto voce*.

We had made it about halfway down the main corridor of the Ryerson's offices before I gave the sound of our footsteps some company. "Listen, Doc, you and me gotta have a talk, man-to-man, about something you lost. Now you can go on and just brush me off like yesterday's lint, but I would be out of line if I didn't tell you this caper may be bigger than the both of us."

Dr. Hammil already gave me the impression he was jumpier than a wizard's apprentice, and about as mousy as one, too. I didn't expect the lashing he suddenly loosed on me like that of a line of skilled archers.

"Mr. Baddings, I do not know for whom you work, nor do I care to know. This is merely a formality—and a warning—asking you not to take this particular matter to the press."

As if to accent his threat (and perhaps the most civil and polite one I've ever received, I might add), he removed his spectacles to polish them with a harsh, sharp breath and a clean silk hankie.

"I warn you that our list of benefactors are incredibly loyal to this institution," he continued, "and they would take it as a personal affront if the Ryerson were smeared by an unfortunate incident such as this. These people," he delivered imperiously, "could make your life very uncomfortable."

I really don't like being threatened.

"Capone could do the same to you," I replied with a deadpan expression.

His vigorous buffing came to a sudden halt, the glass spectacle having just snapped between his finger and thumb. He was no longer sweating, but with the paleness in his skin growing paler yet, I thought he was going to fade away in front of me. Nope, he never thought someone of "that element" would be involved, and from the look on his face, he couldn't understand why Capone would suddenly turn his interests on the Ryerson. Poor scholar. So smart, he was completely clueless.

"Look, Doc, why not drop the pretense?" I shrugged, pulling out a small notepad and pen. "I don't intend to tell you who hired me, nor do you want to know, but I'm here as a personal service to the pursuits of higher learning. I may not look it, but lemme tell ya, I got nothin' but appreciation for the books. Research and private investigating go hand-in-hand, so how's about we work together on this, eh?"

With the now-broken spectacles in hand, Hammil's hazel peepers were either narrowing on me in some weak form of intimidation, or merely attempting to focus on the four-foot, one-inch pain-in-the-ass that showed no signs of getting any better unless he played by its rules.

Taking a deep breath, he cast a squinty glance from one end of the corridor to the other. So far, it appeared that no one but us had heard the Boss' name dropped, or the reason why I was there. That reassurance gave him enough courage to keep his shield up…battered and dented as it might have been.

"Mr. Baddings," he asserted in his best "official" voice, "as curator of The Ryerson, my priority is this institution. I am not obligated in any way to divulge confidential matters to hasten your current investigation."

"And being a private eye doesn't obligate me to let you know that Capone is watching this precious institution of yours, and has been for a long time," I fired back. "Now you know who's the visiting team in your ball park. You might even live longer because of it. So *quid pro quo*, Doc, and I give you my word as an honest dwarf, it stays with me. Tell me what I want to know: What was lifted?"

Judging from how fast those gears in his noggin were working, Dr. Hammil was caught between a rock dragon and a hard palace. He didn't like it, but he knew he owed me, and he could tell I wasn't one to be two-timed. Perhaps he had been thinking of going to the police, or even hiring some of my competition to recover this package. But if he truly wanted to make The Ryerson his priority, why hadn't he called anyone yet? Seeing as how the Doc was being so secretive, whatever DeMayo pinched must've been one hell of a score.

Dr. Hammil replaced his spectacles on the tip of his nose, the thin crack across the left lens catching the late-afternoon sun filtering in through the cathedral-like windows. Loosing a heavy sigh, he motioned for me to follow him into his office.

For a scribe's office, *this* was impressive. The room resembled one of Dunheim's main reading rooms, a veritable fortress of books in which you could virtually feel the magic in the air. Most of the wall space was taken up with awesome oak towers of bookcases, and where the shelves were full, other books were stacked horizontally across their brethren. The vaulted ceilings looked closer than they truly were, and any sunlight coming in through the windows appeared as flying buttresses of light, lending an air of romantic mystery to this cramped cubbyhole. (Had Dr. Hammil's office housed apprentices muttering ancient languages to create balls of fire or to turn toads into bats, I think I would have shed a tear out of sheer nostalgia.)

On the bookworm's desk, a tiny fan's futile attempt to circulate the still air was overpowered by the smell of mold from long-unopened books and the fresh ink of new editions. The books covering most of his desk were thick and monstrous, with a dozen or so bookmarks stuck at various points. Five huge tomes remained opened and stacked on top of one another. Dr. Hammil set three of these volumes aside, still opened to their respective places.

I recognized this kind of setting straight from my own office, only with fewer bookcases and a little less impressive of architecture. It looked like I wasn't the only one handling a tough case as of late.

I could tell the crack in his eyeglasses was making it hard to read what appeared to be long Latin passages in the open book before him. Emitting another heavy sigh, Hammil shook his head, looking up from the book and then down to me.

"To be frank with you, Mr. Baddings," he began, keeping his finger at the last place he had read, "I wish I knew exactly what *was* stolen. I know what the artifact was, of course, but as to its origins and its proper name, I have no earthly idea. I do know this much: There is no documentation of this piece anywhere in recorded history. If something like this turns out to be authentic, it would completely turn the academic world on its ear."

"You mean your museum got a hold of something that ain't in the history books? Some kind of Grecian urn, or something prehistoric?"

"No, this artifact was forged well after the Bronze Age, and perhaps even the Iron Age. If we could only authenticate it with a written reference or even a simple hieroglyph, this find could predate the Scottish Rebellions of the thirteenth century. In short," he concluded exasperatedly, "this artifact is either one of the greatest mysteries of our age, or an extremely elaborate hoax intended to discredit the Ryerson."

Standing on tiptoe to get a glance at the open books surrounding Dr. Hammil, I was surprised to find that they were all turned to sections concerning weaponry...*my* kind of weaponry. He had marked passage after passage on swordmaking, styles of blades, and the application of various edged weapons.

These etchings and woodcuttings brought back memories of my part in Acryonis' Great Race Wars, when dwarves battled against elves, elves battled against humans, and then finally the Allied Races battled against the Black Orcs. Days like that began with pristine armor, kissed with that smell you can only find in leather. On the setting of the sun, the leather's deep, rich brown color was soaked with a darker red, giving your armor a brilliant sheen of black, and that comforting smell of leather was replaced by the sharp tang of blood belonging to you, the enemy, and your buddies. Death always covered you, one way or another; when you bowed your head and closed your eyes to give eternal thanks to the Fates for making it to the end of the day alive, you would find graphic images awaiting you behind those closed lids of yours, goblins' howls of horrific surprise at the feel of a battle-axe to the chest faintly echoing in your ears.

Yeah, those were the good times.

"This might surprise you, Doc, but I've got a bit of a background in...*ancient* weaponry." Hell, this had been Basic Training for me. "Mind if I ask about the particulars of this 'artifact'? Are we talking about a sword here?"

"You are a perceptive one, Mr. Baddings," Hammil remarked with a sneer as he motioned to all the sword-related books and papers about his desk.

"That's what I get paid the greenbacks for, Doc. Now how's about dropping the Enchanted Gauntlet of Snobbery and telling me something about this item you've lost track of?"

You know, people who think they're better than others never like being called on it. You ever want to cut someone down to size (and with a comment like that coming from a dwarf, pardon the pun), just call them on their bluff. Makes you a hell of a card player and an even better private dick.

Problem was, a guy like Dr. Samuel Hammil had the power to escort me out of the prestigious Ryerson Library. He was the clout and the authority. On the other hand, he now knew he had Capone keeping an eye on his hallowed halls, and he could tell I had no problem standing up to Capone...all four feet plus one inch of me.

Hammil went to say something. Paused. Then went to say something again, but paused again. Finally slumping his shoulders, he handed me a series of notes scribbled onto a couple of yellowed sheets of paper.

"These are notes from an archeological dig in Egypt from two years ago," he began.

I could barely make out the chicken-scratch, but what I think he really wanted me to eyeball was the sketch. The Doc walked behind me and ran his finger along the length of the drawing in my hand. "As you can see by this rendering, Mr. Baddings, this sword uncovered at the site is anything but Egyptian in its make."

Once I had gotten into the seventh- and eighth-grade level reading in the library, I did some research on the weapons, both past and present, of this world. Being a soldier, you ought to know who's armed with what, wherever you're hanging your shield and battle-axe. I learned that Egyptians, Persians, and folks of that area preferred scimitars—real skinny, long curve, and light. And I remember seeing depictions of Chinese warriors charging into battle with similar blades, drawn and held high above their heads.

I use blades like that to butter my toast.

Anyway, the sword in this sketch resembled a two-handed broadsword, more reminiscent of European than Egyptian make. Now I knew the Persians and Chinese liked their swords pretty and elegant, but this one was decorated beyond the point of gaudy, with jewels all over the guard and carvings along the blade and the hilt. There was no chance it was a true battle weapon, although its size and visible sturdiness suggested it could take a solid hit from my battle-axe. Nah, I figured this weapon was better suited as a wall hanging in some Prince's bungalow, something to impress one of those virginal princesses before taking them to bed and making them just a princess. With this sketch, the ambiance of Dr. Hammil's office, and all these books on weapons,

Miss Lesinger's case was adding some serious asphalt to this Memory Lane of mine.

"There is very little we can tell about how a sword of obvious Anglo-Saxon style and make found a home in Ancient Egypt, ages before the Crusades," Dr. Hammil remarked. "Since its discovery, we have been trying to find any reference to this weapon in the tomb's hieroglyphs."

"The Romans made it to England. Maybe the Egyptians did it beforehand and brought back some souvenirs?"

"If that were the case, this would suggest the existence of an Egyptian empire older and larger than Caesar's!" the curator replied with more than a measure of skepticism. "This would have to be an occupation that, once it fell, had all signs of it eradicated. Tell me, Mr. Baddings, of a civilization that could simply revert to its origins after the fall of a regime?"

He had a point there. During the Elvish Occupation years, the haughty ones imposed a lot of their culture on us. Some of it—such as how to build structures into a mountain as opposed to on top of a mountain—was useful. Their wine? Well, it made a great cleaning solvent, I'll give it that. We still have some structures in our villages with Elvish carvings and their haughty mottos and philosophies. If the Egyptians were feeling that ambitious, there was bound to be some lingering influence in both the conquered and conquering lands.

"And so therein lies the mystery," I mused, flipping through the notes associated with the sketch. "How does a sword of European make find its way across the continent to finally come to rest in Ancient Egypt?"

"This is just the top layer of the mystery, Mr. Baddings. According to the amount of sand and dust on it, the sword had not been there long compared to the other items we have found at the site. A few years, at most. It was as if it just happened to find itself there in the middle of the Valley of Kings, inside a sealed tomb. Our original goal for the excavation was to find out more about the dynasty associated with our site, but now we are simply trying to find any reference that could authenticate this sword's presence. If we do that, we could find an entirely new avenue to explore in Ancient Egyptian civilizations. Perhaps this is a bit over your head, Mr. Baddings—"

I looked up from the archeologist's notes with a grimace. I'm short. Not stupid. "Try me, Doc."

"The possibility of discovering dynasties or empires that stretched farther than Alexander the Great or Genghis Khan? From an anthropological and archeological point of view, this is quite exciting. It could completely change what is currently accepted in academic circles as the history and evolution of civilization."

"And you've lost it."

Dr. Hammil gave a deep huff, as if insulted by my limited vocabulary. The temptation to just sock him in the mouth and end this once and for all was there, and it was strong. Instead, I turned my attention back to the archeologist's rendering. "What else can you tell me about this sword? Any other outstanding qualities about it?"

"Apart from being found in a sealed tomb?" he countered, flipping through a stack of papers on one corner of his desk. "I have a photograph in here somewhere that will show you a bit more detail. Very distinguishing. There is also the crafting of the blade itself. According to some of the participants of the dig…"

Hammil gave out a little "Ah!" as he produced a photograph sandwiched between the illegible chicken-scratch of notes. Then he paused for a moment, staring at it intently for a moment. It was the most enlightened look the dear professor had worn on his face since my arrival.

"According to some of the participants at the dig…?" I asked, reminding him where he left me in this chat of ours.

Hammil blinked. "Oh?" His eyes returned to the photo, then back to me. "Oh, yes, yes, yes, of course." Clearing his throat, he looked at the photo again. "Yes…" The look of inspiration disappeared from his face as he continued. "According to some of the participants at the dig, the sword creates some odd harmonic anomaly when someone wields it."

I stopped writing for a second, first trying to figure out how to spell 'harmonic anomaly,' then trying to figure out what the hell that was. "You want to try that again, Doc? This time in the common tongue, not in Ryerson dialect?"

He sighed heavily, rolling his eyes. "It made a noise, Mr. Baddings," he continued, his tone now slow and deliberate, as if I were a mere apprentice to his all-powerful sorcery. Pompous ass. "Our team could not understand how or why, but theorized it was the engravings in the blade, along with its unique metal composition and the blade's angles, that made it do so."

"Unique metal composition?" I asked.

"It was in a sealed tomb, but there was only dust along the blade. No signs of rust or decomposition. And there were incidents reported from team members that the sword emitted harmonized tones as it cut through the air." He let out a dry cough that I soon recognized as an academic's chuckle as he handed me the photo with a few documents still paper-clipped to it. "It may sound a bit silly, but we call it the 'Singing Sword' around here. I suppose calling it that is not extremely professional, but much easier than referring to it by its catalog name 'Item #EW234450-112-MM' especially in communiqués and conversation."

"And how about these markings?" I asked, my eyes straining to see them on the wide-angle photo. "You said they were glyphs?"

He bent back the photo and a few more pages to a second photograph concealed within the notes. "This is a better photograph of markings along the blade. They appear to resemble Ancient Chinese calligraphy, but only in their writing style. They match no symbols known for any kind of ancient language we have on record."

I took one look, and my blood ran cold.

Dr. Hammil was right about the markings. They didn't resemble Norse Runes, the Greek alphabet, Egyptian hieroglyphs from the Rosetta Stone, or even those cave drawings found in Arizona. Nope, that would be way too convenient, and way too friggin' easy on a dwarf like me.

I closed my eyes for a few seconds, praying everything the Doc was telling me and what I was looking at was all part of a really bad dream. But instead of waking up with my battle-axe under my pillow and a shapely redhead bringing me breakfast in bed with a smile, I was still in the Doc's moldy, cramped office in the Ryerson, the dust from volume upon volume of references, journals, and encyclopedias just catching the rays of a dying afternoon as I held on to a photograph that trembled lightly in my hand.

The writing was *Elvish*. No question. The words were definitely written in an obscure Elvish script, not known in my parts for well over a millennium. A lot longer for downtown Chicago and Ancient Egypt.

Without bothering to ask, I tucked the close-up photo into my coat pocket along with my own notes. This time, I was the one who was sweating.

"Mr. Baddings," Dr. Hammil finally spoke, a little confused (and maybe a touch curious) as to what I was doing. "That photograph is museu—"

"Doc, I'll bring it back, but I've got a need for it!"

His eyes grew as huge as a Kummerian swamp lizard's; if they were to have grown any larger, they would have probably popped out of this poor bookworm's head. "You know what the inscription says, don't you?"

I now had won the last thing I wanted from Dr. Hammil right now—his undivided attention. "Mr. Baddings, what is it? If you know something about this matter, I must hear what it is! This is a find of incredible signif—"

"I am sure you could win yourself and the Ryerson a goodly amount of publicity and patronage with this discovery of yours, Doc," I said sharply, trying to mask my fear with a much-needed warning. "Just listen to me; this sword is something you don't want to mess with."

With that, I left his office almost at a dead run with Dr. Hammil close on my heels. "You cannot leave here with that photo!" he shouted. "I'll call the police!"

Now, unless you've got a set of hooters that I can rest a shot of bourbon on top of and a tight little butt in need a good spanking, I'm not too crazy about being touched. When I felt the Doc's grip on my shoulder, I instantly turned into him, grabbing his wrist and striking his chest with my opposite forearm.

Dr. Hammil was hardly needing the force I exerted to pin him against the hard marble wall, but I didn't spare a thought on how hard his head bounced against the wall, how winded he was when the air got knocked out of him on impact, or how hard his butt hit the floor after sliding down to the ground. The only thought on my mind was the writing on the blade.

"Fine!" I barked in his face. "Call the police. Then *they'll* call Capone. After you talk to Chicago's finest, you can be sure that Chicago's muscle won't be too far behind."

I left him slumped against the wall, confident that I'd got in the last word. But I got to give the Doc credit: He was able to catch his breath a lot quicker than I had anticipated. He was back to shouting at the top of his lungs again, over the hurried footfalls of concerned colleagues now racing to his aid. Over the murmurs of worry and sharp exclamations at my "outrageous behavior" displayed in the hallowed halls of the Ryerson came the one thing I really hoped wouldn't.

"Mr. Baddings, what is that writing?" Hammil shouted. "I need to know!"

"Trust me, Doc…" My voice reverberated down the hallway, *"You don't!!!"*

I think I slipped the cabbie a twenty, and the words *"Step on it"* came out of my mouth. I think I was thrown to the back of the passenger seat as he took off. I don't remember. All my attentions were devoted to the Elvish script in the photograph. I knew enough of the language to work with it back in the day when elves and dwarves were working together for a common goal. It seemed like a lifetime ago when I was translating scrolls that held new orders for me and my boys. Since we were the Allied Races then, the orders were sometimes written in Human dialects, but occasionally I would be called in to decipher the overly flowing calligraphy of the elves, who were calling most of the strategic shots.

Let me just say that translating Elvish script is tough. You have to take a simple phrase like *"Go get me a beer"* and elevate it to a proclamation of universal importance. You also have to add in a few more words—all of the multi-syllabic variety—to this five-phrase request, and then adopt an air of *"Do you have any idea of how important I am?"* when speaking. After interpreting Elvish for a meeting of the military heads,

I usually downed a tankard of the local pub's hardest ale to counter my splitting headache.

When I finally looked up, the cab was idling in front of my office building. Knowing the driver and I were more than square (the cab ride couldn't have been more than five dollars), I placed the photograph back in my pocket and bolted upstairs for my office. Miranda was there, letting the bill collectors know we would be square for the next two months. She had that smile on her face to say that it was, for a change, a really good Monday for us.

Well, it *was* a good Monday until she saw me.

"Billi? Billi, you don't look so good, hon."

"Miranda…"

I stopped for a moment at the door frame of my office and finally took a breath. I know I was probably a mess of sweat, paleness and downright terror. I'm just thankful I hadn't pulled a "Benny" in my pants yet. "Even if it's Joe McCarthy offering me the position of shortstop, you hold my calls."

"Billi?"

"Just do it!" I yelled.

Miranda knew that if I ever yelled at her, she would get an extra week's pay as my way of saying I was sorry for my temper. She also knew one of my outbursts was a sign of a serious case of dragon shit hitting the fan.

The office door shut behind me, the *"click"* of the lock making me stop for a second. In the perfect quiet, I could hear my heart pounding in my ears like pixie wings against windowpanes. I closed my eyes tight and gave my head a shake, trying to recover a bit of that calm, cool reputation that had taken me a year to build as a private dick. But all I could see in my self-imposed darkness were the characters engraved on the sword in that photograph.

Elvish writing in Chicago, 1929? No. Please, for love of the Fates, no. It couldn't be.

In the corner of my office stood a tiny icebox that kept a few consumable odds and ends, aside from the obvious. I pulled out a small block of ice and gave it a few whacks with the icepick, chiseling out enough hunks to fill a tall tumbler. Soon, my office was filled with the cracks, pops and hisses of warm bathtub gin covering the ice, followed by a few quick gulps that polished off half the drink. Downing alcohol this fast always made me light-headed, but it was helping me to calm down…sort of.

The chilled glass felt good up against my temple, giving me a moment's peace before I turned to the modest bookcase in the corner. No, my library was not as extensive as Dr. Hammil's, but it was just as essential to my work and recreation. Right now, I was focused only on one book: my private log from my service in Acryonis, shelved in between a few literary classics I had enjoyed in my time at the library and a couple of books on baseball.

I forced my legs to walk over to the bookcase so I could retrieve the old weather-worn journal. "Go to the desk," I said out loud. "Turn on the lamp," I told my hand.

So far, so good. With the ice chunks providing a reassuring *"tink-tink-tink-tink"* music in the background, I flipped through the journal till I arrived at an entry that would either confirm or deny a growing hunch: my last assignment, the raid on the Black Orcs' Keep of Tyril in the Dark Realm of the North.

Back in those days, we had been told that the Nine Talismans of Acryonis were various ancient relics and baubles, all possessing magic qualities. Separately, they could do some damage. Among them was a ring that could unlock shadows, giving the ring's bearer total control of them; a chalice that could give whomever drank from it the power of a God; and a medallion that controlled time itself. Together, those nine different doodads promised the world on a string, but that string was always attached to some provision that cost you hard. A few years of life, if you were lucky. Your soul, if you weren't careful.

Among these talismans was the Sword of Arannahs, a weapon of immense power that called upon the elements of Darkness and could command demon armies to wipe entire realms clean of life. Its wielder would know no enemy. Anyone standing before the Sword of Arannahs would be laid to waste, and those behind it would either live to serve, or feel its touch of death.

The entry soon confirmed my worst fears. The Elvish writing recorded in my journal (which I occasionally used as a reference for my translations) was a perfect match with the glyphs etched into the flat of the found in Egypt: *"The wielder meek shall possess this blade and bring about the servitude of a world."*

Even in my world, we didn't really understand what that meant. I do remember the same conclusion everyone in my team from the Allied Races reached: This whole *"servitude of a world"* thing was a bad idea, and the Sword of Arannahs was a dangerous weapon in the wrong hands.

As this case had now become one of *those* cases, I knew at last what I never wanted to know: The Sword of Arannahs was in fact the Singing Sword, and now two of America's biggest crime bosses were looking for it.

That was when I puked into my office wastebasket.

A light rapping sounded on my office door as I gave a few more heaves, the bathtub gin leaving my mouth as quickly as it had entered. The room was spinning, partially from my home mix of gin, but mainly due to everything from the afternoon now coagulating in my head like a severe belly slash on the mend.

It was not out of the ballpark that the Talismans could have surfaced here. I mean, among some of these "rare" books severely undersold in nearby dealers' shops were the words and chronicles of my time. And then there was me, the dwarf-now-dick in Chicago. So yeah, why not?

Then again, what did I know about that magic shit? Not enough to fill a fairy's codpiece, I'm here to say. But what were the possibilities of another "banished talisman" finding its way into this realm and being christened, for example, "Excalibur?" Could the people who were burned at stakes and left hanging at the gallows on trumped-up accusations of witchcraft actually dumb mooks who had been sucked into voids of oblivion before me? How about this world's Chinese culture, filled with dragons? Could those dragons have been unfortunate beasts on the wrong end of some wizard's spell?

Stumbling away from the foul stench of my wastebasket, I picked up the photo I'd dropped—this photo of a sword that had just happened to pop up in an archeological dig in Egypt, out of the blue.

"*According to the amount of sand and dust on it, compared to the other items we have found at the site, the sword had not been there long. A few years, at most...*" Dr. Hammil had told me. Should I guess, around the same time I arrived here?

I heard the rapping again. Miranda's silhouette was flanked by two others, which were a little larger and fainter because they were farther away from her and the door.

"Uh, Billi, you okay in there?"

"Yeah, Miranda," I grunted, "but I really don't want to see anybody right now."

"Billi..." her voice quivered lightly, and then fell silent.

She couldn't hide it that time. Fear. I looked up from the photo to see the other two shadows move closer to her. Shoving the photo into my pocket, I fought to walk a straight line to the coat rack. My hand had just made it around Beatrice when the shadows halted their advance and Miranda found her voice again.

"Billi, it's the cops. They want to talk to you about Benny Riletto. They just found him dead in some alleyway."

I let go of Beatrice and shook my head, hoping that the twerp hadn't gone to the trouble to change suits.

CHAPTER SIX
SUITS AND SAPS

The alleyway I had seen up close and personal earlier that morning was now crawling with flatfeet of all kinds, with the neighborhood's more inquisitive types camping out on their stoops to watch the sideshow. Not that there was a lot to see from where they were sitting—due to the safe distance at which coppers were keeping the motley assortment of bystanders, all anyone could see of the crime scene were the cops, their cars, and a lot of flashes coming from the alleyway. People with a good view were catching quick glimpses from their windows, but with a flutter of curtains or a good yank against a set of blinds, they were gone. The best way to know nothing is to see nothing, even if you can hear it over the radio.

The way my uniformed escorts were hustling me through the barrier of cops holding back public eyes and curious mob fans, you would have thought I was some kind of Police brass. The crowd we were muscling our way through was now screaming even louder at the sight of a dwarf flanked by cops and getting a front row to the crime scene. I kept the peepers forward out of habit as the voices behind me grew more distant and the murmurs of detectives and uniforms in the alleyway became more intelligible.

Suddenly, my stride was halted by a fresh-faced young kid careening around the corner of the alleyway. Sporting freckles across his nose and cheeks, he looked barely above the age limit for joining the Academy. I had to stifle a snicker under the dire circumstances, but it really was hard to take the look of a farm kid in the black duds of the 15th precinct seriously.

Once I saw his eyes, though, I gave him plenty of room. I knew that look extremely well. Wore it myself decades ago, and later, I found that all the green recruits wore that face in their first few battles. The first time you watch a buddy get torched by a rock dragon or an orc drive its fist through a comrade's chest, you can't be expected to keep your food down for long. (I still manage to get all queasy whenever I catch a whiff of breakfast sausage.)

I took another few steps back, adding to his already-generous amount of personal space. Good thing my instincts were on the mark: This cop set a new distance record in cookie-tossing. It would have cost me a few of the Lesingers' bills to get what was coming up out of him off of my shoes.

Just then, my shadow appeared for a second on the wall the rookie was holding up with one hand. Then again, and again. I could only shake my head and feel for this poor constable. His first picture in the Chicago papers wouldn't be apprehending the low-lifes threatening Chicago's innocents, nor would it be busting one of the biggest illegal bootlegging networks working out of his precinct. It would be upchucking his lunch in front of a dwarf detective.

"Well, well, well," huffed a thick brogue from the alleyway. "If'n it ain' tha littl' Circus Freak o' Chicago, comin' ta jine us this fine afternoon. Wish I cou' say I was surprised ta fin' out y'was 'ere this marnin'."

"Is that what you heard, O'Malley? Well, thank the Fates you finally got those damn potatoes out of your ears. I bet you're hearin' all kinds of stuff now."

What little civility he had in his voice dissipated like a mist after a warlock takes his leave. "I 'eard enuff ta haul yer fat arse down 'ere, ya freak ya!"

I shot a glance over my shoulder at the rookie, who was still trying to collect himself. "And with your boys extending such a friendly invite," I replied to O'Malley with a wink and a smile, "you think I'm going to stand you up? After all, this is our first date. People are going to talk."

Still nothing. His face didn't budge. I wondered if some wizard had, once upon a time, slipped through a portal and cursed him as a child to grow up without a sense of humor.

This mirthless creature towering over me was Chief John O'Malley, a crusty Irishman who—regardless of the prejudice I'm sure he encountered on the trip upward to his lofty office—could not care a succubus' pimpled ass whether he insulted me or not.

I first met O'Malley while working on yet another divorce case, during which my client had suddenly fallen ill with a severe case of murder. (Being pushed from the top of a four-story building will do that to you.) O'Malley, who had just received his Police Chief appointment, wanted to make his first case an open-and-shut one. The press quoted his claim that the jilted ex-wife had taken matters into her own hands and let gravity do the dirty work.

Tribune newshounds were about to run a story on the ex-wife's arrest when "an anonymous source" sent in photographs of her enjoying some extra-curricular business. Seen clearly in these photos of the couple enjoying a romantic afternoon in Hyde Park was a large clock, keeping perfect time in the background. In another photo taken from a different angle, an outdoor concert provided their afternoon's entertainment. It also confirmed her location at the moment of my client's fall.

The story swept across Chicago faster than an ogre horde blinded by blood lust. When the article ran, I chuckled at my reporter-pal's final comment: *"If this is any indication of what we can expect from Chief O'Malley, perhaps we will have to place our faith in small wonders."* It was a pleasant nod to me, and subtle enough that you would have to be pretty clever to pick up exactly to whom he was referring.

No sooner had I finished reading than the phone rang. O'Malley was a lot more clever than he appeared.

The Chief had kept a giant black mark by my name ever since, taking bizarre pleasure in trying to put a chink in my chain mail whenever he could. Note, I did say, *trying*. His cleverness did little to make up for his lack of wit. However, his inability to get under my codpiece only egged on his attempts at insulting me, and I enjoyed watching him take a swing only to swing. Poor mick couldn't knock one out of the park if I told him what pitch I was throwing. Whenever our paths cross, his face gets a little harder and his hair is graced by a few more white hairs in that sea of red.

"Listen, Chief, if you hauled me all the way down here just to practice your battlefield insults on me, I'm flattered that you invited all the press. You must have an incredible verbal infantry at the ready. Since I'm *not* thinking that's the sole reason you called me here, how about explaining to me why I'm in the middle of a crime scene by invitation, provided you talk slow so your brain can keep up."

O'Malley beady eyes never left me as he walked over to the freckled cop and slapped a hand on the rookie's shoulder. "Go home, Donovan. Ya've seen enuff for a day."

The rookie was breathing evenly again, his pallid look accented by those freckles of his. He was one of Chicago's Finest, and now his picture was probably going to wind up on the front page of the *Tribune*, the *Daily Herald*, or—Fates forbid—one of those smaller, independent rags that aren't worth the paper they are written on. (Yeah, I know I don't talk like a scholar, but when you are weaned on the classics and the finest voices in literature, dime-store newspapers hammered out on basement typewriters are an insult in every way.)

"Right, then. An' now t'you, Shorty." O'Malley stared at me for a minute, an eyebrow rising slowly as he studied me standing underneath him. "If i' t'were any other crime scene, I'd toss y'outta here wi' tha bathwat'r…but as i' t'is, I t'ink I'm gonna need yer perfessional opinion on this."

I felt a chill run down my spine as I watched what he did next. Motioning with a gesture to the alleyway, O'Malley smiled at me. At that moment, I decided that I liked him better when he was stone-faced.

The remaining rookies all looked like that kid Donovan, but they were still managing to keep their lunches in their stomachs. Even the seasoned cops were looking a little rough around the edges. One way or another, everyone in the alley had that green look—and we'd already celebrated St. Patrick's Day, so I knew that wasn't the reason.

Well, not everyone was celebrating the luck of the Irish. There was a pair of suits I didn't recognize. They weren't Chicago's Finest. That much was plain from the quality of suits and shoes they wore, compared to that of the other detectives on the scene. Everyone seemed to answer to them—even O'Malley, who gave them a nod as I came around the corner. They reminded me a little (too much) of Imperial Watch Guards of Trysillia. Good fighters, don't get me wrong…but Watch Guards were nothing less than mindless drones who follow orders and ask no questions. Everything was carried out by the book. If not, they were writing the book.

These suits looked up to give me the stare, pencils in their grasp and pressing against their memo pads, ready to pick up where their last scribbled thoughts left off. I kept my own baby blues locked with theirs. When you're four-foot-one, it doesn't do you any good to be intimidated.

These guys were good. Usually when humans of this realm get into a staring competition with a dwarf, the dwarf wins. My best opponents for this contest back in Acryonis were elves. It is easy for elves to play this little intimidation game because of their omnipotence. Elves know everything; just ask them, and they'll tell you. We used to be pretty chummy, the dwarves and the elves, but we had a falling-out once. Lots of races all tried to guess why. A disagreement over battle strategies in the Great War? Bad business surrounding a mining contract?

Actually, if you really want to know, it was over a malt-beer recipe.

Anyway, while I kept walking with O'Malley in my peripheral, these guys and I were enjoying our own stare-off. Whoever these suits were, they must've taken lessons from the elves. They didn't blink. Statues. I had to wonder if they were still breathing. I felt my own fists tighten. Ain't no way I was going to lose this stare-down with these chumps.

Then it dawned on me: These were the same chumps that crashed my detective's breakfast party at Sal's. I hadn't found out yet who these yahoos were, but it was going to take a little more than a corpse at a crime scene to break that stare-off we had going.

Benny's corpse, it turned out, was more than enough.

O'Malley walked me right up to Benny, putting me so close to his face that if I had puckered my lips I would have given that wop a wet sloppy right on that dirty cheek of his. Carved into Benny's mug was a face of terror, his eyes literally bulging halfway out of their sockets, a scorched tongue reaching out of a mouth stretched open in the most unnatural of screams.

Now that I had my wits about me, I could only stare in fascination. His features appeared chiseled as if from granite. The mouth looked as if it had been torched, it and what I could see of his throat all blackened like his tongue.

I summoned up the courage to gently touch Benny's cheek. (Yeah, it was a little weird, and I think it even shocked O'Malley. What he didn't know was that I'd seen worse.) The visible skin made it out of this fight burn-free, but it had lost its elasticity—not from *rigor mortis*, but from the intense pain he must have experienced at his death. Poor Benny must have seized so hard from shock that he locked permanently into this gruesome position. The cherries on top of this grotesque banana split were a pair of swollen, bloodshot peepers staring upward at the point where his outstretched hands were frozen, fingers splayed and slightly curved, as if whatever hit him caused them to curl.

Had I not felt a twinge of pity, I would have worried. Not even a sap like Benny deserved a death like this. What the hell could have torched him like that from the inside?

I stepped back, pushing up my black fedora and stroking my beard. That was when I noticed the sunlight catching his shoes. In the trash can next to Benny were those imitation Italians, still sporting that professional shine and still on his feet.

Summoning up the courage Chicago's Finest lacked, I took a closer look inside the other can. Whatever hit Benny had sliced him across his torso into two pieces. His feet, legs, and waist were slightly bent in this second trash can, and from the burn marks on his slacks, I could see without tipping the legs to one side that the wound was sealed: a clean, white-hot burn that cauterized as it sliced.

Benny would have been happy, at any rate. His imitation Italian loafers made it through the attack unscathed.

The little start I gave at the beginning must have given that stupid mick a hard-on. "You get your jollies for today?" I quipped at O'Malley, who still wore a smile I found far more unsettling than Benny's current condition. "Now how about we drop the Halloween hijinks and get back on the clock, Chief, or are you ready to explain to all those public eyes around the corner how one of Capone's runners wound up looking like an apprentice's final test gone horribly wrong?"

The smile melted from his face. Now it was my turn to enjoy getting this dink's goat.

"I shoulda known ya wouldn' be shaken by this, ya lil' circus freak!" O'Malley seethed. "An' I jus' might go on an' slap tha cuffs on ya, due ta tha nature o' this crime. It's *odd*. An' seein' that yer tha las' ta see Benny Riletto alive, Shorty, I t'ought I'd bring ya back ta tha place o' yer deed!"

"Now that's hardly fair, O'Malley," I replied, feigning a severe blow to my feelings. (He couldn't score a blow on me, even if he took a deep breath!) "What makes you think I've got anything to do with this?"

"This has got yer name written all over it, freak!" he shouted, causing everyone—even those mystery suits—to stop and look our way.

O'Malley took a few steps closer. The chief wasn't "tall" as humans go, but hey, everyone's a beanstalk to me. Only thing is, *this* beanstalk had a lot of his pods growing on the *inside*. If he took two more steps forward, I'd have disappeared under that gut of his. "I don' like this kinda garbage in ma precinct. I don' like dealin' wi' tha press!"

"You don't like dealing with the press when you don't have an easy answer, you mean," I replied as I calmly produced my pipe from my coat. "Remember the last time you slapped the cuffs on one of your 'quick deductions'?"

O'Malley's patience was growing so thin right now that it appeared transparent. Judging from his next move, he must've hit a whole new level of frustration. He slapped the pipe hanging in the loose grasp of my teeth. It broke in two against a brick wall, narrowly missing some rookie taking pictures of the scene. It wasn't a favorite pipe of mine, but pipes weren't cheap.

"Watch yer step, Baddings, or I swear I'll 'ave yer ass hangin' from a flagpole!"

I could have taken a cheap shot to his jimmies, but we had too many onlookers.

"Now, talk!" he bellowed. "What d'ya know 'bout this? Y'were tha last...person...seen wi' Riletto when'e was alive."

"Yeah, I was having a chat with Benny. No big to-do. We were shootin' the bull this morning. I had a couple of questions for him."

"Oh, really? And jus' what might y'be askin' tha likes o' someone like Riletto?"

"I'm not at liberty to give the gory details…and that's a good thing, because this crime scene is gory enough. I can promise you that it wasn't about anything illegal. If it were," I spoke evenly, my eyes never leaving his, "I'm sure you'd have heard about it, right?"

A staring match with O'Malley could last a solid minute…maybe two if he was particularly pissed at me. I don't know if it was a flash bulb or the day's tension that caused him to blink, but this stare-down ended as soon as it began. His pause—not tense so much as awkward—did catch my attention, though. "When I left Benny," I continued, "he was pickin' lettuce and orange peels out of his greasy hair."

"So t'ings got a littl' rough, eh? T'rew 'im inta tha garbage, did ya?"

Yep, Chief O'Malley provided living proof that just because you got height does not guarantee you got brains to go with it.

"Hold your foot up, Chief."

He leaned his head to one side. "What?"

"You got dungeon muck in your ears? I *said*, 'hold your foot up, Chief.' "

O'Malley never likes it when I asked him for a favor, and a favor includes asking him something as trivial and passing as the time. Fortunately his Irish curiosity kicked in at this point, and he brought his loafer up.

Reaching into my own coat pocket where I once kept my now-broken pipe, I brought out a tiny box of matches. I struck one across his sole, tipping the stick down at an angle to allow the flame to catch and grow along its thin, wooden shaft. Before O'Malley could ask *"Now jus' what tha hell are ya doin'?"*, I flicked my match at him. Instinctively, he brought his hands up to shield himself from the already-extinguished match that bounced harmlessly against the thick cuff of his coat.

"Hold that pose, Chief," I told him before he could throttle me. "Now look at your hands. You see they're only waist-high, right? If I had been your height or taller, your hands would have been higher up, wouldn't they? Well now, there you go. A clue. On the house."

"Waist-high? Yer tellin' me—" O'Malley paused in his tirade, realizing he was still holding the silly pose. He lowered one hand while another thrust a beefy finger at me. "Yer tellin' me tha ma hands 'waist high' proves y'ain't got nothin' ta do wi' this?"

"Not unless I sprouted wings and took flight, or I grew ten feet only to shrink back again to a height the ladies love!" was my smug reply.

I walked around O'Malley to the top half of Benny's body, getting a lot closer than any of these weak-stomached cops dared. "See? He held his hands up high over his head. Whatever did this came from way above him."

"Aye," he conceded with a curt nod, "an' if'n a man Riletto's height were ta drop ta his knees, as 'is bent legs insinuate, then a nipper tha likes o' ya would tower over 'im, now wouldn't ya?"

I took in a slight gasp, as if impressed. "Hey, Chief. *Insinuate.* You've been hitting the dictionary again, haven't you? Can't wait to hear you when you crack a thesaurus, you wordsmith, you!"

I could feel his glare boring into me as I turned back to Benny's other half. "Check the pants, Chief. His knees never hit the ground. Whatever hit him—" I turned back to O'Malley, catching myself in my mistake. "Okay, whatever *sliced* him, did so quickly. He was probably about to beg for mercy, but was cut down before hitting the grovel position. I threw him into the trash, sure, but he was still in one piece when I did."

I took a closer look at the back of Benny's torso. "Come here and take a look at this."

O'Malley didn't move. A stomach that big, and it's weak?

"Well, when you feel your lunch will allow it, take a look at Benny's back. He's got mud there. It matches the stains along the side of his pants leg here." I motioned to the thick brown grime soaked into the slacks of Benny's bottom-half, and then pointed to a large patch of mud and grime in the middle of the alleyway. "He must've originally landed here and here. But I left him over *there*," I said, pointing out a couple of overturned garbage cans and street trash scattered around them, a good fifty feet from the crime scene.

O'Malley's face now reached a shade similar to his hair. "Well, if'n y'ain't a reglar Sherlock'Olmes!"

"And I'll give you another one, Chief Watson." Looking at both halves of Benny, I slowly shook my head. "Whoever did this is one cold soul. Benny was *about* to drop to his knees to beg for mercy, and our killer didn't give a troll's ass. At least Capone'll hear you out before he buries a bullet in your brain. This ain't your typical hit."

I turned back to O'Malley with one of those grins you'd see on a dragon's face right before making a final move on a hunting party. I knew this next one was going to get me off this mick's hook and put yet another black mark by my name. "Oh, and one more thing: You might want to check Benny's cheap excuse for a watch. Its face is all cracked to hell, but you'll see it stopped at the moment he was parted like your Red Sea. Give Dr. Samuel Hammil, curator of the Ryerson, a holler. He'll vouch for my whereabouts at that time."

I got that feeling again—that feeling of the hair rising on the back of my neck. Slowly, deliberately, like a valley saber-tooth on the prowl, I turned to look over my shoulder. Sure enough, those square-jaws were starting up that Elvish stare-down again. Were these dinks already up for Round Two?

No, I held their attention for something other than making themselves the big tuna here. They weren't playing the game this time, because I had *caught* them looking at me.

I turned back to O'Malley, who was back to his lovable, Mad-Irishman demeanor. "So, Chief, are we done here? You need my help on anything else?"

"Get out o' here, freak!" he barked, bending down to give my shoulder a deliberate shove.

What, no good-bye kiss? That was a shame. He wasted no time to sic his uniformed escort on me, both of them eager to follow their Chief's orders.

When I came back around the corner, the press started screaming louder. My uniformed escort decided to get a little rougher this time. And yeah, I couldn't slight their gnome-sized brains for noodling this scenario out. They couldn't manhandle me going to the alleyway on the chance it would make the front page. Not the best image portrayed to the public, right? But things were different now. By clearing myself with my "academic" alibi, I had granted these uniforms free reign to drag me away from the alleyway as an unwanted spectator. All bets were off, and now they could put on a little play for the newspapers, to pose for pictures of Chicago's Finest enforcing order.

After the coppers released me with one more shove for the road, I made a quick "about face," issuing these academy grads a silent warning about pushing me around.

That was when the flash bulbs went off. I could no longer hear any of the sweet sounds of my adopted home, like the L or the traffic passing by. I wouldn't have heard a flock of giant mountain condors with the way those reporters were screaming, asking who I was and why I was escorted into (and hastily thrown out of) a closed-off crime scene.

I had to give O'Malley credit. It was a "win-win" for him. If he proved me guilty, I'd get ushered out in cuffs and the chief would score a redeeming front-page moment. If I provided an alibi, he'd order his ogres to roughly toss me out, providing yet another newsworthy moment for the press.

When you're a private dick, the press is not your friend most of the time. Kind of makes the whole "private" aspect of your job a moot issue. This was exactly what I *didn't* need, for now and for future jobs. O'Malley had played this card pretty well. I guess this made us even.

Giving my coat a tug and straightening my fedora, I made a beeline through the screaming sea of reporters. Some of them kept pace alongside me, still trying to get answers to their questions. I left them shouting even after I hopped into an Ace and whipped out my memo pad, intending to get what I had seen and heard out of my head and into my notes while still fresh in the noggin.

The cab dropped me off a block away from Riletto's sorry excuse for a neighborhood. For a numbers runner in the Capone organization skimming off the top as he was, you would think Benny would have tried to live a little higher on the hog. As it was, this would be a quick search, because there wasn't much to where the "dearly departed" hung his hat.

Like I said before, when I was first shadowing Benny, I followed him home after one of his nights on the town (on the princess' purse, naturally). I found it amazing that from where I watched him, I could easily get a guided tour of his place. One bedroom, one bathroom, a couple of closets, and an open room with a couch, a coffee table, and a radio. Hell, Benny's place was an insult to the word "little."

I hoped to beat the uniforms in checking out Benny's place, and it looked like I'd done just that. No uniforms in either eye or earshot, so I knew I had some time. Not sure exactly how much, but hopefully time enough for what I needed to do.

I arrived at the apartment with my wallet of enchanted lock-picks in hand, ready to work some old-fashioned magic. Then on my first glance at his flop, I slipped the tools back into my jacket. I wouldn't be needing them after all, because Benny's door was wide open.

Standing just shy of the doorway, I gave the interior a few whiffs, wincing at the smell of that cheap cologne he wore that morning. I also caught hints of hair cream and the hiding place of a single bottle of Canadian whiskey. Beatrice was in my grip, but the safety was still on. No need to promise her quality time if I didn't have company.

From the hallway, my nose continued to search for telltale signs of anyone else still in Benny's place. With the exception of his signatures, I didn't see, hear, or smell anyone else in the room. Swapping Beatrice for my memo pad and pen, I lightly pushed open the door with my foot, breaking the silence of this pathetic apartment with a long, steady creak.

Something I always gave Benny credit for when I had watched him from my hiding places: He liked a clean flop, and that was going to make searching his place a lot easier. When the door swung back, though, I thought some of my boys from Gryfennos had blown through here. The closet, bed, and what little furniture Benny owned had been given a thorough once-over. Someone had obviously been looking for something, not caring in the least how untidy the place got in the process. (Like Benny was going to complain about it?)

Standing in the middle of all this mess, I steeled myself for something I had been praying to the Fates I wouldn't have to do: I had to think like Benny. I barely stomached the run-in with him this morning, and now

I was going to pay homage to him by getting into his routine? As soon as I called it a day, I was going to have to take a nice, long bath!

No use complaining about it. I was on the clock, and I didn't doubt that I'd be getting a phone call from Miss Lesinger once she saw my mug running on the front page of every newspaper in Chicago the next morning. If I wanted to give her a reason to keep me employed, I needed to find out more about the link between Benny Riletto and the Singing Sword. Seeing that two-bit hood sliced into two bits had made it clear to me that the Singing Sword was somewhere out on the mean streets of Chicago. I needed to find that enchanted letter-opener first, and perhaps string along Miss Lesinger in the meantime. Hopefully, buying myself some more time on her family's payroll would help me come up with a sane explanation as to why her mob boyfriend was whacked. Telling her *"Anthony DeMayo pinched an enchanted sword that would have brought about the Apocalypse…"* just didn't sound credible, true as it might be.

So, on to the task at hand: stepping into Benny's imitation loafers.

Evidently, the bed had been made before the "French Maid of Darkness" visited. The sheets and covers were pulled back, but parts of the bedclothes still remained tucked under the mattress. It was a bed big enough for one only, so whatever jollies ol' Benny scored were not here. Dropping to one knee, I took a closer look at the bedsprings. I would have been surprised if I found something that the earlier visitor had not.

On waking up, the first thing a guy needs to do is take care of "personal issues." Sure enough, by the can, I saw another section of Benny's morning newspaper. Benny, it appeared, was an early riser. Either that, or he'd pulled a long night out on the town that went right up to this morning. Whichever one it was, I hope he enjoyed his last sunrise.

Upon entering the bathroom, I immediately started coughing. From its overpowering presence in the privvy, I must not have been too far off in guessing that Benny bathed in that damn dragon-piss cologne, after all.

So, he got up this morning, gave himself a shower and a splash, and then what? Off to the closet to get his suit and shoes, of course.

I was more than happy to leave the bathroom and cross the bedroom, stepping over Benny's clothes that now littered the floor. I thought about that "shower and a splash" idea for a minute. Whenever I'd rolled Benny for information before, rarely would he stink up the air around me with his cologne. Why would he have *started* the day with slapping on that much scent, unless he was headed somewhere popular with the Night Life types later on? It was hardly out of the ordinary for speakeasies to enjoy the party well into the wee-small hours of the morning. *So, Benny,* I thought as I stared at the empty wire hangers above my head, *what time were you out and about today?*

I was about to step back out of the closet when I caught another blast of the cologne. It was pretty strong, and had I not paused, I would have made a bad assumption that it was coming from his rumpled clothes on the floor. The scent was not coming from outside the closet, though. It was coming from my feet.

Following the dragon piss to a small section of the closet's floor, I found tiny flecks of paint and plaster here. Looked like Benny had cut away a bit of the closet (probably not to the knowledge or the satisfaction of his landlord) and created his own secret panel—not as sophisticated as ones I was used to from my days raiding keeps and castles, but a secret panel nonetheless. Whoever was here before must have been in a hurry to miss this.

I pried the section away, revealing a frame that probably hadn't see the light of day since this place was built. Taking a whiff of the panel in my hand, I recoiled slightly. It looked like the hand he used to slap his "signature scent" all over his face was the same hand that returned this panel back to its concealment inside the closet.

Tucked inside this hidden nook was a small journal that looked no more unassuming than a library book. I smiled as I flipped it open. Not a lot of surprises for me in here, because this book was *the* book: Benny's dirty little secret that only he and I knew about.

As I've said before, I remember catching a glance of this little gem once when I started shadowing him, but I never knew where he hid it. This was the duality of Benny: He was clever enough to hide it completely out of plain sight, but he was stupid enough to hide it in his flop. It was these times when Benny provided me with a good laugh that I would miss the most.

On the left-hand side were the actual numbers from Capone's racket, while along the right-hand side were his own notes on how much to skim off the top. There were also a few contact numbers jotted in the margins. I chuckled at some of his names. Most of these guys were muscle—muscle that wanted a bigger take for doing the dirty work, perhaps. No, I didn't like Benny all that much, but I admire anyone with enough stones to swindle Scarface, and enough smarts to make friends where it mattered most. If Benny was caught with his hand in the cookie jar, he wanted to make sure he had more than enough heat to call.

Close to the end of the journal, the last few pages were dog-eared on the corners. It was clear these pages had been receiving a lot of Benny's attention lately, because they were wrinkled from notes hastily jotted down, erased, and rewritten. At the bottom of one page, I found a note that looked fresh. When I ran my thumb across it, the lead from the pencil Benny used that morning smudged lightly. These leaves held dates and places with Pretty Boy's name jotted off to the left, and Two Times off to the right.

Under Riletto's, DeMayo's, and Bennetti's names was a list of Capone's bagmen and runners. Some of the names—Jimmy Hill, Tommy Ross, Chuck Morris, and Luigi Morrelli—I recognized, but there were names on this list that looked hard to pronounce (and coming from a place called Acryonis, that's saying something!). Jimmy, Tommy, Chuck, and a few others were crossed off the list. (Interesting, as I had not seen either Jimmy or Tommy for weeks.) The star by Bennetti's name reminded me that only a few days before I got on this case, Pauley had met with an "honorable discharge" from Capone's ranks. (Translation: Someone discharged a Roscoe against the back of his head.)

I transferred Benny's journal to my coat pocket and glanced at the modest alarm clock still keeping time, unaware the master served would not be coming home. I'd been there for about an hour. Given the way O'Malley ran a crime scene, I was already on borrowed time.

I walked back to the main living area, and—on a hunch—placed my palm against the radio. Still warm. Yeah, whoever rifled through Benny's place was not your run-of-the-mill dink. He was smart enough to leave the radio on for any newsbreaks. While reporters weren't allowed near the crime scene, the local wire would have picked up enough to know that something was happening in that alleyway. And he listened to the reports, knowing if NBC announced a "gangland hit" in their alleyway, that meant the story reached their news desk anywhere from half an hour to an hour after the body was discovered.

Don't know who you are, I thought with a grin, *but you're going to be a lot of fun to cross battle-axes with, pal!*

Turning toward the door, I heard footsteps in the stairwell. Way too heavy to be that of kids coming home from school, or the lady of the hovel returning from the market. Whomever those footfalls belonged to, they were big.

Guess I'd be taking the servant's entrance.

I quietly slipped out through the closest window and onto the fire escape. Pane was touching sill before the next round of unexpected guests could catch me beating them to Riletto's hidden treasure.

Before I took a powder, I took out a handheld mirror I carried in my opposite coat pocket (because there are times when Mickey's chili tries to stay with me all day in between my teeth. Not a pretty sight…) and angled it to catch a peek at who was on the third watch of Benny's place.

Well, wasn't that something? It was those stone-faced ogres from Sal's ruins and Benny's alleyway. And they were alone. Guess Chicago's Finest were still taking their time in the alleyway. Either that, or O'Malley was still mugging it up for the cameras.

I gave Benny's journal a reassuring pat in my one pocket, returned my mirror to the other, and quietly made my way *up* the fire escape. The suits were stone-faces and they were big, but they were smart enough to leave the crime scene and find their way here. I'm sure one of them would soon make for the window and check to see if anyone was waiting to get arrested, or interrogated. It was only one flight to the rooftop, so I hoisted myself up to get a more scenic look at the neighborhood. Then it was across the roof to the opposite fire escape, and a casual descent back to the Chicago streets.

CHAPTER SEVEN

WORD GETS AROUND

"So, Mr. Baddings, what other surprises do you have for me this morning?"

My day typically started with a coffee and bear claw delivery from Mick's. After that gourmet breakfast, I planned to stay behind my desk armed with my case notes; the personal journal I'd kept while in the Emperor's service during the Great War of the Races; the photo I had pilfered from the museum; and a prized tome that covered two-thirds of my desk all by itself.

I had called Miranda the night before to let her know it was going to be an early start, so she was swinging by Mick's to pick up my breakfast while I opened the office at 8 a.m. sharp. A good thing I chose to rise with the Risian icarai, too, because at 8:05, Julia Lesinger came storming into my office hotter than a brimstone she-demon, and I don't think she was joining me for breakfast. My ass was not so much of a morning's cup of coffee to her as it was a huge, fresh-from-the-bakery muffin that she could slowly tear apart and savor all the way into the afternoon.

"Is *this* how you run a private investigation, Mr. Baddings?" she continued in the same vein, slapping a copy of the *Chicago Tribune* on top of my notebooks. "By having your picture appearing in the city newspapers?"

Really, I couldn't blame her for being so pissed. As I'd expected, on the front page of the morning edition was a picture of me, flanked by Chicago's Finest, with a headline screaming:

GANGLAND THUG AND CHICAGO POLICE COME UP SHORT

Clever. Whoever came up with that one probably got an earful of guffaws and slaps on the shoulder. If I ever find him, I'll make sure to hand him an exclusive on how hard a dwarf can punch.

"Miss Lesinger," I began with a heavy sigh, sitting back in my chair, "I can assure you that your name was nowhere near that crime scene. I was called in on a matter of unique circumstances for the 15th Precinct—"

"Unique!" she huffed, taking out a silver cigarette case and slipping a tobacco stick into her mouth. She was about to dig out some matches until a *click* from my desk caused her head to snap up. I knew the sight had to be comical, if not disarming: me standing up in my chair, holding out a lighter and giving her the big ol' puppy dog eyes. Nobody in Gryfennos could do the "puppies" better than me.

As she bent low to catch the flame in my outstretched hand, I caught a quick glimpse at her chest. Look, if I was being sentenced to the rack, I might as well die with a smile on my face after a quick glance at *hers*. Oh, yeah…definitely a good, healthy girl, that Julia Lesinger.

The resulting grin on my face quickly faded as she straightened up once more, her anger still present but far more subdued.

"Forgive me, Mr. Baddings," she said suddenly.

Good thing I was hanging on to the desk. Otherwise, my surprise would have made me shift too sharply, sending my chair one way and me the other.

"My concern for discretion, you understand. If my father knew that I was here…"

"No need to apologize, Miss Lesinger."

"Actually, there is." She took a long drag from the cigarette, the scent of freshly lit tobacco lingering as she took a seat opposite my desk. "My father viewed my relationship with Tony as an embarrassment to him, the family, and his business. If he found out about my dealings with you, I might not be able to settle the final bill."

"Disinherit you, would he?"

"First, he would disinherit me. Then you would conveniently pack your bags, go on vacation, and never come back."

I had just gotten comfortable in my office chair when she launched that catapult of a statement on me. "Didn't realize Daddy Dearest was so…"

"Ruthless?" she completed with a mirthless laugh. "Mr. Baddings, regardless of what image is perpetuated by the press, my family didn't acquire its wealth or privilege through generosity. My father has carried on my grandfather's and great-grandfather's legacy of earning money and holding on to it. If anyone threatens the Lesinger name, retribution would be so quick that Al Capone himself would wince."

As she paused to take another puff, her eyes softened a little more. "You are a good man, Mr. Baddings. Good men are hard to come by in this day and age."

"Good dwarves, even harder." I smiled, giving her a wink.

The quip earned me a smile. "I can only imagine, Mr. Baddings, what was so *unique* about a gangland hit that would make the Chicago police feel obliged to call on your services."

"I can tell you right now, Miss Lesinger, that after one look at *that* crime scene, the boys at the 15th knew they needed some outside assistance on this!"

"Well," she replied with another smile, "Unique, indeed."

"That's a nice way of saying 'too weird' for the boys in blue. And the 15th would like to think that when it's weird, the weirdo of the Windy City—yours truly—is behind it. It was a pleasure to disappoint them."

Pulling myself closer to the desk, I flipped over the *Tribune* and linked my fingers together, staring for a moment at my pudgy digits interlocking and flexing. Since she was here, it was time to play the library card.

"Miss Lesinger, I need to ask you something that could sound like I'm digging for court gossip, so bear with me."

"Court gossip, Mr. Baddings?" she repeated, her curiosity clearly aroused. "Sure."

"Is there a reason why the Ryerson omits the Lesingers from its mailing list?"

"Ah, good Dr. Hammil and The Ryerson Museum." She sighed heavily. "It all started when my father hired the doctor's staff to research our genealogy, in the hopes of confirming his oft-repeated claims that we sprang from European nobility."

"And Hammil couldn't prove it?"

"He could only find mentions of the name 'Lesinger' in one family's ledger...they were on staff."

"Ouch." I shook my head. "And from what I know of the good doctor and his lack of tact, he probably shared this with your father."

She nodded. "Ever since then, my father has threatened harassment charges if he ever receives another invitation to a Ryerson exhibit." She gave me a wry grin. "My father is quite good at holding grudges."

"And his daughter?"

Miss Lesinger took another slow drag, nursing this dramatic pause for all it was worth.

"I think you'll find out soon enough," she finally said.

For a response, I grumbled something I wouldn't say in polite company.

She arched a meticulously sculpted eyebrow. "My Norse is a bit rusty, but something tells me I'm better off not knowing the details."

My head slowly turned back toward my grinning client. It was easy to forget that the Norse language of this world was close to my own Gryfennos dialect…so close that you could pick out the gist of full-out Dwarven speech if you were fluent with the Vikings' lingo.

Guess Julia Lesinger had her own surprises for me.

"Sorry about that," I said, feeling my face turning red under my beard. "Knew you were cultured, but didn't know you were *that* cultured!"

"I have soft spots for history and mythology, and it is always a benefit when you can read legend and lore in its native tongue. To that end, I took a few linguistic courses in college," she said while tapping her cigarette into the ashtray at the corner of my desk. "These soft spots are why, regardless of my father's feelings, I volunteer much of my time at the Ryerson." She sat back with her smoke delicately balanced between two fingers, the freshly exposed tip sending a serpentine wisp above her head. "So, what does the Ryerson and their falling-out with my father have to do with my case?"

"In a minute," I stalled, tapping the face-down *Tribune*. "Do you know a numbers runner named Benny Riletto?"

"Benny Riletto?" Her mouth twisted in the effort to get the name out. "I had the *pleasure* of meeting him one night," she replied with more than a hint of sarcasm. "He never made any overture to pay for drinks, I noticed. Tony noticed, too, but he didn't seem to care. He told me that Benny served his purpose. That wasn't uncommon."

"What wasn't uncommon?"

"Tony believed everyone had a purpose, and the ones whose purpose most benefited him, he kept close."

Yeah, and it would make sense that a dame like Lesinger served a very important purpose to him. She was a fine-looking lady, but I'm sure the connection with the Ryerson merely topped the ice-cream sundae that was Julia Lesinger. The girl was smart, though. Did she know DeMayo had been playing her finer than a bard's mandolin?

"It would seem, Miss Lesinger, that you made quite an impression on your ex-boyfriend. I am still trying to find out all the details, but DeMayo's trail keeps coming back to the Ryerson. I've got a lot of hunches, but nothing solid to pursue…that is, unless, you've got something to tell me?"

"I'm sorry, Mr. Baddings. What do you mean?"

What I *meant*, of course, was did she know the Singing Sword had been pinched? Since she spent time at the Ryerson as an active volunteer, couldn't she be in the know about this missing artifact?

It was a pitch I wanted to take a swing at, what with her name popping up at the scene of the crime and all. But looking into that confused gaze of hers, I had to wonder if the good Dr. Hammil was keeping his office staff in the dark on this one. It would make sense that he would want to avoid adding to Daddy Lesinger's grudge, plus to ensure that the Lesingers' friends didn't catch wind of the Ryerson's incompetence.

"I guess I've got a little more investigating ahead of me," I hedged, "but now, you know what I know. The trail that eventually leads to Sal's, where Tony DeMayo met his demise, is currently stalled in the corridors of the Ryerson. Still, it's definitely a few steps forward…dwarf-sized as they may be."

"It's progress, Mr. Baddings," she said pleasantly, slipping out a few more Franklins—a little more than half of what she had originally left for a down payment. "More progress than I anticipated. With what you've told me so far, I know I made the right choice in whom to trust. I wouldn't want to start again from scratch, so please, Mr. Baddings, be more careful in the future."

Sure, lady. "Careful" is my middle name.

A few minutes after Miss Lesinger took her leave, Miranda poked her head into my sanctuary.

"You okay, Billi?" she asked, appearing with a brown paper bag holding my breakfast. "Anything I can do for you?"

"Yeah, hon, there is," I replied as I swapped the *Tribune* on my desk for my long-awaited morning's delight. "Find a birdcage to line this with, okay?"

A little guardian angel, she is. Just making sure that everything was Jake. After glancing at the front page with an impish smile, she shut my door and fielded all phone calls. And yeah, we got a lot of them! Every ring was met with Miranda's *"I'm sorry, he's out ..."* dodge, and I could only pray her voice would hold out for the day.

Thanks, O'Malley. I owe you one.

Taking a sip of my tepid coffee, I turned my attention back to the various notes in front of me, all of which somehow tied back to the Sword of Arannahs—now known to this world as the Singing Sword.

Hard to believe that a bog rat like Benny would have been involved in pinching something as powerful and dangerous as the Sword of Arannahs. He had liked the numbers racket because it was the "safest" of Capone's businesses; in order for Benny to have gotten mixed up in this, DeMayo must've convinced him the coup was planned out to the last detail. (I don't doubt it was, except for that one stray detail of DeMayo having Sal's Diner collapse on top of him.) If only Benny had kept to his pedestrian-like ways like the good spineless goblin that he was, he would still be above ground without the charred innards.

In the final pages of Benny's journal, now joining the mountain of resources on my desk, it looked like Pretty Boy, Benny, and Two Times were gradually covering their tracks. But why did Pauley's name get a star and not a line through it? Had Benny known more about Pauley's sudden demise than he had let on in the alley? If so, did Benny also have an inside on Tony? He had been as deep into this scheme as Tony and Pauley had, but when I chatted with him, he appeared to be cool and collected. "Cool" and "collected" are two words to describe anyone else in Capone's crew, but not Benny.

If I was reading Benny's notes correctly, anyone handling the Singing Sword eventually had his name struck through with a line. No doubt these poor saps were the enlisted of Capone's army, probably offered higher positions in the New Order once DeMayo took over. A small part of me understood why these guys followed DeMayo's orders without question. It would be easy to grow tired of being cannon fodder for the Gang Wars. At any rate, these unlucky bagmen were answering to either Bennetti, Riletto, or DeMayo, thinking they were on an easy street to life in the palace.

So much for rewarding loyalty in the New Order.

As Benny had told me before, the plan was that the three of them—DeMayo, Riletto, and Bennetti—would call on one of Capone's groundlings to pick up the Singing Sword, keep it on ice for a day or so, and then move it to another locale. And according to the dates, and drop points in Benny's journal, this Sword really enjoyed Chicago, jumping from one side of the city to the other.

After successfully moving the Sword twice, the name of each bagman simply disappeared from the book. As they were simple soldiers in the Organization under DeMayo's command, they wouldn't be missed if they weren't mentioned. So it went that the Sword hopped from place to place, and never did all three of them know at one time where the sword was hidden. Of the three, DeMayo always knew where it was kept.

It was a plan with a body count that would make an orc nod with approval.

According to Benny's journal, the last two foot soldiers to see the Singing Sword had been Two Times and Jimmy Hill. One was pushing up the daisies, the other was missing in action. I would make a wizard's wager Hill was probably sharing room and board with Two Times.

At this moment, I wanted to hit the streets and look deeper into Bennetti's recent movements, but asking questions about a soldier in Capone's army killed in the line of duty would attract the kind of attention I didn't want or need. Another option would be looking into this other man, Jimmy Hill. As he was only missing, the police really wouldn't care. And as he was barely a foot soldier, the mob wouldn't pay attention, provided my questions didn't get too close to the personal matters of the throne.

Setting aside Benny's book, I returned to my other sources: my notes from the crime scene and the museum, my journal from Acryonis, and a massive volume that I had nicknamed "My World Book Encyclopedia"—a little play on words from a set of books in the Washington Street library that had done a bang-up job acclimating me to this realm.

I found this monster in a pawnshop's display window while searching for dealers who would buy the Acryonis memorabilia I had brought with me from across the portal. What caught my eye about this curious item, proudly displayed among bric-a-brac, knick-knacks, and odds-and-ends, was the Elvish script and Dwarven glyphs burned into its worn leather cover. Sandwiched in between these unintelligible (well, unintelligible to anyone who didn't know Elvish or Dwarven) markings was a single word: *Chronicles*.

The price tag on it was steep, but still a fraction of what this book was worth to a guy like me. While the shopkeeper assessed the worth of my gauntlets (a Gryfennos pack-beast's hide—softer, but more durable than this world's leather—decorated with purest platinum), I sneaked a few more glances at the book in the window. As soon as I had enough greenbacks, I bought it, much to the owner's surprise.

"Thing was becomin' an eyesore," he said joyfully as he counted my cash. He was convinced he was getting a sweet deal, and that couldn't have made me happier. Nothing wrong with being an ignorant human, mind you. Hey, ignorance is bliss, right?

Trust me, if you knew what I knew about this book, you would pray for such bliss.

These kinds of tomes alternated in their languages. Certain sections were written in the Dwarven glyphs, while other passages featured various languages of Man and Elvish. It was kind of a "minimum security" for secrets, plus a way to make all the races feel they participated in the recording of history.

A few pages later, I was staring at passages devoted to the Sword of Arannahs, thrilled to find this particular section written in my native tongue. I needed a lucky break, and I had found it in my own native tongue. Good thing, too—apart from labeling various goods in my kitchen and trying to rewrite a copy of *The Red Headed League* in Elvish,

I was getting a little rusty. Maybe I'll get lucky one day and run across an Elvish cookbook that was, for whatever reason, sucked into a portal. (It would be easy enough to pawn it off as Chinese calligraphy.) Not only would an elementary book like that help dust off the cobwebs, but elves have one mean recipe for peanut butter soup.

Following the dawn of the First Age of Peace between the Realms, these parchments chronicle the forging of the Talismans of Acryonis. As the green of life continues to return across the moors, highlands, and valleys of our lands, whispers of the Darkness spawned from the hatred nurtured between the Races draw strength in the night, murmuring plans of bringing forth another scourge to the realm. Therefore have the Elders of each race now come together once more. Blessed be that we all meet not drawn or haggard by the toils of war, but as Kindred of Peace.

Kindred of Peace? When dwarves try to write like elves, they just come across sounding stupid. I gave my eyes a quick rubdown, knowing this chunk of pretentiousness was merely the start of a long day's reading that would probably stretch into the night. I wondered if I should ask Miranda to get me a fresh cup of Mick's java, along with dinner, before she left for the day.

The Darkness is what was created from the bitterness we Races carried as unseen weapons in our Great Wars, and so have the Elders created the Nine Talismans, sacred objects that will banish that which makes us susceptible to our most primal of desires.

Were these dinks serious? These elders truly believed that they could channel all the hate, lust, greed, and ambition of men, dwarves, and elves into nine charmed hood ornaments? And then what? The world would be a better place? Yeah, sure.

This is exactly why magicians of any race never held my trust. All those damn necromancers, enchanters, and sprite-oil salesmen bending the rules of Nature. If their magic succeeded in anything, it was in pissing off the Old Lady. What really bristled my beard were the sorcerers' justifications in their tampering. Yeah, you heard me right—*tampering*. That's exactly what these pricks did on a daily basis. If it weren't for the "Old Boys' Club," there wouldn't be half the problems we faced in Acryonis. Hell, I would still *be* in Acryonis, maybe getting cozy with that cute little red-headed elf over a nice pint, if it weren't for dark magic.

The Dwarven runes started to dance on the giant leaves of parchment in front of me, slowly blurring into a series of lines and dashes that closely resembled the etchings of a dungeon wall where prisoners kept track of days past. I managed to labor through fifteen pages—fifteen *really big* pages—and was only on the third talisman. I'm sure all this detail was useful to someone in another world, in another time. My priorities were on this world, right now, and the Singing Sword. The day already felt as long as the Summer Solstice, and reading verbose, flowery passages of Acryonis' brush with an apocalypse was only making it longer.

And I was getting cranky. That was not helping.

On the last sip of Mick's strongest, I struck paydirt.

From the lands of Arannahs, where the Goddess of Shu-Mei, the Bringer of Life and the Harbinger of Death, protects and reigns over Her Children, the great masters of the sword crafted a blade of sturdy make and of great power. Upon the Sword of Arannahs, the Master Mage decreed that only the nature mild and gentle should wield this blessed weapon. He, not of this nature, who calls upon its power shall suffer its wrath.

There it was: Confirmation. The Sword of Arannahs. Now that is one serious bowling trophy! Considering who its makers were, it was a given there were going to be some details kept hidden, even from the authors of this book.

In my world, very little was known about Arannahs. The people who dwelt there were human, but before I left, rumors were bouncing around that some disenchanted elves had also slipped into their communities. (The elves never did put any credence into these rumors, but they didn't bother to discredit them either.) But the Elvish script along the Singing Sword's blade seemed to support those rumors that perhaps the *Fethrysma*—the exiles—had found a home, after all.

Far from social, the Arannahi barricaded themselves inside their lands with great stone battlements that either rose high over the rolling landscapes, or were built into them. The traders who managed to get in and out spun a good yarn on what the Arannahi did to wile away the hours within the city walls: Mastering sword-making and sword-wielding techniques, plus developing arts both of the natural and supernatural kind, unique even to Acryonis.

The Arannahi first made a show of collected force in a war that pit the humans against the elves. (This was one of those wars you hear about when sitting by the hearth during the holidays. Lots of legends, lore, and all that.) The humans found themselves on the losing end pretty quickly, their ranks falling by the wayside like a ball team lacking a decent shortstop. Imagine the surprise through Trysillia when the secluded Arannahi offered their allegiance. No one really understood why they came to the aid of their human brothers. It wasn't like they weren't part of the Trysillian realm. The best anyone could figure was that the borders of the human realm ran beside the Great Walls of Arannahs, which protected a people who cherished their solitude. Now the elves threatened that solitude.

Their skill on the battlefield wasn't anticipated, nor matched.

When the Council of Light was founded, Arannahs did not reject the invitation to join—again, something that was unexpected. Their representative indirectly became the inspiration for peace between the races. If the shire of Arannahs was willing to come out of its isolation to join the Council of Light, then it must be a good idea. Representatives of each race, each shire, coming together to serve as a monitor, a peacekeeper over Acryonis...yeah, it was a great idea.

So was the League of Nations.

Still, generations of us working stiffs in Acryonis looked at the Council of Light as a good thing. After all, their first act was to set up protections against evil, and anything that takes on evil has to be good. Right?

Let's just say that I got a more honest look at the Council just before being sent on the "Nine Talismans" mission. Our little party was finally granted access to the Council's Hall of Records, following a heated debate and a close vote. I figure we won the privilege on some Council members' assumptions that no member of one race, especially a dwarf, could effectively read multiple tongues. They apparently knew nothing about my job—a knack for the languages.

I was granted access to records, but not *all* the records. We were given just enough information to know what we were looking for. That's it.

Kind of hard to prep for a mission when you've got a six-foot Valley Elf hovering over you. (To keep the "stupid dwarf" illusion alive, I asked for this council member's help on a couple of stanzas. I don't know which was harder: pretending to not understand what I was reading, or laughing in her face at *her* translations.) Even with my second shadow checking to see if I could "handle" the volumes, I managed to read between the lines. By the time I left the Hall of Records, I not only knew what to look for, but also that the Council of Light wasn't all *that* pure, and our mission was to clean up a serious mess they'd made.

I heard a light rapping on the door, a pause, and then a louder knocking. This was Miranda's code for *"Billi, there's someone here. Hide whatever you're working on and get ready!"*

Miranda's figure was barely visible through the frosted glass, but I could see she wasn't alone. The second figure behind her was obviously not one of O'Malley's dinks this time. Way too many curves.

I slid *My World Book* back into the false panel behind my bookcase, where I kept this volume under lock and key. When the bookcase closed with its soft click, the office and my desk lost that "Wizard's Study" look, returning to a 1929 state of disarray.

I was sliding my own journal back into the bookcase when I finally responded, "S'okay, Miranda. Come on in. I'm decent."

The woman behind Miranda was cut of the same cloth as Miss Lesinger, but that was where the similarity ended. Her ice-blue eyes were set in a delightful face—perhaps not as angular or defined as Miss Lesinger's, but still pleasing to my peepers. When I caught a glimmer of golden locks under her hat, I gave a barely audible groan. Blondes are always bad luck for me; when I'm in the company of a golden child, really awful things come my way. Seeing how things were progressing in this case so far, getting mixed up with a blondie at this point came as no surprise.

"Mr. Baddings?" she asked, clutching her purse tightly. There was a slight tremor in her voice. Sounded like this little number was about to fall apart right then and there in my office. "My name is Eva Rothchild. Do you have a moment?"

Eva Rothchild?!? Did I just hear this broad right?

"I'd like to hire you for a case."

No hesitation. No double-take. This lady didn't care that I was a dwarf. But with some of the things she'd seen in far-off places, she probably wouldn't have cared if I were a goblin in an evening dress.

Eva Rothchild was the conundrum of Chicago's upper echelon. Although she was rarely in Chicago these days, the local rags occasionally ran pictures of her posing with various tomb raiders in front of archeological digs. (A strange kettle of fish, this world. Here, tomb raiding is considered an exact science. Back in my stomping grounds, if you were caught breaking into a sacred burial place, they would simply reseal the crypt...with you in it!)

This young socialite would have been considered one of the leading authorities in obtaining rare antiquities had it not been for the night life in which she continuously indulged. If the photos weren't of her displaying a priceless jade container, gold burial mask, or ancient parchments, they usually revealed a flapper in the throes of a really good time, her company usually someone far from the academic type. These pictures and idle chitchat suggested the real Eva Rothchild was the one in the hiked-up evening dress, not the one in the pith helmet and jodhpurs.

Both Miss Lesinger and Miss Rothchild were featured in pictures of gala events, museum wing dedications, and other socially redeeming functions, but it didn't take a private investigator to see right through those smiles staged for the public eyes. While the Lesinger family owned half of Chicago, the Rothchilds owned the other half. These daughters to Chicago's crowns shared a serious rivalry, both in being social miscreants and in being the darlings of the city.

As she stood there waiting for my reply, I wondered if I should change the title on the door to "Billibub Baddings, Private Investigator to Chicago's Wealthiest."

The fact that Eva Rothchild was in town, let alone in my office, was enough to give me pause. Something else giving me pause was her perfume, a scent very familiar to me. Miss Lesinger had been wearing the same brand the day she came to hire me. Expensive as the scent may be, it was no big to-do for her—this bird was a Rothchild, after all.

I caught Miranda, from her modest desk, giving Miss Rothchild the hairy eyeball. It took a lot to impress my girl Miranda, and Eva here wasn't even close. Then again, she gets a little protective when it comes to clients and clients-to-be throwing their weight around. I'm sure if Miranda had been around for Miss Lesinger's stormy entrance, that same eyeball would have been cast.

"I see. How's about we chat in my off—"

"I want you to look into the death of 'Pretty Boy' DeMayo."

I wanted her to ask me to help her find a pair of lost earrings or maybe follow an unfaithful boyfriend, just for a change of pace. That would have surprised me, and it would have been a surprise most welcome. But this? No, this was no surprise.

"Look, Miss Rothchild, I've got what you would call a conflict of interest here. I'm already under hire by another client—"

"Who?" she snapped.

Now her pretty face, inviting cleavage, and curve of the cute derrière lost my attention. I don't like being cut off when I'm talking, and by my count, that was her second cut against my armor. First off, you don't do that to a dwarf. Not in my culture. Especially when you're a dame. The other reason: It's just plain rude. I guess Little Miss Eva was used to getting her way, and if you got the means to live that high on the hog, then by all means do so. But if you really want to rub my beard the wrong way, keep cutting me off. Eventually, you'll get four-foot-one's worth of etiquette lessons that those to the manor born must have skipped.

"You see the sign on the door, sister? I'm a *private* investigator. Private, as in between me and my client. Private, as in not public knowledge. Private, as in none of your damn business!"

She nearly dropped the purse, her mouth opening slightly. No, she was not used to hearing the "little people"—a literal analogy in my case—talk like that.

We just stared at each other for a minute until the loud *pop* from Miranda's chewing gum made her jump. She shot a glance toward Miranda, and my girl didn't budge one inch.

I tell you something: I am convinced Miranda has some elf blood in her veins.

Miss Rothchild turned back to me, her tone still insistent, but not as sharp as before. "I am willing to double whatever your current client is paying you. It's important to me that I know the reasons behind the murder of my boyfriend."

Her boyfriend? Time to go fishing.

"I'm sorry Miss Rothchild, but there is little I can tell you because my client must remain confidential. I can tell you this much: Pretty Boy was not killed for reasons involving infidelity. Something I understand he was good at."

"Mr. Baddings, *please!*"

While Julia Lesinger had been cool as an Arctic bear on an ice drift, this tart could barely contain her emotion. From the way her bottom lip was pouting, I was waiting for this intrepid explorer of civilizations past to start stomping her foot. (Talk about a great press agent!)

"I don't appreciate you trivializing this request. I need your help, your expertise in delicate matters. I cannot afford to have my name dragged through the papers any more than usual."

Didn't I just hear a conversation like this earlier this morning?

Then Miss Rothchild added a final touch that Miss Lesinger had notably avoided. "Please, Mr. Baddings, I want to know who would kill..."

She paused for a minute and, with a sudden sniffle, reached into her purse for a handkerchief. Miss Rothchild dabbed her eyes, but there really was no pressing need to do so. I doubt if any tears had fallen from them in recent years.

"...my sweet Tony."

Right. I couldn't help but stifle a chuckle as she took the seat in front of my desk. By now, Eva Rothchild seemed pretty certain that when she left my office, I was going to toss my client aside and take her on as my benefactor. Although she really laid on the huffing and sniffling thick, Miss Rothchild was no Mary Pickford. I'm sure she was hoping those baby blues and that buxom bustline would win me over.

If she was a redhead, maybe...

"Look, toots, knock off the Minotaur tears. Maybe Daddy Rothchild can employ some of his goons down at City Hall to look into the matter for you. I'm sure they owe him some favors."

Without missing a beat, Miss Rothchild put the handkerchief away and produced a silver cigarette case that was probably worth more than all the furniture in my office. Placing one of the smokes between her lips, she leaned into the light I offered. I think that the gesture surprised her, but I had my reasons.

Soon the case disappeared, her purse closed with a snap, and Eva Rothchild's eyes fixed on me once more. "Mr. Baddings, I assure you that I can make your life extremely uncomfortable if I leave here without getting what I want."

"Sweetie," I grunted, placing the lighter back on my desk, "I can give you what you *need*, but what you *want* may be a problem. And while I know you got a father with friends in high places, I also know I could make a few phone calls to my pals at the press. A good-looking girl like you loves to paint the town with Daddy's money, am I right?"

Eva's motions slowed to the crawl of a bog snail, the cigarette smoke barely seeping out from between her painted lips. Her eyes narrowed and those rosy cheeks darkened as we looked at one another. (Nothing like getting into a pissing contest with a woman.)

I was the first to break the silent standoff. "How about we cut to the treasure and have a little chat, you and me? First off, I can understand how a dish like you gets all heartbroken over Pretty Boy DeMayo, but why you are so interested in Benny Riletto's death?"

Her eyes went wide with the mention of Benny's name.

"Oh, come on, sweetheart. You blow in here like the winter wind from Death Mountain and offer to hire me, and you're not bothered in the least that your private dick is no taller than an end table? It was as if—" Slowly I reached for her hands, gloved in the finest white cotton, "—you knew exactly what I looked like before you came in here."

Her gloves were a stark white. I mean, so white that they were blinding. Well, they *were* white until you saw the fresh grey stains evenly running across the fingertips. My eyes were tired from reading *My World Book,* but I wasn't blind. I got confirmation once I got her gloves under the light of my cigarette lighter. The pristine fabric was marred by ink residue from the newspapers she had been reading. By the amount of smudge, I would guess that she had picked up every rag this morning after reading the first one that mentioned Benny. How many people in this great city had woken up this morning to a picture of me? (Damn! That must've packed a stronger punch than a cup of Mick's coffee!)

Guess it must've been easy for this dame, as rich and connected as she was, to track me down. How many dwarves are there in Chicago, anyway? Probably had no clue that I was a private gumheel. And when she did find out, it probably unsettled her something fierce.

"Now, sister, I'm sure before you walked into you this office, you were used to getting whatever you wanted if you wanted it bad enough." I gave her my million-dollar smile with my eye-twinkling chaser as I leaned in closer. "But you see, you're in *my* castle now. You're talking to Ol' Billi Baddings, and when you talk to me in my place, we play by my rules. So it's like this. You can talk to me about your involvement with 'sweet Tony' and Benny Riletto, and we can part as friends. If we can't do that, you can find the same door you came in. I don't think we want to go out of our way to make one another uncomfortable, so how about we have a little share time? Whadya say?"

Little Miss Eva did not care for being put in her place, but she could appreciate it to an extent. A small extent, but it was there. She took off her hat, allowing her hair to spill across her shoulders. The brilliant spun-gold locks framed an angel's face, her baby blues softening the insolent demeanor she so proudly wore about her like high fashion. Yeah, even easier on the eyes, *sans chapeau*. I could tell she was measuring me up from the opposite side of the desk, and if that made her feel better about herself, I was happy to oblige the princess. It was her move. She was just trying to figure out how much she wanted to play with me.

"I know you're working for Julie."

"Julie?" I asked innocently. "Who is—"

"Julia Lesinger."

Okay, once more with the interruption and I was going to bend her across my knee and slap her across her rump with the flat of my short sword.

"I know she hired you because I had Julie followed here this morning. And as you share a front-page picture with what is left of Benny Riletto, I can only assume that Julie hired you to investigate the death of 'Pretty Boy' DeMayo."

"Yeah," I huffed, "and those public eyes didn't bother to catch my good side."

"I know Mr. Riletto was one of Anthony's associates. He would occasionally join Tony and me when we would be out on the town with a group of people."

No surprise there, seeing as I recognized her from the mob-party picture at the Assistant D.A.'s office. "Enjoying that dangerous lifestyle?" I fished. "Lying down with the mob?"

Her upper lip curled with disdain. "On the contrary, I found Tony repulsive. You can throw as much money as you like at a greaser, but it won't change what he is." A fleeting smile crossed her face. "However, my keeping company with Tony repulsed my father a great deal more. That was enough of an incentive for me to be seen in public with him."

Well, now. Isn't she charming?

"Just seeing?" I asked casually, my eyes twinkling with mischief.

Eva tensed on that statement, gripping her purse more tightly. It was a surprise to us both when she found her voice. *"Just...seeing."*

"Daddy would be so proud," I purred with a grin rivaling the cat's after it had dined on the canary special.

If there had been a pit of ravenous goblins nearby, Eva Rothchild would have found great pleasure in throwing me into it. By the tautness in her jaw, I was convinced any cracking sound would be coming from her teeth breaking under the strain.

"His relationship with Julie was a bit more involved than the one with me. There were a few mornings I had my driver take me by Tony's place, and Julie's driver would still be impatiently waiting out front. I noticed that her driver appeared less concerned about the well-being of his boss' daughter, and more about being seen by anyone. The press, for example."

"Or worse," I scoffed, "you."

The smile returned to her face. "Perhaps, Mr. Baddings."

I shook my head, clearing my throat with a tension-breaking cough. "Miss Rothchild, you missed your calling. You should have been a detective. If you know so much about Julie and Tony and this love triangle between the three of you, why are you knocking on my door?"

"I assume you know of my involvement with the Ryerson."

"That I do," I nodded, a civil smile spreading across my face. Didn't this lady think I could read a newspaper?

"I have been concerned over the institution's competence in handling acquisitions for some time now. From the company I've kept of late, I suspect that Mr. DeMayo and Riletto have been involved in illegal transactions; while I cannot prove it, I suspect Miss Lesinger is at the center of it. I want to hire you to dig for me." Eva extinguished the cigarette—her butt falling idly next to Julia's, as a matter of fact—and then reached into her purse for a compact, splitting her attention between me and her make-up. "After all, that is what your kind do."

Your kind. Those two words were this girl's subtle reminder to me of the pecking order. I'm a working stiff. A servant to the one with the greenbacks. I do the work that is beneath her. I get my hands dirty while she goes to some hoity-toity spa and has hers massaged and lotioned.

Eva continued her quality time with the compact mirror, apparently figuring that talking at my reflection instead of conversing with me as an equal would throw me for a loop. She was trying to play the same control games that elves and humans go toe-to-toe in back home. Problem was, she was in control of a carriage without a horse team. She suspected Julia Lesinger of—what, volunteering her time at the Ryerson? She could have always let it slip to Daddy Rothchild, thereby letting it slip into "civil meetings" between him and Daddy Lesinger. No, Eva wanted something tangible that could get Julia into a world of trouble and out of the Ryerson. She suspected Julie of something all right, but exactly what it was, only Eva knew.

One thing was clear: Eva wanted Julia as far removed from the Ryerson as possible.

Too bad I knew the rules of the control game better than she did. Trust me. You can learn a lot about these games when you work through Bill Shakespeare's stuff.

"So what exactly am I digging into, Miss Rothchild?"

A smile lit up her face. The shoulders relaxed. Her head tipped back as she looked down the length of her nose, savoring her victory. Yeah, she did love the "Miss Rothchild" touch, my indication of acquiescence. It was Little Miss Eva's bone to gnaw on for the moment.

I kept the illusion alive with my polite delivery. "If you want me to do what I do so well, I need to know what buried treasure I'm looking for."

With a quick *click-click*, the compact snapped shut in her gloved hand. Her make-up was perfect once again, her eyes flashing like brilliant water-stones in the Se-Irya River that twisted through Acryonis, marking a border between races as well as lands. For a moment I thought she had been transformed into a statue of Goddess Vanity herself.

Then she had to ruin the illusion by speaking. "As you make it your job to meddle into the private affairs of others, I am willing to take advantage of your talents where Julie is concerned. Find out what she knows. Find out if she is, in fact, trying to sabotage my reputation at the Ryerson."

"Now just a moment, Miss Rothchild..."

"Mr. Baddings, you may think that Julia Lesinger's intentions are honorable, but I assure you that she has her own agenda in hiring you. I want to know if that agenda includes smearing my name. I may not be the heir apparent in my father's eyes, but I am still a Rothchild," she hissed. "I plan to protect that name by every means within my grasp. Am I clear?"

"As a seer's ball, toots." I swallowed hard. I was going to need a drink after this one. I thought Julia Lesinger was going to be a handful, but this one was trouble. Here she was, spouting about protecting her "family's good name" when she mocked it in one party photo too many every chance she got. Perhaps it wasn't the family, so much as it was her allowance, she wanted to protect.

Still, I'm not one to turn my colors to the Visiting Team when the Cubs are suddenly losing in the bottom of the Ninth. No different when you're on the battlefield with the axe in hand. Go down swinging.

"I don't know what kind of private eye you expected to find here, Miss Rothchild." She started to speak, but I immediately cut in with, "But I'm not some bog leech that'll suck blood on command! I'm spoken for. If you want to sic your royal hounds on me and make my life uncomfortable, you go ahead and try. I guarantee you a lesson hard learned not to cross a committed Highlands Dwarf. Unless you have another reason to hire my services that excludes the Lesinger family, I bid you a pleasant day."

Her eyebrows raised slightly, the pair of full, red lips parting again in shock. I guess when you're royalty, you just don't get rejected by the lower classes. So I was bracing myself for more of her "making my life uncomfortable" threats. (Like dealing with this case couldn't make it more so?)

But then, her lips curled up in a slight smile. I spent a few missions scaling Death Mountain, its talons of stone and ice serving little to shield me from the bite of the frigid winds. When she looked at me, the chill I felt was colder than my bleakest night on that faraway ridge. She held that look as she placed the hat back on her wavy blonde mane.

"My father is co-hosting a reception this Saturday night. Perhaps I could include you on the guest list?"

Now, think about this for a moment. I am a four-foot-one dwarf among a realm of humans, so that should give you an idea of how hard it is for me to get dates. Add to this how hard I have just spurned one of the richest women in this town. And now she's inviting me to a party?

"You want to run that by me one more time, Miss Rothchild?"

"I am not one to take rejection lightly, Mr. Baddings. I get what I want without question, but I respect your integrity. I see so little of it from where I am in the world. I still wish to win you over, and perhaps if you got to know me better, I could change your mind."

"Lady, my loyalty won't be changing until the case is closed, but if you want to make your possible business venture a social engagement, then I'll be there. Black tie?"

"But of course. Seven o'clock. I'll send a driver. Until Saturday."

"Sure, toots. See you then."

Miranda's *scritch-scritch-scritch* of the nail file went quiet as the blonde princess passed her without so much as a glance. Then the door to my office closed behind her. My eyes were fixed on the chair where she had sat, the sheen of its finish catching the glow of pink, light blue, and green across it. I couldn't help but be surprised that Miranda was still here. It was getting late.

Counting up all the similarities between Miss Rothchild's and Miss Lesinger's first visits, right down to the way those two debutantes clutched their high-fashion purses, I gave a weighty sigh as I shook my head. I hate *déjà vu*. I really hate it. Why? Because every time I experience *déjà vu*, it usually serves as an omen to something bad. And I mean, *bad*. The kind of bad that makes you wish you had stayed in bed. This was the kind of bad that brought to the surface a regret that I didn't listen to my mother and go into the brewing and tobacco business. It was at times like this that I wished I had no skill with a battle axe, that I had no clue where the weak spots on a Forest Dragon were, and that my only desire for excitement involved a particularly good mix of malt beer cooked up in my own brewery.

"Billi?"

I was resting my forehead in the palm of my hand. I parted the fingers, peeking through the V-opening I'd made. "Yeah? Who's at the door now, Miranda? One of the Rockefellers?"

Miranda is a good kid. You know that by now. But did I happen to mention how savvy she is?

"You know that raise I've been wanting, Billi?"

"Yeah, hon," I muttered, barely audible to even myself.

"I don't want it if it's going to put my boss at the bottom of some river."

I turned to look at her face, white as a Forest Banshee. She was afraid. I really began to wonder about that elf blood again, because she definitely had their intuition. "I don't like this, Billi," she said, walking up to me at my desk. "I don't like this at all."

"If you don't like the idea of getting a raise, just say so."

"I didn't say *that!*" She gave me a playful shove. I could tell she was trying to be serious, and I wasn't making it easy for her. "You know what I mean, Billi. There's something really wrong with all this."

"You're preaching to the Cleric, darlin'."

Hopping down from the chair and slipping on my jacket, I placed a pouch of tobacco into my coat pocket, giving it and Beatrice two reassuring pats. I then removed a pipe from the tiny tree at the corner of my desk and cast a quick glance over the Chicago streets. "Two of society's finest coming into this office today, both with connections to the Ryerson and the mob. I'm thinking I need to pay my intellectual pal Hammil another visit."

"Billi, don't you think you should lay low for a couple days?"

"Miranda," I replied with a grin, adjusting my hat and giving her a courteous tip of it, "as Little Miss Eva said, this is what *my kind* do."

"I couldn't give a rat's ass what Miss Moneybags says!" The protective "big sister" side of her had now kicked in. Ah, she's cute as a button when she gets like this!

"All right, you win. I'll just go home for the night, maybe stop by Mick's for a quick bite..."

In response to Miranda's look of warning, I tucked my thumb into my palm and rested my four fingers on my heart, a sign of the Dwarven Oath of Loyalty of Service. "I swear I'm going to take your advice this time. Seriously. I guess the Singing Sword can wait one more night, but no matter what, I'm going to be the first to find it."

"The Singing Sword?"

I then realized I had just mentioned the Sword by its nickname. I didn't want to mention it around my girl, but I could tell Miranda wasn't going to take something with a name like that seriously, anyway.

"It sounds important to you," she observed with a tinge of curiosity in her voice.

"You have no idea, nor do you want to know." I motioned for her to bend down closer for a quick pinch of her cheek and a wink—my way of saying "End of Discussion."

"Now, time to take a break from our business of poking around other people's business," I announced. "I'm calling it a night. Okay, hon?"

Between reading melodramatic Dwarven runes and receiving visits from Chicago royalty, it had been a long day for me...so long that, just shy of five, I was still craving Mick's "Lunch Hour Hot Plate," a special Reuben sandwich recipe and a cup of chili so hot that a cup is all you can handle.

Even though the Lunch Special was now nothing more than a distant memory for Mick, he'd be glad to whip it up special for me. I always hated putting him out in his own place, but the craving was stronger than usual, and I thought that tonight—along with that glance down Miss Lesinger's blouse—I'd earned myself an indulgence.

Being a dwarf in a human world means that subtlety of any kind is hard to pull off around me. I'm a novelty in this town, whether I like it or not, and it's just plain awkward when people try to pretend otherwise. No other way to describe it. On those rare occasions when someone does manage to pull off an act of subtlety with me, that individual earns my respect.

So I couldn't help but respect the two ogres standing behind me. I couldn't turn around and get a closer look, because one of them—I think it was the ogre on the right—was pressing the barrel of a .45 into the back of my neck. Now, I had to give this guy credit because I could feel the fabric of a raincoat draped over the pistol, but still the move was subtle. It didn't even knock my fedora out of place.

"I sincerely hope I can help you, gentlemen," I spoke pleasantly, the slight chill from the gun's metal causing the hair on my arms to rise.

"You look hungry," the voice behind me grunted. "How's about we treats yous ta dinnah?"

"Hey, boys, that's real nice of ya." I replied with a friendly smile, my insides already churning.

I got into the car first, giving a polite nod to the goombah already sitting in the back seat. He responded by patting me down, removing Beatrice, my pipe and weed, and the hogleg from my person. (I might as well be naked!)

The mook behind me removed the raincoat from his piece and sandwiched me in between him and his fellow gangster. Not on purpose, mind you. I'm just a little dwarf with a big waist, and these dago-ogres were no petite sprites themselves. Yeah, you could say we got close to one another without getting to know one another.

The last mook, still outside the car, closed the door behind us and then wiggled his fingers at me in "toodle-loo" fashion before we three sped off to destinations unknown…well, unknown to me.

Like I said, I hate *déjà vu*. Always led to something bad.

My Dinner with Alphonse

Nobody said anything, the tension in the car growing so thick that a two-handed broadsword would have a problem getting through it. Not that I expected stimulating conversation or anything like that; if they wanted me to know where we were going, they would have told me already. And judging by the looks of these ogres, stimulating conversation probably consisted of extremely short, single-syllable words.

I could see the hood ornament through the windshield, and I focused all my attention on it. This was not the time to take in the sights. Right now, I just needed to keep a cool head and hope I'd not pissed anyone off too high in the Organization.

Thanks to Chief O'Malley, I was now an instant celebrity whom everyone wanted to meet. The press kept calling to find out why a little tyke like me was the best friend of Chicago's Finest; a Rothchild wanted to outbid a Lesinger to have me, "Snoop to the Snobs," dig up quality dirt on her rival; and now, flanked by two palookas, someone in the Business wanted words with me on one of their fallen foot soldiers.

If I lived to see the dawn, I planned to mark this day in my calendar as the day to close up the office and stay in bed.

Our destination established itself as an upper-tier hotel from the moment we rolled to a stop. A doorman, sporting a polite grin, tipped his hat to each of the ogres as we followed the red carpet to the doorway. Even for this dwarf, his obligatory expression and gesture were extended. I guess I was expected to remember that so I wouldn't stiff him on a tip when I left...provided I left on my own accord.

As we entered the lobby, dark-wood fixtures providing the only warmth in this cavernous expanse of marble and brass, the receptionists and bellhops didn't raise an eyebrow or give a second glance to my personal Neanderthal escorts. They did, however, nearly inflict severe whiplash on themselves when they caught a glance at the dwarf in their midst. Ditto for the guests milling about in the lounge or waiting at the reception desk. On noticing my companions, bystanders quickly retreated into their own personal solitudes, but not before I picked up on their shared thought: *Better him than me.*

Now we were going up a red-velvet staircase decked out with polished fixtures and black-and-white marble panels that shone as smooth as glass. I started to hope and pray that somewhere between telling Miranda I was going home and reaching the sidewalk outside my building, I had taken an arrow in the chest and I was actually wandering through the Sacred Hall of Furrow Fillenstub, the Keeper and Supreme Guardian of the Everlasting Fields of Yernase. Here I would stand judgment for my lives in Acryonis and in America, held accountable for my deeds. Did I fulfill my duty to His Holiness, the Emperor? Did I serve as a good example to my people, never surrendering the pride of the Dwarven Empire? Would the Great Guardian grant me lands of my own in the Everlasting Fields or turn me out of door, his judgment unquestioned and final?

My prayer was answered with *"Billi, dammit, you aren't dead. Now focus!"* when I saw the kid in the elevator. He had it all: Freckles, buckteeth, and a frame so skinny that a quick look at him would break a bone. He didn't bother to look at any of us as we got in, and didn't say anything as he closed the door. He was no different from the doorman in the way he moved like clockwork, preferring to remain oblivious to the outcome of his actions. While I knew this elevator didn't deliver me before the Great Guardian, it was clear I was about to face a judgment of some kind.

Several floors later, the cage shut behind us with a loud *clang* that reverberated through the corridor as we walked down a carpeted hallway that closely resembled the Halls of Hurrenheim, our footsteps resounding as soft, dull thuds.

I fixed my gaze on the distant door at the end of the corridor, figuring that was where we were headed. Instead, we stopped before a pair of double doors halfway down. One of the ogres turned to face the hallway, looking left and right with a casual pat against his jacket's left breast lapel. Probably making sure his boom-dagger was where he last left it in case anyone stopped by for unscheduled room service.

The other ogre opened the right-side door, and looked down at me. Guess it was my turn to take the lead.

First I saw a desk, pristine and well-organized, second only to Miranda's. No one was sitting behind it, so I surmised this meeting was not going to be recorded in a ledger somewhere.

Continuing forward into the next room, I heard the footsteps behind me cease. I removed my hat as the light behind me dimmed, followed by a soft *click*. The only sounds I heard now were the light scraping of silverware against a plate, coming from somewhere in front of me.

He sat by himself at a round table large enough for eight. There were a pair of guards stationed at the door behind me, a pair of guards several paces from the table, and one guard occasionally peering out from the drawn blind to catch a glimpse of the street. I couldn't help smiling at the sight of the man enjoying his dinner in the midst of a small army. From his size, you wouldn't think he needed guards; even seated at the table, it was pretty apparent that he could take care of anyone wanting to start trouble. It was also apparent that if you did start something with him, he'd be the one to finish it.

This was a big man who obviously enjoyed his Italian food, his Italian wine, and his Italian arias, which were softly playing on a nearby phonograph. I'm not a huge fan of the fat chicks strapping themselves into costumes two sizes too small, donning a ridiculous helm, and then belting out an hour-long goodbye after being supposedly poisoned. My advice to those operatic villains: Use faster-acting poison.

This particular aria, though, was different. Soft. Subtle. The melody was tragic but didn't overwhelm the listener in its emotion, creating a rich tapestry of notes seamlessly woven into the orchestral accompaniment. That was nice. I needed something to relax me right now.

This situation was a tough one to call. I could just go ahead and take a seat opposite him, showing a bit of balls...which could lead to them being removed if he perceived my *hubrimaz* (Dwarven word for *chutzpah*...) as a threat or challenge. Or I could just continue to stand here like a total mook, providing some dinner entertainment for a while until boredom settled in, and then face a quick end on an empty stomach.

Being in his presence meant waiting on a word, so I'd have to play tonight by his rules. It was no different from the rules of royalty: Speak only when spoken to, and move only when told.

As a waiter brought in a second plate, I lowered my defenses ever so slightly to savor the sharp, tangy scent of tomatoes mingled with earthy aromas of oregano, basil, and the ambrosia of the culinary gods—garlic. A sweet tinge of cinnamon was also present, and I wasn't used to that in a red sauce. A secret ingredient, perhaps?

Now, the waiter was grating fresh Parmesan cheese over the dish. A simple dish for a simple taste. Sometimes, it is the simple things you crave (even when you have everything, as this man did) that make life worth living.

Contemplating the man at the table more closely, I realized that he didn't "have everything," so much as he rented it for the time being. This man of girth would fall one day as would a star from the night sky, making people stop and stare in wonder, only to burn out and vanish with no fanfare. Empires like his believed themselves to last a millennium, only to fade into history tomorrow. (Yeah, not that far a stretch from my old stompin' grounds, this place called Chicago.)

"Your plate's gettin' cold. Pull up a chair."

My waxing philosophic immediately screeched to a halt on the sound of his voice, his chewing as he spoke giving it a casual, muffled sound. The invitation could only mean that for the time being, anyway, I was a guest.

He didn't hear it, but I let out a soft sigh of relief. Okay then, all bets were off. I could loosen up a bit…well, to a point. I was a guest as long as his temperament and attitude approved, but that could change in a heartbeat.

The waiter pulled back the chair and, on measuring me up, added a couple of throw cushions from a nearby couch. I hopped up and adjusted myself to be on a decent level with the table. The pressed white linen over the waiter's forearm was draped across my lap before he moved me closer to my dinner. With that same artificial smile the rest of the hotel staff wore, he took my hat out of my hands, gave me a nod, and then excused himself from the room.

It was to be a lovely night of good food, good music and good conversation. Just me, the guards, and my host: Alfonse Capone.

"This is real generous of you, Mr. Capone. My original dinner plans were for something a bit less complex."

He gave a chortle and glanced at me while holding a fork of pasta halfway between his mouth and the plate. "Spaghetti? Complex? Lemme tell yous, wheah I come from, dis is just comfort food, y'know? Sumtin' I throw togeddah when I wanna fill up quick. Now if ya want *complex*, y'oughta have my chef whip up a tortellini dish fa yous sometime." Alfonse shoved his mouth full of spaghetti, finishing his thought as he chewed. "I'm to da prosciutto an' chicken he's got down. Covah it wit Alfredo sauce. Knock ya socks off."

If this was the meal of a condemned man, I was not going to let it get cold. I dug into the small mountain of pasta before me, twirling my fork into the steaming noodles. Up close, I caught some of the sauce's subtleties, a signature of his chef that distinguished him as a master. Italian food, at least for me, was always a fare that you either got right on the first try or not at all. You might go too heavy on the salt, get chintzy with the parsley, or use the wrong kind of basil and throw off the balance. (Now me, I'm a purple basil dwarf myself. It's got a sweet aftertaste and plays well with other herbs, in particular the oregano and garlic.)

This spaghetti, a simple "comfort food" of the Italian cuisine, was nothing less than a masterpiece. *Buono pasto!*

"Your chef knows his sauce, Mr. Capone." I nodded in approval.

"He'd bettah," Capone chuckled. "It's me."

The guy who ran Chicago cooked, too? Damn, I was impressed! On the second bite, I chewed a bit slower. This was the best spaghetti I'd ever had. *Period.*

"You missed your calling, Mr. Capone. You would have made a chef worthy of a royal entourage."

"Nah, nah, nah," he dismissed with a wave of his hand. "My chef handles da tough stuff. I just have dose times, like t'night, when I wan' sumtin' simple an' don' mind clutterin' up a kitchen. Just 'cause I got off da boat an' out heah ta Chicago don' mean I gotta fuhget wheah I come from. Take my word fa it. Nuthin' more important den remembrin' wheah y'come from."

Capone held the dark red-purple wine underneath his nose for a moment, enjoying its aroma while eyeballing me. "Ya shortah den I thought. Mus' be tough bein' a little guy like y'self in a town dis big, huh?"

I wasn't returning the stare, but his stare wasn't what made me uncomfortable. It was the direction he was already taking with our dinner chitchat. "I manage."

"I bet ya do, ya little sprite ya!"

My fork paused for a second. That dig didn't ruin my appetite or the taste of the spaghetti, but I didn't want to see this pleasant scene go bad. I'm sure he caught my hesitation, so now he knew what button to push if he wanted to get in a last word, or just see what a pissed-off dwarf looked like.

"Yeah, I bet ya do," he went on, "an' y'know what? I *respect* dat. I do. Ya facin' an uphill battle, Short Stuff, an' ya not lettin' anyt'ing slow ya down."

I'm not much for the wine. It's an elf's drink. As I took a sip to wash down the spaghetti, though, I couldn't deny it: The wine suited the sauce. One exceptional table Capone set. Come on, Al, don't spoil this dinner with the height jokes.

Capone nodded with a smile, waving a beefy finger. "*Yoooouuu.* You are *very* good, you. Y'got balls, an' y'got heart, an' dat is worthy of my respect."

I inclined my head modestly. "You're making a great wall out of pixie bricks, Mr. Capone."

He shook his head after the wine glass left his lips. The same finger he just waved at me pointed up, to let me know something important was about to be said. "Nah-nah-nah, I jus' said y'earned my respect. Please, honah me by callin' me Al."

Ho-boy, did I really want to cross this line?

Hastily finishing my mouthful of pasta, I lifted my glass in a toast. "Only if you return the favor and call me Billi," I replied with a grin.

"Heah's ta you, Billi," he smiled, returning the toast.

It amazed me that I could enjoy this meal under the circumstances. The wine was good, as I said, but after that last exchange, I really wanted something stronger. I was not only having dinner with Alphonse Capone, but now I was on a first-name basis with him. I think a bullet to the head would have been easier to deal with than this.

"No, Al, you honor *me*." By the Fates, that just felt wrong in so many ways. "You're treating me to a terrific dinner you yourself cooked, with good wine, and I would be the last one to flout this honor by not being an appreciative guest."

"Flout?" Capone chuckled. "*Flout?* What? Sumtin' in dat sauce givin' ya gas?"

"No, Al, I mean, throw it back in your face." As if I couldn't make this dinner more awkward, I had to pull out a word from the library stacks and teach it to a gangland boss. "Far be it from me, a working-class dwarf, to break bread at a king's table and then take a battle-axe to the hand that's feeding me."

He nodded, I thought, in reply to my comment, but then he said it again. "Flout." He kept nodding. "Flout. I like dat. Dat's classy. Flout."

"Seriously, Al," I continued, "I'm just a working stiff. I do what I do 'cause no one else is gonna do it, or *wants* to do it. I was just telling my secretary that today—"

He sat back in his chair with a long, contented sigh. At first I thought it was in response to the wine or the meal, but then I caught the leer on his face.

"Aww, now dat Miranda Tanner is one nice piece, Billi. I'm s'prised she didn't get inta pitchuhs, or sumtin' like dat."

No. No, he *didn't* just do that.

Humans—in particular, the really menacing ones—love to play this game. I feel the same way about it here as I did back in Acryonis. It's a coward's ploy. Face me in the field like an equal. That's a code we dwarves live by. You touch my family or those close to me, and I got only three words for you: *better be sure*. Better be sure I don't get up. Better be sure I don't get over a severe case of death. Better be sure I can't find you.

"She's a good girl, Al." My voice was calm, but my intent was as crystal-clear as the Jewel of Shri-Mela. "I love her like family."

That was going to be his only warning.

"Yeah." Capone nodded, my tone clearly registering with him as he paused for a moment. "An' bein' a little big man like y'are, I can't help but respect how ya comin' up in da world. Front page of *three* newspapuhs? My hat's off t'ya, brownie."

With the mention of the newspapers, I knew we were finally getting around to what he wanted to know: My connection. To deal with the "brownie" insult, I just shoveled more pasta in my mouth to shut myself up. (I was just silently hoping dessert was going to something other than cannoli. Too much cheese gives me the kind of gas that would make a rock dragon turn around and shout, *"All right, that wasn't me!"*)

I had known all along that this case would eventually bring me here. After all, I was getting involved with the Business. However, I had been hoping for that involvement to be more on my terms, preferably with someone close to Capone. But sitting down with Capone himself? Over a dinner he cooked? Now that was something I didn't count on.

As "nice" as our dinner had started, though, he had begun playing games almost immediately. The second insult was no slip. Then a mention of Miranda—extremely intentional. If his hospitality had caught me completely off-guard, the games sobered me up pretty quickly.

"You set a terrific table, Al." I broke off a piece of bread, dipping it in the sauce remaining outside my pasta. "I can't help, though, but worry that I'm taking up your valuable time."

Al's smile softened as he helped himself to a hunk of bread. His plate still had a bit of this sauce left on it, but not for long as he ran the bread across its surface. "What makes ya say dat, brownie?"

Yep, he did it again. Time to swallow hard and keep going.

"Well, just that you're a man of extremes. You either enjoy the lush life, or you're keeping to yourself. Tonight, you're dining here in this ritzy hotel. Big room, sitting at a table for eight, and your guards are on the clock. Dinner at what I'm guessing is your office? Kinda tells me you didn't feel like being social tonight."

Capone gave a laugh and nodded. "*Veeeeery* good. Very good, you. Guess bein' a private eye, it's hard ta turn dat off, huh?"

"I just watch and learn, Al," I replied with a shrug. He was right, but I wasn't going to let him in on that. "I watch and learn."

"And how 'bout *teach*, Billi?" His plate now clean, he shot a glance to the waiter hovering in the doorway before picking up his wine glass. I watched as the employee disappear the moment Al took a sip, his glass nearing empty. "Y'evah teach?"

I finished my own glass. I could see a trace of a grin on his face. "Well," I replied, "I don't so much *teach* as I *inform*."

Al nodded slowly, turning his attention to the window opposite. A car honked, its engine revved, and then faded into the distance. He looked back at me. "T'ink ya could *inform* me, den?"

Capone's waiter reappeared with an open bottle of wine and a second. As he refilled the glass, the other waiter appeared with the pipe removed from me earlier (already packed with my weed) and a good-sized cigar, already cut and waiting to be lit.

"You see," Capone continued, "I'm lookin' fa some infahmation, and I can't t'inkah no one bettah ta inform me den a private dick from da front page."

I could have come back with that "private investigator" line I used with Miss Lesinger and Miss Rothchild, except that here, it would be my ticket on the Wise-Ass Express to the Afterlife.

"All you have to do is ask, Al," I smiled as I mopped up my plate with the fresh baguette, its thin crust melting in my mouth. The wine steward offered a refill, but I shook my head and took my pipe. "You've been a gracious host and a stand-up guy for inviting me to dinner."

I wasn't lying there. Insults aside, Capone *was* being gracious. After all, I was still breathing. Pretty damn gracious, if you ask me.

Capone laughed, his laughs sounding closer to pig's grunts as he placed the stogie in his mouth. "Ya know sumtin', Shorty, I'm likin' yous da longah we sit heah!" He drew from the cut end as the waiter held a small lighter to the cigar, causing the lighter's flame to flare with each of his deep drags. "Na...don' geh me w'on..." he continued, still lighting the cigar. I guess he felt like he had to get his thoughts out, regardless of how much the cigar hindered his speech. "I unna-sta y'goh ob-la-gai-sha…" One more long drag and the cigar was lit, his speech clearing up. "An obligation ta keep t'ings private an' all. So do I. I got obligations. Obligations ta da people dat work fa me. Obligations ta my family. Obligations ta my friends."

"Obligations to friends, Al?" I placed the pipe stem in my mouth and, on cue, the wine steward ignited the lighter, catching the contents of my bowl. Once the weed glowed softly, the servant gave me a courteous nod and cleared my side of the table. "Some friends. Asking obligations of *you?*"

With the second already heading for the kitchen with Al's dishes, the butler took my plate and empty glass, gave a nod to us, and we were alone once again. Just us and Capone's hired muscle, their attentions divided between the world outside the hotel, the corridors outside our suite, and me.

I removed the pipe from my mouth, sending a light puff above us. Didn't want to be rude to the host. "What kind of obligations are we talking about?"

"Favuhs fulfilled, Billi. Promises kept. An' if I make a promise, my honah, my children's honah, and da honah of my family is challenged. I'm not one ta back off a challenge, no mattah wheah it comes from."

Capone reached for a folded-up newspaper, letting it fall open to the front page. This headline was about as clever as the one I'd read this morning:

HALF AND HALF

The headline blared in huge letters above the picture of me leaving Riletto's crime scene. This public eye, though, got lucky. Along with revealing me being escorted from the alleyway, the photo included the bottom half of Riletto stuffed in the trash can behind me.

"An' dese people I got obligations to?" Al went on. "Well, Billi, dey wanna know who's issuin' da challenge."

Big Al had a point. All I could do was remove my eyes from the newspapers and lock on his. "I can understand that."

He kept this stare with me for a moment, and then turned back to the picture, puffing the stogie in his mouth. "Mmmm…I figyuh y'wou'. Ya smah gah." After appearing to memorize every inch of that front page, he took another drag from the cigar, shaking his head disapprovingly.

I gave my pipe a long drag too, sending a few smoke rings to one side. I find smoke rings make great tension-breakers. "So, Al, these obligations to these friends of yours, your crew—how do they involve me?"

"Now da private dick. I t'ink ya can figyah dat out."

"Oh, it's a *test*," I said with just a touch of facetiousness, not that I was expecting Capone to pick up on it. He didn't, thank the Fates. "Well now, let's see. *The Defender's* photographers couldn't get too close to the crime scene in question, but they *did* manage to get a shot of a rather handsome dwarf. Now, if this handsome dwarf is coming from a crime scene that public eyes couldn't get up close to, he must've been invited by Chicago's Finest to give them some pointers on the crime scene." Replacing the pipe in my mouth, I concluded, "And when you got a mick like O'Malley running the fuzz, Chicago needs all the help it can get."

Al gave a few healthy guffaws, the cigar still lodged in between his teeth. "So, ya go back a ways wit O'Malley, eh?"

"We've danced a few times. He's got two left feet."

Capone gave few more chuckles. Paused. Puffed. And then asked, "But he still invited ya ta have a look at what happened ta m'boy, Benny?"

"Yeah. Apparently, I was the last one to be seen with him."

"And den Benny winds up dead in an alley?" He folded up the paper and set it on the table, rubbing his forehead with his palm while the cigar continued to smolder between two fingers. "Dis upsets me. Dis upsets me like y'wouldn' believe, Billi."

"Yeah, it upsets me, too." I took another slow drag as I studied Al, who remained engrossed in the newspaper. "Benny was a good guy. A real pal. I'm sure you feel a loss…"

He finally looked over. "I just learned da guy's name a coupla days ago," he remarked, his tone a bit cold and callous. "Still, he was a loyal soldjah an' all. But since *you* knew Benny so well, how 'bout ya tell me what yous two talked about?"

Finally, we were getting down to business. I was going to 'fess up that I'd been poking my pudgy nose into Al's affairs.

Now that we were facing the real reason why I was there, I knew I needed to tread lightly unless I wanted to make a bad situation worse. Although he was Public Enemy Number One, Capone never forgot "the big three." Duty. Honor. Family. If you asked him what got him up to where he was, he would have given "the big three" all the credit. (Well, most of it anyway. I'm sure the bullets and the brutality were a big help, too.) If you betrayed any of Al's Holy Trinity, you'd better have a Portal of Oblivion to get sucked into, because there wouldn't be anyplace you could hide from him in this world.

"Al," I began, adopting the casual approach. Now, I was friendly, chummy, and relaxing with an old friend…an old friend who wouldn't hesitate to use me for his private boat's anchor. "We've been sitting here, breaking bread and sharing wine as friends. So, how about we talk like friends, *capisce?*"

Capone didn't budge.

"You know what I do for a living," I explained patiently. "People pay me to find answers to questions. All kinds of questions. Why? Because I ask the questions no one else will ask, to people no one wants to be seen or associated with. I'm on a case right now, and the question my client asked led me to Benny Riletto. I asked the question. We talked a bit. And we didn't talk about anything in your business, save for one thing: one of your generals, Anthony 'Pretty Boy' DeMayo."

I noticed Capone flinch on hearing DeMayo's name. Interesting reaction to his former right-hand man. He puffed on his cigar, still avoiding any eye contact. Maybe he was thinking about DeMayo? Looking back on their years together? Whatever trip my new friend Al was taking down memory lane, it was not a pleasant one. His eyes darkened slightly. Now it was my turn to watch him in silence, trying to figure out if I was going to leave on my own accord, or be carried out by four of Capone's boys.

"It's one thing to hit one of your own. But you brought that whole building down with not one, not two, but *three* bombs?"

Capone nodded. "I was tryin' ta prove a point."

"Prove a point, Al?" I leaned forward, fishing for a certain response. "Or trying to bury something you couldn't control?"

Maybe he knew more about DeMayo's plan than he was letting on. Did Capone think that DeMayo had the Sword and figured he would bury both traitor and trinket, making sure neither would move against him? Did Capone know something about the Singing Sword that he wasn't admitting?

He raised a dark eyebrow, a smile accented by the cigar between his lips the prelude to a soft laugh. "I'm impressed," he finally said, removing the stogie and tapping it free of ashes. "A little private-eye Tom Thumb, aintcha?"

The ogre at the door was snickering. Now we're back to the name-calling? Bad direction, Al. Don't do this.

"Y'got balls. Serious balls for a small fry, Billi."

"Yeah, well, when you only come up to the waistline, you got two options to do with what the other guy's shovin' in your face. Me? I choose to punch 'em. The Catholic Church is always in need of good sopranos."

Oh, he found that one funny. "Good one, Billi. Good one. But ya know, I'm *not* a violent man. I'm not. I jus' have a tempah." He shrugged, gesturing with his hands, his smoke sending wisps around his head. "My boys know it. Chicago knows it…"

His voice trailed off as he leaned forward, the cigar now pointing upward like a defiant "one-finger salute." He wasn't smiling anymore. "But I'm thinkin' maybe *you* don't know dis. Shorty, ya just need ta ask if ya really wanna screw wit me?"

This intimidation game was getting dull. "Okay, I'll ask. Do you really want to screw with me?"

Capone didn't laugh. I didn't expect him to.

"You asked me what I talked about with Benny. I told you. And as I told you before, Al, I'm not stupid enough to lie to you. I'm telling you the truth about Benny and my morning. Now you're fishing for—what—details? Then, I went on a research trip to the Ryerson. What more do you want?"

"What do I want? *What do I want?!?*" Capone was on his feet now, his face a deep, mottled red. I knew what he wanted. It had nothing to do with details. I just wanted to be sure.

"Y'know what I want!" he shouted. "I wanna heah it! I wanna heah what ya found out 'bout da t'ing!"

I kept my eyes locked on him, sending a set of smoke rings his way.

"Y'know sumtin', Baddings?"

Okay, that's his windup. I'm thinking his fastball is next.

"For a pixie, you're a handful."

Fine. Time to send this pitch deep into center field. "Yeah, but even being a dwarf, I still stand toe-to-toe with you, Scarface."

I heard the ogres' hammers pull back. They must've pulled out their heaters when Capone exploded, thinking I was on borrowed time. Maybe I was close to taking the dirt nap, but I really didn't care now what line I'd just crossed. I knew he killed people for calling him that, but he wouldn't stop pushing. (Something else Al didn't know about me…I can handle being called an elf before being called a pixie.)

"You lose that temper of yours, kill me now, and I take what I know with me. Now maybe you're thinking, 'So what?' Well, how about I tell you exactly what?"

He was about to pop, but I just wasn't all that impressed. I've seen orcs up close and personal, feeling their breath on my face and smelling their sweat in the heat of battle. You think this fat human is going to intimidate me?

"Let's say you find whatever you're looking for. I can tell you this: You're not going to know what the hell it does, or how it works. I'll make a wizard's wager that no one *in this world* is going to know what the hell it does, or how it works. So that leaves me."

I gave a nod to the steward and held out my pipe. After his eyes darted nervously from me to Capone, he quickly turned to fetch me an ashtray. (Poor guy was sweating harder than a fully armored foot soldier in summer.)

"I'm not from these parts, Al. Like you couldn't have guessed that. So when you finally find what we're both talking about, which is…?"

I wanted Capone to say it. I didn't need to ask myself if we were talking about the same thing. Coincidence was a fair-weather wench in my life.

"Da Singin' Sword," he finally said, his voice just audible over the outside traffic.

A piercing *tink-tink-tink-tink-tink* filled the room as I rapped my pipe against the thick marble tray. I gave my bowl a quick check before giving Al the final score in this pennant playoff.

"Then you're going to need an expert from the outside. And I'm here to tell you, Al, that they don't come more outside than me."

The cigar smoldered between his pudgy lips, but I could tell from the occasional glow of the embers that he was still breathing. Calling Capone the name he hated was a stupid thing to do, but what I was offering him was far beyond the borderlands of his imagination. It was also my bargaining chip with the Big Man. What I knew about the Sword of Arannahs would wrap Capone around my finger until I became useless. Then, he would bring up the "Scarface" comment and take me for diving lessons off the Reliance Building.

I knew that this was a serious bluff, but I wasn't showing my cards. Capone wasn't the only one who knew the gargoyle's stare.

He finally moved away from the end of the table and leaned in close to me. If it had been just the two of us, I would have slapped that stogie out of his mouth. His eyes narrowed slightly, as if trying to bore through me with his steely gaze.

"And why d'ya t'ink ya can stand up ta me, Baddings?"

I conjured up the best shit-eating grin I could muster. "Because *I* know what the word 'flout' means."

Okay, it was his move. I didn't have to glance at Al's muscle to know they were just wanting the nod. I hadn't heard their boom daggers slipping back into their holsters. A single gesture stood between me leaving here on my own accord and that long car ride out to the country where three leave, and two come back.

He grunted. Okay, not what I expected, but it was better than having him give the command to his boys. Again, he grunted...and these grunts eventually turned into a good, healthy laugh.

"You—are funny. Yeah, youah funny guy, Billi!" Capone nodded approvingly, still laughing at me as if I was a court jester who finally got in the big score. Even over his guffaws, I could hear the guns behind me slipping back into holsters. "And I like funny guys, Baddings. I do. Yeah, deah's too much tragedy in da streets."

"Listen, Al," I volunteered, "I don't know if you were on top of this, but you may not be the only boss looking for the Singing Sword."

His laughter died down as he put out his cigar in the massive ashtray on his end of the table. "Really? What gives ya dat impreshun?"

"Couple of trolls dropped Bugs' name to me a couple of nights ago. Consider that a free bit of investigation from me."

Capone nodded. He didn't seem surprised at all, but he did appear disappointed. "So, I take it y'gointa come work fa me if I get da Singin' Sword first?"

"If you don't, I'll get it for you. You got an idea what it can do, and I know *exactly* what it can do. I'd rather see it in your hands before Moran's. No offense, but you're the lesser of two evils."

My second bluff. I just hope he took it as well as the first.

"None taken," he nodded.

"Al," I went on, "Chicago is yours. And I respect that. I'm going to make sure the Singing Sword goes to the right people, and the right people are in this room."

Yeah, the right people were in this room, all right. It was me.

He was quiet, thinking over my offer. For the second time tonight, the chances of me seeing the sunrise tomorrow rested with his decision. Guns out or not, the ogres were still on the clock and waited on that decision, right along with me.

"Den I'll bid ya good evenin', Mr. Baddings. I hope y'enjoyed dinnah."

"Mr. Capone, the pleasure was all mine." I slipped my pipe back into my inside pocket, gave my tie a slight tug, and fixed my stare with Capone's. Yeah, it was my pleasure that I was walking out and not being carried out. "If you come across the Singing Sword, Mr. Capone, you go on and give me a call, and my services are yours."

"Count on it."

I fought the instinct to run, keeping my strides relaxed but long. One of his orcs took me back to the elevator, handing over my guns and tobacco pouch before shutting the cage on me and the freckled kid. As our descent began, I wasn't planning to let this thug enjoy watching me breathe a sigh of relief. He was already shouldering the disappointment of seeing my face leaving the same way it went in. And this lovable mug of mine didn't have a split lip, black eye, or switchblade scars across the cheek.

Right before he slipped out of view, I give this mook a wink. *Be seeing you*, I thought with a grin. I probably would...seeing as I was now a valuable commodity to his boss.

I maintained my calm, casual gait to the outside (where I tipped the grinning doorman a fiver) and hailed the cab that would get me home. I whispered a quick prayer to Dunnagor, one of the Dwarven Guardians of Yearnese, that if he were going to raise his battle-axe for anyone, to let it be for my girl, Miranda. I was confident that I'd charmed Capone and figured he wouldn't play that card...at least, right now. I had to keep him and his goons at arm's length and string him along while I figured out what the hell to do with the Singing Sword once I got it.

Yeah, once *I* got it. There was no room for "ifs" and "mights" here. Either I got it, or the world I now called home was going to be in for one rough, bumpy ride.

CHAPTER NINE
ANY FRIEND OF LOU'S...

The best after-dinner mint I could think of after my face-off with Capone was a long, hot shower. My clothes reeked of garlic, along with traces of pipe and cigar—not a sweet-smelling combo.

After a soothing moment under the warm water, I decided to make the shower cold to counter my adrenaline rush. Shivering under the bombardment of frigid droplets that bit into my skin like a swarm of flesh-gnats, I confronted the reality of what I had just stepped into.

Just what I needed: a good, old-fashioned slap in the face.

My fast-wrinkling fingertips passed across a trio of permanent welts starting at my lower back and abruptly stopping just short of—well, where a human's kidney would be. The cold water was turning them a darker shade of pink, making them look a lot nastier that they were in truth. Still, on certain days—usually before a snowstorm—I still feel a tingle from them. I felt that same tingle now, the sensation taking me back to a battlefield and a thunderstorm with rain as cold as the stream I was standing under.

A few years before the big mission for the Nine Talismans, the Black Orcs had overrun a number of elf villages along the border realms, and we were called in to take them back. As far as the Elvish Intelligence (in all their *infinite* wisdom) reports went, the Black Orcs had not yet discovered the libraries in the villages of Aeryn's Harbor, Chi-ya-Nah, and D'Hargoh Pointe. The Elders kept many of their more powerful spell books in these three villages, making them very strategic territories. Fortunately, what Black Orcs have in strength and ferocity, they lack in brains. In other words, we had time on our side.

Fighting orcs is a lot like facing off with Capone or Moran and their boys. You go in with a simple strategy: Hit these bastards with everything you got. We planned a full charge on these border villages, starting with Chi-ya-Nah because their libraries' spell books would prove to be the most dangerous if read by the wrong set of peepers.

I was fighting alongside this human by the name of Kev, a swordsman with whom I had two big things in common: We both enjoyed an evenly matched fight on the battlefield and a passion for our favorite weapons. Kev took his broadsword technique seriously, often needling me with his remarks that a battle-axe was best used for chopping wood. (I always fired back that broadswords made for great back-scratchers.)

So, we made a bet before this great push: Whoever killed the most orcs would buy the drinks afterwards. We kept score during the fighting, and Kev could not help but be impressed by my numbers. I'll admit I was having a particularly good day. My battle-axe was cutting down orcs like wheat at harvest time.

We remained neck-and-neck through most of the battle, the rain showing no sign of letting up. The bad weather was actually driving us harder, I think. By now, I had taken down my twentieth orc, and was really getting into the love of the kill. So, I started to showboat a bit. Twirling my axe in one hand or swinging it around my body before striking an oncoming orc was for no one's benefit other than mine.

This showboating would normally get a laugh from Kev, but I didn't hear a lot of anything going on right then outside of my own private euphoria. As my axe hit orc number 25, I felt a guttural cry tear through my throat, already tasting the beer that would be free all night.

That was when the axe disappeared. It just wasn't there anymore. By the Fates, how could I be disarmed? This made no sense! I was unstoppable. I was untouchable.

I was wide open.

The axe was still lodged in the fat orc's gut. He was losing plenty of blood, but he hadn't lost all of his fight. With a single turn of his torso, I'd lost my weapon. And after that, this weird tingling swept across my side. I remained on my feet, suspended by sheer will and perhaps a hint of fascination that this dimwit had actually disarmed me!

Kev's scream sounded as if it were coming from a million leagues away as he buried his broadsword into that beast's chest, his grace reminiscent of Hack Wilson diving for a high fly ball and catching it tight in his mitt. There was a slow fluidity to Kev's movements that was just beautiful to behold.

By the time the hilt reached its chest, the orc dropped hard into the mud. So had I. I don't doubt our simultaneously drop looked like a pair of marionettes after their strings were cut. I was now aware of the rain, because the drops hitting my face made me wince. When the thrill of the kill finally faded, I noticed the orc's claws. Now what was an orc doing with claws? After staring at them a little longer, I eventually figured out the claws were his weapons—metal gauntlets with fingertips filed to fine points and edges, capable of doing some damage.

Then I looked back down to my side. It all came to me in that moment. Pain. Awareness. Anger.

Yeah, anger. I could not believe how stupid I had been.

Hard to believe that wasn't even ten years ago by this realm's calendar. The Great War of The Races had been going on for so long, it was easy to lose track of time when it came to battles like those. Yet that particular memory remained crystal-clear, leaving me to wonder whether these goose bumps covering my skin were coming from the cold or this unscheduled journey back into my past.

I retraced my scars, tasting the icy water as it trickled from my head, down my temple, and eventually into the corners of my mouth. Those scars were a reminder of how dangerous having an attitude can be. I had gotten lucky that day, and I was even luckier tonight.

Those scars also reminded me of friends like Kev. Damn, I wonder what that big blonde knucklehead is up to these days.

The towel didn't do much to warm me up—bad news for my mace and stones, which had shriveled up and were making the walk across the flop a little uncomfortable. I crawled into bed, letting the warmth of my blankets bring me down from my rush. Silently staring at the ceiling, my eyes followed a hairline crack that began at the light fixture and disappeared into the shadows. I must've followed that crack back and forth a hundred times. Better than counting sheep.

I still couldn't believe I'd managed to con safe passage out of Alfonse Capone's lair...after entering a pact with him, no less! If Capone and I had been talking about a shipment of booze or gambling profits, I wouldn't be taking a shower—I'd be taking a nice long bath in the Chicago River.

What I had going for me—my upper hand on Capone's battlefield, if you will—was knowing his unknown. He knew guns and knives, sure, but *swords*? Maybe he'd read about them in storybooks, but something told me he didn't spend a lot of time in the tomes. Nevertheless, he was smart enough to know that he was in need of an expert, and one look at me in the newspapers told him that I was his man.

For years, I had resented being a dwarf in this realm because I was out of place and disadvantaged everywhere I went. Tonight, it saved my ass.

Gradually, the thoughts and recollections of the evening faded save for one: Somewhere in Chicago, the Sword of Arannahs waited for a wielder—a *true* wielder. Benny's crime scene was a rock dragon-sized clue that a "worthy" opponent had gotten his mitts on it, all right. However, the lack of similar deaths since then left me to wonder if the Sword was up for grabs again, or if its current keeper was having trouble controlling its power. One thing was clear: Once that magic was effectively harnessed, it would be anyone's ball game as to what would happen next.

I hadn't found anything in *My World Book* yet about just how meek you had to be to command the Sword, or how exactly the Sword would call upon the forces of Darkness—only flowery allusions to what it would leave in its wake. (Like I really needed reminders.) Tomorrow, *My World Book* was going to stay in its hiding place. I needed to walk the path of captains and corporals who wanted to be kings.

Nuzzled deep in the Southside was this hole-in-the-wall Italian bistro, widely considered to be the only place in Chicago for a cappuccino. (Now I like a strong cup of java as much as the next guy, but this stuff reminded me of the venom that marsh slugs spit on unwanted intruders. These crazy Italians were drinking it to get a swift kick in the ass!)

There was nothing unique about this little family-run shop: Traffic in and out of this coffee shop was steady, the suits coming in and out were all in a hurry, and I didn't note a lot of friendly chitchat going on between the customers and crew. There was, however, a checkmark next to this place in Benny's memo pad, which is why yours truly was there to check it out.

Enduring the usual round of stares, I hopped up in a chair and perused the modest menu. (The menu was in Italian, so I just pretended to know what it said.) Meanwhile, I felt myself waking up just from the fumes of cappuccino wafting in my direction.

A hefty Italian mama fixed her beady little eyes on me. "Littah man, wha' you wan' dis mornin'?"

Blunt. To the point. Something to be said about these Italians.

"Never been here before, ma'am." Ah, the Baddings charm, at work so early in the morning. Damn, I'm good. "But my friend Benny loves the coffee here."

On dropping that name, I held her undivided attention, even with the hustle and bustle going on around her.

"He described this kind of coffee he got here," I went on, "but I don't think I'm awake enough to pronounce it. It's…ummm…cap of…cap-poo…?"

She nodded. "Yeah, I know wha' you wan'. I'll-a make it for ya reel niiice."

I watched Mama with a falcon's stare as she muttered something in her native tongue to a kid standing next to her—probably some second cousin or nephew trained to jump when this battle horse whinnied. Mama then ducked into the back room while this young apprentice worked his magic behind a mechanical cauldron.

Now that's disappointing. Here I thought Mama *was-a gonna make it-a reeeal niiice*, but then she disappears into the storeroom instead? At this busy time? Then again, even with the bistro as busy as it was, a few seconds is all she would need to tell someone to scram harder than a gnome when slave traders hit the groves.

Following this early-a.m. hunch of mine, I slipped off my chair (since it was busy, no one heard my feet hit the floor) and quietly made for the door.

Very few alleyways allowed access to the back of this joint, so my time was short. Moving as fast as my little Dwarven legs would carry me, I took a pass-through and emerged into a wide alleyway behind the Southside shops, a place for deliveries and trash. Along with a few alley cats, I observed crates of different produce stacked behind what should have been the grocery. I caught the scent of fresh bread coming from another doorway. The bakery.

Then, with the same effect as downing fire whiskey brewed by Mountain Crossbloods, I was knocked back a step by a whiff of freshly ground coffee beans. A back door flew open a few feet away, soon followed by the sound of rapid-fire Italian. My big bistro mama was whapping some kid against the back of his head—a kid far too old to be working in a coffee house. Maybe if he were a few years younger, I could see him helping out his mama when the hired help couldn't make it, but his street clothes had seen a lot of hard work elsewhere. Whether that work was legitimate remained to be seen.

I didn't understand what they were saying to one another, but I still understood them perfectly. From his shrug-responses to mama's railings, he didn't see the big deal in a little guy coming in to the bistro for a cup of Italian java, and she wasn't too crazy about anyone asking questions about a dead mobster. It came as no surprise to me that he stayed outside when the conversation—and the door—came to a close.

"Yeah, my mother always won the arguments in my family, too."

He looked my way, looked down the other way, and then ran. Why do these mooks always run?

I removed a lid from the trash can next to me and gave it a good, solid hurl. Watching the lid's trajectory reminded me of why I didn't really like discus-style weapons in my world. I'm horrible at throwing anything outside of an axe. Between my lousy release and the ill-timed breeze, the lid sailed up high above him before dropping like a stone. Even so, I was still blessed with a bit of the Fates' Luck: After landing on its edge, the lid continued to roll fast enough to catch up with my mark, trapping itself between his legs. He fell hard to the ground before skidding to a stop.

At the present time, Beatrice stayed snug as a bug in her holster. This guy was not high enough on the Capone food chain to warrant such attention. I wasn't going to give him a chance to get up, though, placing my foot between his shoulder blades and keeping him pinned to the ground.

"Good morning, pal. My name's Billi. What's yours?"

"M-M-Mario," he stammered.

This is Mario as in Mario Pezza, a mook from Benny's list I'd never met before. What do you know? A name had survived up till now without a star or a line through it.

"So, you understand English. You speak English, too?"

"Well, yeah. I'm an American. Whadya t'ink I'm gonna speak? French?"

I gave a chortle of approval. "Finally, an Italian who bleeds red, white, and blue. Smart boy…but not so smart that you couldn't say no to Benny Riletto?"

The kid groaned and looked down the alleyway. I could see in his face his longing to have been just two steps faster. "Benny told me he had a lot goin' fa him," he finally got out. "Said I could get a piece a' da action if I helped him out."

"And how were you, not even a two-bit hood, helping him out?"

Mario moved as if to get up, but I pushed my heel a little harder in between his shoulder blades. He sank back down into the alleyway asphalt. (Well, he just *said* he wanted a piece of Benny's action; now, just like Benny, Mario was getting a good back-alley grilling from The Gryfennos Kid. He couldn't say his mentor didn't deliver on at least one front.)

"Deah was dis package Benny had," he reluctantly began. "Said it was important. Said we hadta keep it movin' at all times. So dat's what we did. Benny'd call me at da bistro, lemme know da when and wheah, and den we'd make da switch."

"Well, ain't that a cozy arrangement?" I lifted my foot off Mario's back and hauled him up by the cuff of his vest to a sitting position. The shove I gave him against the brick wall was a reminder not to try and make another run for it.

"Now, how 'bout you tell me who's 'we'? Are you talking like the royal 'we'? Think you're the heir apparent to a throne or something?"

"Nah, nah, nah. Dis ain't a single-man job. I'm part of a crew now. A coupla guys, y'know?"

I gave Mario another hard shove against his forehead, bouncing his skull against the wall. "If I knew that," I barked, "I wouldn't be asking, now would I! Are you being a wiseguy because I'm a dwarf?"

Mario looked at me blankly. I gave his forehead another push, his skull knocking against the bricks a second time.

"I said, *are you being a wiseguy because I'm a dwarf?*"

"Nah-nah-nah, I'm—"

"*No!*" I snapped, shutting him up. "You're not doing much right now apart from keeping out of sight and hoping Capone doesn't come knocking down your mama's door! So just be happy I'm here instead of Capone's boys. Now let's try again. Who is 'we'?"

This is usually the point of the investigation where I'm going beyond giving out headaches. Right now, I'd be busting noses or handing out the odd black eye. Just part of the job—a part of the job that, on some occasions, I don't mind so much. But I could see that little Mario here had a bit of the mage in him from the way he was tuning in to all my silent warnings. Weighing the look in my eye, the arched brow, a slight tilt of my head, he knew if he wanted to walk out of this alley without looking like a wild boar's half-eaten lunch, his next words needed to be the ones I wanted to hear.

"Jus' a coupla guys I work wit," he replied with a shrug, his voice reaching that higher register of nervousness. "Jimmy Hill, Tommy Ross, an' some guy I didn' know…Chuck something."

"Chuck Morris?"

Mario nodded. "Dat's da guy!"

"And lemme guess…you all worked with Two Times and Benny."

Suddenly, he went quiet like the good little soldier he was. I don't know if Mario could handle an interrogation from the Black Guard of Hannerith, but he was planning to go the distance with me. This kid possessed a fair measure of strength, stamina, and loyalty. What a waste to dedicate all that to a couple of orc-shits like Riletto and DeMayo. Though to be fair, he didn't have a clue that all this loyalty and dedication was to be rewarded with a bullet with his name on it.

"Kid, you don't have to worry about ratting anyone out. You're hiding, right?"

"Mama told me I hadta," he said, puffing his chest out a bit. I suppose that was his way of saying, *"I'm a good boy 'cause I listen ta mama!"* The truth, though, came out in his face—this poor kid was running scared. Mario was trying to act like the head rooster, but he had probably figured out he was in *way* over his head.

"Word on da street was dat Riletto got taken out wit da trash," he added, a slight tremor in his voice now.

Got to love the street's grapevine. Faster than a hawk flies.

"So how long has it been since you've heard from any of your pals?" I asked.

"Well, 's been a while, but I ain't worried 'bout it." His chest puffed out again as he went paler. "Riletto was tellin' me las' time we got togeddah I was suppos'ta get outta town. Like da uddah guys did."

"Really? You're the last one in town, huh?"

"Yeah. Riletto wassa little worried when Two Times was found by th' docks. So he called an' lemme know I was gonna hafta take a powdah."

"So where were you supposed to go?"

"Riletto was suppos'ta pick me up las' night aftah we made da switch. He was goin'ta take me out t'some safe house wheah da guys were layin' low."

It wasn't like Benny had lied to him there...the other guys *were* laying low. You don't get much lower than six feet under.

"Mario, Mario, Mario," I chided, "you're getting mixed up with the wrong crowd, and I don't think your mama would be too happy about that. Bad enough you're working for Capone, but right now ain't such a good time to be known for keeping close company with Riletto and DeMayo, either."

"DeMayo," Mario huffed. He shook his head and spat. "DeMayo was just a punk wit a nice face who Riletto played for da suckah he was. Nah, Riletto had it all figyahed out. He was goin'ta see dis plan out wit DeMayo an' his partner, whack 'em an' whack 'em hard, den run Chicago wit me an' da guys as his generals."

While this kid wasn't dim, he didn't strike me as creative enough to cook up a cockamamie story like this. Benny Riletto, planning a coup of his own? It didn't make sense when I was searching his place, and it *still* didn't make sense. He was the kind of dink born and bred to follow, like most goblins I had the displeasure of crossing paths with. So could Benny, as Mario was telling me, really been playing DeMayo all along?

I took a few steps back, giving this gullible kid a little more breathing room. (With the new insight he was giving me on Benny and this case, I figured he had earned it.) My goodwill gesture was accented by that final touch of my pipe appearing from my coat pocket.

Mario didn't move. Finally, he was using that brain the Fates had blessed him with. He wasn't going anywhere until I was long gone.

"You're a good boy, Mario," I said, scratching a match against the bistro's bricks and taking a few deep puffs. "Regardless of what your mama thinks."

He huffed again, but I held up my hand. "Look at who you're talkin' to, kid. It wasn't easy growing up where I did. I did what I had to do for my family. Then, when I…lost my family and found myself on my own, I did what I had to do to survive. I'm just like you. Only shorter."

Feeling the full weight of that truth, I took another drag, watching Mario patiently. "Too bad you and Benny didn't hook up so you could pass that package on to him. Can't be safe, what with Ness and his boys raiding the warehouses."

"Yeah, but da Feds are avoidin' da speakeasies right now, so I'm—"

The poor wop froze as he grasped what I had just pulled over him. He slowly tipped his head back, lightly rapping his head again and again against the brick wall for that slip of the tongue. Between the two of us, he was going to wake up with a severe knot on the back of his noggin.

"Which one?"

"Cornah of 20th an' Clarendon," he mumbled in resignation. "Two alleyways if ya walkin' toward 21st. Take da second one, and s'da t'ird door on ya right. Password's 'I'm a friend of Lou's,' and y'wanna ask fa Daphnie."

"Daphnie's your contact?"

"Yeah," he nodded. "If anything goes screwy, I'm suppos'ta give her a call."

"Good boy, Mario." I smiled warmly, clapping him on the shoulder. "So maybe you didn't do as good as a job for Riletto as your buddies did for Bennetti, but keep your chin up. Right now, you're better at one thing than all those dinks put together."

He lifted his eyes from the asphalt and looked me in the eye, mustering up a final ounce of defiance. "Oh yeah? What's dat?"

"Breathing."

I could tell Mario didn't like the fact I was getting in the last word, but hell, what do you say after something like that? This kid just heard he was part of a regime that ended before it truly began. Just as first morning's light slips across the moors, it dawned across his face that he was a living reminder of this scuttled plan to take down Capone. I wondered (no doubt, as he did) how much borrowed time remained.

The bistro's back door suddenly flew open again, making us both nearly jump out of our skins. In the door frame stood his big Italian mama with a stone-cold look that could have stopped an advancing army of trolls in its tracks...and make them run away. In one hand, she held a small cup of cappuccino.

When I pulled out a Washington and held it out for her, she broke her stare with Mario and looked at the bill for a moment, almost forgetting why she had the cup in her hand. Finally, she took the bill and I took the cup. Even trade.

Setting the cup gingerly on a nearby crate, I then pulled out a Jackson. A few seconds later, the kid was gaping at the twenty I had just slapped into his hand, his brain and mouth trying real hard to form a simple question.

"Before you take a long vacation from Chicago, place that on a puppy. Any puppy you pick at any track you visit. You can't miss." I took a sip of the cappuccino and blinked quickly. Damn, this stuff was going to keep me awake for days. "You have no clue how Luck is your mistress right now. Enjoy it while it lasts."

I left Big Mama and Mario in the alleyway, the coffee and the cup it was in paid for with interest. Instead of taking a cab right away, I chose to walk the Southside streets, sipping my cappuccino and digesting the latest revelations.

As I've said before, Benny Riletto was the closest thing to a goblin that I've found in this realm. Goblins aren't as stupid as trolls, and I've always given them credit for that, but they can barely lace up their own boots without someone commanding them to do so. Many times, the orders they get from their orc commanders are, *"Charge ahead of us,"* which they obey with weapons drawn and running full speed into ranks upon ranks of the enemy. (Yeah, not the brightest candles in the cathedrals, those goblins.)

Benny was cut from the same cloth in that he didn't command. He followed. Outside of his daring creativity with the numbers, he was hardly the type to develop a scheme of his own. Oh sure, the guy had dreams of being a big spender and living the lush life, but that would have meant showing some initiative. (I don't think Benny could pronounce that word, even if he had a *Webster's* in front of him.)

Mario's claims about Benny double-crossing Pretty Boy threw a screw loose in this machine of mine. If it's true I'd been wrong about Benny's waiting-for-an-order personality, I'd been wrong about Benny since I met him. I'm dwarf enough to admit when I'm wrong, but to be this wrong about someone for this long?

Like I said before, Benny never showed guts of any kind unless it was a sure thing, and apparently there was something about the Singing Sword that told him it was a sure thing. He carefully plotted his every move in his journal—everything save for how to stick it to the guy behind the whole operation, Tony DeMayo. I kept flipping through his meticulous notes, looking for any thought he might have jotted down concerning that final hurdle, but nowhere did I come across Benny plotting Tony's untimely death. Still, Benny did seem to understand that anyone remotely involved with this "sure thing" eventually wound up dead. That didn't seem to throw him. He still planned and plotted... his part of this operation, at least.

Could Benny have been in cahoots with another party apart from DeMayo or Capone giving orders? Moran's boys were back in the neighborhood. Their meeting at Mick's was appearing less like a coincidence, and more like a quick bite after a meeting with Benny. Was Moran closer to the Singing Sword than Capone?

From Benny's notes and my friendly chat with Mario, I had only three leads left who knew anything about the Singing Sword and still had a pulse. In the past twenty-four hours, I had enjoyed dinner with the Boss and breakfast with an Italian knucklehead who was hopefully heading out for an extended weekend in the country. Guess it was time to have lunch with some dame named Daphnie.

I sent a quick prayer to the High Warrior: *Please, let that girl be alive.*

When the cab dropped me off at the corner of 20th and Clarendon, I slipped the cabbie a Jackson and told him, with just enough of an edge in my voice, "You never made this fare, and you never saw me."

The guy looked at the twenty in his hand and then back to me. "First dwarf I've never had in my cab before. I don't see ya. I don't know ya."

Chicago taxi service. Nothing beats it.

A few minutes' walk later, I found myself standing in the second alleyway just before 21st Street. It was high noon, not much activity happening there. No garbage men picking up the evidence from last night's revelry. No deliveries, yet. Maybe closer to dusk, but not in broad daylight. All was quiet for now on this Midwestern front.

The closer I got to the door of the speakeasy, the lighter Beatrice felt in my holster. That was my premonition that I was going to need her in case things got hairier than my beard. I stood at the large metal hatch for a moment, my boom dagger feeling light as a feather. I couldn't figure out why. By now, the party would have wound down to cleaning up from the night before. *If anything*, I thought to myself as I gave the door a few good pounds, *there's no better time for a working-class dick like me to ask a few questions.*

I heard the metal peephole slide back, followed by a few seconds of silence, and then another quick *"ssssshickt!"* followed by more silence.

Like I was surprised.

I gave the door a couple more hard hits. On the third rap, the peephole slid open again.

"Down here, pal," I called up.

Again, I heard the *"ssssshickt!"* (a little louder and harder this time), followed by sounds of the door being unlocked from the inside.

One look at the guy behind the door explained why my instincts were making Beatrice float in my holster. This troll manning the hatch just stared at me for a moment. I could see those gears turning in his brain, but alas the motor just wasn't up to Henry Ford's specs. He probably thought (or hoped) that I was just some hallucination brought on by a bad batch of White Lightning. He went to slam the door again, but I grabbed it by the edge, and there it stopped.

At first, he looked surprised when he found he couldn't close the door on my chubby fingers. (No doubt, he thought I was some kind of easy mark on account of my height.) Then he looked disappointed, then just plain pissed that he couldn't budge that door one inch with me hanging on to it.

What a dink.

"Don'ya got some circus t'be at, Shorty? Beat it!"

"Now is that any way to treat a friend of Lou's?"

The troll broke into a gravelly laugh, but his hand was still trying to pull on the door. *"You're* a friend-a Lou's?"

"Yeah, I'm a friend of Lou's *and* Daphnie's."

"Well, Lou's gone ta bed," he said, giving the door another tug. The door surrendered a bit, but not enough for him to close it on my fingers. Yeah, he really didn't like me one-upping him like this. "He don' wanna be disturbed, so take a walk, munchkin."

Didn't these trolls have anything better to come back with? Come to think of it, calling this hired muscle a "troll" was an insult to trolls everywhere. Sure, trolls were pretty thick in the head, but at least they struggled to say something clever right before eating your face. These mob types never even bothered to try.

He leaned forward, placing his head between the opening of the doorway and the door itself, his voice only audible to the alleyway rats and me. "You still heah, munchkin? I thought I told ya t'make tracks!"

Yeah, I had to give trolls credit. Trolls weren't as stupid as this guy.

"I just can't help but look at you, pal, and wonder."

He leaned in closer. "Wonduh what?"

"How thick your skull is."

It must have slipped his mind completely that he was still pulling on the heavy metal door. When I let go, the hatch came at him faster than a saber-tooth on the hunt. The guy's head was first knocked by the door itself, and then by the doorframe. Because both were made of thick metal, the double-rap to his temples gave him enough of a hard knock to make him sway back. Then he started coming forward again, and that was when the door, back in my control, slammed hard into his forehead, sending him back into the speakeasy and backwards over the small staircase leading to the main casino. From the hollow sound of his bald skull hitting the floor, I could tell that the carpet was way too thin to cushion the blow.

A couple of cigarette and playing-chip girls raced past me to check on him, while ahead of me, the bartender reached under the bar to clear the stores if needed. At first sight of me, he moved away from the speakeasy's remaining stock, reaching for what looked like a shotgun behind him. I just shook my head and gave him a little warning waggle of my plump finger, and he got the message: *I just took out your muscle with a door. You sure you want to point a gun at me?* I could see the bartender think about it, and then go back to cleaning glasses left over from the night before.

I glanced over to where my door-troll fell. He was down, but not out. Anyone else would have been unconscious if hit that hard with a hatch that sturdy.

I was impressed. That palooka's skull was pretty thick.

Turning around, my eyes were blessed with the sight of a sweet little thing in an outfit that would have become part of her skin if she wore it any tighter. The girl was well-endowed to begin with, but the bustier she had laced herself in now made her bosom impersonate the thick head of ale poured too quickly. It was hard not linger on her breasts as she leaned over the lip of the bottom Dutch door, trying to find out what all the hubbub was without leaving her coat check station. It was also hard not to linger because, on account of her leaning, I was eye-level with her chest.

Damn, I love being a dwarf!

"Daphnie?" I asked.

The girl's baby blues were radiant, much like the thick mane of flaxen hair falling lightly about her shoulders in ringlets. Unfortunately, the radiance didn't make it to the *inside* of her head. She stared at me, maybe trying to figure out how a little guy like me could be causing so much commotion. Whatever mill was slowly grinding wheat in that head of hers, it wasn't working hard enough! Not that I minded her hesitation…just meant I scored more time to enjoy the view.

This sweet picture of leaning out that Dutch door, which she created so well, was soon ruined with two words: "You're short," spoken with a voice that could shatter freshly blown glass.

My impulse reply would have been, *"And you're dumb, but you don't hear me announcing your faults to the world,"* but I had to think about this one. This was a girl who, every night, squeezed her slender self into this tight-fitting bar wench's get-up, probably cutting off what little blood flow she had to her brain, and then spent said evening smiling for hours and saying *"Take your hat and coat, sir?"* She was paid for that shelf she called her chest and for looking good.

Then it dawned on me. Was this girl completely snowblinded, or was she smarter than she let on? After all, her job was easy money, and presented the potential of meeting Mr. Right and his robust bank account.

Fighting my original impulse, I turned my reply around. "Actually, I'm Billi. Billi Baddings. I'm hoping you're Daphnie."

At that, she straightened up and rested her hands on the Dutch door. I could tell Daphnie didn't like the fact that this guy—this *short* guy—knew her name without a proper introduction made. She clearly preferred the penguins with their slicked-back hair and expensive colognes, and I didn't have a problem with that. I *did* have a problem with this girlie's attitude, which was making my job as much of a bitch as she was.

"Look, Daphnie, I'm not going to keep you long, so long as we talk like pals and you be honest with me. Otherwise, I'm going to have to come back here at another time. Say, during your shift?"

"You wouldn't get past the door."

I looked over my shoulder to the doorman, still on the floor. I could see his arms reaching up for a makeshift ice pack the bartender threw together for him.

I turned back to Daphnie with a wry grin. "Wouldn't I?"

Frowning, Daphnie opened the door for me and disappeared into her makeshift office, a tiny table with stacks of cash and an adding machine. I watched her return to her desk in the corner of the now-empty coat room, situating herself in as comfortable a manner as her snug wardrobe allowed.

After loosing at me an extremely apprehensive look, Daphnie hiked up her already-short skirt, and I now lingered on her legs, which looked powerful. (Even the definition in her calves had definition!) With no further regard to me, she resumed tracking different tickets from the previous night's clientele, separating from a rather healthy cash pile the pay going to numerous club employees. A lot of things went down in these keeps of bootleg booze, gambling, and just about anything else the President would prefer not to have in his beloved realm. From the look of her tips, she apparently did a bit more than check hats and coats, and was very good at it.

"You know something?" I spoke over the sounds of her adding machine. "For a dancer, you're a real whiz with the numbers there."

Daphnie froze, the money still in her hands (and I don't doubt she knew exactly what the count was before she stopped). She turned around and looked at me. "You've seen our show?"

"No," I replied, flashing her an appreciative nod and smile, "but you got the kind of legs that ladies would kill for and men only dream about."

I meant it as a compliment, but her eyes were sharper than any daggers I'd faced in a tavern brawl.

"So because I've got a big chest and nice legs, I don't have a brain?" she fumed. "I'm good with the numbers, and I earn a few more greenbacks for helping out with the cash count. So what do you want, Mister?"

"You can call me Billi if you like," I answered pleasantly as I pulled out my memo pad.

"I don't like anybody who knows me but I don't know them." This girl was talented. She kept on counting out bills and making notes, never missing a word with me. "So I'm going to ask you one more time, Mister Whateveryournameis. What do you want?"

"Well, I just had a chat with a kid who goes by the name of Mario. You know him?"

Now here is where I wait for the moment's hesitation or fumble, followed by, *"Nope, never heard of anyone by that name…".*

Instead, she kept on working the numbers. "Mario. Cute kid. Does a bit of running for us. Yeah, I know him. Real nice kid, now that I think of it. Too bad he's poor. I'd pay him a little attention if he had more going for him."

A comment like that gave me pause. That, along with the Louisville Slugger leaning against her desk. She wouldn't need a lot of technique to grab a baseball bat and impersonate Big Apple's Freddie Lindstrom if she didn't like the way this talk was going. In the past, I'd been punched in the jaw once or twice on account of looking at the notepad and not at my interview subject, but so long as I heard her working with the numbers from the night, I figured I was safe.

This next comment would be the test, though. "Mario was telling me you were helping him case some stolen goods."

"Really?"

She paused in her money counting to glance at the bat for a moment, then over at me. "And you believed that Italian cockroach?"

From "real nice kid" to "cockroach"? Wow!

"I'm not saying I believed Mario about you aiding and abetting him in his side business," I assured her, although a girl this savvy should be smart enough to know who and what she was getting mixed up with. Yeah, I don't doubt she knew there was something a little shady about

Mario. "I'm just saying he dropped your name, and that's why I'm here. I'm just asking you some questions. That's all."

"Well, I don't like your questions." She pushed back a loose lock of blonde hair before returning to the money in front of her. "I don't have to answer them."

"No, you don't," I sighed, "but you could make my job a lot easier. And you might also get a little something out of it."

She laughed at that one. "Like what?"

"Like another day above ground."

That comment made her hesitate. From the way her head turned ever so slightly, I knew she was looking at the two-handed broadsword of Wrigley Field once again.

Before she set down the cash in her hands, I spoke up. "Now, toots, you can just calm yourself. That's not a threat. That's a friendly warning I'm giving you. Whatever you were helping Mario with has got some seriously bad ma—" Hmmm...maybe *magic* wasn't the right word to use here. "—*luck* about it. Right now, I've got you and Mario being the only two folks still breathing after handling whatever this hot item is."

As Daphnie turned around, I felt myself taking a step back. There was something really, really wrong with this girl. I had just told her that she was involved with something that left only two people alive: Herself and Mario, the really nice cockroach. She didn't seem to care. If anything, she seemed annoyed. At me? I don't know. Only thing I was sure of was this lady was giving me a serious case of the heebie-jeebies.

"So what was this thing that I was supposed to be helping Mario out with?"

This time, her grating voice came as a blessed relief. It meant she was willing to talk, instead of using me for batting practice.

I cleared my throat before speaking, just in case there was any hint of anxiety left there. Daphnie didn't need to know she gave me the creeps. "It was lifted from a museum, and that's all I can tell you. Mario told me he was supposed to pick it up from you. I'm assuming tonight was going to be the pick-up night. He also tells me you were doing this favor for him and a guy by the name of Benny Riletto. You know Benny?"

"You mean Benny 'Tight Wad' Riletto?" she quipped. "Yeah, I know him. Oh, sorry, I *knew* him. Saw in the papers that Benny is no longer with us." She shrugged. "No great loss, except for the fact he wasn't bad in the sack. He was fun when I need to take care of some girlish impulses."

An image of Benny riding this girl like a fine Elvish stag popped quickly into my head, and I nearly lost my cappuccino breakfast. "Anyway, I didn't really like the guy," Daphnie went on, "but he did promise me some green if I was to help him and Mario out with this score he pulled off." Her eyes suddenly brightened for a second as she blurted, "Hey, you're that short guy on the front page of the *Tribune*, huh?"

Goddamn newshounds.

"So Benny dropped off this score with you," I said, wincing at the recognition, "and Mario was supposed to pick it up tonight?"

"Nah, it never happened. Benny called me at home and told me he'd be around and asked me if I would be on the clock that night. Usually I am, so I told him so and he said to expect him. Like he's so important. Well, Mr. Important never showed. The next morning on my way home, I read about him in the papers."

Then, without shedding a tear for her bedroom buddy, Daphnie returned to the numbers, adding and subtracting with all the finesse of a crossbreed moneylender. This girl never missed a beat or a dollar bill.

"So, I guess you do all right for yourself. A coat check girl *and* a dancer, eh?"

She froze again. This time, she was pissed. "I'm also the accountant."

"*You* handle the books?!?"

For a moment, I thought she was going to throttle me with the fistful of fives and tens in her hand. I held up my own mitts in surrender. "I'm sorry. I know about your Women's Movement and all, but a dame working as a bookkeeper for one of Capone's speakeasies is just something you don't come across every day. Still, there are stranger things in Chicago. Hell, I'm living proof."

"I'd agree with that."

Eh, I gave her a pass on that one. I had it coming to me.

"Now, Mr. Private Dick, I would really like to concentrate on tonight's take, so are you finished with your questions?"

"Yeah, I'm done," I confirmed, closing my memo pad and slipping out one of my business cards. "I tell you what, though: If you think of anything that could help in finding where Benny kept this stolen trinket, or if you feel threatened at any time, don't hesitate to call."

I placed my card on the corner of her desk, out of her way but well in her sightline. She didn't react to it. From the looks of how fast her hands were working, she wanted to get home yesterday. Without so much as a goodbye, I turned around and left her to the night's take—not a King's ransom, but definitely worthy of an heir's.

The troll guarding the door was sitting up now, still holding the ice pack on his head. On seeing me he went to rise, but then his eyes rolled up into his head and he returned to the ground with a dull thud and a deep groan.

"Don't worry about seeing me to the door, beautiful," I said to his crumpled form. "I know the way out."

CHAPTER TEN
HITTING THE BOOKS

After visiting the speakeasy, I zipped over to the office to pick up the Singing Sword photo. I had gleaned everything I needed from it, and if I didn't return it to its rightful owners today, there would be another death.

And I had a feeling it wouldn't be a pretty one. Beaten to death by a Smith & Corona is not the best way to leave the corporeal world.

Ever since I walked out of the Ryerson a few days ago with the photo snug in my breast pocket, Dr. Hammil had become a regular phone pest. While Miranda knows exactly how to handle assorted press reporters, clients, and authority-types over the phone, Dr. Hammil was her first-ever bookworm, and he was starting to replace Capone in Miranda's book as Public Enemy Number One.

At first, he was blunt and abrasive, as most bookworms often are. Miranda, trying to soften him up and buy me some time with the photo, made mention of her own interest in higher learning. (She really knows how to play a guy.) Well, the conversations got a bit longer after that. And then a bit longer. After one hour-and-a-half long stretch on the phone, I heard the soft thud of a forehead against a desk, followed by, *"Hey, Billi, you wanna hear about the role of women during the reign of Cleopatra?"*

Yeah, yeah, I know…technically, I'm a bookworm, too. And yeah, I'm blunt and abrasive to boot. But unlike Hammil and his ilk, I only read out of necessity. For these Sages-in-Training, reading is beyond any passion that a Bard could write a play on! I'm not in their league. Hell, I'm not even in the same sport as these academic types.

Dr. Hammil must have been returning to his abrasive demeanor when I came in the office and found Miranda on the phone, nodding in what had become a reflexive action while saying things like, *"Really? Legal action?"* and *"Yes, I'm aware of how valuable museum property is,"* all the while tacking onto her bulletin board a picture of a man (well, a stick-figure of a man) in glasses with "Dr. Hammil" penned underneath it. I watched as she drove two pencils deep into the heart of the sketch. If I didn't remedy this situation soon, I was afraid where the next couple of pencils would go!

When I got out of the cab twenty minutes later, the sun was just beginning its daily descent in the west, the shadows of the buildings behind me stretching across the street toward the Ryerson like the talons of a dragon reaching for a sacrificial snack.

Before the doors closed behind me, the receptionist I'd crossed battle-axes with on my earlier visit was already on her feet and hustling down the corridor. (Geez, doesn't that harpy take any time off?) Guess there must've been a change in their policies on dealing with dwarves. I hadn't even reached the reception desk before I saw Dr. Hammil waving at the end of the corridor, his face bright and spectacles repaired.

"Mr. Baddings," he beamed, thrusting a hand out to welcome me. "A pleasure to see you again."

"Sure, Doc," I nodded, shaking his hand. His palms were soaked! Either he was nervous about something, or he was *really* excited about seeing me. "I appreciate the loan of the photo. I hope you weren't too inconv—"

"No need to worry about it, Mr. Baddings!" He gestured down the corridor. "Care to join me in my office? I would like to talk to you for a moment, if you have the time."

"Yeah, Doc," I said apprehensively. "Sure."

There was something different about the good Dr. Hammil today. I couldn't read the academic from the back, but his cheeriness unnerved me.

"Glad to see that your glasses were repaired," I ventured. "Hope it didn't set ya back too far."

"What?" He managed a nervous titter. "Yes, well, I managed for as long as I could, but sometimes you do have to pay the piper, as it were."

What a difference in his office! His desk was much less cluttered, and the chair opposite was now cleared of the volumes that occupied it on my last visit. Hopping up in that now-vacant chair, I straightened to my full height so I might catch a peek at the book he had open this time. I was a little disappointed (for a number of reasons) that the volume was not some mammoth, leather-bound tome with pages so worn and frayed that a dirty look might make its spine collapse. This time, it was a simple notebook, open to a blank page with a date—today's date, the ink still fresh on the paper. Looked like it was going to be the good doctor's turn to ask the questions today.

"So, Mr. Baddings, I would like to talk to you about—"

"Thanks, and you're welcome."

Hammil stopped for a moment. "I'm sorry?"

"You didn't know me from Prince Liggermaut, and you could have called the cops for stealin' property like that, but you didn't. It gave me some quality time to research this enigma of yours a bit. I appreciate that, almost as much as you should appreciate my care in handling this photo and returning it intact. Wouldn't you agree?"

"Oh, um, yes, well…" Easy there, Doc. "…no matter, then, is it, Mr. Baddings? I do hope that we can—oh, I'm so sorry, would you care for tea or a coffee? I was just about to brew some up for myself."

"No, thanks."

When we first met, I was barely worth the mud on his doublet. Now, I was being elevated into the same company as his equals. He was offering me a place to sit, offering to brew me a cup of tea…*tea?!?* Nah, I didn't have time for this superficial crap.

"So, Doc, what do you want?"

He clinked the mugs together clumsily, his coordination taking a brief holiday. Again, he laughed nervously (as bookworms often do when called to the carpet) and turned to face me. "What do you mean, Mr. Baddings?"

"I know crossbloods who get better treatment than I did the last time I was here."

"Oh…well, you have to understand that Miss Pendergraft is a very busy woman, and she does face quite a few questionable sorts. She tries very hard not to offend, and she has only the best intentions where the Ryerson is concerned."

"Like you, Doc?"

As his smile started to melt like snow under dragon's breath, I took another look around. "I meant to tell ya, this is a nice office. Cozy. But I don't know if a guy crammed in such a tight space as this could afford new glasses so quickly. Even where I'm from, specs like yours don't come cheap."

Dr. Hammil loosened his tie and took a deep breath. He was about to say something, but I wasn't going to allow him a word until I was done.

"You got to understand that I'm still a bit perplexed about why the cops didn't pay me a visit after I walked off with that photo. That's property of the Ryerson, and valuable property of the Ryerson at that." I paused for a moment. "Then I got to thinking that maybe you didn't want the attention—"

"Mr. Baddings…"

He had found his voice, dry as it was. By the amount he was sweating, his voice was the only thing dry about him.

I pressed forward. "And now I have to think why you wouldn't want that attention, unless you didn't want anyone else to know about the Singing Sword."

Again, I paused. Builds the tension real nice. "Or the other thefts you've suffered here at the Ryerson."

"How did—?"

There it was. Confirmation.

"Yeah, Doc, because people would to ask. People would ask who's running this show, and people would wonder why no one was asking after all these other missing artifacts, wouldn't they? They would wonder how a guy wearing frayed cuffs and hems can afford a brand new pair of glasses! Yeah, I bet you have a few other surprises in your bank account, don't you?"

I watched the poor sap try to brace himself against the small table with the teapot and mugs on it, his academic career now flashing by him with the speed of a human cavalry. He then dropped heavily to the floor, his body trembling so hard that he was an earthquake unto himself. I was waiting for him to burst into tears.

Hopping out of my chair, I leaned in close to Hammil and locked my gaze with his. "So here you are, selling priceless heirlooms on some kind of black market to the socially elite. Then, the Singing Sword comes across your desk. Oh, and I bet you got the offers before it ever reached Chicago, but this was going to be your ticket out of this tiny office, wasn't it? A sword of this make, found sealed in an ancient Egyptian tomb? This mystery, provided you could solve it, could serve as your academic pass to wherever you wished. Hell, you play your cards right, you might even enjoy dinner and cigars with ol' Al Einstein himself. All you need is to crack that little mystery of the Singing Sword, right?"

"Mr. Baddings, please, just hear me out." He was terrified, but of exactly what remained to be seen. "I am facing difficulties in the circles I travel in. While the Ryerson has been very good to me for years…"

"Your academic ascent has stalled a bit, hasn't it?"

"Exactly, Mr. Baddings. I needed to win certain influences that would garner attention and patrons to the Ryerson. There is a business to what I do. It can be very…"

"Political?"

He nodded. If I kept giving him rope like this, he was going to be swinging in the breeze by tomorrow morning.

"And so you figured that when those new acquisitions came across your desk, you could make a few calls and supply some of Chicago's privileged with some one-of-a-kind paperweights and centerpieces in exchange for their loyalty, huh?"

"My intentions were to help the museum—"

"Don't give me that!" I snarled, grabbing him by the tie and pulling him closer. "The only dink you were looking out for was the one you see in the mirror! Once the Singing Sword arrived, you planned to shut down this racket and reform to a more respectable trade among your bookworm friends, and what better way to retire than to stash the Sword away for yourself and tell your back-door clientele that the Ryerson had been hit!"

"No, Mr. Baddings—"

I tightened my grip on his tie, cutting him off in mid-comment. "Nice way to cover your tracks, Doc! You can't be blackmailed by any of these elite types because reporting the Sword's heist would bring in the press. As far as they were concerned, you just had to shut down operations for a time in order to protect them and their methods of illegally obtaining rare antiquities intended for the masses."

I shoved him away, still keeping my eyes fixed on him. "Then when you met me and figured out I was your key to solving the mystery, you let me get away with thievery in broad daylight. Today was going to be the day I got you out of the Ryerson and back on your academic track, wasn't it?"

"Mr. Baddings, *please!*"

"What?"

"If you would shut up and give me a chance to correct you on a point!"

Now, that's what I wanted to hear! If anyone else had told me to shut up, I might have been offended, but I'd been pushing this bookworm hard. It was about time he busted open. Now he was going to set me straight...which is exactly what I wanted him to do.

"Mr. Baddings," Hammil began shakily, "when I tried to win over my patrons, I did not count on any of them using my business transactions against me."

"Someone putting the thumbscrews on you, then?"

"An interesting way to put it, Mr. Baddings, but yes. I now have a very exclusive relationship with this...particular patron, involving rare antiquities."

"Including the Singing Sword."

"You were right in that respect, Mr. Baddings. Just when I was starting to lose faith in this patron's supposed sway over my peers, the communiqué from Egypt came across my desk concerning the Singing Sword. I was trying very hard to keep this find outside of the administrative circles here. Provided I was the only one who knew about it, my patrons would not ask. However, a find of this magnitude is hard to keep secret. The phone calls started the day it arrived, and I did my best to put them off. A few days after I catalogued the Singing Sword in the presence of essential museum staff only, it went missing. The Board of Directors immediately convened, and I convinced them to keep the news a secret. The team in Cairo would remain there, and I knew exactly who at the Ryerson knew about the Singing Sword. I assured these people that if word leaked out to the press about the Singing Sword's disappearance, their curriculum vitae had better be in order!"

"Careful, Doc," I smirked. "You're starting to sound like a Capone of Academia."

From the glare I just received, I don't think Hammil liked the comparison between himself and Capone, but he had a nice little operation going, and his people followed his orders without question, so the analogy was apt enough.

"We're keeping the Sword's disappearance a secret because we can't afford the bad publicity before our Summer Gala."

Featuring that "Chicago's Who's Who" list I saw on my first visit, no doubt.

"And this patron who has the 'exclusive relationship' with you?" I asked. "How did he feel about not getting his mitts on the Singing Sword?"

"Not happy in the least," Hammil sighed.

"But the good news, if I'm following you right, is that your exclusive patron couldn't do a thing about it because ratting you out would mean losing his dealer of fine acquisitions."

That is something you can count on with nobility of any kind. They do love their baubles and bangles; the harder-to-come-by the possession, the bigger the bragging rights they hold over their buddies. Dr. Hammil lacked street sense, but he was smart enough to make himself important enough not to lose.

"So does this exclusive patron have a name?"

"Absolutely not," he said, pulling himself up to his feet. "Absolutely not, Mr. Baddings. Revealing this patron's identity would only make this mess worse, and I simply cannot afford that."

"No, Doc, you can't…just like I can't afford to tell you anything else about the Singing Sword." I shrugged. "I tell you what: You hang on to that picture and your notes and keep on doing what you do best—and I *don't* mean fencing archeological finds to Chicago royalty." With that, I made for the door. "If I need to chit-chat with you about this case, I'll give you a call. And don't you worry about me flapping my gums to anyone. As I like to say, there's a reason why I'm a private investigator."

I had just touched the doorknob when I felt a sharp pain against the back of my head that sent me forward into the door, knocking my fedora into my face. Turning around, I saw the leather-bound book right before its spine clocked me in the noggin. The last time I saw that many stars, my regiment's encampment was deep in the Messina Plains, the night sky was so bright that I could read my journal at any hour I wished. As I landed among a few tall stacks of books, all of which toppled on me, I had to admit it was a good hit. Hammil would have been good with a battle-axe or an ace hitter for the Pirates with a swing like that. I was fading fast, but not before I heard him one last time.

"As I said before, Mr. Baddings, I cannot afford for this mess to get any worse."

That stinks!

A strange thought to wake up to, but those two simple words screamed out what I couldn't in that moment. The smell was coming from formaldehyde, or some other kind of preservative used for specimens and acquisitions. By now I'd remembered that I was in the Ryerson, but I knew that I was not in Hammil's office.

I tried to blink, but that sent a sharp, piercing pain into my head—a souvenir from the temple strike, no doubt. I went to check and see if I was bleeding, but my hands were tied at the wrists. Apparently, the Doc knew his knots, and my bonds weren't going anywhere.

At this point, my eyes finally focused and I realized exactly where I was ...or, rather more to the point, exactly what I was *in*.

I was tied up inside what looked like an Egyptian sarcophagus. Towering over my coffin was a nearby shelf unit containing other ancient coffins from the desert regions of this world. The stacks of caskets looked uncannily similar to the final resting places of Dwarven miners and builders in Acryonis, where holes were chiseled out of the stone walls in whatever location these loyal subjects of Gryfennos happened to drop. There they lie forever, a tribute to what they died to create.

Egyptian royalty, stacked in a warehouse like common folk. Wouldn't that bring those Tutankhamens and Nefertitis back to life in an uproar?

As I gave the ropes another tug, I heard movement close by. Didn't have to take too many guesses as to who it was.

"Hey, Doc, you're pretty good at tying someone up! Should I ask what you're up to in your private life?"

"You will forgive me, Mr. Baddings, if I ignore you for the moment," his voice filtered back in reply. "As soon as I am finished here, I'll be giving you my undivided attention."

Back home, bookworms were usually the last to join up with my cross-country missions. When they *did* join up, they tended to stay in the back during skirmishes because they didn't like to besmirch their lily-white hands with blood. (Made it a lot harder for turning the pages of their spell books.) But this Dr. Hammil had not only sucker-punched me with the tools of his trade, but also stripped me of my jacket and shirt, leaving me with only a tank top to cover my hairy torso. (I really wasn't sure why I was down to my undershirt, but considering my earlier question and the tightness of the ropes, maybe I didn't want to know.)

I slowly worked myself up to a sitting position, grimacing at the pounding in my head. Damn, the Doc had really dealt me a hammer's blow!

Now that I was upright, I could see that Hammil had his back to me, working at a table across from my private casket. He was fiddling with a syringe, mixing various vials of clear and not-so-clear potions. From where I was sitting, it looked pretty full.

"So, you're a bartender, too? What's that cocktail you're mixing there?"

"Something I've been reading about." Holding the syringe up to the light, Hammil laughed, the sound emerging as a series of high-pitched squeaks. With a slight nudge to the rubber bulb, he sent a few drops of his potion running along the length of the needle and out through the tip. "I'm not sure if you would appreciate its scientific name, so I will give you its simplified name: truth serum. This will allow you to relax and talk a bit."

"You are just huesia-bent-for-leather in finding out about the Singing Sword, aintcha?"

He didn't answer. I gave another tug against my ties. The rope wasn't that heavy—all I needed was a rough surface. An edge.

"So, Doc, how much do you know about Dwarven biology?" It never really held my attention at the public library, but I understood enough to know that it's mighty different from the human variety.

"Tonight, instead of adhering to scientific facts, we are—you might say—playing it by ear, Mr. Baddings," he said, giving the syringe a few taps. "There, that should do it."

My throat felt like it was filling with sand and grit. In the next few moments, I was going to become a living witch-doll. I knew that certain things in this realm didn't affect me the same way they affected humans, but there was the additional problem of the opposite being true. When I got a nasty paper cut in the office one day, Miranda insisted I dab some iodine on it to make sure I didn't get a nasty infection. Instead, I was laid up in bed with a fever for a week because of a bad reaction to that stuff. So I tend to stay away from seafood and such, but because I'm a constant enigma with the medical types in this realm, I still don't know what will and won't set me off.

Fortunately, Mick's chili was a-okay for my system.

That was my last passing thought before taking Hammil's needle in the arm. If I struggled, I would only make this bad situation worse; a broken needle in a vein wouldn't do much for me at the moment.

"We'll start with a mild dosage. See where that gets us."

"Great," I winced as he pulled the needle free.

Either truth serum works fast, or a Dwarven bloodstream takes to it like a nosferatu to the darkness. I suddenly tasted salt in my mouth…a *lot* of salt, like over-seasoned pork at the dinner table. My mouth watered, but my throat remained dry and rough. I don't know how much of that stuff the doctor pumped into me, but for a minute there, I thought I had just downed an entire keg's worth of malt beer on my own.

"Haaaaaammmmmilllllllll…"

Okay, mouth and brain not playing well with each other. Come on, Billibub, keep it together.

"I think…yoooooooouuu ussss't plenty."

"We will see, Mr. Baddings."

With that, Dr. Hammil (or at least the blurry form that could pass for Dr. Hammil) took a seat next to the sarcophagus and pulled out something that bore a marked resemblance to the journal I saw on his desk earlier.

"Now, listen to me carefully, Mr. Baddings…"

"Billi. C'mon, Doc," I giggled. (I was *giggling*? Now that was just wrong.) "We're pals now."

"Very well, then…Billi…tell me about the Singing Sword. You know, the photograph you borrowed from me?"

"Photograph…photograph…?" I knew what he was asking, but I didn't really want to tell him the truth so much as I wanted to take a nap. I was having a tough time holding my head up.

All of a sudden, the image of the Singing Sword popped into my head, clear as a Spring day. My head jerked up and I shouted it out. "The Sssssssssword of Arrrrrrrrrrrrranah-ha-ha-haaassss, you mean?"

Was my voice just echoing in my head, or were the acoustics in the room that good?

Then I heard what I thought was steam escaping from a radiator, but it was just Hammil shushing me. Were we not alone in the museum, then?

"Is that its name, Billi? The Sword of Arran—Arran—?"

"Ass!" I snapped. "Arrrrrr—hhhhhhannnnnnn—ASS!" I sniggered like a pimply-faced schoolboy. "I said a *naughty* one, didn' I? Don' tell Mama Baddings, 'kay? She'll tan my bott'm!"

"No need to fret, Billi," he said. I think he was getting slightly annoyed with me, but I warned him about the dosage! As it turned out, he'd given me all I needed and then some. "Now then…"

"MY TURN!"

We both stared at one another for a second, neither one of us expecting that to come out of me.

"What?" Dr. Hammil finally managed.

"S'my turn." Now *I* was annoyed. "Is my turn t'assa queshen. No fair if you ass'all th' queshens."

I could feel a fog slowly consuming my brain—no doubt the same fog that was messing with my vision. If I didn't try to fight through this ogre piss in my bloodstream, I knew I was going to be in trouble. I could hear in the Doc's tone he was losing patience. Fast. Still, I wasn't loopy enough to forget I had something he wanted.

"Very well, Mr. Baddings," he conceded with a frown, "I will play your little game. Ask me a question."

"Whhhhhhhhy…okay, whhhhyyyy…" Damn, this crap really made talking hard! "Why am I in a carsophagas?"

"You mean a *sarcophagus?*"

"Yeah…that, too."

His civil smile sobered me up a little, but not as much as his next words did.

"It's my own little tribute to you, Mr. Baddings. I've got a cable here, written by the Egyptian Ambassador, demanding the return of this most hallowed artifact. It's false, of course, but I'm intending to seal you inside this casket and ship you off to Egypt so that you will be put on display in the Museum of Cairo. If you survive the journey to Egypt, perhaps they will open the sarcophagus up and rescue you before you starve to death, but I happen to know that the curator there is so backlogged in his work that he will be most fortunate to catalog you by May…"

What, it was March now? That didn't sound so bad.

"…1935."

All right, six years without food: Bad. Six years without a beer: Worse.

"WOW! Tha's a loooooong time!" I shook my head. "I'm not gonna feel so good when they fin' me."

"Indeed, Mr. Baddings, which is why I'm going to empty this syringe into your veins once we're done. If you're fortunate, you will slip into a coma before tomorrow morning."

"Heeeyyyyy, than's, Doc. I 'preeshiate y'lookin' out fer me!"

"Now, the Sword of Arannahs?"

"Oh, that!" I motioned with my head for him to come closer. "S'a weapon of ainshent power…a power that c'n ooooooonly bee desssscribed like…" My head drooped a bit. By the Fates, I was really feeling worn out. "Like…"

Hammil leaned in closer, his whisper matching mine. "Like what, Mr. Baddings?"

"Like thissssss…"

I brought my head up into his jaw with everything I had. I knew that I'd pay for it tomorrow, provided I would even see tomorrow. The pain helped me focus enough to see Hammil stumble back on the table where the syringe sat.

With a groan, I pulled myself up to my feet and jumped out of the sarcophagus. When I landed, I realized that I was still lacking a bit in the coordination department. I didn't know how hard I had stunned the Doc, but I didn't have time to think much about it. I slowly pulled myself up to my feet and made a break for the darkness.

Whatever this place was, it was cold, dark, and completely foreign to me. I took refuge next to shelves of what looked like Roman pottery. Using my chin, I nudged a particularly large urn over the edge, shattering it against the floor. The crash provided the Doc with my exact location in this warehouse, sure, but it also provided me with a shard sharp enough to start cutting the ties around my wrists. Still cutting, I continued into the shadows with the telltale footsteps of Dr. Hammil right behind.

"That was a find of incredible worth you just destroyed, Mr. Baddings," he called out in my direction.

"You can bill me!" I barked back, feeling the rope start to slacken.

Despite the blood-rush of my escape, I still felt a bit tipsy. What few wits I kept about me led me back to the sarcophagus. I hoped the doctor—being inexperienced at handling hostages and prisoners—would have left the rest of my things there, including Beatrice.

On my way there, I caught a glimpse in between the shelf units of a figure with what appeared to be a weapon in his hand. The Doc wasn't serious, was he? Did he really think he could handle my girl?

I was still tugging at my ties, still moving the sharp clay shard back and forth, when suddenly the ropes broke free with a dull *pop*, sending my wrists flying in opposite directions. One wrist went through a glass windowpane of what looked like stained glass. Stained glass, the way I knew it back in the mother country. Nice to know the craft made it to this side of the portal. Broke my heart that I just destroyed it.

I heard the window above me crack and finally shatter from the gunfire. The pitch of the gun was too high for Beatrice. Reaming low to the ground, I felt the holster still strapped around my calf. Empty.

"Do you know how rare it is to find such samples of Tudor glasswork?" Dr. Hammil screamed from some distant part of the warehouse.

"Tell you what, Doc!" I shouted back. "How about you stop shooting, and I'll stop breaking your priceless artifacts?"

I continued crawling toward the sarcophagus by homing in on a pair of desk lamps, the only light illuminating this dingy space. Hammil was moving a lot faster now because his long legs covered more distance than my smaller hands and knees.

Reaching my coat, I felt for the shoulder holster draped over the same chair with the jacket shirt, and tie. There she was. My girl, Beatrice. Guess the not-so-good doctor felt a little intimidated by her size.

I had just slipped Beatrice free from her scabbard when Dr. Hammil emerged from the shadows, my .38 in his hand with two rounds left. I slowly started to back away from the table, but the *click-click-click* of the pistol's hammer pulling back stopped me in mid-step.

"That is far enough, Mr. Baddings."

I didn't know what to keep an eye on—Hammil himself, or the trembling pistol in his grasp. If it shook any harder, I thought it was going to go off on its own accord.

"Place the gun at your feet."

I lowered myself slowly, the fog of the truth serum beginning to settle in again as I did so. Placing a hand against a nearby shelf unit to steady myself, I noticed that the structure swayed ever so slightly, despite the weight of the massive coffins stacked there.

"Now, get up. Slowly, Mr. Baddings."

I started to rise, but then quickly ducked into the dark side of the aisle closest to me. I think Hammil got off a shot, but I didn't hear it because I was giving a good, old-fashioned Dwarven battle cry as I braced my back and threw all my stockiness into the heavily laden shelves. Sure enough, I felt the whole unit go down like a giant oak tipping over after a woodsman's work. I heard the doctor screaming over the sounds of sarcophagi sliding from their respective shelves, and not surprisingly, his screaming stopped when the explosion of stone hit the floor.

The dust clung to the still air of this warehouse, and now the earlier smell of formaldehyde was drowned out by the combined scents of mold, decay, and time-treated corpses. Buried under several slabs of stones that once guarded the dead was a pile of ancient corpses, still wrapped in their tattered linens, and Dr. Hammil, still clutching onto my.38 with the hammer pulled back to fire that last shot.

I felt the remnants of the serum still trying to make a final rally in the bottom of the ninth. The dust really wasn't helping to clear my head, but I had enough presence of mind to appreciate the irony of the Hammil's death alongside his treasures of the past.

"Figured you for a mummy's boy," I quipped before everything went blurry again.

"Yer mine, Baddings!!!" Any minute now, he'd start dancing like a leprechaun. "Ah, sain's be praised and may the blesséd Muthur Mary smile on me tomarra as she's doin' tonight! Yer all mine, freak!"

The security guard heard the hoopla (guess the first gunshot woke him up) and was on the call box to Chief O'Malley's flop in two snorts of a goblin's nose. I was found unconscious next to the rubble of the Ryerson's sarcophagus collection. Or at least, that's what the cops told me. The last thing I remember was pushing pretty hard against that wobbly shelf unit, saying something that I thought was relatively clever. When I came to, I was in a cell, still in my filthy undershirt and slacks, under the watch of that same cookie-tossing redheaded rookie from Benny's crime scene.

Still, could have been worse. I could have woken up in a sarcophagus as a featured exhibit somewhere in Egypt.

Now I was in Chief O'Malley's office, nursing a hangover unlike any I had ever felt following my regiment's all-night victory celebrations. An ice pack rested on the knot where my noggin had clocked the now-deceased Dr. Hammil. The Chief could not have been happier to see me because *this* time, I was caught with my hand in the biscuit jar. There was no question about it: I had killed Dr. Hammil, sure.

"There's this thing called self-defense," I groaned. Damn, I wish the drummer would stop sending the war-charge using my brain! "I think you'll find I didn't gun that bookworm down in cold blood."

"You're na' weaselin' yer way outta *this* one, circus freak! I gotya dead ta rights! You killed tha doct'r aft'r stealin' an' destroyin' propertee o' tha Ryerson!"

"Did someone write that motive up for you, O'Malley, or did your boys at the crime scene trip through this one as they tripped through Benny Riletto's?"

The Chief was about to launch into The Riot Act, but I spoke up before he uttered a sound. "The good Dr. Hammil was about to seal me up and have me impersonate King Tut! He was filling me with something called truth serum, and to tell you the truth, it's given me one beauty of a hangover!"

"So you two were takin' it in th' arm ta'gether an' y'shot him because y'were 'igh as a kite!"

This mick couldn't be that stupid. "O'Malley, if you notice something, he wasn't shot. In fact, he was shooting at me with my piece!"

"Y'could've planted that!"

Doesn't give it up easily, does he? "No, O'Malley, I didn't plant my gun on him. I planted a couple of stone coffins on top of him because he was trying to kill me!"

"A confession! Jus' wha' I was—"

The door to his office flew open, and in walked a gentleman dressed in a sharp-looking, expensive suit, his hair slicked back as if expecting to be in O'Malley's office at 12:14 a.m. As he handed his card to O'Malley, he gave me a nod of reassurance.

"This interview with my client is over."

O'Malley went pale at reading the name on the bone-ivory card in his hand. "This circus freak is yer *client?*"

"Mr. Baddings is one of many clients I keep an eye on, and I will not have you degrading him with such slurs. If this treatment reoccurs, I will—"

O'Malley slapped the card on his desk and stood nose to nose with this slick-suit (as I like to call the barristers of this realm), spraying the guy with his spittle as he ranted, "Now wait jus' a minute, ya fancy pants boy-o, I gotta confession outta him jus' a momen' ago!"

"Out of duress, from the looks of him."

This guy wasn't conceding an inch. This slick-suit had orc blood in his veins! "And as his attorney was not present for this interview, he was not advised properly as to what questions were appropriate to answer, considering the circumstances."

"There's a dead man in tha' morgue tonight 'cause of 'im!"

The slick-suit smiled politely and walked around O'Malley to stop at the chief's desk. "According to your police reports," he continued calmly, opening his case and producing several documents that joined his business card, "there was evidence of a syringe containing traces of a mixture of barbiturates that my client could still very well be under the influence of."

"I can assure you, Counselor," I grunted, shifting my ice pack from the back of my head to my forehead, "I am."

Sharp as a broadsword, well-informed, prepared for any sliders from O'Malley's mound. Who the hell was this guy?

"Considering the influence of said drugs that Dr. Hammil was administering and my client's current physical state, do you seriously believe that his confession would hold up before a grand jury? If you submit this confession to the D.A.'s office, I will have you laughed out of the courthouse and this precinct." He then fastened the clasp on his briefcase and sighed heavily. "Do you really want a second black mark by your name, Chief O'Malley?"

Damn, this guy's got a set!

I turned my attention to O'Malley, expecting him to be deep in the throes of a demonic possession as cast by Ressican necromancers. I had a feeling I was going to be treated to the main event between "Mad Irishman" O'Malley and "El Boy-o de Slick-o" going the distance over little ol' me.

But damn all the luck, O'Malley was throwing in the towel. His shoulders dropped and his skin continued to flush in color. His Irish eyes weren't smiling, that's for sure.

"Please return Mr. Baddings' possessions immediately, or else we assure you that your poor handling of this delicate matter will reach tomorrow's papers."

Hey, pal, I thought in a panic through my head's incessant pounding, *don't tempt the Fates! I know you got a set that would make a Valley Giant envious. Now let's get my things and scram!*

I really didn't think this could get any weirder, but it did.

O'Malley looked at me, swallowed hard, and said, "Sorry ta've inconvenienced ya, Mr. Baddings. I'll have yer things in a moment."

Okay, that settled it. I was dead. The whole thing with covering the doctor in the sarcophagi, waking up in a jail cell, and this meeting with O'Malley was my final test. I could now walk out of the precinct headquarters and accept my estate upon the Everlasting Fields.

"Mr. Baddings," my newfound attorney spoke, "if you will follow me?"

I hopped out of my chair, hissing slightly at how much I hurt. This was definitely an all-over hangover I was suffering. At that moment, a uniform showed up with my stuff: my shirt, jacket, fedora, and arsenal. I followed the mystery slick-suit to the double-doors of the precinct where I slipped on the jacket and wrapped up my pieces (in their respective holsters) in my shirt.

"Look, pal, I know it's late, but thanks." I put on my fedora. "I don't mean to question the Fates, but who the hell are you?"

Again, he produced a bone-ivory card and handed it to me. "Michael Ahern, attorney at law. And you're most welcome, but you should also thank my employer the next time you see him. The driver will see you home."

He motioned to the waiting car. Even through the blinding headache I was carrying away with me, I still recognized that particular car at a glance. It was the same car that had delivered me to my private audience with Al Capone.

GIVE MY REGARDS TO ELIOT

Thursday, I woke up feeling like I'd gnawed too deep into a Gryfennos Woods Boar. (Certain cuts of the meat can give you the runs for weeks.) Thanks to his truth-serum experiment, the Doc had left me a parting gift in the form of a hangover that just wouldn't lift, no matter how many home remedies I threw at it. So I phoned up Miranda and talked her into taking a day off. (Why not? I certainly was.)

The next day, I woke up to the sight of Chicago's street sweepers being given a power assist from the Forces of Nature: The rhythmic *pip-pip-pips* of raindrops straight from the Everlasting Fields, giving sidewalks, passing cars, and brownstones a brilliant silver sheen, even though the sun remained shielded behind its armor of steel-grey clouds. (Yeah, snobby as they are, those elves possessed a way of polishing their armor that made them glow even in a moonless night. Problem was, it made them easy targets.)

This morning, while enjoying my morning coffee, I idly turned the pages of both the *Daily Tribune* and *Herald Examiner*. Apart from yesterday's tiny blurb on a "freak accident" at the Ryerson that claimed the life of its curator, Dr. Samuel Hammil, there was no investigation or even an inquiry planned. Guess that slick-suit of Capone's covered all the bases, making sure the cops and the museum's security stayed tight-lipped about me so I could work free and clear of any unwanted press. Nice to have high friends in low places, I guess.

The clean scent in the air took me back to bright spring days in Gryfennos when my mother would come in with our clothes, sun-dried and smelling of the fresh outdoors. In 1929 Chicago, this scent was seasoned with car exhaust, a couple of nearby bakeries, and the uncovered trash can or two, but it was still a "waxing poetic" moment so I enjoyed it for what it was.

Sadly, this innocent euphoria wouldn't last.

"Billi?" Miranda asked, rapping lightly on the door to my office.

"Yeah?" I asked over my shoulder, still enjoying the sound of the rain.

"You got visitors."

I turned from the open window to stare at two extremely tall, square-jawed gents whose faces were devoid of enthusiasm for the simple pleasures of the morning. Matching their nondescript personalities were their dark, charcoal-grey suits—hardly the tailored cuts of Capone's boys, or even Moran's. They also didn't sport the "hard" look of a typical mobster that boasted they could walk into a barfight with an average orc and win. These guys, from the looks of them, couldn't intimidate orc, cave troll, or mountain dragon.

Then it hit me: These were the same suits I'd had the staring contests with at Benny's crime scene, and then caught nosing around his flop later on.

The awkward silence was finally broken with one them asking me, "Mr. Baddings?"

Now there's an original introduction. "Last time I checked, yeah."

These guys didn't work for Chicago's Finest. O'Malley's flatfeet would have made themselves thoroughly at home by now, checking behind all the pictures for hidden booze or some other contraband to add to their private stashes. These suits just stood there, silently looking the room over until finally their eyes came back to me. I merely crossed my arms with a wry grin. If they wanted posturing, then by the Fates, I'd give 'em posturing.

"So, who you suits working for? Treasury Department? Bureau of Alcohol Violations?"

"I'm sorry, Mr. Baddings," the lead suit replied stiffly, "but I'm not at liberty to discuss what organization we are affiliated with."

The military. Definitely.

"Okay, Army or Navy?" I inquired, laughing gruffly as they shared a nervous look between them. "Look, guys, I'm former infantryman. I know the talk. I also know if you wanted to come here and give me a good old-fashioned, bare-knuckles interrogation, you could do so and have the United States Government backing you in the name of freedom and preservation of liberty. How about you cut me a break and let me know who your boss is in Washington D.C., and I'll tell you whatever you want to know."

From the way the square jaws looked at me, and then back to each other, it was really clear they found it hard to believe that someone like me had served in the armed forces anywhere. It was also really clear that they didn't know how to handle me. They reminded me of how the mountain trolls crossed with elves, creating an Elvish breed taller, stronger, and denser than your usual elf. The resulting mountain elves looked as if they possessed all the answers to Acryonis' deepest, darkest secrets, but they would have problems crossing a forest footpath just to reach the other side.

The military was interested in a mook like Benny Riletto? It couldn't be for past service to his country. Benny was the type of dink who would make certain if his boys were charging into a fight, he would be there, right behind them, every step of the way. *Way* behind them.

The lead Mountain Elf finally spoke up again, producing a thin billfold from his coat pocket. "My name is Jackson. My partner here is Miller. We are with the Department of War."

Department of War, still enjoying their victory from The Great War, looking into the Gangland Wars of Chicago. Well, don't that just beat all? Their identification papers appeared legit, but what really sealed the deal were the imitation-leather billfolds. Definitely U.S. Government, all the way.

"Department of War. Okay, then. You boys have any rank there?"

"I'm sorry, Mr. Baddings," Jackson replied in the identical manner to which he had a moment ago. "I'm not at liberty to discuss what rank I hold in the department we are affiliated with."

"I see."

Oh boy, were these guys stealing the wind out of my barge's sails! I was all ready to offer them a drink, from military man to military men. I could already hear the reply: "*I'm sorry, Mr. Baddings, but I'm not at liberty to imbibe any contraband, as it is against the regulations of the organization we are affiliated with.*"

Neither of them wanted to be in my office, although it was not as evident in Jackson's face as it was in Miller's. As a matter of fact, Miller looked downright pissed. It wouldn't surprise me at all if a single nod from Jackson was keeping Miller at bay like some angry warhound.

"How can I help you gentlemen?" I asked pleasantly as I leapt into my office chair.

"We understand you were in contact with a Dr. Samuel Hammil of the Ryerson Library last week," Jackson began, his voice lacking anything remotely resembling spontaneity. He knew exactly what to ask and how to ask it, and he was looking to walk away with all the answers. "Two nights ago, he died in a bizarre accident that apparently involved you."

"I was there. As far as my being involved, that is a matter of perspective."

He watched me in silence for a few moments, maybe mulling over the flash of attitude I'd just thrown his way. "Mr. Baddings," he continued, "we are very curious as to what a private investigator's interest is in the curator of the Ryerson."

"I'm a patron of the arts," I smiled, leaning back in my chair.

"Mr. Baddings, we do not appreciate your levity with us."

"Well, since we're both military types in suits now, let me be frank with you. I don't appreciate you two coming into my office and asking questions about my business. Read the door, because it says what I do for a living. If you don't like it, then scram!"

Miller stepped forward, but Jackson stopped him with a look. As they continued to stare me down, I began to wonder whether were trying to establish their dominance over me, or working up the nerve to ask me out on a date? Did they want me to enlist? Did they want me to fart *The Star Spangled Banner*? (If they came back after Mick's Lunch Special, I'd be happy to oblige!)

I really didn't have the time for an old-fashioned Elvish stand-off. "All right, boys, how about we have a trade-off of information? You tell me the sudden interest the War Department has taken with the Ryerson Museum's recently departed curator, and I'll try to answer your questions within the scope that my profession allows."

They could have arrested me and dragged me into a setting a little less familiar and friendly to find out what they wanted to know. They were the U.S. Government, after all. Fortunately for me, they decided to play by my tavern rules

"Our intelligence operatives intercepted a communiqué concerning an archeological dig in the deserts of Egypt," Jackson began. "This team, sponsored by the Ryerson Museum, discovered an item cataloged under the identification number #EW234450-112-MM. Dr. Hammil informed us that this find was a sword of ancient origin, and that it apparently was stolen from the Ryerson before it could be properly cataloged for the museum's inventory. It was also apparent to Dr. Hammil that you possessed in-depth knowledge of said item #EW234450-112-MM."

Ah, how the military loved their numbers—the pencil-pushers, anyway. I preferred the actual point of the military as opposed to the regulations of administration and formalities of ceremony. Just hand me a sharpened battle-axe or a nice, thick-headed mace and point to where you want me to charge. To me, *that* was the military.

Another very military thing was the amount of information they had for a theft that The Ryerson was keeping under wraps. I didn't doubt for a moment the government's ability (and their justification in doing so) to intercept a communiqué between an archeological dig in Egypt and an institution in the US. The details these government employees had seemed to be originating from the dig itself; no doubt "a bizarre artifact" surfacing in sands outside of Cairo must've caught their attention. They tracked the Sword from the desert to the museum, and now they were wondering why it hadn't been revealed to the public as some sort of exhibit. Then I showed up. First, on a crime scene. And then, at The Ryerson. A dwarf in the middle of all this oddity? I wondered how long they'd been casing my ass.

"Well, yeah, as you can see," I said, motioning to my weapons mounted on the wall. "I have an interest in ancient weapons and artifacts. Safe to say, I've got a lot of hands-on experience with them."

"We also understand that you relieved Dr. Hammil of a photograph of item #EW234450-112-MM and kept it for an unspecified period of time." And like a peacock that held full reign over a courtyard leading to a King's Palace, both Jackson and Miller arched their backs ever so slightly to give themselves a hint more height. (I know that trick well.) "We are here on matters of national security to collect your data concerning #EW234450-112-MM."

And they did their little posturing maneuver together again. How cute. I bet these government dinks do *everything* together.

I was trying really hard not to snicker because I knew they could, if given the green light from The White House, tear up my office without so much as a worry for my individual rights. Power is power, regardless of what freedoms are promised to people. All it would take to turn me from Billibub Baddings, Private Eye to Billibub Baddings, Enemy of the State was a single phone call to the great Ivory Palace of the East. Still, that didn't mean I had to blindly roll over and play dead for these clowns.

"I gave the photo back to Hammil already, so if you guys flash your badges to the Ryerson or the Chicago Police I'm sure they'll grant you two access to whatever you want. As far as access to my personal notes, I'm afraid that is classified."

"Classified?"

"Yeah, classified," I echoed Jackson. "I knew that's a word you two would understand. There are already two deaths that I know of linked to item #EW234-blah-blah-blah. That's enough blood spilled for my taste, so I've got my notes stored away in a safe place so that no one else will come to harm." I then leaned forward, slowly lacing my fingers together. "As far as turning over my own personal notes without question, that gets a little complicated."

"Complicated?"

I paused for a moment, looking at Jackson as if he had suddenly grown a third arm from his forehead. "You should change your last name to 'Canyon.' It suits you better."

He didn't get the joke. I didn't expect him to.

"My own notes are linked with a case," I went on, "and because I am a private investigator, it really would not do a lot for business if I went and released my findings to anyone…even ol' Uncle Whiskers himself."

"Watch your step, Shorty!" Well, what do you know? Miller had a voice. "You're working with the G here, and we don't take kindly to that kind of talk!"

"Where'd you hear that tough-guy talk, G-man? Listening faithfully to *True Detective Mysteries,* are we?"

Miller's beady eyes narrowed. If these boys were with Alphonse's or Bugs' crew, they would be taking me for a one-way scenic ride through the more rural spots in Illinois by now, and I wouldn't be making the fitting I had scheduled at Sergio's after lunch.

No, these guys wanted to keep a low profile, and for good reason. Because Chicago was creeping up more and more in the trouble department lately, the Feds were now poking their noses into business that local law enforcement couldn't handle. While mobsters were able to deal with local cops—easily adding them to the "business expenses" of the operation—the Feds were gumming up the works with reps like Eliot Ness. Apparently, Ness had recruited himself a sharp little team, all of them following the same codes and edicts of refusing bribes and remaining out of the Organization's influence. (I hope those "Untouchables" are as squeaky-clean as their press makes them out to be.)

As Jackson cleared his throat to speak, the sound seemed to give the invisible chain connected to Miller's neck a bit of a tug. Not too much, though. The dink still wanted my head as his pike ornament.

"I don't think you understand the present situation, Mr. Baddings. We are not *requesting* information from you. We are merely extending a courtesy in telling you that you *will* hand over *all* information concerning Ryerson's missing item #EW234450-112-MM."

When you're dealing with dwarves, the best way to completely shut down the negotiation channels is to make demands. Never tell dwarves that they are going to do something, because whether you insinuate it or not, we will add "*…or else!*" on the end. I have seen peace negotiations degenerate into barroom brawls simply because the party opposite the dwarves worded their terms as *"You will do this,"* or *"You will do that."* And so, the rumor (probably started up by the elves) grew that dwarves are rude little twerps at treaty talks.

"Really?" I countered. "Then how about I extend to the Department of War a little courtesy of my own? If any agent of the Department of War—or any other United States Government agency for that matter—attempts to relieve Gryfennos-born dwarf and United States citizen

Billibub Duronhoumus Baddings of any information he is not willing to part withal, then said dwarf cannot and will not be held responsible for damages or injury to the government agents in question."

This was the challenge Miller had been waiting for. As he leaned over my desk, tipping his charcoal-grey fedora back to the top of his head, I could make out the roscoe under his now-unbuttoned jacket. While I mentally painted the bull's-eye exactly where my fist would do the most damage to that square jaw of his, I sent the High Warrior and His Second a prayer that "Tough Guy" Miller was going where I hoped he would.

"That sounds like a threat, Shorty." He rested his fists gently against my desk. "You threatening us? You threatening Uncle Sam?"

I had to give this ogre some credit. Every time his mouth opened, another line from some dime-store detective magazine came out. For a government agent, that's talent.

"It isn't a threat, tough guy." I smiled. "Like you said before, it's a courtesy."

"Really? Well then, maybe we should dig deeper. Maybe we shouldn't just take your classified notes, but everything here. Find out exactly what brought this courtesy on." Miller looked over at my battle-axe and war hammer and gave a nod to them both. "I think I'll start with these trophies of yours over there. They look dangerous."

As Miller strode over to my former tools of the trade as if he were the herald returning with the enemy's surrender, I nodded to myself in satisfaction. Apparently, my prayer had just been heard.

"Hey, Miranda!" I shouted, causing Miller to freeze in midstep. "Make the call!"

Just as I heard Miranda pick up the phone and ask for a connection, Miller's hand touched the handle of my battle-axe. My *charmed* battle-axe.

This weapon was forged by the best in the business, a big, burly dwarf by the name of Dursley Dingelhorff. This guy crafted one-of-a-kind battle-axes that could slice through metal armor like a knife through warm butter. Once Dursley finished this little gem of a weapon for me, I took it to a wizard whose forte was casting charms for weapons and asked him to give my battle-axe something that would make it work for me instead of against me. Let me just say that I've got to be damn more careful what I ask for from a friggin' mage! The old coot took my request literally and charmed the axe with a spell that prevented anyone else to wield it, outside of yours truly. This way, no one could use it against me. Not what I expected, but a handy charm nonetheless.

As I was saying, Miller's hand touched the leather-wrapped handle, just long enough for him to feel the tanned animal hide against his own fingertips. As I watched him fly across my office and through the frosted window that separated my office from Miranda's reception area, I remembered how my pal Kev had described being on the other end of my battle-axe's charm. Once, when he and I were well into our kegs of malt beer, I dared him to try and take my battle-axe from me. When he landed on solid ground and sat up, laughing in a drunken stupor but also grasping his ribs, he described a sensation of being back-kicked by a pack beast in a very bad mood. Now Kev was a big guy, though not as big as "Tough Guy" G-man now landing in front of Miranda's desk with a hard crash.

If I remembered correctly, Kev managed to walk away with a couple of broken ribs. I had no doubt Miller had the wind knocked out of him, but chances were good he'd just be sore as hell for the weekend.

"Hello, Mr. McWilliams? It's Miranda over at Baddings Investigations." She nodded. "Yeah, someone touched the wall décor again." She called through the open hole that once separated her from my office, "Who does he bill this time?"

Jackson turned back at me, his pistol out and pointing down at me. I was still at my desk, fingers laced and smiling wide at the somewhat befuddled government agent. I had made my point. There was no need to bring Beatrice or even her little sister into this standoff.

"The Department of War, Washington, D.C." I sat back in my office chair, giving my beard a few strokes. I took a moment to wonder what was running through that highly militarized mind of Mr. Jackson's. This grain-fed human knew nothing of magic, necromancers, and charmed weapons. How could Jackson, who accepted only what regulations and training had taught him, possibly reason his way through this display of sorcery before him?

I shrugged. "Go ahead. Shoot me. Shoot Miranda to cover all your tracks, if you need to, but you can tear up this office and still not find any more answers to the questions you and your crew are asking. How about you lower that heater of yours, and we talk like a couple of military types?"

Jackson was really working the brain muscle pretty hard. On one hand, he really wanted to check up on his bull-headed partner. At the same time, he didn't want to turn his back on me for a second. The poor sap really didn't have a clue what I was going to do next, or what I was capable of.

As far as Miranda knew, this was just a booby trap I'd rigged up in my office in case anyone tried to pinch my weapons. *"So where is it?"* Miranda would ask me. My reply was always, *"You won't see it coming,"* and that was good enough for her. I figured the booby-trap story would be easier for her to swallow than explaining how my battle-axe's charm worked.

"Hey, Miranda?" I asked, casually taking my eyes off of Jackson. Not like he really wanted to take a chance and lay a finger on anything else in the office, present company included. "How's our pal looking out there?"

"He's moving. Not much, though."

"Give Dr. Roberts a call." I turned back to Jackson and picked up my desk lighter. "He's across the street. He'll give your boy Miller the once-over, and be discreet about it. Now, you got to make a choice here, Agent Jackson. What's it gonna be?"

He slowly returned his piece back to his shoulder holster, and I masked a relieved sigh by stretching across my desk for the pipe tree. I packed the bowl with fresh tobacco from a nearby box. Savoring the sweet mixture of leaf and earth in my bowl that I'd just ignited, I blew out a smoke ring with the second puff. Jackson wasn't impressed.

"Now, Mr. Jackson, I'm not one for being told what I'm going to do. I'm my own boss, and I answer to only one person: me. You try to muscle your way through my office, case files, and personal details, and you got one seriously pissed-off dwarf on your hands. I extended a courtesy to you and Miller, and I'm real sorry that Miller took that header through my window. This friendly meeting didn't have to play out like that, you know?"

"Mr. Baddings, you are making things more difficult than they should be."

"Maybe I am," I conceded with a long drag from my ornate pipe, "but as you witnessed with my battle-axe, I've got a handle on matters like Ryerson's missing artifact, the Singing Sword. A much easier name referring to it, wouldn't you agree?"

"That may be the way you understand the situation, Mr. Baddings, but you have no idea what you are getting yourself into."

"Really?" I fought back a laugh. "I was just thinking it's your War Department that's stumbling into a dungeon without a torch and a clue." I slid a pen across my desk. It stopped by a blank memo pad. "So how about we educate one another? I'll give you a better idea of what exactly was stolen from the Ryerson Library, and you tell me why the United States military is so interested in this trinket."

I watched Jackson consider the offer on the table, silently considering what would be safe to talk about with me, and what should remain under Uncle Sam's red, white and blue top hat. After a moment or two of getting comfortable in the seat across from my desk, he finally spoke. "Since the cessation of hostilities in Europe, we have been keeping a close eye on developments overseas."

"Not a bad thing to do. I know you guys had your hands full with the cleanup and all."

"In every war, you always have a losing side, I'm afraid."

"Yeah," I replied, a bitterness forming in my mouth. "All part of war."

"As you are a civilian and unfamiliar with the aftermath of a war, Mr. Baddings, I don't expect you to truly understand the reconstruction of a nation. Germany has been slow in putting itself back together since the end of the war. These past few years, however, have shown developments requiring our attention. There is this fringe party that appears to be pushing somewhat radical platforms. The followers of this movement seem to have very particular, if not peculiar, attitudes toward race, politics, and national pride. According to the limited intelligence we've gathered, their party leader is a charismatic individual, harping on the vision of what Germany was in its heyday," he ended with a scoff.

"I'd keep an eye on this guy, then," I replied. "Take it from me: When all you have left is pride, you can build a lot more than a nation."

That wiped the ignorant smirk off his face. Not bad for a "civilian," eh, Jackson?

"So what does all this have to do with the Singing Sword?" I asked.

"Our intelligence also reports that this individual shows a preoccupation with historical artifacts of a supernatural nature."

Now it was my turn to scoff, listening to him try and explain the Singing Sword in terminology he could understand. "Historical artifacts of a supernatural nature?"

Jackson looked away for a moment. "Do you read the papers, Mr. Baddings?"

"In my business, you got to."

"Do you recall in last week's paper an article concerning the Smithsonian?"

Ah, the Smithsonian: an institution of higher learning that would make bard, mage, cleric, and sage alike clap with glee and believe it was Christmas every day. While the Ryerson was the gem of Chicago's academia, The Smithsonian was considered the gem of the whole country, the kind of place that had everything under one roof. And when I say everything, I mean *everything*!

"Yeah, I know the place. Was thinking about taking P.S. 35 out there for a field trip. You know, do my good deed for the local kiddies here."

Nope, still no rise or reaction from Jackson. He was a tough crowd in himself.

"Do you recall a story about its temporary closing to the public for cataloging new artifacts?" he asked.

"Yeah, buried in the national news section. Not much to tell."

I pushed myself free of my desk and hopped out of the chair as I watched old Doc Roberts arrive with his trusty black bag in hand. He took one look at Miller, and then looked over at me through the broken pane with a hint of a scowl. For a second, I thought I was going to get a scolding. Instead, I got a rueful shake of his silver-haired head as he knelt by the groaning patient. Chances were I'd get an earful from the Doc at the next change of the seasons, when my knee always acted up.

I returned my attentions to the dink in my office. "As I recall, the article was to inform tourists and the like that if they were going to D.C., they'd better not plan a visit to the Smithsonian."

Since Jackson was seated, we were seeing eye to eye. His voice dropped to a level only I could hear. "What the article didn't report were the murders of several Smithsonian staff."

I took my pipe out and cast a casual glance at Miranda, who caught it better than Kiki Cuyler out in Right Field. Continuing to file those nails of hers, my girl struck up a conversation with Doc Roberts. The Doc needed to be preoccupied not only with his patient, but with her as well. It was for privacy's sake. A bit of a challenge right now on account of Miller's quick flight through my office window.

I motioned with my head for Jackson to join me by the window. The rain still came down steadily, the *pip-pippty-pap-pap-pip* symphony now giving our conversation a little cover.

"Several staff members, huh?" I couldn't mask the surprise and confusion in my low voice. This news, if not a front-page item, should have been at least a lead story in the national news. Instead, it ran as more of a side story for the folks who read a *Tribune* or *Chronicle* from beginning to end, and apparently the story was incomplete.

"How did the news wire miss that little detail behind the Smithsonian's closing?"

"Because, unlike you, they were cooperative," Jackson answered. "What I am revealing, I am doing so with discretion. Mr. Baddings, you have given me no reason to trust you unconditionally, but with this collection you have on display here, I cannot completely dismiss your knowledge on this matter. I will warn you that if these facts I share with you are made public, I will practice the same discretion in how I make you, your business, and your staff disappear."

Back to threats, are we? Jackson, I must admit, did have something that could scare the bathtub gin out of me. He had resources even Capone wouldn't be able to call on. And while Capone's displays of enforcement were usually public, messy, and downright nasty, this chump was the G. Jackson could make Baddings Investigations a front for organized crime and vilify Miranda and me to a point where the general public would scream for us to make an appearance at Chicago's answer to "Executioner's Square."

"You know, Jackson? We got this saying from my parts: *Ke mach be-nesh fa denarg, fa re mach desatch.*"

Jackson looked down at me blankly. Guess his investigation into what his team labeled "the supernatural" didn't include translation of Dwarven dialects.

"And that means?" he finally asked me.

"Don't screw me, and I won't screw you."

The honest, yet crass, statement sounded better in my own tongue.

"The murders were of two archeologists and a student, all recently arrived from an archeological dig in Greece. These gentlemen were apparently celebrating a recent discovery of lost satyr plays and rare pottery, still intact. However, a communiqué sent a month before the incident at the Smithsonian mentioned another artifact discovered that shouldn't have been there."

"Really? Why not?"

"At the time of the satyr plays, the Greeks wielded weaponry of a specific style and metal composition. This team came across a weapon completely different in its origin. Descriptions made it out to be crescent-shaped, no longer than a forearm. The inside angle of the weapon…"

"…kept an edge, still sharp. And let me guess—it was a brushed silver color, wasn't it?"

Finally, I got a reaction out of Jackson. Could have knocked him over with a dragon's scale. I think he was expecting me to keep going in the description of this doohickey, but no such luck. I vaguely remembered what this "unique find" looked like because I had caught a glance of it before pitching it into that portal. Guess I just caught up with talisman number two.

"So this boomerang of death, which those scholars and you military types knew was more prevalent in a completely different hemisphere, wound up in a dig in Ancient Greece. Did those scholarly types get this trinket home?"

"Archeology is not a priority of the Department of War, you understand, Mr. Baddings. We are hardly interested in clay urns and images of gladiators depicted in various forms of combat. What caught our attention was the communiqué our European intelligence operatives intercepted a few days before the Smithsonian incident."

"No, wait, don't tell me. You can't give me the particulars of that telegram because it is considered super-secret, and not for the ears of 'civilians' like me."

"Correct, Mr. Baddings." He was back to his rock-demon self once again. If it weren't for the fact that he was speaking, I'd be holding a mirror under his nostrils to see if he was alive. "I can tell you the intercepted message made reference to an archeological dig somewhere in Greece, and was extremely clear in its order to obtain this artifact at all costs."

"So this character you're keeping an eye on gets his jollies off of ancient good-luck charms? Do you have any real evidence that this political party was behind the murders?"

"We have evidence that this political party not only carried out the murders, but have some sort of inside advisor who is currently assisting them in their investigation of these said artifacts."

I shook my head amid a cloud of pipe smoke. "Now why are you doing this to me, Jackson? Why? You've got *what* that tells you this? Come on, a little faith between us. This is getting us nowhere."

"On the contrary, Mr. Baddings. I have already told you a great deal, and you're the only one of the two of us benefiting from this conversation so far. I am willing to tell you more, but you cannot blame me if I wish to keep a few details to myself. Out of good faith."

Good point. Hell, there are times I don't even trust myself.

"Fair enough," I conceded. "The Singing Sword is actually called the Sword of Arannahs."

Jackson began feverishly jotting notes on his memo pad, hanging on every syllable coming out of my mouth. I probably could have blurted out Gabby's batting average in '28 and he would have made a note of it.

"What you have to understand about the Sword of Arannahs," I continued, "is that it's actually part of a collection of talismans."

He paused and looked me incredulously. "Talismans?"

Ain't that just like the government? Still, I couldn't ignore the reality that the Feds were now officially in the middle of my investigation. These boys at the War Department probably had eyes and ears everywhere. Between Jackson's operation and the Treasury Department keeping an eye on Al, Bugs, and his boys, Chicago was now a regular Secret Policemen's Ball. Without trying, these government suits would trip over each other. Talk about making my job tough!

"The Sword itself is more of a ceremonial piece than a weapon, and there is an inscription along its blade." I chose not to tell him it was Elvish. That would just make this chat even more complicated. "The inscription is part of its prophecy that only the mild and the meek can wield it."

"So what if someone strong were to handle it?" Jackson looked up from his memo pad, unable to mask his curiosity. "I don't mean someone strong in build, mind you. Let say, someone strong in stature, like say…"

"The current Commander-in-Chief of the United States Armed Forces?" Humans are so thick! They really feel entitled to everything, even when it comes to wielding talismans like the Singing Sword. "I'm not going to lie to you about this, Jackson. I don't know all the details of what it can do. I do know that armies following the chosen wielder went unchallenged. Those who did challenge the Sword fell before it, subject to the whims and darkest desires of the blessed that wielded it. Something to that effect, you know? The prophecies from my parts tend to sound a lot like that *Revelation* chapter."

I turned from the window to glance out to Miranda and the little party in my waiting area. Miller was fighting to stay on his feet while Doc Roberts gave him a quick eyesight check. Never saw one guy try so hard to keep his peepers on a single finger.

I turned back to Jackson and added, "As far as what would happen if our man Hoover got a hold of the Sword, I can't say for sure. When wizards and mages perform their hocus-pocus…"

"Wizards and mages?" Jackson interjected sharply. "You're not serious about that, are you, Mr. Baddings?"

"Ask your partner. He just found out firsthand just how serious these charms and curses on weapons can get." I could see the denial building in his eyes. With a shrug, I turned my eyes back to the rainwater slowly running down the glass in front of me. "If you really want to understand what you're dealing with, first you have to open your mind to the oddball and just plain weird, and you might be able to hang on to your sanity, Jackson. When wizards and mages work their charms and-or curses over a talisman, be it a ring, a gauntlet, sword, or even a battle-axe—"

We both looked over to Miller, now taking a seat next to Miranda's desk as she came in from outside the hallway with ice pack in hand.

"—you probably won't know the results of their work until it's all said and done. You just don't know for certain what will happen in the long run. I've had that battle-axe long enough to know how it reacts to other people's touch. Your boy out there was just a little too eager to answer Uncle Sam's orders. Best to look carefully before crossing any unknown streets. Agreed, Mr. Jackson?"

Gently placing the pipe on my desk, I hopped back into my chair while Jackson went out to take a closer look at his partner. Evidently, Miller was already returning to his former charming self, snatching his fedora out of Miranda's hand and grunting at Jackson. (Guess that was War Department code for *"I'm okay."*)

Jackson then turned back toward me. The size of this suit rivaled some kings I've stood before, but even with the roscoe resting snug and secure in his shoulder holster and the War Department covering his expenses, I refused to forget that it was *my* tax dollars that paid for his cheap-ass suit and morning java.

"If you're waiting to find out why I'm looking into the Singing Sword alongside you," I told him through the now-open window, "that ain't gonna happen. You saw the name on the door, and I made it clear to you when you got here. My clients remain private. If you can spare the manpower, maybe you'll find out whom I'm working for; that's going to be the only way you're going to find out anything else from me."

Jackson gave me a nod. "We'll be in touch, Mr. Baddings," he spoke flatly.

"I'm a detective," I replied in the same tone. "Kinda figured that one out."

He was almost out the door when I spoke up again. "Hey, Jackson. Before you go, I do have one more thing I want to know. Just a little detail that's gnawing at my craw."

Jackson turned back, more out of curiosity than courtesy. "Yes, Mr. Baddings?"

"You said you intercepted that message concerning the Smithsonian folk a month before the murders." I paused for a moment, making sure I had his undivided attention. "Tell me. Why didn't you warn them?"

"We needed to find out how real this threat was, and how far they would be willing to carry out orders."

I nodded slowly. "And you can sleep with those deaths on your conscience?"

Jackson's expression didn't change as he turned to join Miller by Miranda's desk. Miller gave me a final cold stare before tossing Miranda his ice pack. Then they both made to leave, the glass that used to be my window grinding and crunching underneath their steps.

Suddenly, Jackson whirled around and retrieved his notepad, flipping a few pages forward and reading the notes there. "Where exactly is..." He paused for a moment and slowly formed the word, "Griff-ANN-us?"

"It's a small town in Missouri, about an hour outside of Shelbyville," I replied. "We're very traditional in our ways when it comes to folklore and all that, so that's how I come across stuff like this," I said, motioning to my weapons. "It's an out-of-the-way sort of place, so you may find it hard to come across it on a map."

"Shelbyville."

"Missouri," I confirmed. "I could have told you I am from a realm of wizards, dragons, and trolls, and that I got here by slipping through a Portal of Oblivion." With a gruff laugh, I added, "but that's about as believable as a division of the War Department devoted to the study of magic talismans, huh?"

He didn't say anything as his notepad closed with a barely audible *snap*. A few seconds later, my office door closed behind them quietly.

Old Doc Roberts still packing up his bag. I waited until Uncle Whiskers' pals were out of earshot before loosing a long, heavy sigh.

The Feds. Shit. I really could have done without this new addition to the roster.

Then again, if what Jackson said were true, gangsters weren't the only ones on a quest for the Singing Sword and its fellow talismans.

"As you are a civilian and unfamiliar with the aftermath of a war, Mr. Baddings..."

I grimaced at the bitterness forming again in my mouth. Jackson didn't know just how familiar this citizen was with the aftermath of losing a war.

"Take it from me," I had replied, *"when all you have left is pride, you can build a lot more than a nation."*

When we lost the First War of The Races, the elves introduced doctrines forbidding dwarves from holding assemblies. But our newly appointed figurehead (and he was barely that) called his court in secret, and could this guy talk! This emperor was a wordsmith, and he appealed to the Gryfennos Empire's glory days. Word passed from family to family, and slowly we regrouped.

Twenty-five years later, the elves decided in closed council to fully restore our emperor's power as a "gift" to us for serving their royal house so diligently over the years. (It really was their way of admitting defeat when our underground's blockades and declining productivity in their mines had starved out their supply lines.) With the guidance of our emperor, armed only with motivation, we had ultimately won the war against the elves without swinging an axe.

Yeah, Jackson, I thought as I paid Doc Roberts for the visit, *I know all about war, its aftermath, and that one guy who can make a difference.*

I glanced at the clock. Sergio had asked me to come around lunchtime to try on the tux he was stitching together for me. In answer to Miranda's uncertain look, I fired off a quick wink and returned to what was now a *semi*-private office.

Through the curtain of rainwater running slowly against the windowpane, I watched Miller and Jackson cross the street and climb into a parked car that had two others in the front seat. My moment in front of the window turned into five minutes, and five minutes turned into ten. Apparently, they weren't making plans to leave anytime soon.

Guess I'd be taking the back door to Sergio's.

CHAPTER TWELVE

I'll Live a Lush Life

One of the few things dwarves do because they have to—not because they want to—is attend fancy-dress events. Break out the kilt, find the medals and pendants of past glories, and then it's beard-braiding time. The dwarves of Gryfennos only pulled out the formal military duds from the mothballs for royal appointments, a presentation of a family crest, or the coronation of an emperor. We never did this sort of thing for "fun." When we threw a party, we dwarves liked to be comfortable. (Trust me, it's never a good idea to pass out in leather armor and a kilt.)

Perhaps I was really tempting the Fates by attending this dinner party. But here's the thing—I'm one of those few dwarves who really enjoy getting dressed up for no good reason. Because of that, and because my pal Sergio handles a needle with the same flair as a blademaster with a sword, I couldn't help but wear a smug little grin. I didn't have to ask—I knew I looked good.

Promptly at seven, a scarecrow of a chauffeur knocked on my office door and accompanied me down to a sharp silver and steel-grey limo idling at the curb of my building. Damned impressive sight. When I arrived at the party, the valet didn't seem to care that I wasn't up to par (or height) with the other guests. I could have been a mountain troll stepping out of that ride and he would have still greeted me with the same look. He had a job to do, and intended to do it to the best of his ability so that the Rothchilds would invite him back to the estate…whenever they needed a valet, that is.

As my feet lightly scuffed against the stone surface of the manor's wide steps, the tall, double doors in front of me opened wide like the jaws of a great dragon in full roar. I couldn't help but dwell on that image for a moment…the prospect of entering this beast of splendor and indulgence was giving me a severe knot in the stomach.

No doubt Miss Rothchild had an agenda in inviting me to her hallowed halls. Maybe it was just to aggravate her old man. That was fine with me, because I had my own reasons for being here, too. All I knew was this: Once I stepped across her threshold, I had to be sure I could handle whatever waited for me on the other side.

I don't know how long I stood there. I think three couples passed by me. They could have been laughing at me, or enjoying an early start to the evening's revels (I preferred to think the latter). Inside, I could hear a string quartet striking up a movement from *The Four Seasons*. "Winter," from the sound of the slow, relaxing melody. Probably the Largo movement, so the cellist could steal a bit of the spotlight. Why should the violins have all the fun?

Hey, I'm a tough-talking detective, not some socially challenged orc who can't appreciate a good tune.

The enthusiastic proclamation, "Mr. Baddings, you made it!" pulled me back from my own private abyss. Before me stood Eva Rothchild, extending a flute of champagne to me with a bright smile.

As for my hostess, she was very much like the house: classical caressing contemporary. Her long blonde tresses were swept up and away from her face, now fresh and soft-looking. While she didn't sport the bob that many women of this world embraced, she evidently had no qualms in embracing the latest fashions, if her plunging neckline number (probably the latest rage from Paris) was anything to go by. An interesting contradiction Miss Rothchild was proving to be.

Smoothing out the front of my double-breasted tuxedo as I walked up to her, I couldn't help but smile at her approving look. I took the glass from her, raised it in a silent toast, and took a sip. Even filled with the fine sparkling wine that carried a light, slightly floral bouquet, the glass was as light as a feather. Best crystal that money could buy.

"Yeah, well, usually a big Saturday night for me involves a talkie and a soda. This is a step up for me, so if I seem a little shy, bear with me."

She giggled, smiling even wider as she toasted the couple who followed my entrance. "Mr. Baddings, you hardly strike me as being shy about anything."

"Is that a fact?"

I followed her eyes to the couple she was toasting—a couple I recognized (only by face, not by name) from the society pages. Their bright smiles dimmed a little as their eyes fell on me, the dwarf in the tux. While I could dress like their kind, it was clear that I was still far from blending in.

"Whatever the reason your father had for throwing this little party," I ventured, "it must be a big deal." I motioned to a group of couples talking and laughing in the grand foyer. All the gentlemen in this group I recognized as members of the District Attorney's and Mayor's offices. It would have not surprised me at all if the Governor of Illinois were in the next room.

"So tell me, Miss Rothchild, is my presence here specifically to push Daddy closer to a coronary, and you a little closer to the family inheritance?"

"Now, Mr. Baddings," she scolded, resting one of her delicate, bejeweled hands on my shoulder. "Your invitation to this gathering is merely a gesture of appreciation."

Appreciation? I didn't buy it for one minute that this lady appreciated anything beyond her own wants. Sometime tonight, I was certain the punch line to this joke of me being here would present itself.

Until that time, though, I decided to play along. "Well, in light of that, I tell you what, Miss Rothchild. You call me Billi, and I'll drop the shy, wide-eyed dwarf routine."

"Very well then…Billi." She touched her glass with mine. The tone rang lightly, a perfect tone that continued to echo like a death toll through the surrounding din of the party. "And you may call me Eva."

With her hand still resting lightly on my shoulder, we went for a stroll around this grand palace. The stunning ornaments along the wall, and statues proudly displayed on pedestals in the foyer and adjoining chambers, were impressive…but merely the warm-up for what was in the main banquet room. Illuminating the party was a breathtaking crystal chandelier, a fixture casting more than enough light on the various cuisines offered, the bar (Like the Feds were going to raid this place when the D.A. and police commissioner were hobnobbing with potential backers?), and an impressive collection of pieces that looked like they would be more at home in a museum somewhere. There was no real unifying theme in the pieces here, other than they were rare.

After we passed an urn that curators would have begged to prominently display in their own institutions, I turned my attentions back to Eva. She saw the pieces as well, but I saw no appreciation in those crystal blues of hers. In fact, her disregard struck me as rather odd. I could at least appreciate the history behind said artifacts, and the events of this case were only adding to my interest in Rothchild's collection. But Eva seemed more interested in being seen with the dwarf than appreciating the spoils of her numerous digs in Egypt, Europe, and the Orient.

When my eyes fell on a beautifully carved jade dragon, I tapped my escort on the wrist and pointed up to it. "Now *that* is a beautiful find, Eva."

She shrugged. "If you like that sort of thing, I guess."

All right, it was time to play *"How Thick Is Eva?"* and find out how much of a sham she really was.

"But the *history* behind this piece," I persisted. "Just think about it: Ages ago, artisans could craft something like *this*," I motioned to the serpentine creature, "out of a block of pure emerald."

"Yeah. That's really…" Eva paused as she stared blankly at the dragon, "…something."

And so the painfully small talk went as we passed various relics, with this intrepid, high-society archeologist missing every contradiction and error I threw at her. Clearly, Little Miss Eva couldn't tell the difference between a Ming vase and Mick's plateware. Guess the apple didn't fall too far from the tree. Much like her ruthless robber-baron ancestors, Eva was enjoying her success on the backs of scientists, scholars, and local workers. (I couldn't help but wonder how many of those dinks were enjoying fine champagne in expensive crystal goblets tonight.) Daddy Rothchild would have really nailed an impersonation of a berserker if he'd known exactly what a waste Eva's education had been in reality. He always made it clear to the papers how much he loathed wasting his money, especially in light of how hard his family had worked in earning it.

The Rothchild fortune was built in the oil industry. The family took part in the Great Land Rush and managed a few acres of farmland. Well, as the Fates would have it, oil was discovered on their property—not enough to build the fortune that the Rothchilds currently enjoyed, but enough for Granddaddy Rothchild to invest in Missouri's mining industry. I give ol' Granddad credit—he didn't put all his eggs in one basket. He invested in several mining operations, and they all brought him a solid income. The harder the Rothchilds' miners worked, the better the Rothchilds lived...and it was apparent that the Rothchilds' miners were working very, very hard.

As we passed various pockets of people, my ears picked up bits and pieces of conversation that wasn't far off from the talk I'd hear at Mick's. Only difference was in the details. I caught a few words spoken about a close polo game, which didn't sound very different from talk over the Cubs going into extra innings.

Before too long, I heard the *ding-ding-ding-ding* of a small spoon striking the side of a glass. Conversations came to a halt, the music stopped, and guests' attention gradually turned to the room's large, elegant fireplace, where it looked like a small group of people was preparing to speak.

Eva turned to me. "How about I get you a better seat for this moment in Chicago history, little man?"

Little man? This was definitely not the same Eva Rothchild who had visited my office the other day.

"Sure, *toots.*" That was for the "little man" comment. Normally, something like that would have pissed me off, but this was a social event. No need for me to get snippy. "How about you get us a place in the front row?"

As we worked our way through the crowd of tuxedoes and evening dresses, I could hear the voice pretty clearly now. While he was getting up there in years, the speaker's deep, confident baritone and dry wit still commanded respect. It was a safe bet that the man flapping his gums would be Franklin Rothchild, the lord and master of this estate. He cracked a joke that I didn't get, but the socialites seemed to get a kick out of it. The politicians I caught sight of laughed politely, but I could see it in their eyes: They didn't get the joke either. What a surprise.

When we finally made it to the front of the crowd, I saw Rothchild and his wife standing there, quite self-assured in their stance (both physically and socially). From his toothy, Cheshire-Cat smile, it was clear that he was no longer the one doing the talking. No, the guy now addressing the crowd was roughly the same age as Rothchild, but looking as if he could easily dance the Charleston into the wee-small hours of the morning. I knew his face from the papers, but I had already seen so many familiar mugs from the Society section tonight that my memory had left the castle for a quick smoke.

But the third figure standing next to them, I knew at first glance: a shapely socialite with a dress and cleavage that definitely gave my date Eva a run for her money. This raven-haired *femme fatale* proved to be the punch line to a really bad joke.

"So tell me, Eva…did you and Miss Lesinger arrange this little *rendezvous*, or is her presence at your house and home one hell of a coincidence?"

"Who said this place was *my* home? I never made mention of that when I invited you. I just told you I'd send a driver and gave you a time. Nothing more."

This bitch was so lucky there were people around. While I don't believe in hitting women, there are some unique members of the pack who really beg for it. Eva just became the leader of said pack!

"So, this is the Lesinger estate, huh? Nice digs." My eyes narrowed. "You are a true game mistress, aren't you?"

She merely grinned, quite pleased with herself. "Now Billi, do you think I would intentionally try and start up trouble between you and your client?"

"No…provided you nurture some kind of bizarre fetish for four-foot-one guys with thirty-six inch waists, bushy red beards, and hostile attitudes toward goblins." If only the edge in my voice were sharp enough to draw blood. "I *do* think you are capable of painting a picture of me hobnobbing with you in order to outrage your social rival over there, getting her to drop me harder than an elf taking an orc's arrow to the chest."

Her smile softened for a moment, only to flood back more radiantly than before. "You are good, Billi." She bent down to place a gentle kiss on my cheek. "I look forward to having you on my payroll."

I remained indifferent, along with the rest of me. The kiss was specifically for Miss Lesinger's benefit, because she had just caught sight of me in the tux. It was a shock, I'm sure, to find me there; that shock increased tenfold at Eva's empty gesture. Shaken, my client returned her gaze to the onlookers as Henry Lesinger continued to address the party.

"…but as I grow older and wiser—well, all right, as I grow *older*—I'm finding it harder and harder to move forward on my own. Lesinger Industrial & Technological Development has provided jobs for the workers of America and advancements for the world, but lately I believe we are growing too comfortable. We are not moving forward fast enough, and I believe that two kings work better than one. Alliances have always proven to be the future of business, society, and nations. After all, it was an alliance that brought an end to the Great War in Europe."

Yeah, a war that America refused to get involved in until their hand was forced. And what was with the "two kings" comments? He apparently didn't know the kings of my realm, who went to war over the position of a tree stump and an invisible line in the ground. I'm sure he meant well, but ol' Lesinger really needed to lay off the booze, because his tipsy state was altering his take on reality.

Franklin Rothchild, the earlier voice we heard, now chimed in. "Therefore, for the betterment of the country and for the future of my children and—" He quickly glanced over to Eva with a transparent smile, "—perhaps one day, grandchildren—"

She returned the nicest *"Screw you and the mount you rode in on, Dad"* smile I'd ever seen on a lady.

"—I am announcing tonight the partnership between Rothchild Oil & Mining Industries and Lesinger Industrial & Technological Development."

There was a slight gasp from the assembled guests as the men clasped hands. Flashbulbs burst around them like Forest Pixies who, at the time of their deaths, explode at night in a fleeting brilliance and then return to earth in a shower of sparks. The smiles and nods the two tycoons shared were sincere…so sincere that I think it frightened many of the partygoers. Even outside these upper-crust social circles, it was well known what bitter business rivals these men were. This announcement was marking the end of an era of underhanded, cutthroat struggles for financial supremacy in Chicago. Whether or not this new relationship would usher in a new age of cooperation remained to be seen.

Raising his own glass, Henry Lesinger grinned for the public eyes who were continuing to capture the moment for tomorrow's front pages. "I do not doubt that this partnership will prove beneficial to all of you who invested in us as individual entities. Now, it's time to send the news to Wall Street and enjoy the windfall of this merger. Ladies and gentlemen, here's to 1929. May it be one unforgettable year for us all!"

Flutes were raised in a unified toast. "1929," echoed the crowd.

As Lesinger and Rothchild continued to pose for pictures and the crowd dispersed to discuss this development, Eva gave me a pat on my head (All she was missing was a snout and a bushy tail, wagging wildly behind her!) and then disappeared into a grove of penguin suits and evening dresses, beaming more brightly than a broadsword fresh from the forge and polished to a fine sheen.

The message was clear: I had served my purpose, and I could now leave whenever I felt like it.

The quartet started up again. This time they were performing Mozart, a composer I especially liked. Other composers, from both my world and this one, seemed to go easy on the notes and melodies, but this guy really knew how to make his musicians work for their applause.

"Mr. Baddings," came the familiar voice I was hoping to talk to first thing Monday morning so I could explain everything.

"Miss Lesinger...believe me when I tell you this is an unexpected pleasure."

"Really?" Oh yeah, she was in a lather, all right. "Is there a reason you are here...with Eva, no less?"

"Actually, I'm on my own now," I replied with a slight shrug. "Miss Rothchild invited me here, so I showed up in my best double-breasted to what I thought was the Rothchild mansion and hoped for the best. It wasn't until I saw you that I realized I was being played for a sucker. Looks like Eva was intending for you to drop me, and drop me quick. I would like to think that, in light of my past service to you, I can continue to disappoint her."

I motioned to a grand patio that presented no real view, apart from a grove of trees. There were a few guests out there enjoying the clear night sky, their smokes, and quiet chitchat. "Perhaps we should get some fresh air. No offence, but I find the surroundings here…"

"Stuffy. I know." Miss Lesinger turned up a nose and, with a final disdainful glance at the party around her, led the way outside.

The conversation out here was even less substantial than the talk I had eavesdropped on earlier. What I noticed here were the boys in their slicked-back hair determined to enjoy the company of whatever lady they happened to be chatting with. This, I could only assume, was the optimum place to close a deal and bring home the goods, "the goods" being anything from marriage to a business merger, or just a good night of *grunde'malking*.

"So, Miss Lesinger, concerning Tony…"

She was about to place a cigarette between a pair of freshly decorated lips when her head turned down to me sharply, her voice a harsh whisper. "Mr. Baddings! This is not the time—"

"Well, if you whisper like that and attract attention to yourself by not acting normally, then yeah, this isn't the time nor the place. Or did you notice that when you came out here, no one seemed to care?"

I watched her resume the lighting of her cigarette, nonchalantly looking around her as she blew her first drag's smoke away from us. I didn't have a care about becoming the focus of the others' attentions. Judging from the amount of pheromones being exchanged between couples, we were the farthest things from their minds.

"Just keep the tone down," I advised, "act as if you don't care, and enjoy your smoke. I'll do the talking."

From my inner pocket, I produced my mini-pipe. Little indulgence was about the size of my palm, and good for social situations like this. Then I pulled out a small pouch of weed and packed the bowl. I was relieved when she struck a match for me and lit my smoke as I suckled on the other end of the pipe; she was still miffed, but maybe not as much as I initially thought.

"Thanks, Miss Lesinger." I finally got a taste of the sweet leaf and, with a nod to her, I also puffed out a cloud of smoke to the shadows nearby, just to make certain no one was listening in on us.

"You wanted to know why Tony was bumped off," I began, "and while I've got a handle on the 'why', I'm not so sure about the 'who' anymore. Seems that Tony wanted to enter the antiques business. His first score, though, was an item in popular demand. In fact, the supplier Tony tried to connect with—your good Dr. Hammil at the Ryerson, in fact—was already in bed with many of the folks here tonight, selling off quite a few museum finds for a tidy profit, then rewriting history in the Acquisition Department."

"No!" Miss Lesinger's mouth fell open in surprise. "Dr. Hammil was illegally selling off some of the Ryerson's inventory?"

"Maybe not the most premier ones, but yeah. He was enjoying his own little side business and some of the perks of upper-tier society besides, unbeknownst to the Ryerson staff. And this is where we get confused with the 'who' behind Tony's death."

"But we know that Capone was behind it." She shrugged.

"We know that, but someone had to nock that arrow and light it. It could either have been someone inside Tony DeMayo's inner circle, or the supplier himself."

"Dr. Hammil could have killed Tony, you mean?"

"He could have been instrumental in some way. It wouldn't surprise me if he was the one who ratted out DeMayo to Capone's organization."

I paused to draw from my pipe, studying her partially-lit face. With her volunteer connection to the Ryerson, it was hard to believe she was entirely in the dark over Hammil's shenanigans. "But something tells me that some of these facts come as no surprise to you."

She balanced the cigarette between two fingers, her expression grew pensive. "You're referring to 'the score.' I imagine you mean the Singing Sword, don't you?" She then threw a slider that only Bruce Cunningham could conjure. "I saw it when it first arrived in Chicago."

I nearly coughed on my weed. She *saw* the damn thing? I think I liked this case better when it was just a mob hit. Now my client was linked to this talisman from my old stomping grounds. Just at the point where I thought I had this case closed…

"Really, Miss Lesinger?" I said evenly, trying not to give away my total astonishment.

"Julie, please. Miss Lesinger makes me sound like my mother."

"Okay, Julie." I replied with a nod. Gazing up at the stars for a moment, I decided to keep her talking about the Sword. I needed to find out how much she knew…which, I was praying to the Fates, wasn't a lot.

"You know, I keep feeling as if I'm on the verge of opening a case within a case. What's with all the fuss over this particular trinket?"

"It's a find that archeologists dream about, Billi." Her eyes caught the light from the mansion, and I could hear it in her voice: This was something that fascinated her unlike anything she had ever known. "Imagine a sword of European design, discovered in a sealed tomb of Ancient Egypt. Mysteries like the Singing Sword are cornerstones that theses, symposiums, and careers are built on." Then her tone changed. She sounded disappointed. "But sadly, it was Eva who found it. This was going to be her greatest find, provided that she took care to consult her on-site archeologists about what she found, that is. "

"You insinuated in my office that Eva was a bit of a loose cannon at the Ryerson."

"She supposedly studied history at the finishing school her father shipped her off to, but I doubt that she'd know the value of a true find unless it came from Tiffany's. That doesn't deter her from being a little too quick in alerting the press sometimes. Since the tomb of King Tutankhamen was discovered back in '22, archeology has become all the rage. Eva convinced her daddy to finance her overseas adventures. I was privy to the reports from the Ryerson staff she only showed up on site when something was discovered, ready to take the credit for it. I also learned that the real archeologists were thrilled whenever Eva was somewhere other than the site." She shook her head in exasperation and contempt. "I still remember the day we received a wire declaring that Eva had discovered the 'true' resting place of King Tut."

"Safe to assume that her revolutionary find was nothing more than a scam cooked up by the local boys?"

Julie nodded, taking a quick puff of her cigarette. Did little to mask the bitterness in her face.

"If she had succeeded in going public with the discovery, it would have been the iceberg to Ryerson's *Titanic*. She's a benefactor, and that gives her some sway…but I have watched Hammil and his staff avoid potentially disastrous situations. Once they received Eva's wire about the Singing Sword, it became top priority to keep her quiet."

Filing that nugget away, I went on. "So being the lowly volunteer, how did you manage to get a glimpse of it, let alone get access to these sensitive wires?"

"You've met Dr. Hammil. You've seen the condition of his office. I tried to find reasons to go there so I could catch a glance at what was on his desk." She chuckled, quite pleased with her resourcefulness. "I assure you, Billi, I wasn't supposed to be on the inside of anything. Hammil loved to make it clear that I was only a volunteer. When acquisitions arrive from various digs, I merely assist with the registering and tagging. Nothing more than busy work, but it would still infuriate my father if he were ever to find out I'm connected with an institution he despises so much. It was an opportunity I couldn't pass up, menial as the administrative work is, because any experience at The Ryerson is bound to lead me on to bigger and better things. Besides," she added with a suggestive wink, "sometimes I could push that envelope with Hammil and extend the boundaries of my position."

Being the looker she was, I bet she pushed pretty hard. "So how much could you get away with?"

She grinned modestly. "Oh, not as much as you would think. But I did get an inside peek at Acquisitions from time to time. When the Singing Sword arrived, I was at the right place at the right time. I was the only volunteer in Acquisitions that day, along with two full-time staff members." She paused, a smile absently forming on her face at the memory. "Billi, you should have seen it. It looked liked as if it had been created only yesterday. Not a single scratch, blemish, or mark on it. All of us were taken by it."

The smile faded, and so did the wonder in her voice. "Hammil was apparently expecting its arrival, but he'd gotten caught in traffic across town. I'd never seen him so angry when he caught us cataloging it. He swore to fire all of us—even me, the volunteer—if word got out that the Singing Sword had arrived. It was pretty frightening, Billi. For a moment, I thought he was actually going to use it on us!

"The next day, I was barred from Acquisitions altogether. It was back to sorting books and taking head counts of school groups."

So, Doc Hammil wasn't beyond threatening a Lesinger? He really did think this Sword was his ticket. And to assure her silence along with two other staff members? He must've been a real demon that day!

"Doesn't sound like the most exciting of jobs." This girl could have whatever she wanted in life, and yet she chose to suffer in the trenches at the Ryerson. She had to have a good reason. "So why did you stay?"

"Because my father has mandated that I stay in Chicago," she replied with a sigh. "If I leave, I am on my own…financially as well as personally. I've been fascinated by ancient cultures and relics ever since I was a little girl, visiting the castles of Europe and the pyramids of Egypt, and I excelled in art and anthropology classes at college. The Ryerson is the best place to explore all of those interests at once."

"Not the only place, Julie."

"No, but the *best*, even as a volunteer cataloguing rare finds. Had Dr. Hammil simply told my father what he wanted to hear about our family's lineage, I could have held a very prominent position at The Ryerson." Her face twisted in disgust. "But my position—such as it is—was still lofty enough to catch the attention of a mobster. I guess it's true what they say about institutions of higher learning."

"What do the all-knowing 'they' say?" I asked.

"That you trade common sense for a college degree," she smirked. "You would think I am smart enough to tell when I'm being played."

"Considering the way tonight went for me, I can tell you this: It happens to the best of us."

Julie winked at me. "I should have warned you about Eva. She loved to join Tony and me whenever she was in town, and she was either Benny's date or some guy named Paul…Pauley…something like that. It was pathetic watching her try and wedge herself between the two of us. I put nothing past her."

After tonight, neither would I.

I also wouldn't have put anything past Julie Lesinger. Not that Julie was in the same class as Eva, mind you; I'm just dwarf enough to admit that my first impression of her being the "spoiled rich bitch" was far from accurate. For one thing, I hadn't pinned her as someone passionate about academic pursuits. From the pictures in the news rags, she seemed more prone to hot jazz, cocktails, and parties that outlasted the night—not researching and identifying treasure from ancient tombs. Second, I had to grudgingly acknowledge the luck she possessed. To be a volunteer who, at best, was given the grunt work no one else wanted, and she winds up being one of the few people in Chicago to see the Singing Sword? Not bad, Julie. Not bad. Wish I had that kind of luck when rolling the bones!

"You know, Julie, just because ol' Sam Hammil believed himself on a higher plane didn't mean it was the truth. I think the Doc was as much in the dark on the Singing Sword mystery as anyone."

"Really? What makes you say that?"

"Let's just say we had a heart-to-heart over it before he died. All he was certain of was its worth to his reputation. If he were able to figure out how the Singing Sword came to appear in an Ancient Egyptian tomb, it would be an accomplishment that would shake things up in his academic circles, plus it would get him out from under the thumb of whoever was keeping him in the black market."

I took another long drag before continuing with a hunch I needed to play concerning Julie and her take on tonight…not to mention her earlier comments about Hammil. "Like this merger between your father and Rothchild. Quite an accomplishment, it sounds like."

As she looked down on me (strictly a height thing, in this case), Julia kept her cigarette close, the smoke easing its way from between her lips.

"A blessing?" She shook her head, trying not to laugh. "Do you know why this merger is happening?"

I didn't bother to shake my head. I had a feeling Julie was going to tell me either way. She was wound up like a clockwork scene moving as fast as the music and its gears could run.

"Neither the Rothchilds nor the Lesingers had boys. Just me and Eva. Our fathers, in between their bouts of outdoing and out-donating one another, have been trying to figure out what to do with the empires they have built. After all, women do not make good businessmen."

"Does Eva share your disdain of this merger?"

"You were standing next to her when her father made that 'grandchildren' wisecrack. Both our fathers are hoping beyond hope we'll get married before they die, so they can pass on the business to their sons-in-laws or male grandchildren." Julie gave me a smirk. "I suppose we turned out to be disappointments, Mr. Baddings."

"Billi. Mr. Baddings makes me sound like my father," I said with a wink.

"Billi." Her smile suited her. *She should do it more often*, I thought to myself as she went on.

"My father would have been a happier man if I were his son, and not his daughter. But at least I am my own person, and not pretending to be something else merely to please daddy...unlike my counterpart."

"Well, your counterpart will be facing a disappointment in her future equal to that of discovering the Singing Sword without getting the credit. I'll bet you a coffer of gold coins she'll be sauntering into my office first thing Monday morning, so sure I have lost a somewhat profitable client that she'll probably try and undercut my normal fee."

"What makes you think I'm not going to fire you now, Billi?" Julia asked, a dark eyebrow slowly arching as she took another long draw from her cigarette, bathing her face in a warm orange glow.

"Well, the fact that you're calling me 'Billi,' that you're still talking to me, and that you're wearing a sweet smile are all subtle hints that you're not too pissed. So now that you at least know the 'why' behind Tony DeMayo's passing, I guess the only thing for me to do now is close this case and bill you for services rendered."

She took one final puff of the cigarette before dropping it to the stone floor of the patio, grinding it out with a single, quick twist of her high-heeled foot. "You're right, Billi. At least now I know that Tony was killed over the Singing Sword, even if the rest of the answers remain out of reach."

"Spoken like a true apprentice," I said with a confident nod.

Her eyes stayed with mine for a moment, and I gave a delighted chuckle. Julie had just unwittingly quoted a good number of apprentices I've known in my day. It was always the apprentice's duty to shuttle weapons, books, and the assorted talismans back and forth from a study to a battlefield, always watching from the dugout when the mages cast those "home run" spells. It was not out of the ordinary to hear an apprentice say something like *"The Stone of Ifyea remains out of reach."* Gotta love those apprentices.

"Sorry, that's just a saying I heard a lot when I was growing up," I explained. "About things being out of reach, I mean."

"Must have been one interesting place where you grew up, Billi." She smiled warmly.

I decided to test the waters. "Well, I won't lie to you...mountain dragons were a severe pain in the ass."

Julia let out a titter, shaking her head in exasperation at my hometown references. "Billi, *what* are you talking about?"

"Those things get cranky and stay cranky until food is brought to them, and in many cases, that food takes the form of some virginal sacrifice. Still, an easier choice compared to the other option."

"Okay, I'll play in your imagination for a spell." Her head tilted to one side, sending a few locks of midnight-black hair across her forehead. "And what was the other option?"

"Send in the exterminators."

I tapped my pipe on the heel of my polished black shoes and placed it back in my jacket's inner pocket. It was time to head on inside, if not head on home. "Julie," I said with a polite smile, "it was definitely an experience working for you. I'm going to call a cab, then call it a night. I'll write up a final bill for you Monday morning."

"Billi, there's no reason for you to call for a cab. Considering how dull my father's friends are, you will probably be asleep somewhere in the estate by the time it gets here. Believe me, I know these types. The Egyptian mummies I cataloged for the Ryerson are livelier than this crowd. I'll have my driver take you home."

"I appreciate that, Julie." And I did. A cab ride from here would severely bite into the profits of this case.

"Look for a silver-grey car, black top, pulling up in, say, ten minutes?"

"See your driver in ten." I nodded. "Good night."

Julie seemed to float back into the party like a wraith across the battlements of a haunted watchtower, her head lifted slightly and a gentle hand raised in greeting—a greeting that eventually came to rest on another's shoulder. One of those obtuse "friends of the family," no doubt. Now that she was in the light of the Lesinger mansion, I could enjoy the sight of her before she moved off to call for her driver.

She was still my Lady Trouble, I knew that for sure, because she was bringing back to me an aspect of my life that I thought was far behind me and best left there.

The final bill from Julie would hold Miranda and the business well off for a few months, and I didn't foresee any extravagant expenses in tracking down the Sword. I had to keep a profile so low that a Trysillian swamp worm would look tall to me. Still, there was some solace in realizing I had closed this case and managed to stay above ground. I must be getting better at this detective thing.

Too bad the whole "private" part of this job prevented me from sounding my own war horn over this. *"Yes, Ladies and Gentlemen, hire the only dwarf able to poke his pudgy nose into Al Capone's business and live to talk about it!"* It would make one hell of a radio advertisement.

Just thinking his name slapped me harder than a mace. Capone would probably give me a few weeks of peace, and then expect me to begin my new job as his personal advisor in finding and handling the Singing Sword. What the hell did I really know about it? Not much, other than *"only the meek and mild could wield it"*, the body count was rising, and no one—including the self-proclaimed expert—knew where it was in the Greater Chicago area. Now, I could see that black sand of Death slowly slipping from the top chamber to the bottom in the hourglass of borrowed time, and it was slipping pretty fast.

A crisp chill, probably coming off one of the Great Lakes, pinched me on the cheek as I stood once again on the stone steps of the estate's entrance, where this evening had started for me a few hours ago. I had to give Little Miss Eva an amount of credit for dreaming up this evening, a sure-fire way to get me right where I live. Instead of parting with a chunk of change for a tux, a client, and a taxicab ride home, I was getting a chauffeur for the return trip too. *Not bad, Baddings, I thought to myself. You were riding with the Guardians tonight.*

The silver-grey limousine pulled up, its lights flashing for a moment in my eyes as it pulled around the circle of the driveway. A ride worthy of a Dwarven emperor or Elvish king, only nicer! The limo stood out from the other ebony chariots patiently awaiting their masters. I got a nod from the driver, who stayed put and readjusted his grip on the steering wheel. With a soft *click-click*, the passenger door opened automatically. *Neat trick*, I thought. *The driver didn't look like a magician.*

The magic that opened that door had a different kind of power altogether, and I paused before climbing into the cabin of the limo, raising a bushy eyebrow at the sorceress responsible for the trick.

"Sorry for the wait, Billi," Julie Lesinger smiled. "I had to say goodbye to some people and then sneak out the servant's entrance so I wouldn't get an earful from Daddy."

"He won't mind you coming into town at this hour?"

"I'll be surprised if he notices my absence. Right now, my father's priorities are getting the best photo opportunities." She slid to the opposite end of the long seat. "Your chariot awaits, Mr. Baddings."

Step into my parlor, said the *drinék* to the *valley thir*.

CHAPTER THIRTEEN

THE THINGS YOU HEAR AT MICK'S

The limousine rocked lightly as I hopped inside. Once the valet shut the door behind me, I gave the driver my home address—modest in comparison to the mansion I was leaving behind, but still my own little hovel in the great concrete grove that was Chicago.

Even with the absence of street lamps and interior lighting, I could still make out her form across from me. Wearing a dark crown of curls that gently cascaded down the back of her neck and across her shoulders, she was a vision that I wouldn't doubt could persuade men to charge into battle, straight to their deaths. It was the kind of beauty that inspired loyalty, devotion, desire. (Well, the last part, for sure. I couldn't help but feel an urge kicking up from parts of me that hadn't known a woman's touch for quite some time.)

Julie Lesinger was still cut from the same cloth as Eva, so I couldn't let that urge for even a tiny "tavern tickle" throw me off-guard. She had her reasons for accompanying me all the way into town. It was hardly for my company, stimulating as it might be. (She didn't strike me as a baseball kind of gal.) I wanted to know why she was here, and I knew if I were patient enough, she'd come around and tell me.

All right, screw patience! Hell, I'm a dwarf. We aren't known for it.

"Mind if I ask why you're taking this ride with me, Julie?"

"Perhaps I wanted assurance that you made it back to your place safely."

"I'm a big boy; I can take care of myself."

She gave a snicker. Probably at the *"big boy"* comment. Eh, let it slide, Baddings.

After a few moments of staring at the distant city lights, she finally said, "Perhaps I've been thinking about your closing the case on Monday."

I tugged at my bowtie, letting it fall loose around my neck. "Julie, you wanted to know the why behind Tony's demise, and you got it. What more do you want?"

"Billi, this Singing Sword that Tony died trying to steal is nothing more than a catalogue number, some inscriptions on a blade that no one can read, and a mystery without an answer. Why would Tony risk his neck on something like this? Why would a mobster like Capone want something like the Singing Sword? And why would Tony double-cross his boss when he was next in line to succeed him?"

She turned away from me again, and I could just make out her ghostly reflection in the car window. "This must be the frustrated academic in me. I'm not satisfied with the answers, so I continue to ask questions."

"I wish I could tell you more."

Yeah, I did. I wanted to tell her that DeMayo bit off more of his boss' power than he could chew, and Capone made him choke on it. I wanted to tell her all about the Singing Sword and its immense power—power that was attracting the attention of everyone from Gangland bosses to our own beloved Uncle Sam. How could I explain to her, an inquisitive mind in a society ready to keep her barefoot and pregnant in a glitzy castle somewhere, that what she already knew was more than enough?

She spoke up again before I could. "In some strange way, I loved him. I truly did. It wasn't true love, nor was he a prince on a white horse, but that didn't mean I slept with him because he was convenient. When we were alone, things were…different. I suppose I let myself believe he was genuinely interested." She bowed her head with a spiteful laugh. "The higher you ascend in social circles, the harder sincerity is to come by."

"It's harder still when you walk among thieves, rogues, and highwaymen, Julie."

She turned to look at me. "Perhaps you're right. Perhaps I believed we had something that was never there. Or maybe I'm just trying to convince myself I wasn't part of Tony's plan to break into the Ryerson."

"What's done is done," I said gently, trying not to sound like I was some kind of know-it-all Elvish holy man. "From what I've found out on this case, Tony got himself killed over an over-decorated letter-opener. His choice."

"I suppose." I picked up a slight tremble in her voice.

We were nearing the city limits now, the trees now registering as momentary interruptions of the Chicago skyline. Once again, I caught the faint apparition of Julia Lesinger lost in contemplating the skyscrapers now surrounding us like the towering bluewoods of Sorcerer's Grove. For a moment, I wanted a quick peek into this girl's soul, to find out what truth resided there. She was searching for something. Damned if I knew what it was, but it wasn't beyond Julia Lesinger to come out and tell me. This girl was far from dancing around her desires, even if the drum circle did lay down a heavy beat.

City traffic was still steady, even though it was nearing the witching hour between Saturday night and Sunday morning. My flop was now only a few blocks away. Whatever she wanted to ask of me, her time was running out. After this, it would be a Monday-morning formality of closing the case and settling the final invoice.

At last, she turned to me with an odd smile that conjured up more images of those pain-in-the-ass mountain dragons I had mentioned earlier, sunning themselves in a glen after devouring a herd or two. (I'd swear they'd smile in contentment at times like that.)

I don't think Julie would have appreciated the analogy between herself and a dragon, but both beauty and beast had their poetic grace about them. Apart from the obvious differences (Julie was scale-free, as far as I could tell), both shared the look in the eyes: A desire to always stay in a moment of bliss and comfort.

In the dim light that filtered into the car from the streetlamps, Julie took my hand and began studying it, perhaps wondering what kind of life had roughened my skin. As she turned my hand over and opened it, gently stroking it, letting her long, tapered fingers run the length of my short, stubby ones, I was reminded of just how long it had been since I had known the fun and the physical gratification of a good *grunde'malking*.

Honestly, I didn't think I was her type. What was that human saying about curiosity and a cat? Kitty here was daring to go where few in this world would even think to tread.

The driver slowed down the car in front of my building, hazarding a nervous glance in the rear-view mirror. He seemed to know this pattern of Julie's. I pulled my eyes away from the back of his head to meet her gaze.

"James," she spoke up to the driver, not taking her eyes off me, "Mr. Baddings and I have some business to discuss tonight. I will give you a ring tomorrow morning."

"Miss?" he asked nervously. "What should I tell Mr. Lesinger?"

"Tell him whatever you like."

For a suggestion, it sounded awfully like a warning.

Poor dink. What was he going to tell Daddy Lesinger? *I'm sorry, Mr. Lesinger, but your daughter Julia is currently getting the hardest, wildest tavern tickle by a four-foot-one dwarf from an alternative universe.* Nah, I didn't think that would go over too well, and I didn't relish the idea of taking on his hired muscle outside my flop at four in the morning, wearing only a bath towel and wielding the axe kept under my pillow. (*That* was sure to get the neighbors talking.)

I got out of the limo and turned to offer Julie a hand. When she stepped out into the streetlamp's harsh glare, it was the first time I had ever seen her drained of color and emotion—a fleeting moment but a sobering one, nonetheless.

I looked over at the driver, who was still trying to figure out what to tell Daddy Lesinger. "You heard the girl," I said before closing the car door, locking it with a lift of its handle. "Home, James."

I remember hearing my keyring hitting the small table by the door, the same table where I keep a yardstick so I can reach light switches. However, I didn't get the chance to grab the ruler this time. Julie had already kicked off her high heels and reached over me to shut the door.

Feeling the softness of the tiny area rug underneath her feet, she dropped to her knees (I know, this would be a dream come true for humans, but Julie would have to be a gifted contortionist to give me such a delight) to kiss me. Her tongue was soft, and I savored the sweetness of her mouth as I would a fine stout aged and brewed by masters of the masters. She gripped my shoulders tightly, and only the sound of her taking a deep breath filled the room. Once she got her fill of air, a sigh escaped through her nose, accompanied by the gentlest of moans.

Perhaps you're thinking that *grundle'malking* between dwarves and other races is an acquired taste. Ah, but ask another race about the experience, and all they can do is smile at the memory. Yeah, we're short. We're fat. We've got hair that remains total strangers to combs, and beards so thick that you could lose wood sprites in them. So why was she doing this? Perhaps it was my attitude. We're the bad boys of the good guys, and I don't doubt there was a curiosity factor working here. For her, anyway.

As for me, I wasn't going to turn down a night between the sheets with Julia Lesinger. Are you kidding? Our professional relationship is over. We're consenting adults. No problem.

Dwarves are underestimated for a lot of things because of their height, one of the biggest myths being that we don't know our way around a woman. The average Dwarven family—and let me stress that, *average*—is ten dwarvlings. There is a reason why Dwarven families are so large, and it is not because we love to procreate. Well, we love to procreate, obviously, but that's just it. We look at *grundle'malking* not as a duty nor a chore, but a passionate, full-contact indoor sport.

And I'm here to tell you: I am the Big Bambino of *Grundle'malking*.

Julie pulled me closer, refusing to let this lip service cease as she shimmied her way out of that fine evening dress. It became ever clearer that the "kiss at the door" was merely me "swinging two in the batter's circle" before taking the plate. The frantic stripping of our clothes brought back a lot of memories of *grundle'malking* in this world that had been hasty, impulsive, and fleeting. Tonight was a step closer to home, where we dwarves took our time in making these intimate moments last.

Still, I had to be careful. I kept wanting to lose myself in her arms, to try and grasp some kind of belief that she wanted me. I couldn't deny wondering about her intentions, her real reason for tonight. The more I lingered on this, the harder I kissed her. The harder I kissed her, the harder other parts of me became.

Julie stepped back, gasping for air. The blinds of my apartment cast horizontal shadows across that beautiful face of hers, and in her eyes dwelled a blind fury of emotions. She had to be wondering what was turning her on, but by the way she had just ripped open my shirt, I don't think she cared. Her hands brushed along the bushy auburn hair covering my chest and followed the curves of my belly with a fairy's touch. That was when she gave a slight gasp—whether from the size of my beer gut, or the reality that she was molesting a Highlands Dwarf, I couldn't say.

Julie stared at my body with morbid fascination. "I don't normally like hairy chests," she whispered.

I slipped off the suspenders, letting them hang from my waistband as I removed the rest of the dress shirt. "Just wait until you see my back."

She finally stood up and looked over her shoulder at the modest bed silently calling to us both. It was big enough for two. Not because of the frequency of my nocturnal guests, mind you. I tend to roll around a lot in my sleep. (Not tonight, though. Not tonight.)

Julie took a few steps further from me and quickly slipped out of her camisole. Even in the medley of light and shadow, I could tell her body lived up to everything I had imagined. Her toned legs seemed to have no end, but where they finally did was a destination that promised sweet pleasures that would last well into the morning. The same horizontal shadows that touched her face also adhered to her stomach, curved and tight in all the right places. Her breasts were now in the open air and from the looks of her tight, hard nipples, they were all the happier to be free of concealment. Plus, my earlier assumption was confirmed: Julia Lesinger's body was indeed devoid of dragon scales.

I must've been eyeing her like a gourmet meal, because when I finally made eye contact with her again, she was smiling. A strange form of flattery, but I could see she enjoyed being fawned over. Most of the guys at Daddy's party—Daddy's party that was leagues away from us now—played that game of disinterest, of *ennui* in the presence of undeniable beauty.

From the upper-crust pretty boys to a dwarf detective, huh? All right, Julie, I'll play your game tonight. She needed some education anyway, and class was most assuredly in session.

I took her by the hips and pushed her past the bed, not stopping until we hit the wall. The impact earned me a delighted cry from my new pupil. In the moments that slipped by after I parted her legs, she discovered one of the reasons why I loved being a dwarf. By the sound of her moans—moans that grew into louder and louder wails of excitement as I continued to savor her—*she* couldn't help but love that I was a dwarf.

Julie nearly collapsed on top of me as her body shuddered from waves of erotic spasms that hit her hard, again and again. Her harpy imitation now subsided into gasps and sighs of relief, pleasure, and expectation for what was to come.

Taking another deep breath, she pulled herself free of the wall and staggered to the bed where she crawled on top of the covers, turning to face me. (Not that I would have minded if she faced in the other direction. Even walking away from me, the view was lovely. A reminder of the rolling moors and breathtaking valleys of Gryfennos.) She gave a purr while on all fours, her hair falling like a veil across half of her face. She looked at me and sighed as another aftershock passed through her body.

"Billi," she whispered.

She wanted me to drop the boxers and let loose, but first, I wanted to make sure she knew what was heading her way: *"Billi's Battle-Axe,"* I called it when scouring the taverns with my drinking pals in search of a quick *grundle'malk*. Slipping my hands inside the waistband, I pulled the boxers down just low enough for them to be loose, and then let them fall.

The light from outside was hitting me just right, and I watched Julie's jaw drop slowly at the heat I was packing.

She blinked, and then finally swallowed the lump that was forming in her throat.

"*Billi!*" she exclaimed.

This was the worst assumption that human women always made about dwarves. There's no real way to prepare a woman outside of my race for the hard reality. It is a truth that so many races are oblivious to, and this ignorance continues in this world to mislead the opposite sex. Tonight, Julie Lesinger would discover the third advantage in being a dwarf...

There is a difference between being short and being small.

My eyes opened slowly, the sunlight streaming through the blinds rudely reminding me that it was time to get my ass out of bed and get a head start on the final paperwork for the Lesinger case. I was sore. Last night, my Lady Trouble performed contortions and acrobatics that would make a court jester green with envy. I couldn't recall the last time a woman had given me a workout like that. I know it was back in Acryonis and she might have been a crossblood, but Julie had outshone them all. As I stretched like a mountain lion after enjoying its prey, a single thought repeated again and again in my head:

Worth the wait.

A cursory glance at the surrounding walls reassured me that the paint was still there. The worry that her screams were going to remove it off the walls crossed my mind several times last night. I moved to get up, but my muscles let me know just how stupid of an idea that was. Guess Julie Lesinger wouldn't be the only one walking funny today.

Eventually, I rolled over to the edge of the bed and gave another good stretch, locking my fingers and reaching above me with a hearty groan. I tipped my head as far to the left as I could, and a very satisfying *pop-pop-pop-pop-pop* resounded in my head. Nothing like a good night's *grundle'malking* to rejuvenate the spirit and ease the brain. I felt like a new dwarf, ready to receive the last payment from Miss "Now I Know

The Truth About Dwarves" Lesinger and then find the Sword of Arannahs before Capone or the Feds. Yeah, Sunday was going to be a good day, provided I didn't get thrown out by the landlord for making too much noise the night before.

I opened the window slightly. An advantage to where my flop was located in this modest building was that I could usually catch the breeze off the lake, and on a day like this, it would freshen up the place.

I then noticed another pleasant scent tickling my nose, that fresh-ground scent that greeted me on the mornings when I'd have breakfast at Mick's. My coffee pot was already on the stove and still warm with the burner underneath at its lowest setting. Next to an empty mug sat my sugar bowl. In the center of the modest table—where on mornings like this I would usually treat myself to a Cream of Wheat topped with honey, a strong pot of tea, and some toast lightly buttered—the memo pad I kept in my kitchen for grocery lists, messages, and the like waited for me with its pencil resting across it, placed very purposefully so I wouldn't miss it. The message was written with a refined hand, a hand that had grown up surrounded by privilege and elegance at all times. Either Julie must have been one early riser, or able to wear me out to the point of me being lost in a deep slumber. The note brought a smile to my face.

> Billi,
>
> To say last night was incredible would be an understatement. I was not sure about where we were headed last night, but it has been a long time since I felt that good. Something in your touch showed me I needed a little more than just a private eye on the payroll. You're not what I expected, and I hope last night won't be our last. I'll call you Monday, Big Red.
>
> —J.
>
> P.S. I helped myself to some coffee and sugar. I brewed enough for you, too. I hope I didn't make it too strong.

Big Red. Hey, I liked that. Never been called "Big Red" before.

I ripped out the note from the memo pad and walked over to the corkboard I had by the door, laughing to myself as I crossed the modest flop. Even on its last day, this case was getting crazier by the minute. Okay, sure, maybe she was just interested in another repeat training session with "Billi's Battle-Axe," but I was intending to enjoy this for everything it was worth.

The corkboard, high enough for me to notice it as I was going out, had numerous scraps of paper. Some of the scraps were reminders of rent and other bills due. My eye fell on the reminder to keep an eye on Benny, just in case he was deciding to branch out in his moonlighting to other areas of Capone's business. *Why stop at embezzlement,* I had written on this scrap of paper.

I guess that note could come down.

I pushed the thumbtack into the cork surface with a good, solid shove. With a self-gratifying nod, I stared at the note. The morning breeze played with the paper, gently lifting it against the thumbtack along with the other notes surrounding it.

Yeah, today was going to be a good day.

"Well, well, well," chided the man over the jingle of his diner's door. "If it ain't the Sherlock Holmes of Chicago! Good to see ya walking above ground, Scrappie."

"Good to be above ground, ya crazy Pollack!" I snapped back, taking my usual seat at the end of the bar. "Think ya got a Sunday Special back there with my name on it?"

"Lemme take a look."

Sundays were always slow in the city, but after spending quality time with the clerics, priests, and other holy men of this realm, spending an hour whipping up a lunch for the family just didn't make anyone rejoice. Mick's Diner was a popular stop for the families in their church best, and today was—as I mentioned before—a good day. For me, it was the end of one of the riskiest cases of my career. For Mick, it was business as usual...and as usual, business couldn't be better.

"Okay, Baddings, here you go." Mick presented a modest toasted sandwich before me with a side of what looked like a hearty chicken-noodle soup.

"What—" I stared at the soup. "—the hell—" I peeked at the sandwich, burning my fingertips on its melted cheese. "—is this?"

"Billi," Mick shook his head, clicking his tongue. "You shouldn't be talking like that on The Lord's Day."

"Well, some God-fearing Christians would have a problem with *you* earning a living on The Lord's official day off."

Ah, the shrug. I love Mick's *"Whadaya talkin' about?!?"* shrug, his magical shield against my verbal slings and arrows. "Hey, c'mon, Billi...I'm doin' the Lord's Work here, encouragin' fellowship outside of His house and feedin' His flock."

"A regular Good Samaritan, ain't ya, Mick?" I sighed heavily, motioning to the dish. "And now I ask again, what the hell *is* this?"

"Today's Special." Mick rolled his eyes at the expression I was giving him. "Billi, man does not live by Reuben and chili alone. That goes double for a dwarf," he said proudly, poking me in the chest. "That is homemade chicken soup, and *that*," he said motioning to the sandwich, "is a ham-and-cheese, toasted on the grill just enough so that it melts in your mouth."

"This is not the Sunday Special." I grumbled.

"This is *this* Sunday's Special." Mick slapped me on my arm and beamed. "Dig in and enjoy."

Giving another disgruntled grumble, I took a spoonful of the chicken-noodle soup, which had cooled to a comfortable temperature by now.

I must admit...not bad.

"So, Sherlock Scrappie, d'ya think now you can talk about this hush-hush case of yours?"

You would think Mick would leave well enough alone, but not this crazy Pollack. "Now what part of 'private' in my vocation completely eludes you? Mick, I've gotta—"

"Nah-nah-nah, I don't want names or anything like that, just some of the details, y'know? C'mon and lemme see what it's like in your world."

My *world*. A funny choice of words there, Mick.

"Let me tell you something, pal: My world is definitely not for the faint-of-heart."

"How so?"

Ever see a guy in full armor bitten in two by a low-flying dragon?

"It's complicated, Mick. Very complicated." I slurped down one of the longer noodles and chewed on it for a moment while eyeballing Mick. I wasn't going to get off the hook that easily. "Okay, I could probably get away with telling you this. Those troglodytes who paid your place a visit earlier?"

"You mean..." And then Mick leaned in, his voice dropping to his detective's whisper. "Moran's boys?"

"Yeah," I whispered back. "Those guys. They're not going to be bugging your establishment in the future."

Mick cocked his head to one side. "Now how can you be so sure?"

"Well, when I had dinner with Capone..."

"Capone!" he shouted, causing many of his diners to stop and look our way.

"And this," I nodded, giving my chicken soup a break and picking up a still-warm slice of the sandwich, "is exactly why you are not a detective, but still one of the best cooks in town."

I took an orc-sized bite of the ham-and-cheese (as I had worked up a healthy appetite from the night before), and in about my third chew I paused. I gave another chew. My next one was a bit slower, and I could feel a somewhat pensive look creeping across my face.

Mick noticed. "Billi?"

"Well, okay, maybe not the best cook anymore," I said, my mouth still full of sandwich.

"Problem with the sandwich?"

I nodded. "You got the melt-in-your-mouth part right," I replied, chewing as I spoke, "and this is definitely cheese, but it ain't cheddar... and this ham tastes a lot like salami."

"What?!?"

He immediately tore the second half of the sandwich apart. "I swear," he growled, "sometimes I wish I wasn't a sucker for the hardships!"

I swallowed down the first bite. Couldn't help it. I was hungry. "Well, it's not a bad taste, just unique. Guess nobody said anything because you are the master of the chili. They probably thought you were trying something different."

"I am," he grumbled. "His name is Petro. Good kid, but a little lacking in communication skills. He tends to be hanging on to the ways of the Old Country, know what I mean?"

"Yeah," I chuckled, venturing another bite of the odd-tasting sandwich. "I know." This time, it was harder to finish. I turned back to the soup. "So, this kid charmed his way into a job, huh?"

"Well, he whipped that soup together, and I was pretty impressed, so I told him what I wanted for this Sunday, but he kept insisting on the salami instead of just plain ol' ham. And I got a little gruff with him and he started saying why it should be salami and not ham, and the longer he argued with me, the more Italian he threw in. We got to a point where that was all he was speaking!"

"That's my Mick," I said with a grin. "Lord and master of his castle, but still willing to let the servants get in the last word!"

"Well, I didn't think I was letting him get the last word," Mick scoffed. "I didn't understand a damn word of that Italian. It was all Greek to me."

Now there was a new one on me. "Come again?"

"Oh, another saying you're not familiar with, huh?" he chuckled. "Well, unless you're really educated or you're from Greece, you can't understand Greek. Right? So if you don't understand something, we say, 'it's all Greek to me.'"

I sat there, noodling through the quirky saying. *It's all Greek to me.* If no one else understands it, it's all Greek. But what about the other way around? You stick with a language near and dear to you because no one else understands it. The Italians. The Chinese. Even I do it sometimes. Why? Because it's all Greek to everyone else. Everyone else, save for those few who know Greek. *It's all Greek to me.* Heh, that's a good one.

Holy shit.

I slapped a Lincoln on the bar. "Keep the change."

Mick blinked. "Billi, I just flipped through the other half of your sandwich as if it were a good book. I owe you."

I adjusted my fedora and hopped down from my barstool. "No, my friend, I'm the one who owes *you!*"

"For what?"

"For a bit of higher education from the streets," I smiled, tipping my hat to him. "Talk to you later!"

CHAPTER FOURTEEN

NOT THE SAME OL' SONG & DANCE

It's always tough to get a cab on Sundays, but pay a cabbie enough moolah and they will take a priest to the gates of Hell and back in time for morning Mass. When my ride finally arrived two blocks away (the second shift from Miller and Jackson, Inc. was parked across the street, so I had to take the back door and a few shortcuts to my pickup point), I made a quick stop at my office before rolling back up to the corner of 21st and Clarendon, where I had been "a friend of Lou's" and talked at length with Daphnie of the book-balancing and *grundle'malking* talents.

For another twenty, I had my cabbie leave the motor running. If my suspicions were true, I would need this driver's talents on call. That hourglass of borrowed time I pictured the night before was pouring a lot faster now.

I pounded on the speakeasy door, my breath still labored from the sprint across the street and down the alleyway. The hatch slid back and there was my favorite doorman, peering out and then down to see me.

"Y'got balls," he slurred through his still-healing jaw.

"Nice to know there are some things in this world we can agree on. Now we can either make this easy, or I can break your other jaw so you got a matching set. Open the friggin' door!"

In case the dink had a good grip on his heater this time, I used the awkward silence to enlighten him. "Look, pal, if you call your boss, he will tell you that filling me with lead would be a colossally bad career move on your part. If you want to enjoy a permanent early retirement, be my guest."

As he peered through the peephole at me, thinking about calling me on my dare, I could see the hourglass' bottom chamber continue to fill.

"I ain't got time to dick around!" I exploded. "Either pop me or let me in!"

The peephole lid shut, the door latch slid back, and there he was staring at me, the red in his face growing like the fire of an oncoming missile launched from a distant catapult.

Of course, I had to fan the flames. "I hate to ask you for a favor, mac, but is Daphnie around?"

"Y'gotta be kiddin' me…"

I took that abrupt answer as his trollish way of saying, *"No, Mr. Baddings, I'm not going to help you."* So dismissing the door troll, I took the detour to the stage where the band and showgirls put on productions that stretched well into the wee small hours of the evening. There were fresh scuff marks crisscrossing older scuff marks—the only remnants of a grand spectacle of jazz and flappers, all set on a stage where I barely had room to change my mind.

"Y'got ten minutes, Short Stuff!" came the doorman, summoning up his courage now that I was a good distance away.

There was no point in haggling with this dink like some common peddler at an open bazaar. Ten minutes was really all I could spare, anyway, so I had to make this time count.

I climbed up the small riser and walked around the stage for a moment, following the scuff marks as best as I could. At certain points in between where feet had been, there were gouges in the stage. I lowered myself to one knee, probing the tiny pinpricks in the wood with my fingertips. Whatever props were causing this kind of damage on a nightly basis were gradually drilling holes and cutting grooves into the stage. The damage was everywhere, but carefully sweeping the riser with my hand, I could tell they were happening within close proximity of one another.

"Lookin' for an audition, little fellah?" asked a voice behind me.

She wasn't as busty and curvaceous as Daphnie, but even in her modest street clothes, she boasted a fine athletic frame. (Her dress hemline was also high enough to give me a nice look at her defined calves). Although the bags under her eyes were so deep that groceries could be carried in them, there was still an impish glimmer in her dark gaze and an edge in her attitude.

I also felt my smile get a bit brighter. The girl was a redhead. Nice.

"Well, I don't think I would look quite right in the outfits you girls wear," I said, giving her a playful wink. "Been a long night, I gather?"

"If only you were to slip into my shoes, pal. Last night was murder," she huffed as she pulled a box of cigarettes from the inside pocket of her coat. I struck a flame for her, to which she nodded as she took her first drag. "Thanks," she said, blowing the smoke over my head. "So, you a talent scout or an undercover Fed?"

"If I answer with the first, you're going to be a lot nicer with me, aren't you?"

She chuckled as I stuck out my hand and introduced myself. "Billi Baddings. Private eye."

"Glenda."

"Hey, Casanova," the door troll howled across the club, "Five minutes!"

Glenda lifted a thin eyebrow as she looked over to him, and then turned back to me. "Let me guess. You're the guy who did that to Bruiser?"

"*Bruiser?*" I asked.

I shot a glance of my own at the doorman (for which I got a scowl and a tapping of his wristwatch in return). "Well," I said with a shrug, "I guess the nickname suits him now."

I took a seat on the riser, looking up at the flapper with my charming Baddings smile. "I'm on a case that keeps bringing me back to this club. Just so you don't worry yourself over whom you're swapping words with, I'm not working for the Feds. All I'm doing is asking a few questions. Not the kind of questions that get people arrested."

Glenda's mouth twisted into a grimace. "How about getting people canned?"

"That all depends on the questions I ask," I replied with a gruff laugh.

"If you're investigating something that happened here, try investigating where the hell Daphnie was last night!"

Bingo. "Oh, Daphnie was AWOL last night?"

"Yeah, me and the rest of the girls were covering for her last night. Third time this month, too! Little bitch better watch herself. She may be in with the management, balancing the books and all, but we lowly entertainers aren't so attached to the Dancing Bookkeeper." She took a quick drag before continuing her rant. "She didn't bother calling or anything, and so here we are trying to make up for this gaping hole in our number."

I was about to fire off another question, but out of the corner of my eye, I caught movement at the door. Bruiser's wrist came up to his face again, his eyes fixed on his wristwatch. That dumb mook was actually counting down the last minute of the ten granted to me out of the goodness of his heart.

"Listen, Glenda," I said, still watching Bruiser mouthing the seconds. "You wouldn't happen to know another way out of here, would you?"

"Sure, I was just about to head out that way myself. But," she sighed heavily, "this will mean you'll be buying me breakfast from the bakery."

"The bakery?"

"Yeah." She smiled, taking a final drag of her cigarette. As Glenda crushed the butt out with her sole, she called out to the Bruiser, "I'm taking him out the front door, okay?"

Bruiser grunted, which I recognized as a troll's "yes." He didn't seem to mind the fact I was leaving through the secret door. Instead of being relieved about my leaving he appeared distracted. He kept turning his head back to the main door while trying to make certain I was well on my way out of there.

"The secret door to this place opens up to a bakery," Glenda spoke over her shoulder, leading me past dressing rooms and storerooms all lined with brick. No sound getting through these walls. "Poor guy running our front really wasn't happy about getting mixed up with us, you know? He resented getting bullied into this racket by the mob. He was all upset and rude to us until he started getting our business. It started with the hostesses wanting to offer up some nice desserts and pastries that go well with our cocktails. Then we had folks coming in and out, noticing this guy's work in both directions. Now he's just turning a blind eye, hoping the Feds don't come barging through his store to arrest his upscale customers."

"So Bruiser's okay with me leaving by this route?"

"He's definitely okay with it this morning. We're having some friends from Canada coming in for a brief stay."

No wonder Bruiser was so accommodating, nerve-wrecked, and hostile all in the same lumbering breath that he took with me. He couldn't afford my miniature innards decorating the alleyway on the same day that a truckload of Canada's best was scheduled to arrive. As badly as his damaged pride screamed for retribution, the shipment took priority. Guess I picked the right day to pay Bruiser's post a visit. But this was just the Luck of the Apprentice again, still with me as it was in my own flop last night. I couldn't help but wonder when that luck would run out...and when it did, how bad of a mark it was going to leave on me.

Glenda led me to a thick wall, an apparent dead end, and pointed to a brick just above her head. The cement around it was loosened, deliberately chiseled out so the brick would act as a latch. "Just give this a tap," she smiled, looking down at me.

I raised an eyebrow at her command. "You want to try that again, sister?"

Despite the futility of her request, she motioned again to the brick above her head. Then, as she looked down at me again, I saw the light go on in her eyes. Miss Sleepyhead finally figured it out.

"Oh yeah," she laughed nervously, a slight blush coming to her cheeks, "Sorry."

She reached up and a latch from somewhere inside that wall sounded with a dull thud and the entire wall now served as a doorway to an establishment rich in the smells of hot bread, fresh pastries, and strong coffee. (Guess the "poor guy" running the place had resigned himself to milking this unbidden opportunity for all it was worth.)

Once we were both in the storeroom, Glenda slowly pushed the hatch shut. "We have to be quiet," she whispered. "Just in case he's got early risers. And we have to make sure we hear the catch."

I nodded.

Yeah, the old swinging-wall trick. Damn, that brought back some fun memories of trekking through abandoned keeps in my youth: trying to find those secret passages, praying that we didn't come across any tourists trapped in these trick hatches, laughing when we would hear about groups of these dinks suiting up in their best armor to go rummaging through castle ruins and dungeons for buried treasure, sacred relics, or charmed weapons.

Stupid tourists. Didn't any of them ever stop to think that maybe these sites were abandoned *for a reason?*

With a dull *cka-thick,* the shelf unit now blended in with the rest of the wall again. We then tiptoed through the small storeroom and peered out into the bakery where only a short, portly man in a modest grey sweater and slacks, protected from his craft by a stained apron, quietly took count of the various rolls and loaves on display.

Glenda cleared her throat in the storeroom, twice, and then we entered into the store from behind his counter.

The baker just looked at us quietly, sizing me up while slowly stroking his thick black mustache. As I was a dwarf, there was not much to size up, but I'm sure he was asking himself what other sideshow attraction was going to walk out of his storeroom this morning. He shook his head and muttered something under his breath as he resumed taking inventory.

"Good morning, Sunshine," Glenda beamed, completely oblivious to the look in this baker's eyes. "How's about two coffees and a couple of croissants to go?"

I hoped Glenda was better at dancing than she was at reading people. While my money was as good as anyone else's, I could see in the old man's body language that we were the last people he wanted to serve. Before he became involved with Capone's speakeasy, he probably knew all of his customers by first name. And no doubt, they were more than customers, but loyal friends who were willing to cut breaks for one another when needed. Now his real bread and butter were nameless, faceless, privileged speakeasy customers and Organization members who wouldn't come to his aid if it ever hit the fan, be it the Feds, cops, or Capone himself. If he ratted out the Mob, his next business would involve undertakers and coffin makers. If he continued to play against the G, he faced every day having everything he built taken away. They—both Capone and the Feds—threatened to shut down his American Dream, and now he was trapped.

"Thanks, Gorgeous." Glenda smiled to the storekeeper. This bimbo was starting to lose points with me real quick. She didn't even bother to learn this guy's name? "See you later!" she sang out as the door closed behind us.

The sun was about to hit high noon—a blessing in itself, because there was a slight March chill lingering in the air. Maybe those golden rays would warm up the Windy City just a hint.

"So, Glenda, tell me," I said, taking a sip of the old man's coffee. Strong. "Does Bruiser always work the door?"

"Mondays and Tuesdays are his nights off."

"And yours as well?"

"I'm an honest working girl!" She scoffed. "I'm here, along with the musicians. Every night we can get, although right now we're all taking a couple of nights off and then starting final rehearsals for the new show."

"So maybe you wouldn't mind a little guy like me getting an upfront seat one night? From the looks of that dance floor, you girls really put on some number!"

"Oh yeah, this last one's been a big hit with our regulars, but it was hell on the stage." She smiled, a bit of self-pride giving life to her tired expression. "Once the new stage is put in, we'll start our new revue. Just send word backstage that you're in the house, and I'll have a place for you up front and close. Too bad you missed the last show, 'cause I'm going to miss that one. We literally tore up the stage with those dance numbers!"

"Really? What was the old show?"

"A Salute to Prohibition," she smiled brightly, obviously enjoying the irony of the show's subject matter. "For the finale, we all dressed up as Lady Justice, with swords in one hand and scales in the other. The balances were done up to look like two whisky barrels!"

"Sounds like a riot!" I nodded in satisfaction. "Thanks again, Glenda. You've been a big help. Enjoy breakfast."

She gave me a nod and then started down the sidewalk for home, her hips working like a pendulum with her dancer's derriere serving as a fine counterweight.

I took another bite of the croissant and looked into the bakery window. The old man was staring at me, but this time I didn't bother to go for the subtle glance away. I could see in his eyes exactly what I saw in the mirror this morning before I left my hovel. Strangely enough, we shared something in common. How ironic that the two of us were on opposite sides of this town and sharing parallel lives.

I wish I knew enough Italian to tell him, *"Brother, I know exactly how you feel. You and I are slaying the same dragon."*

If my hunch was right, I was about to enter the dragon's den tonight.

The cabbie was thrumming nervously against the side of his car door when I came around the corner. With a flash of my Lincoln, the cabbie gave a nod and drove up to the front of the bakery.

"I've been sitting here with the motor running," Driver #2347-5 grumbled over his shoulder, "and you know gas ain't cheap."

He was looking for an out, regardless of how much I was paying for his cab and his time. As I had said before, Sunday was a tougher day to get a hold of a cab. It was not impossible or out-of-the-ordinary, though, for a cab to be seen alongside the road with the motor running. He was probably a little nervous already when, out of all the establishments opening its door on an early Sunday morning, I chose to duck into an alleyway. Then I reappear outside a bakery opposite of the same alleyway? You didn't have to be as clever as a Wright Brother to know what I was up to.

I handed the cabbie my Lincoln. "Give me a little more of your valuable time, mac, and Lincoln will have some company. I hear Alex Hamilton is looking for a pal right now."

This cabbie already had two Lincolns in his pocket, and I was getting ready to throw in a ten. He would be sitting pretty after this fare, maybe even able to call it a day before the afternoon was done, provided the speakeasy's crew didn't catch us.

"Where to?" he said, putting the cab in gear.

"Around the block."

The cabbie turned around to look at me. "Say that again?"

"Around the block, and then we sit tight. You just wait on my word, and we move."

The cabbie nodded, still trying to noodle through what I was asking him to do. In a few minutes, we were back around the alleyway by 21st and Clarendon, but this time parked at the top of the block. We sat there with engine running, watching the front end of the white bakery truck sticking out of the speakeasy alleyway.

I could see an orc dressed all in white sitting in the driver's seat, sucking on a product of Phillip Morris, occasionally checking his watch as if he had to be somewhere soon. I'm sure if anyone were to ask, he was picking up a delivery for a Sunday night service or maybe a wedding celebration somewhere on the outskirts of town. If we were in a small town somewhere, this much activity on a Sunday would warrant lots of questions from the local law enforcement. That was one of the beauties of this shire. Even on the human's "day of rest," something was always going on in Chicago.

"How long are we sitting here, Shorty?"

"Until Abe, Alex, and I say so."

The cabbie turned around to eye me suspiciously. "Look, mac, where I dropped you off is under protection. Everyone knows that. I'm not going to cross Big Al. So either we go someplace other than here, or you get the hell out of my cab!"

Damn, I was hoping to avoid this. Guess I was going to have to change the rules on this poor mook.

"Okay, okay; let me make this worth your while." I pulled out a handkerchief from my coat pocket and opened it up to reveal a beautifully engraved gold coin wrapped up in it.

The cabbie was fighting to keep his deadpan, but I could see his pupils dilating in anticipation, his eyes squinting at its unexpected brilliance.

"Would this change your mind? It's worth a couple of Franklins. I need to keep an eye on that bakery truck, and if you help me with this, it's yours."

"Let me see it," he said gruffly. He took the coin in his hand, palming it to feel its weight. He flipped it over, trying with little success to read the various glyphs stamped into its smooth, polished surface. "It's heavy."

"Yeah," I nodded, my attention returning to the orc behind the wheel of the bakery truck. Unloading was taking longer than I expected. I wondered if there were any pals from Scotland or Ireland paying a visit, too. (Can't let the Canadians have all the fun.) The guy turned around again briefly, just checking the progress of his pals and the out-of-town guests. He was getting nervous. Any minute now, he was going to be underway whether the shipment was off completely or not. They were already pushing their luck because they were making this drop in broad daylight and on a Sunday. So far, no cops or Feds in sight.

Finally, I watched the goon reach under the steering wheel and start up his truck. It was time to go for a ride.

"Okay, cabbie," I said, "time to go."

"You bet, mac," he replied.

The bakery truck pulled out of the alleyway just as my driver got his cab in gear. We were about a half block away, playing second shadow to this truck that worked its way through the streets of Chicago.

"How am I doing?" My cabbie glanced in the rear-view window, trying to catch my reaction. "I'm not crowding him, am I?"

"You're doing okay. Keep this distance, and you should be fine."

I glanced for a moment at the cabbie and gave a heavy sigh. I'm not one for changing the rules like this, but I couldn't afford to lose this lead. Didn't make me feel any better playing the magic card (or coin, in this case) on this poor sap. The coin—a one-use-only charm engraved with each races' native tongue—was issued to all of us who assaulted the Black Orcs' keep on Death Mountain.

The humans had a name for a mineral that had suckered in a lot of "forty-niners" into thinking they struck the mother lode: "fool's gold." I called this trinket "the fool's gold coin" because it really wasn't gold, and it made people easy marks. My driver was now susceptible to my commands for a period of time, and once the spell wore off, he wouldn't remember a thing between taking the coin and snapping out of the trance later.

"All right, traffic's starting to thin out," I said as we neared the warehouse district. "You think you can give him a little more room?"

"Sure thing, pal."

Although I couldn't help but like this guy's hospitable disposition, the spell was unsettling nonetheless. It was a temporary, altered state of being, and it was that "altered" part that was making me more and more uncomfortable. In my world, there was a basic Law of Magic: The longer an exposure to a spell, the more unknown a spell's counter-effect would be. Magic of any kind tends to completely skew nature so that an individual's reactions become harder and more unpredictable than a cranky swamp serpent. This was the caution we were always given when the mages would impart their "gifts" to us in the form of a fool's gold coin, or even something like the Sword of Arannahs. In using magic, a chain of events is set into motion, and if you're not careful, you could quickly lose control of those events.

And then, you're truly screwed.

The cabbie started whistling cheerfully as we crossed over another pair of railroad tracks, behind us the skyscrapers of Chicago several city blocks away. The buildings around us now were short, squat buildings, large only in their width as opposed to their height. Far ahead of us, the bakery truck began to slow.

"Give him more room, cabbie," I said, placing a hand on his shoulder. "In fact, go on and stop here."

We pulled over to the curb and watched our bakery truck pass two more warehouses before stopping. Even though it was two in the afternoon, the truck suddenly turned on its headlamps, then off they went, and on again. One row up, a large warehouse opened its doors. The truck revved its engine and then disappeared in the gaping maw that slowly shut once the truck was safely inside.

"All right, cabbie. That's it," I said, opening the door and stepping out. "You can go home."

"You need any help with your bags, sir?"

I took a deep breath of the dockside air and felt my stomach roil. The smell of the docks always made me queasy.

"Nah, just give me a moment to get it out of the car, and then you can get out of here before things get ugly." I needed to chew on a bit of rubenna root, provided I still had some in my backpack. Best thing for a stomach that wasn't settling right. "This will only take a sec."

The cabbie began whistling once more. That hadn't bothered me when he was driving, but now with his window rolled down, I wasn't certain how well sound carried around here.

"Hey," I said around the open trunk, "you mind keeping the musical mouth concert to yourself?"

The cabbie glanced back at me apologetically. "Sorry, sir."

From the open boot came my trusted backpack of worn leather and suede. It didn't really go with the brown pinstripe I was wearing, but the backpack was not for making a fashion statement. The soft clinking of metal against metal from the weapons once hanging in the office reassured me that I was as prepared as I was going to be for whatever I might find here. I reached into one of the outside pockets of the haversack and found a collection of small, thin roots no longer than an elf's index finger.

I began to chew on the end of the rubenna root and smiled at the sugar-sweetness in it. In a few minutes, those butterflies in my stomach would settle.

I closed the trunk with a quiet thud. One last thing for me to do. "Okay, here's what you're going to do," I said to the cabbie. "Turn the car around and drive out to your favorite restaurant. Buy yourself a nice meal. Just relax. And when this spell wears off, I don't want you to worry about a thing. You've had a long day and lost track of time, okay?"

"Yeah, you're probably right." He suddenly gave a healthy yawn. "I've been working pretty hard lately."

"So go on. Treat yourself to a nice meal."

"Thanks, pal!" he smiled. "Can I do anything else for you?"

"Yeah," I nodded, holding out my bare hand. As the magic was in tune only with him, it couldn't do me any harm. "Give me that gold coin back."

"Sure." He reached into his pocket and dug out the fool's gold coin. It covered my palm and I was impressed at how quickly it had changed. The coin was lighter, and its original brilliant sheen now appeared dull in the intermittent sunlight.

"Did we settle on the fare, sir?" the driver asked.

I had promised him a Hamilton, but he was already several Lincolns in the black after picking me up this morning, waiting all afternoon, and then getting me out here. Did he really earn Alex's attention? I'd been hoping to keep that charm for later tonight. Looking at the tarnished piece of metal covering my small palm, I breathed heavily.

"Yeah," I said. "We're square."

"Good night, sir," he replied happily.

I watched the cab disappear back into the thicket of brownstones and skyscrapers, and then I cast a glance ten warehouses down to where the truck now kept safe harbor. It was still too early to poke my head in Capone's storage unit and take a look around. I had to wait until tonight. While it takes a serious pair of stones to bootleg in broad daylight, it wouldn't be the same for the Singing Sword. Tonight was going to be when everything went down.

Shoving the spent magic item into my pocket, I darted for the warehouse next to the one with the white truck. Thanks to the enchanted lock picks, I was on the other side of the door in two waves of a magic wand. This warehouse was nothing out of the ordinary. The smell of sawdust hung in the still air. It would have been nice if all the wood stored in this unit brought back the sights and sounds of sleeping in the unmarred groves of my own realm, but instead there was a sharp, sterile scent of cut wood. I chewed a bit more on the stick in my mouth, suckling a bit more of its sap.

I settled against the door I came in, glanced at my wristwatch, and waited.

CHAPTER FIFTEEN

HELL, HELL, THE GANG'S ALL HERE

So there I sat, my favorite tobacco offsetting this particular warehouse's sharp lumber smell. Twice, I needed to disappear into the shadows when a wide-shouldered, fedora-wearing silhouette stopped by to make certain the door was locked. No doubt it was Capone's boys checking to see if any of the neighbors were home.

As the sun began its descent, the ivory-white panes of frosted glass high above began to yellow. Yellow deepened into red, and the red cooled to indigo, until I was left with only the glow from my bowl illuminating my wristwatch. When even the weed in my pipe was nearing its end, my final drag produced enough amber light for me to glance at the time once more.

It was just past ten o'clock, and my hourglass of borrowed time had finished pouring.

When I opened the door a crack and peered outside, the docks were clear in both directions. Capone's warehouse was dark, save for the windows to the left (the back of it, if you were facing its front doors).

I stealthily closed in on its nearest side door, keeping an eye on its front to see if any thugs were out taking the night air. As it happened, I'd donned the brown pinstripe this morning, making it easy for me to slip in and out of the shadows unnoticed. (Gotta love that Apprentice's Luck while it lasts...)

Just when I reached the warehouse, I saw the door handle turn.

Had he not been chatting over his shoulder to what sounded like two others still inside, the orc in fine Italian duds would have caught me ducking behind an empty barrel. Closer to the waterfront now, I retrieved a fresh rubenna root from my pants pocket and bit down hard. I couldn't afford my gag reflex to give me up now.

That accomplished, I peered through the crack between my hiding place and the warehouse to see what this dink was up to. Hopefully, he would still be stationed outside the door and not casually pointing his piece at my skull.

As it happened, the goon didn't hear me breathing because he was breathing pretty heavily himself. His plump fingers fumbled for the final cigarette in his pack, crumpling the empty box and dropping it by his feet. The tiny flame of his match lit his double-chinned profile for a second. From the number of crumpled packs and flattened cigarette butts littering the pavement, it had been a long day for him and his pals, too.

Pow-pow-pow!

If the warehouse's acoustics hadn't amplified the sudden gunfire into a deafening roar, I'm sure "Fat Man" would have heard me jump. As it was, I doubt he would have noticed me anyway because the shots were soon followed by a thunderous Tommy gun's reply.

For a proud member of the big man's club, Fat Man moved fast. (I didn't even see him draw his piece.) The door was opened, and only a few seconds passed before two more shots exploded from inside. Then one more. Then, all I heard was silence…well, silence apart from a soft rattling that sounded like someone trying to reload a Tommy gun in the dark.

I dared to step out from my hiding place, giving myself some elbow room as I got my gear together. From my haversack came my charmed battle-axe. I spun it lightly in my hand, smiling in satisfaction at the light hum it made. Setting it down for a moment, I slipped two smaller throwing knives into the back of my belt. (They would have normally gone into boot sheaths, but as these loafers I was wearing weren't exactly calf-height, I had to improvise with where to keep these little gems.)

The windows flashed twice, closely followed by the sound of two more gunshots. This time, the Tommy didn't answer.

I picked up the battle-axe again, working the rubenna root from one end of my mouth to the other like a toothpick. My stomach was okay for now…provided you didn't count those damn butterflies that you feel right before the call of your regiment's ram-horn.

In his haste to re-enter the building, Fat Man had left the side door open. I gave it a push with the head of my axe and crept inside, keeping low (not too hard for a guy like me) with my choice weapon clasped in both hands.

Once I found cover in between two stacks of crates, I hazarded a quick glance around the corner. There was the first body—the driver, his white bakery disguise now stained with red. Pretty doubtful it was cherry-pie filling he had accidentally brushed up against. Whoever shot him got close. He didn't even have his heater out, so chances were good he knew his killer.

The hush was broken by the sounds of someone rummaging through wooden crates, and it seemed to be coming from somewhere further back in the warehouse. I homed in on the noise, choking up on my weapon as The Babe would when he stepped up to the plate. By the volume of the commotion, I didn't have to worry too much about being sneaky. Hell, the racket being made not only covered my movements, but also gave me lots of time to take in the carnage left behind by the gunfight.

Close by the dead deliveryman was a trail of bullet holes extending across several crate towers. Many of them were leaking salt or sugar, but some were leaking a strong-scented clear liquid: gin.

And there was gunfire in here?

At least, the dink on the Tommy gun had played it a lot smarter by holding his fire the second time. Perhaps he was planning to flush the shooter out in the open, away from anything remotely flammable. He knew what was in these crates, while his opponent was clueless.

Not a surprise. As I'd deduced by now that the shooter was blonde, I didn't expect her to think out this situation completely.

Creeping around the rows of crates toward the noise, I felt that goddamned *déjà vu* coming over me again. Only a few days after my last chat with Hammil, here I was in another friggin' warehouse. Just lovely.

Finally reaching the back of this place, I paused at the sight of another dead mobster, still gripping his Tommy. From the look on his face, he never knew someone was drawing a bead on him either. Next to the Tommy Gunner was Fat Man, a bullet between the eyes and a cigarette still lit between his lips.

Yep, this Little Miss was full of nasty surprises.

And here she was in yonder dimly lit corner, tearing through a second crate like a pack of wild *huffas* on a downed *grumbi* beast. From her total abandon, it was clear she didn't have the foggiest idea which one held the Sword of Arannahs. Her ignorance hardly deterred her desperation; she was ready to open up every crate in this warehouse until she found it.

A determined grunt escaped her as she pried off the top of the third crate. Just like the wooden lid now slamming against the floor, she was about to crack.

When the crate revealed its contents, her gasp reverberated throughout the warehouse. I heard the light tinkle of metal against metal as she pulled out a variety of stage prop swords from beneath the top layer of wood shavings, trying to get a better look at them in the dim lighting. One by one, the cheaply made, gaudily adorned props hit the wooden lid lying at her feet. The light tinkle of metal swelled into the sound of blade striking blade, filling our ears with the resounding tintinnabulation. (Maybe even the ears of the dead. The noise was that loud.)

I couldn't see a pistol in the small of her back or in an ankle holster. Neither was it lying about on any of the surrounding boxes. That left only one other place: concealed.

This could get tricky.

"You know something…" I ventured as the *clang* of the last sword strike died away, "I never thought a girl like you would lower herself into paying a visit to the docks."

She froze, one hand inside the crate and the other holding on to the box's open lip.

"You give a whole new meaning to *femme fatale*, you know that?" I remarked, still keeping my axe at the ready. Her gun had to be somewhere within reach. "Capone's boys do now, that's for sure."

The warehouse was so quiet now that I could hear the wood shavings settling inside the crate, along with the soft buzz from lights above our heads.

Then, her reply echoed around us. "They got in my way."

"They didn't get in your way," I scoffed. "They got in the way of your bul—."

Daphnie suddenly turned, her gun aimed low. This would have been the last case for ol' Billi Baddings had I left my axe on the wall of my office.

Like a sword in the hands of a knight on the battlefield (or a bat in the hands of my boy, Gabby), I swung the axe over my head in a sweeping arc and let fly. The axe's hum became a loud, high-pitched whine as it hurtled end over end toward Daphnie's pistol.

She never saw the axe coming, but she did see her .38 Special dropping to the floor...

...along with her right hand, still gripping it tightly.

Daphnie tried to scream, but nothing came out. In her eyes, there burned an incredible determination to somehow command her disembodied hand to pull the trigger. Then she sunk to her knees, giving way to a weak moan as the pain of her cauterized wound began to consume her like the flames around a keep under siege.

"Sorry, kid."

I don't know if I really *was* sorry, but I felt like it had to be said anyway. I took another sharp bite of rubenna as the stench of overcooked meat hit my nostrils.

I flipped over one of the already-sacked crates and slid it next to the one Daphnie had just rifled through. From the wooden creaks I heard escaping when I stepped up on the box's bottom, my newfound stepladder was working pretty hard. Maybe I ought to think about cutting back on Mick's chili specials...

Naaaaahhh.

"You shouldn't be playing with toys like this one," I chided Daphnie as I leaned into the open crate.

Powerful magic—the kind that doesn't come from charmed objects, like my axe—carries an electrical kind of smell, reminiscent of a mixture of hot copper and sulfur. The stronger the magic, the stronger the scent. The deeper I dug into this box, the more pungent the acrid fumes became, causing the hairs on the back of my neck to rise and my eyes to water.

Nestled at the bottom, concealed by straw and wood shavings until my hand pushed them away, was an ornate hilt that could have easily passed for one of the rejects cluttering up the warehouse floor...except this sword's handle was covered in dark, chocolate-brown leather that looked warm before you touched it. As I pulled the sword from the crate, the telltale ring of high-quality craftsmanship sounded clearly in my ears.

Yep, I thought I would never see this stupid ice pick again. (Not that I'd ever wanted to in the first place.) The Sword of Arannahs, along with its talisman brothers and sisters, had cost me my home and my life. Although I'd got a quick glance before chucking it into Oblivion, this was my first chance to get a really good look. The Ryerson sketch and photographs really didn't do it justice. From the intricate engravings along its wide blade and the bejeweled hilt and guard, the Sword appeared to weigh a ton, but actually felt light as a feather. This was not a weapon for the battlefield, but for ceremony; yet, its legend told of power unequalled by any army.

As the magic teeming inside the blade seemed to adjust itself to my own weight and strength, I began to understand why the races of my realm coveted this sword so badly. It was a beautiful piece—a magnificent broadsword that would not be denied in its power.

Clear your head, Baddings, I thought to myself. *You don't want to trigger anything you can't control.*

When handling magical doodads of any kind—weapons, pendants, clothing—a clear mind is always the best defense. Doesn't have to be crystal-clear, but clear enough so that the power of said enchanted item won't get triggered by a sudden powerful emotion or stray thought.

Back home, I remember one campaign where a particularly clueless human grabbed himself a cloak from a wizard's stronghold. Its scent really made my head turn. *"Something's in the stitching,"* I warned him.

"Maybe 'tis a charm to keep mine own person warm," he huffed in that namby-pamby, upper-crust voice of his. *"'Tis so drafty in this accursed realm."*

The next morning, we found "Sir Fancy Pants" dead, smothered in his sleep by—you guessed it—that damned cloak.

So, think about that blank memo pad, Baddings, I reminded myself. *Keep your head clear.*

As I hoisted the Sword, the blade's edge caught a glint from one of the warehouse lights suspended high above us, revealing the Elvish script more clearly.

Daphnie was in agony now, but she was far too pissed to reveal any kind of weakness. I had to hand it to her (no pun intended): The girl had a shitload of moxie.

"Believe me, sister," I told her, "you could lose a lot more than your hand with something like this in your life. Nothing's worth what this sword would cost you."

"You *freak!*" Guess the girl managed to call up some courage now. Must have been the anger keeping her from going into shock. "You don't know who you're messing with!"

"I got a pretty good idea," I replied, hopping off the crate with the Sword. "That's my job: figuring out who I'm messing with."

Resting against my axe's handle, I enjoyed a moment's pride. Through her wrist, and into the crate. Nice to know I still had the arm.

"But I don't buy for one second, Daphnie, that you know what *you're* messing with," I added, nodding at the Sword in my hand.

Daphnie's teeth gnashed as another wave of pain shot through her. Beads of sweat were forming across her brow and upper lip. "You think you got all the answers, don't you?"

"You're a smart girl, Daphnie. A numbers girl, absolutely. And from what I saw of Benny's digs, you definitely know how to trash a place. But masterminding a heist like this? Doubtful. Look…how about we have a chat before you pass out here and wake up in the hospital with Chicago's Finest changing your bedpan? I want to know who's calling the shots here."

Clickity-click-click.

Guess that was a really bad choice of words.

If I were back home, I would have sworn that sound coming from behind me was a marsh cricket, or perhaps an orc toddler breaking the hind legs of a pet dog so it wouldn't run away. However, in this world and in this profession, I instantly recognized that sound as the hammer of a.38 caliber pistol pulling back into a firing position.

I lifted my nose to take a few quick whiffs. A smile crossed my face. "That scent is really popular in your circles," I noted with a nod. "Bet the archeologists appreciate it, too."

"Do you really think I care?"

The warehouse echo distorted her voice. I guess she assumed I was like her...still in the dark.

"Maybe. A little." I turned toward the shadows where the voice came from. "Looks, after all, mean a lot to you."

"And what makes you say that?"

Daphnie now stared unblinking into the darkness, fighting to stay conscious. She must've really wanted to see me buy it before passing out. By the sudden paleness in her face, I could tell it was going to be any minute now.

"Looks do matter to you, toots. You really want to appear being the victim when you're actually the brains behind this little caper. Maybe not when you first saw the Sword, but after you figured out what it could do."

"And now that I figured it out, why don't you slowly walk forward, put it down by your feet, and then back away?"

I started to lower the Sword, but then paused as I heard her whisper *"Easy..."*. Once the talisman reached the floor, she took a few steps forward.

"Pretty strong stride you got there," I observed with a smirk as I slowly stood up.

"I was sore this morning, but nothing a little rest couldn't cure," she answered, stepping into the pool of light where Daphnie and I stood. My Lady Trouble shot a lewd smile at my crotch in memory of the night before. "Still won't take away anything from the wildest romp I've had in the sack for some time."

Glad I could deliver the goods to you, sweetheart. And to thank me, you're pointing the business end of a Roscoe at me? Thanks a hell of a lot.

"Julie, this prick's been on my case!" Daphnie growled as she pulled herself up to her knees. "He knew about the job, and I don't know how he figured out I was coming here tonight."

"Daphnie, he's a detective," Julie said flatly.

"Yeah, a detective *you* hired!" With another wince, she braced the stumped arm closer to her body. "I told you it was a bad idea from the start."

"Maybe, but he did find the Sword, didn't he?"

Daphnie paused, turning her attention back to me. Was she expecting me to answer for her? Don't look at me, you stupid tart. I just took your boss to bed for a good, hard *grundle'malk*.

Through her grimace of pain, I could just make out a glimmer of fear. She couldn't have been afraid of me. I wasn't the one with the gun.

"It's okay. Billi was everything I hoped he'd be," Julie smiled, giving me a wink. "I trust you in taking care of the numbers in our organization, Daph. When will you learn to trust me?"

"I *do* trust you, Jules," Daphnie replied, her voice wavering slightly. I saw her swallow hard, but there was something different about her demeanor now. She wasn't as defiant as earlier. Something was hitting the fan right now. "You *know* that! I just don't understand why we're creating more loose ends to tie up..."

"Billi here is a private investigator, so apart from his client, who else would he confide in? His secretary?"

Nothing is more uncouth than talking *around* someone. So what if they already considered me dead? It's just plain rude. Still, wasn't like I had much to say to either one of these harpies right now.

"Jules..." Daphnie revealed her wound with a sob. "He did this to me. He's just like the rest of them, just like you said..."

"I know, I know. We've got to take care of you, hon. I know who to take you to. She's someone I can trust."

"Okay," she sighed, sinking down a hint. "We just have to—" Yeah, there she goes. She was coming close to passing out. "We have to..."

"Shhh," Julie murmured soothingly. "Just let me take care of this loose end, okay?"

"Okay, okay...just make it qui—"

Julie pointed the barrel at Daphnie and pulled the trigger. The back of the flapper's head exploded, splattering her platinum-blonde hair and the nearby crates with splotches of deep red. After her head jerked back for an instant, she remained upright for what felt like an eternity. Her lips were moving slightly, but only a gurgle escaped. Then the unseen strings holding up this marionette were suddenly cut, and her body slumped to the floor.

"So was that for losing track of the Singing Sword," I asked, the talisman still within reach of my foot, "or for killing Benny Riletto prematurely and then trying to double-cross you?"

I knew that was going to impress the hell out her.

"You are very good, Billi." She nodded approvingly, still holding me at bay with the gun. "When I read in your notes this morning that you found her through Mario—a contact she denied ever meeting—I knew I needed to watch her closely from now on, because the Sword never made the transfer from her hands. Now, step away from the Sword, Billi. Nice and slow."

With a quick glance down at the Sword, I started putting some space between me and it, one small step at a time. "I won't lie to you…you almost had me convinced that Eva was the culprit. Because you two share the same wealth, the same social circles and even the same expensive scents, it would have been easy to jump to that conclusion."

Julie suddenly extended her arm to its full length. "I would prefer if you didn't get too close to that axe of yours," she said, pulling the hammer back once again.

Damn, she was on to me. I took my next steps much slower, putting more distance between me and my weapon.

"Of course," I went on, "Eva didn't help her own case when she claimed to be another girlfriend of Tony's who desperately wanted to understand why he was killed. And because she was the archeologist— and yes, I do use that term *loosely*—who found the Singing Sword, I'm thinking if I confirmed that Tony's death was in fact connected to the Sword, she would have her proof that it was somewhere in Chicago, and then it would become my mission to find it for her. How am I doin'?"

"Excellent work, Billi." Motioning me with her pistol for me to take a few more steps away from the Sword, she started moving toward it. "Go on."

"Judging from her lack of reaction to your family's impressive antique collection, I could see you were absolutely correct in your assessment of Eva Rothchild's archeological know-how. After all, if she *really* gave a troll's toss about the profession that keeps her a front-page favorite, she would have ratted you out to the cops for the little racket you and Hammil were running. No, publicity was Eva's one and only motive. Whether she found the Sword herself, or with a lot of uncredited help, all she wanted was to be recognized in Chicago for the adventurer that she claimed to be. For that to happen, she needed her find close by."

"Goddamn, Billi, you were worth every penny! Keep going."

"You even admitted that Eva wanted to be part of the gang, but I'd already gotten that impression after seeing a press picture taken of you, Tony, and Eva with the rest of the gang. You may not like Eva, but you kept her close. Maybe to see if she had what it took to join you."

Julie stopped at the Singing Sword, glanced at it, and then gave me an affirmative nod. "Eva was a bit of a disappointment, Billi. For what I was planning, I needed people I could trust."

I laughed. Something she didn't expect. "Trust? No, Julie, you needed people you could *control*. Benny was controllable. You knew that from nights spent on the town together. Daphnie's mutiny was a surprise, though, wasn't it?"

For a moment, albeit a brief one, Julie looked almost regretful. "She was incredible with numbers, Billi. While Tony was wrapping up business there early one morning, she and I talked, struck up a friendship…I believed that I had found an ally."

"Yeah, an ally featured in a show with dancers parodying Lady Justice. What better place to hide the Sword than in the epicenter of Chicago's underworld so that neither Capone, Moran, or even you would notice it under their noses? All the while you were searching, Daphnie was keeping the Sword safely stashed with the other props backstage at the speakeasy, making sure it never saw the light of day.

"Now, Benny feeling his oats…that one took a minute to figure out. This was probably where your own plan was in trouble. DeMayo—with a bit of encouragement from you, I'll venture a wizard's wager—wanted to keep the Sword for himself."

"He was ambitious, Tony DeMayo," Julie tipped her head back, the smile on her face one of victory and contentment. "I took creative license with my own findings on the Singing Sword, and convinced him to take what was going to be his eventually."

"A regular Lady MacBeth, you are."

She slowly replaced the hammer of her pistol, and I felt my own shoulders drop slightly.

"You were going to tell me how things started to fall apart," she said, lowering her pistol slightly. Not completely, though.

"Well, I don't doubt eliminating the bagmen was part of the original deal. But Tony getting hit at Sal's was the beginning of the end. When Benny confided in Daphnie his own plans for the Singing Sword, she planned to make him into a human quintain out of loyalty to you. Instead, she unlocked the power of the Singing Sword and used it to strike Benny off his own list. Along with attracting way too much attention for your liking, I'm sure you now suspected Daphnie of hanging on to the Sword for herself.

"When Tony was hit, you subsequently lost track of the Singing Sword's hiding place. Last you heard from Daphnie, Mario was going to deliver it to the speakeasy, but then never showed. Benny's untimely death popping up on the front page of Chicago's papers was your tip-off that the Sword was still in town. And then you panicked, because you didn't want Eva to know it was on the street. Just like your rival, you really didn't care about Tony DeMayo or the 'why' behind his death. You were relying on me to lead you to the Singing Sword, weren't you? If I found it for Eva, it would have granted her credibility. For you, it was the ticket to freedom you've always wanted."

Julie didn't answer that one. "So what was my big mistake? My perfume?"

"No, it was making coffee."

That threw her for a loop. "Making *coffee?*"

"In your note to me this morning, you said you made yourself a cup. Now as you surmised on our first meeting, I'm not from around these parts. To keep my feet rooted in some of my hometown talents, I labeled common things in my kitchen with Elvish script. To everyday people, it would appear like a series of squiggly lines and dots. It would be 'all Greek' to them," I mused with a knowing smile. "But to you, with a flair for the languages? Hardly a problem...especially since you had already seen this script before. My flour and salt containers—even the pepper-jar lid—still had a bit of dust on them. As you might have guessed, I tend to eat out often."

Julie let out a small sigh, shaking her head. "But only the coffee and sugar jars had been disturbed because I cracked the language engraved into the Singing Sword's blade," she recalled, letting out an appreciative chuckle in spite of herself. "Must have been the overwhelming satisfaction distracting me this morning."

Yeah, bitch. Flattery will get you everywhere.

"Yeah, Julie, that was your major slip-up." I gave my jacket a tug and straightened up to my full height, making sure she could take in all four-foot-one of me. "Although Daphnie seemed to think that calling on my services was your first mistake. I tend to agree."

Now that her gun had lowered completely, I could make a move for the axe. But I didn't trust my grace and agility to reach it in time, plus she was within arm's reach of the Sword, making me uncertain how to proceed.

"Daphnie isn't one to talk…anymore," she said with a cruel smirk. "There was a reason I wanted her working for me, but as I've told you before, I've never been a terrific judge of character. Tony, Daphnie, Eva…" she shook her head. "But sometimes I can accurately size someone up. Like you, for example."

Slipping her Saturday Night Special into her coat pocket, Julie took up the Sword in a double-handed grasp. The blade appeared to come alive at her touch, shining brighter than when I had handled it a few short minutes ago.

"Do you really believe I didn't know that you were a two-bit detective?" she said with a sneer. "A *tiny* one at that? I knew if a client like me walked through the door, you would go out of your way to please. And as soon as I saw the wall décor of your office, I knew you were uniquely qualified to help me find the Singing Sword.

"So you used me to get to the Sword…just like you used Tony, right?"

Julie's expression darkened, her grip tightening on the Sword's hilt. *"I* used Tony? You want to make *him* the victim here? Tony's no different from any man in this world. Tony used *me* to get inside the Ryerson. Benny was using *me* to get to the Singing Sword. Dr. Hammil used *me* to reach my father." She gave a harsh, sarcastic laugh. "My father. My father who kept me under his thumb, raising me under his watchful eye, sending me to college, grooming me to be the perfect wife for one of his young go-getters—"

"No one was holding a gun to your head, Julie. You could have left."

"Not with Henry Lesinger for a father. Even if I were to assume another name, he'd find me and bring me back to our Ivory Tower, just so he could get in the final say on my life. Why, Billi, why should I be the fugitive? I've *earned* my legacy," she spat. "I played the perfect daughter, even when Daddy put me up for auction to his lackeys. You can imagine my joy when I met Tony. Then…" Her voice trailed off as she turned her eyes to the Sword and raised it up, a prolonged ringing of metal sounding in the air as she did. "This will set things right."

As I watched her whip the weapon around her body in an advanced form, her swordsmanship didn't impress me as much as the accompanying chorus of notes that seemed to change in pitch and tone when she cut the air.

Funny. It didn't make much of a noise when I held it.

"Pretty impressive," I scoffed.

"I agree," Julie laughed gleefully. "I didn't know I could do this, either. I was right. The Sword and its wielder are symbiotic, provided the wielder is willing."

Symbiotic. Now there's a word you don't hear too often in my line of work. So keeping my head clear must've been the wrong strategy when handling the Sword, because it wouldn't have wanted an unwilling partner.

"So I take it your roll in the hay with me last night was just another ruse? Doing a little recon work to see what I knew about the Singing Sword?"

"And are you going to tell me you weren't using my business to finance your own effort to find it?"

Damn, she had me there.

"As for last night," she continued, "I was willing to make a sacrifice to get the information I needed, but you were definitely a surprise. You have talent, Billi. Talent that a girl should appreciate," she said, keeping her eyes fixed on the blade moving elegantly across her body, its humming growing louder as she stepped closer to me.

Then she paused for a moment in her form to look at me. The smile was surprisingly sincere.

"I'm sure I could find a place for you."

"Oh yeah," I huffed. "Every goddess should have a personal sex-dwarf on call."

The notes were still ringing in our ears as she finished her form with the weapon's tip stopping on my neck. "Now, Billi, how about we go for a walk? I'd like to talk about future plans with you."

"Future plans?" Somehow, I had to get to my battle-axe. It was only a few steps away, still embedded in the crate. It might as well be have been in New York, Miami, or Gryfennos for that matter! "What kind of future plans are we talking about?"

She was about to tell me when two pinstriped orcs stepped out of the shadows, Tommy Guns primed. I raised my hands while Julie lowered the Sword, a very dangerous smile forming on her face as a larger man, armed only with a fat stogie in his mouth and a cashmere coat across his forearm, stepped into the light.

"When nobody called ta tell me how deliv'ries was goin', I figyahed dat sumtin' was up. Maybe I should be a detective too, huh, Baddings?" He chuckled. "Hiya doin', Short Stuff?"

Capone smiled, casting a quick glance over his shoulder to assure himself his other two goons were close by in case things got dicey. "Side door was open, so me and da boys jus' came on in. I'm not interruptin', am I?"

"I never thought I would say this..." I looked to Julie and then back to Capone with a grin, "but am I glad to see you, Al!"

He didn't bother to reply. He was way too preoccupied eyeing up Julie as if she were a side of prime beef. He gave a puff on his thick cigar and glanced at his four gunmen with their Tommys on us. Then finally, a gruff laugh and a nod. Capone believed that all the runes favored him right now.

"Ya pretty easy on da eyes, sistah. Ya smart as y'are cute?"

The rubenna root was dry. Lousy timing, since the butterflies were kicking up again. Considering Julie's animosity to the male gender, it was probably not a smart idea to talk to her like she were some kind of tribute or spoil of war.

A quick look over at her confirmed my fears. Although her expression hadn't changed since Capone's arrival, I watched her fingers splay for a moment around the talisman's hilt. As Julie brought the blade up slightly, Capone's orcs braced their machine guns against themselves, their own fingers around the Tommy's vertical front grips mimicking Julie's.

"How 'bout ya hand ovah dat Singing Sword, sistah, an' I won' hafta make dis nasty?"

Julie tipped her head back, the smile widening across her face. "Oh, you want this?" She followed the blade from tip to tang with her eyes, then looked back at Capone with a light shrug. "All you needed to do, Mr. Capone, was ask."

I watched the Singing Sword fly in a graceful arc across the space between Julie and Capone. He easily caught it by the handle, looking surprised at how light it was. The Tommys were still trained on us, but Capone's boys were paying less attention to us and more on the Sword.

After passing his coat to one of the goons flanking him, Capone gave the Singing Sword a few awkward swings. He was known as something of a knife-fighter in his youth, or so the more-intrepid Chicago reporters asserted in their columns. Watching Capone handle the Sword gave those guys some validity, because it was obvious that Al was no swordsman. One moment, he wielded it like a baseball bat; another moment, it was a golf club. Capone seemed fascinated by the fact he wielded a sword lighter than his nine-iron.

Then I noticed that apart from the typical cutting of the air that swords will do, there were no accompanying tones. No ethereal voices. No haunting chords. Just the typical "*swoosh*" coming from a sword traveling through open space.

I was definitely thinking what nobody was saying: Capone looked like an idiot, swinging the blade around like a war hammer. Maybe his boys noticed it, too, but they were smart enough to stay quiet.

"So *dis* is what everyone's fussin' ovah, huh?" Capone lowered the blade and callously tapped his stogie against it, laughing as he followed the ashes to his feet. "Heh-hey, I guess I've found a use fa it!"

That was his boys' cue to join him in his merrymaking. Everyone was having a good laugh, except me and Julie.

"Are you finished?" Julie purred, extending her hand.

Capone's laugh suddenly broke into a scream so intense that it could have called the demons residing on Death Mountain. After watching him play with the Sword, he now struggled against some invisible opponent for its control. Capone was clearly losing this battle, but didn't surrender his hold. This little show made no sense. If he wanted the pain to stop, all he needed to do was let go of the damn sword.

The damn sword, it seemed, had other intentions.

Two gunmen continued to keep us at bay while Capone's bodyguards pulled against his arms. The scent of burning flesh was getting stronger, but still they couldn't pry his arms free.

His screams finally took the form of an intelligible sentence. *"Get dis fuckin' t'ing outta my hands!!!"*

I was in full support of that motion. Between Daphnie's and Capone's mishaps, the smell of charred flesh was making my upset stomach just plain mad!

"All you needed to do, Mr. Capone," Julie smiled coolly, giving her wrist a slight flick upward, "was ask."

The Sword ripped itself from Capone's grasp, throwing him to the ground as the prize vanished into the shadows above us. Smoke rose from his palms into the air, passing in and out the dim light of the warehouse before disappearing completely. The odor of seared flesh was so overpowering now that one of Capone's lackeys couldn't keep his tough exterior together.

It had to be tough tasting that lasagna dinner a second time.

Then, as the commotion grew quiet, we all heard it: a low, pulsating hum emanating from where Julia Lesinger stood.

The Singing Sword hung above her now, glowing through a thin silver fog that ebbed all around it. She opened her hand wider, and the Sword slipped toward her grasp. The closer the blade got to her, the louder the humming grew. Meanwhile, the fog—comprised of *pure* 150-

proof magic—took on the form of long, opaque tendrils that flowed and fluttered around the Sword and Julie. The tone swelled into a chorus that eventually peaked in its intensity, bursting the lights dangling high above our heads. Sparks fell on us like warm snowflakes, quickly disappearing in the near-darkness around us.

I say "near-darkness" because we were not immersed in total darkness. Julie and the Singing Sword were surrounded now by veils of energy and magic that made every hair on my body—and no doubt, on Capone's and his boys' as well—stand on end. Like a maestro before an orchestra, she lowered her other hand, and the talisman's song softened to a throbbing hum. Through the fog, her eyes appeared as inky black orbs similar to those of a shark—cold, emotionless, dead. She still had that heart-breaking beauty I saw underneath the pale streetlamp outside my flop. Only this time, the enchantress that stood over me on that cool Chicago Saturday night with her pale, cool attitude, now hovered a few feet further above me in the air as the magic of The Sword of Arannahs lifted her, her long black hair whipping around her head like a living shadow.

"Now then, Mr. Capone..." Julie spoke.

And I really wish she hadn't. The silky, sultry voice that once screamed my name in the throes of ecstasy had been swapped out with a collection of voices, each carrying a different pitch but speaking as one through Julie, a thick chorus of mages and witches long dead but remaining as echoes trapped in the Sword of Arannahs. Perhaps on forging this talisman, they sought immortality and found it by trapping what remained of their souls in the magic of this weapon. Now, the condemned spoke through Julie in a dark menagerie that mingled with her own voice.

"After watching you wield this elegant weapon as if it were a simple club..."

She released this sigh of delighted rapture, tipping her head to one side as she brought her free hand up to the Sword's grip.

"...let me show you the *proper* use of the Singing Sword."

Oh, shit.

At this point, my choices were to either get filled with lead from Capone's boys, or become a deep-fried dwarf courtesy of the Singing

Sword. I had absolutely nothing to lose. Spitting out the spent rubenna root, I bolted as fast as my little legs could carry me behind a tower of crates.

Just then, a sound rose like rolling thunder, and then *became* rolling thunder, shaking the thin walls of the warehouse. The Sword's blast shot through one of Capone's goons, the tower of crates behind him, and was eventually stopped by a support beam that buckled slightly, sending an eerie groan throughout the building. The gunman managed to let out a scream before succumbing to the intense energy that now poured out from his open mouth, eye sockets, and ears. He dropped the Tommy gun and, oddly enough, went to cover his ears, perhaps wanting to cut off the sound of his own unnatural death.

One twist of the blade later, the poor sap was ripped in two. No blood. No macabre display of anatomy. Everything inside of him had already been burnt to a crisp.

The remaining three guards looked at their fallen pal (both pieces of him), then to each other, and finally at Julie, who now looked them over one by one. They didn't need the order, but it came anyway.

"Whack da bitch!" Capone shouted.

I wish you hadn't said that, Al. That was gonna just make her mad.

As machine-gun fire tore through the warehouse, Julie merely repeated the basic exercise the Sword had taught her earlier. I couldn't tell if the bullets were being deflected or merely pausing in front of her—but, as she was still standing, it was safe to conclude they were not doing their job. I waited for the momentary pause in gunfire to move from one tower of crates to another. Regardless of what was going on around me, I had to get to my battle-axe.

Capone's boys were reloading, but not fast enough. Julie brought the Sword around, a bolt of energy extending like a bullwhip that sliced through two gunmen, both repeating the same gruesome death of their fallen brother.

Two guys at once. It was the angle from where Julie stood that made this magical trick shot of hers possible. Unfortunately, Julie's angle was also in line with a tower of crates all marked with a single red Canadian maple leaf.

I saw the last remaining gunman grab Capone and pull him into the nearby shelter of other wooden boxes. And that's when I made a dead-run for my trusty axe. I didn't concern myself with Julie, Capone, or any orc with a Tommy. My priority was getting my axe.

My fingers were already wrapped around the axe handle when the crates went up. The blade removed itself easily from the side of the crate as, in the same motion, I flipped myself into the open crate, silently praying it would be enough cover from the explosion that was moments away. The box slid from the sheer force of it, growing warmer by the second. Once the box stopped sliding, I leapt free of the flames and crept back into the shadows, battle-axe at the ready.

A bonfire now greedily consumed our corner of the warehouse, turning this place into a giant furnace with crates of Canadian whiskey as its fuel source. Remembering there was also gin somewhere in here, it would only be a matter of time before this chunk of the waterfront went up in a blaze of glory.

Standing out from the all-consuming fire was Julie Lesinger, still emitting the brilliant, ghost-white light of the Sword of Arannahs. I couldn't help but find it unsettling that this harbinger of doom was the same nimble minx I *grundle-malked* all last night Saturday and part of this morning.

"*Billllllllliiiiiiiii...*" she, along with her other voices, purred.

Okay, now *that* was unsettling!

"Billi, I could not have ascended to power without you. Because of you, I can now usher in a new order." And she held the Sword above her and trumpeted in her full voice—or *voices*—whatever you want to call it. "My order!"

"Glad I could oblige!" I shouted over the roaring fire. "But you've still got some payments outstanding, you know that?"

I could see flames licking against another tower of crates, their wood slowly turning black from the heat. Then I caught sight of little fire-trails along the sides of crates that had been pierced by early gunfire. Any minute now, it was going to be the Fourth of July in here.

"But Billi, your translation of the Singing Sword's blade needs work."

Excuse me? She's possessed by the spirits of dark mages and witches…and she's giving me a lesson in Elvish translation? You've got to be kidding me!

"In your notes, your translation read, '*Only the nature mild and gentle shall wield this blessed weapon.*' My translation reads differently: '*Only nature's gentle maid shall wield this weapon.*' Your Elders were right. Only a woman could unlock the power of the Sword of Arannahs!"

I guess that explained the lack of humming when Capone and I held it. On account of our equipment, the magic went dormant. My Elvish must have been rustier than I thought!

The light began to outshine the fire around her, leaving Julie as a dark cutout against the power building behind and around her. "For your service to us, you will be spared. You will serve us in the new order, and now shall the women rule under the guidance and awe of this blessed talisman!"

Now she was talking about herself in the plural. This situation just went from bad, to worse, to a day in the stables with a herd of diarrheic horses.

I fixed the grip on my axe, hoping that I was going to time this moment of sheer insanity right. What I was counting on was Julie's ignorance when it came to magic, charmed weapons, and where the two shall meet. When charmed weapons meet other charmed weapons in battle, magic could be shielded or deflected. It all depended on the execution and skill of those wielding said supernatural arsenal.

I wasn't looking for either. I just wanted to drive the Sword's magic back to its source as hard as I could.

Choking up on the handle once more, I emerged from my hiding place. "I got news for you, Julie and friends," I shouted over the flames and the Singing Sword's magic. "It's the bottom of the ninth, bases are loaded, and the Cubs need to come home!" I brought up my own weapon in challenge. "Batter up, bitch!"

With my regiment's guttural yell, I charged with the hopes that her defensive nature would kick in. It did. As she extended the Singing Sword, a shaft of pure destruction came barreling toward me.

That was when the flat of my battle-axe came around in a hard swing. Without the sorcery protecting it, my axe would have shattered like a plate-glass window struck by one of The Babe's grand slams. Instead, I made contact with the Singing Sword's magic. For a moment, I didn't see anything except a blinding white light. I felt myself floating in the air, and couldn't figure out how in the hell I was pulling off this levitation act. When my eyes finally stopped burning, I realized that it was the magnitude of the magic-on-magic blow that was hurling my little Dwarven self across the warehouse.

My "first flight" didn't last long. After slamming against a far metal wall with a hard "clang," both my axe and I fell to the concrete floor hard. (I don't think the axe felt it as much as I did!)

Now came the deafening roar of crates exploding from the heat, their contraband contents finally igniting into bombs of glass and flame. I covered myself with my arms, my only shield at that moment, as burning embers hit my skin and lightly covered parts of my back. But I was far away enough and low enough to avoid the blast's full force. My burning coat, which was cast off pretty damn quickly, didn't frighten me as much as the realization that there was *still more* alcohol in this warehouse.

I had to get out of here, but not empty-handed.

Going against the survival instincts, I moved toward the fire. The white mists of magic were no longer visible. Neither were Capone and his remaining royal guard. Smart guy, that Capone, unlike yours truly who was getting closer to the inferno. Regardless of how stupid it was, I crouched lower and paused. My gamble must have paid off, because the supernatural charge once lingering in the air was gone. Heat now distorted everything in front of me, and the air was quickly becoming harder to breathe.

Then, movement just ahead of me. I lifted up my battle-axe, the quick gesture earning me a quick, ethereal hum from my own blade.

Julie was still alive, but doubly marred by the explosion of alcohol and the magic literally turned against her. The once-pristine flesh I savored the night before was now either blackened, or torn to reveal glistening patches of crimson that caught the light of the surrounding flames. Every move, no matter how minute, caused her unconceivable anguish. But her eyes—eyes that were now normal again—were blind with determination. Her unscarred hand was not trying to remove the burning planks of wood from her body, or beat away the smoldering debris that fused the fabric of her fine Italian dress to her skin. Escape was no longer her priority.

With that good hand, she struggled to reach the Singing Sword, which emitted a light hum as her fingertips brushed its pommel.

She smiled as I approached, wincing slightly at the pain her expression caused. I bent down and picked up the Sword in my own hand. Apart from the ring it made when scraping lightly against the floor of the warehouse, the only music was coming from the fire around us. Its magic was not for me, and I was just fine with that.

"Billi," Julie grunted. The good hand now reached for my feet. Well, I think she was reaching for my feet. I was also hanging on to the Singing Sword. "Help me."

The front entrance was now cut off by a barrier of flame. So was the side door I originally came in. I turned back to where I landed after taking on Julie and her sword. The air was still fresh back there, sort of. If I couldn't reach an exit, I guess I'd have to make one.

I hadn't made it that far when I heard her again.

"Billi!" Julie screamed over the fire. "You can't just leave me here!"

I turned around to take one last look, lightly resting the flat of the Singing Sword on my shoulder.

"Watch me."

The look on her face was nice. Yeah, this is the way I wanted to remember her. Just like the way she was last night. Completely and totally screwed.

I don't know if she spent her last precious breaths screaming for me because I was too busy slicing away a section of the warehouse wall with my battle-axe. The indulgent good-bye to Julie Lesinger had cost me precious time; the smoke was getting to me, and I was already low to the ground. Right now, every breath mattered.

I was out of the warehouse in a blink of a sea serpent's eye. Hot damn, that nauseating waterfront air smelled delicious.

The sirens were announcing a strong cavalry of police and firefighters on the way. Can't say that I was surprised by their quick response time. If they weren't careful, especially with the volatile contents of this warehouse (and who knows what else is kept on the waterfront), they'd have a repeat of 1871 on their hands.

My mind kept returning to Julie, still trapped in the structure now beginning to buckle and collapse. There was a good possibility that maybe some people, the Lesinger family in particular, wouldn't mind another Chicago blaze. It might help cover up whatever was going to hit the papers tomorrow.

EPILOGUE
THREE COINS IN A FOUNTAIN

"And so," proclaimed a familiar voice with some of the power and entitlement drained out of it, "in honor of my daughter, Julia Yvette Lesinger, I give this statue to the city of Chicago."

The likeness made me smile.

Although it was only "life-sized," Lady Justice would still no doubt impress visitors to Chicago's courthouse. There were little details—especially in her face—that made her imposing, but still reassuring and accessible. Perhaps she would give hope to those searching for her, while others who had crossed her would finally feel regret or remorse. Whatever the case, this statue, just dedicated by Henry Lesinger, was destined to be another aesthetic jewel in the scepter of the Windy City.

While the resulting applause was polite, it lacked enthusiasm, doing little to dispel of the considerable tension in the air. Many in the crowd were questioning the sincerity of Lesinger's gesture. He had forked over a goodly number of Franklins to alter the statue at the last minute, pushing back its dedication for another month. (Didn't seem to bother the crews working on painting and restoring the courthouse, though.) The newspapers speculated that this statue was his last act of atonement for the sins of his daughter. Instead of appearing energetic and vivacious for a man of his years, he looked tired. He wasn't the same man I saw the night of the merger between his corporation and the Rothchild's.

A merger that never happened.

Once the fire was finally put out, the Warehouse District was still standing, *sans* one warehouse. There was some mild damage to the surrounding storage units, but nothing a little honest work couldn't fix. The cops and public eyes were hardly surprised at finding Tommy-armed thugs among the scorched debris, cooked to the consistency of extremely well-done steaks. When the clean-up crews discovered the bodies of two women, though, the flash bulbs twinkled brighter than a cauldron full of Elvish gems catching the morning sunlight. One of the female corpses, missing a hand and parts of her skull, was sensational enough. When the other charbroiled body was identified, however, respect for the dead took a flying leap off the pier as newshounds nipped at each other's ankles to get the best angle. In the end, *The Chicago Tribune* got the most graphic shot, and the first run sold out within hours.

If anyone else were exploited on the front page like that, folks in this town would have easily lost their appetites for their morning bagels, flapjacks, or Kellogg's Corn Flakes. The fact it was the "wild child" of one of Chicago's privileged changed the rules.

After enduring more than two weeks of sensational press on his daughter's fiery fate, Henry Lesinger re-emerged as quite the philanthropist, contributing to charitable organizations, various community projects, and—in some cases—just outright buying approval. He was determined to show that the apple that was Julie not only fell far from the Lesinger tree, but also managed to roll out of the orchard. His former enemy, the Ryerson, suddenly had more funding than it knew what to do with for staffing, guest speakers, and exhibits. Buses appeared in the slums to take kids to Wrigley Field for a Cubs game, all expenses paid by you-know-who. If a school needed new plumbing or supplies, Lesinger was making a list and buying everything twice. He also became a church's best friend, sponsoring repair work for stained-glass windows, stuffing the poor boxes, and even clocking in face time (and photo opportunities) at soup kitchens. He tended not to care whether the congregation was Baptist, Catholic or Jewish. (I guess he was trying to cover all his bases.)

In the frequent interviews he granted during his acts of kindness, he would comment on how important it was to "give back to the city that gave so much to him." A real turnaround from a guy who, if he didn't buy the little guy outright, would quash said little guy like a forest fairy under his financial thumb. He was so set on buying his way back into the good graces of high-society friends and working stiffs alike that he continued with this magnanimous behavior for a couple of months, all his gestures leading up to this: a final tribute to his daughter.

Problem was, no one really bought into his generosity because it was clear that he was more interested in shoring up his image rather than the community's. It was one thing for his offspring to hobnob with the Underworld, but for her to get caught running illicit business? That broke the highest of implicit commandments among the rich. As knights who dishonored their house were excommunicated in my world, so now were the Lesingers in this one. The social elite now tightened their circles, leaving the Lesingers on the outside. Then, the Rothchild merger hit the skids. Eventually, if Daddy Lesinger wanted to hang on to the house, the Rolls, and the yacht, the only choice he had was to dismantle his empire and sell it off…and I was willing to make a wizard's wager that Rothchild would place the first bid.

I made smiling Irish-eye contact with my boy, O'Malley, who on spotting me turned a darker shade of red than usual. He was probably wondering what the hell I was doing there and why I was grinning. The grin was for Lady Justice, a likeness of my dear Lady Trouble trapped forever in bronze.

Gently stroking one of the braids I'd put in my beard, I couldn't help but contemplate if the artist had somehow caught Julie's soul as well as her face, encasing it forever within this metal homage. Perhaps, on nights when the full moon shone through the courthouse's giant arch-window, Lady Justice's smile would widen and her eyes would turn black as orc blood as she surged to life, a bronze harbinger of darkness and evil.

A fun daydream, but far too close to what could have been.

Miranda, still clapping softly in response to some more of Lesinger's completely insincere comments, leaned toward me. "Billi, I still don't get what Miss Moneybags was doing in getting the mob involved with this Sword thingy in the first place. Since she was already connected with the Ryerson, why didn't she just nab it herself?"

"Julie was smart that way," I replied. "She knew that if she swiped it on her own, it would instantly be perceived as an inside job—and because of her volunteer status and her social association with DeMayo, she'd be right up there on the suspect list. Instead, Julie turned the mob association to her advantage by staying in the background during the heist and then looking duped afterward, thereby acquiring her cherished 'victim' status. Julie also relied on the mob for the dirty work because she needed time to build her own organization. Sadly, her new order started with Daphnie."

"You mean Julie Lesinger was building some kind of mammary mafia?" Miranda chortled. "Snobby ice-queen didn't ask *me* to be part of it!"

What a sense of humor on this girl!

"Well, you would have been the most trustworthy of her minions, I'm sure. It happened like this: Julie cleared a primrose path for Tony DeMayo by persuading him that this score would make him the new boss of Chicago. Then Julie practiced a bit of influence over Benny, a born follower, to talk Tony into eliminating the bagman network one bagman at a time. Once it got down to just the four of them—DeMayo, Julie, Benny, and Daphnie—holding on to the Sword wouldn't be much of a challenge. But then Benny began entertaining dreams of fencing the Singing Sword for himself. Big mistake."

"Double-crossing Julie, you mean?"

"Well, that…and ratting out DeMayo to Capone."

Miranda finally took her eyes off of the Lesinger statue to gape at me incredulously. "Benny ratted out DeMayo?"

"Like a true sewer-dweller! During our dinner together, Capone described this numbers guy he barely knew as a 'good soldier.' And when I'd caught up with Benny earlier, it was clear he knew he was sitting pretty. Think about it: This poor kid Mario had been in hiding ever since Tony's bad morning at Sal's, while Benny was walking around in broad daylight, calmly reading the morning paper and getting his shoes shined. Now that he had Capone off his back, Benny's path to the Sword was short and sweet because he was one of only three people who knew where it was. Charm Daphnie. Get Sword. Pop Mario. And leave Julie in the cold to deal with the fallout. That's why he was talking so big about taking over Chicago during what turned out to be our last chat. He really *did* think he was on to a sure thing."

I shuddered to think of a world under Benny's rule: A world lacking style, charm, and class, but overflowing with enough hair cream and dragon-piss-scented cologne for every man, woman, and child. Thank the Fates it was a world we would never see.

"But I still don't get why Julie hired a detective if she was already playing the mob," Miranda persisted. "And of all the detectives in Chicago, why *us*?"

"Why us?" I scoffed. "Because we're *good*, that's 'why us'!" I gave Miranda a wink. "But why hire a private dick? When Tony took to the Everlasting Fields, the Sword went underground, leaving Julie out in the cold. She needed a lead. I guarantee you she was probably asking every cheap-ass gumheel to take the case, but the bottom line was that no one wanted to even think about crossing Capone."

"So you're crazy enough to take on Big Al, huh?"

Back home, I stood toe-to-toe with trolls. Orcs. Giant swamp serpents. "I've dealt with worse."

With an exasperated huff, she turned her attention back to Lesinger, who now looked as if he would explode with regret over losing touch with his daughter, his precious angel who fell to earth in a blaze of glory.

Poor dink. For a moment, I felt sorry for him. Only for a moment. He would never know how much worse he could have suffered. He would never guess how deep the corruption of his daughter reached, a dark magic that couldn't be cleansed by any exorcism from any religion. Julie was gone. Best to let sleeping dragons lie.

Following the appropriate closing comments, the applause rallied for one last time, and then came the brilliant flashes of camera bulbs, capturing what might very well be Henry Lesinger's last public appearance.

"So Julia Lesinger wanted you to find this Singing Sword, huh?" Miranda mused as we walked through the dispersing crowd toward the new statue. "But you told me that it was Daphnie who had her mitts on it all the time. Why didn't that little flapper make her move when she had the chance?"

"Well, it wasn't that easy for ol' Daphnie," I said, looking up at Lady Justice and breathing a little easier. It worked. Didn't think I could pull it off, but it actually worked. "You remember how I explained to you how the Sword was...unique?"

Miranda nodded, her mouth twisting into a skeptical smirk.

"Well," I continued, "Daphnie unlocked the Sword's..."

Okay, Baddings, what's a better word to use here besides "magic?" Let's try this one.

"...potential. Problem was, she wasn't clever enough to figure out how she pulled it off. So, she kept Julie and me on a wild fox chase while she tried to tap into that potential again. And this time, *control* said potential."

"Do you think Julie knew what...what you believe the Sword could do?"

Thanks for that disclaimer, Miranda. You're not making this any easier.

"That's why Julie kept Dr. Hammil around," I explained. "Julie told me she liked to push the limitations of her position at the Ryerson. Translation: she had uncovered Hammil's secret title of Antiques Dealer to the Rich. She probably guaranteed his secrecy by threatening to go to the cops, the press—or worse—the Ryerson's Board of Trustees. From the look of the Lesinger collection, Julie was bringing home a few of the Ryerson's prize finds before they were tagged. When she made enough off of Hammil's racket, she could leave with her own tidy little nest egg and a note to Daddy saying his personal art collection was courtesy of the Ryerson, an establishment that he and his ego despised. He would have never seen it coming, and being surrounded by illegally obtained artifacts from a place that had proved his family was no better than country peasants might just have been enough of an embarrassment for him to let Julie live her own life.

"When Hammil dared to stand up to Julie and threaten her paltry volunteer position over tagging the Sword, that was her troll-sized clue that there was something special to it. For Hammil, the Sword was a ticket out of Chicago and out from under her thumb."

"How did Julie know this thing was some free ride to the good life?"

"Don't you know, Miranda?" I gave her a bright smile and looked up at the statue. The likeness was incredible. Julie would have approved. "Woman's intuition." That, and the Sword's magic calling to her and just about anyone else of a female persuasion. But I still wanted to avoid the whole magic issue with Miranda for now.

Miranda was about to say something else when she paused. Something about the statue caught her attention for a second. She then looked around at the people also stopping momentarily as they passed by it—primarily women appearing transfixed by the new monument.

"Let's get outta here, Billi," Miranda said nervously, the color suddenly drained from her face. "This thing is giving me the creeps."

Interesting. I didn't count on the Sword continuing to have that effect. "Sure thing."

We stepped out into the brisk, crisp day, taking a moment to let our eyes adjust as the afternoon sunlight reflected off the bright white steps of the courthouse. I never liked that about the government buildings here. The glare was tough on the eyes, especially when you spend a lot of time indoors for a statue dedication. I'm just that type of dwarf who likes to know where he is and what he is about to step into.

And had I known what I was about to step into, I would have waited inside.

"H-eeeeeeeyyyy, Baddings! Howya doin', Short Stuff?"

I don't know if Miranda meant to dig her hand into my shoulder like a falcon's talons into its prey, but her grip only tightened when Capone gave her the approving once-over. With a little wince, I gently patted her hand away. There was no reason for her to worry yet. This was just the next test to pass.

"Mr. Capone," I smiled. "What can I do for you?"

He shook his head and gave that gruff, gravelly laugh of his that made me acutely aware of how close Beatrice was to my breast. "You. Yooooouuuu...you are somethin', Baddings. You're a piece a' work, you y'are! When I heard datcha were still walkin' around, I couldn' believe it!"

"You and me both, Mr. Capone." I motioned to the gloves he wore, color-coordinated with his suit. "How are the hands?"

"Ah, it's still a pain in th' ass pickin' up t'ings, but th' doctahs say I'm healin' up all right. I still don' know what all dat was wit da Sword. I ain't nevah seen anyt'ing like dat befoah. I guess I won' evah see anyt'ing like dat again, seein' as I don't got it."

He held his hand up, the fingers slowly, stiffly opening up enough for one of his pinstriped orcs to place a stogie in his hold. As they cut and lit the cigar, he bent down toward me and lowered his voice. "Y'know, I heard dey found dat Lesinjah girl, th' dansuh, an' my boys, but dey nevah found da Singin' Sword."

"Ain't that something?" I returned in that same hushed manner. "You want to hire a detective to find it for you?"

Capone gave a few puffs on the cigar, the pleasantries now notably gone from his face. "D'ya t'ink I need a detective ta find it, or jus' find th' detective dat's got it?"

I had this urge to get in his face, but why should I? I was the one in control. "Are you sure you want to threaten me, Alphonse? Think about that night for just a sec, and take a good look at who's still standing afterward."

Capone's boys were only an order away from making us a public spectacle, but the Big Boss merely nodded, returning to his full height. He gave a slight grunt as he removed the cigar from his mouth slowly, pointing it at me as if it were a sixth finger. "Okay, Baddings. Okay. But I'll be watchin' yous," he said, still nodding. "Even if I ain't around, I'm watchin' yous."

"What? Taking a trip out of town, are we?"

He couldn't help but smile at the sparring partner who barely made it past his waistline in height. "Yeah. Headin' up t'Atlantic City. Business trip."

"Make sure you don't work too hard. Give yourself a break. Take in a movie or something."

"I might jus' do dat."

With the cigar back in his mouth and a nod to his boys, Capone turned to leave. "Stay outta trouble, Small Fry," he said over his shoulder.

"You, too, Al," I replied.

Not until Capone got into his car did Miranda finally speak. "Billi, what the hell do you think you're doing, talking to Al Capone like that?!?"

"Don't worry about it," I said, watching the King's chariot pull away.

"What do you mean 'Don't worry about it'? I think he just gave us plenty to worry about!"

"Miranda," I sighed. I saw where this was heading. "Capone was there when it all went down in the warehouse. He's seen the Singing Sword, and he knows what it can do. He also knows that after he scampered out of there like a panicked dungeon rat, no one else came out of that warehouse alive, save for one hard-ass dwarf." I gave her an assuring smile. "You think he's going to try and tangle with someone who could survive something like *that?*"

I saw the question forming in her eyes. The wait was killing me, and a strange relief washed over me when she finally asked.

"Billi, what the hell is this Singing Sword?"

"Come on, Miranda," I said, taking her hand in mine. "Let's go for a walk."

We were passing a fountain in Grant Park, a huge mother of artistic and engineering expression. I was afraid that I would have to raise my voice over the loud burble, but Miranda was hanging on my every word. I told her everything. About Acryonis. About Gryfennos. The dwarves, orcs, elves, dragons, and the mission to Death Mountain. It all came bubbling up to the surface, returned to the source, and then came bubbling back out again. (Guess the Buckingham Fountain and I had a lot in common this afternoon.)

From the way Miranda's eyes widened at my telling of what *really* happened the night Julie Lesinger bought the shire, I could tell that in some weird way, she was buying into it. Miranda was throwing me a killer curve ball the like of which would make Lefty Grove green with envy.

"And that, Miranda, is why Capone, the Feds, and Julie Lesinger all wanted the Sword of Aran—the Singing Sword—so bad. Capone now knows what Julie, Daphnie, and Benny took to the Lower Dungeons of Urlinon. He now knows its power, and that a little Scrappie got away with only a couple of scratches and bruises from something that only a select few in this realm—and far too many in Acryonis—know about."

"Wow, Billi, this is…"

Her voice trailed off. Poor kid was quickly approaching that wall folks hit when the brain can't think anymore. She kept looking around the fountain and back at the visible Chicago skyline. Finally, she said in a barely audible, uncertain tone, "Would you please get up here for a minute? I want to look you in the eye."

I knew that tone. It was one I'd heard from a couple of Dwarven heartbreakers just before the end of what I believed was a solid union between a man and a woman. It was that tone of vulnerability and disappointment. Because I had never heard this kind of voice from my girl Miranda before, I knew my confiding in her had turned out to be a good intention gone bad. Damn.

The afternoon breeze swept a couple of my thinner braids to one side while the main ones barely moved. I took a deep breath and looked right into Miranda's pretty peepers. Guess it was going to be time to look for a new secretary.

I shouldn't have started running down in my head the list of potential employment agencies. If I hadn't, I could have stopped her hand from giving me a hard shove in the chest.

It was a beautiful, clear day. I remember this because as I toppled back, I caught a glimpse of the brilliant blue sky, as crisp and clean as the water I landed into. Still chilly from this morning, it caressed me in all my cracks and crevices like a skilled tavern wench. Crying out underwater usually amounts to a mouthful of water and a lot of bubbles, and I didn't disappoint. Then my brain kicked in with, *"Hey, Baddings, you're wearing your best navy blue pinstripe and the shoes aren't too keen on water!"* That was what brought me back to the reality that I was fully dressed and doing the backstroke in Buckingham Fountain.

Now I was back on my feet, drowning out the fountain noise around me with the gush of water pouring out of my clothes. If it weren't for my best suit, the pigeons would have taken me for one of those cherub decorations that made great perches (or privies) as I slowly spit out the water in my mouth.

"*That* was for keeping secrets from me, Baddings!" Miranda snapped, her arms crossed tight across her chest. Even miffed to the degree of a battle-raged orc, she still somehow managed to be a cutie-pie. "Do it again, and I *will* quit. And I dare you to find anyone with looks and brains in a package like this!"

I put my hands on my hips and gave a good, hearty belly laugh. "Swear to the Fates, girl, if you didn't keep my office running so well…" I slowly worked my way to the edge of the fountain, my movement hindered by the wet clothing and my laughter. I must have looked absolutely absurd. (If you think a dwarf in a pinstripe is funny, picture the same dwarf soaked to the gills.)

I gave an exasperated sigh and looked up at my secretary. "I got to stop underestimating you, Miranda."

"That you do, Billi!" she snickered, but still with a hint of anger in her tone. "That you do!"

The stone of the Buckingham Fountain was warm, so I figured I'd let the afternoon sun bake me for a bit before we returned to the office. Miranda took a seat next to me, close enough that I could flick a small spray of water in her face from my fingertips. She chuckled, but then the smile melted away as she turned back to me. "Billi, if you don't have the Singing Sword and both Capone and the Feds are still looking for it, then where is it?"

I smiled with overwhelming satisfaction. "That is a story for another time. The less you know, the safer—"

"Billi…" she warned.

"Okay, okay." I held my hands up, hoping the submissive gesture would be enough to keep me out of Buckingham Fountain a second time. "I told you that Julie figured out only women could wield the Singing Sword, right?"

"Yeah." Her eyes grew wide. "You gave it to some woman you know?"

"Well, you could say I work for this woman."

"But aren't you worried that this dame will…you know…figure out how it works?"

"Nah. *This* lady has her hands full, what with holding scales in one hand, the Singing Sword in the other, and keeping an eye on the lowlifes who thought they could beat the rap."

Miranda had heard so much fantastic stuff from me this afternoon, I feared that this latest bit of trivia would make her head explode. "The Singing Sword…is in the new statue of Lady Justice?"

"I can't think of any lady worthier of wielding it," I declared, wringing out my jacket. "When I heard that Lesinger was holding up the dedication, I made some new friends at the studio where they were creating the old girl. Didn't cost me as much as I thought it would to make these new friends. The Singing Sword is impervious to damage because it's forged in magic, so we dipped the entire thing in bronze. Kinda turning the Sword into a metallic version of a chocolate-covered peanut. And as the artists were all guys, we didn't have to sweat the 'clear minds' issue. Once the bronze shell dried, they worked it into Lady Justice's grasp. We still had enough in the kitty to work in the wee-small hours of the morning when no one was around, and to keep these *arteests* quiet."

"So this sword everyone's looking for is going to be on the front page of tomorrow's *Tribune?*"

I laughed at Miranda's observation. "You're going to need an arc welder to get to it, provided you can identify it. Even the blade's engravings are hidden by the bronze. Julie wanted to wield the Sword of Arannahs, and she got her wish." I gave the jacket a sharp snap and shook my head. "If I hadn't deserved that shove in the fountain, the pressing of this suit would be coming out of your next paycheck!"

I was pouring out the water from my shoes when I looked up to Miranda, who appeared hypnotized by the building tops that pierced the cerulean blue backdrop.

"Go on," said the kind, soft voice that now caught our attention. It was a mother and her kid; the little tyke couldn't have been older than three. "Make a wish."

The child looked at the penny in his hand. He was probably thinking, *"But, Ma, this is a whole penny! Do you know how far I could go on this penny?"* He made a quick, sharp motion with his hand, and the *plunk* of the penny and its slow, languid voyage to the fathoms of the fountain brought a curious smile to his face.

The innocence of the moment brought a smile to Miranda's face as well. She silently pulled out a nickel, closed her eyes, and flipped it into Buckingham Fountain.

"What did you wish for, Miranda?"

She opened her eyes and smiled. "Now if I told you that, Billi, it wouldn't come true. Now would it?" She stared at the nickel's image warping under the cascade of ripples on the water's surface. "Actually, it was more of a prayer than a wish. For Julie Lesinger. I'm an old-fashioned Baptist, Billi, but I have never been a real believer in reaping what you sow. I mean, from what you were telling me, Julie got pushed too far by her father and that bookworm, Hammil. Doesn't she deserve some mercy? No one should die the way she did."

The way she died, I reflected, *or the way I let her die?*

"A question for the ages, Miranda. A question for the ages." I sighed, wringing out my socks. I figured I could change my shorts when we got back to the office. "If you love someone enough, will that guarantee they will turn out right? I've seen humans with real troll turds for parents wind up being the greatest of heroes, and I've seen the wealthiest and highest of nobility turn on themselves like a pack of rabid wolves delirious from hunger. Did I want Julie to meet her end like that? Hell, no. Did she bring it on herself? Well, maybe. Magic and the power it promises does strange things to people." I slipped back on my socks and shook my head. "Sometime I will have to share with you what I know about it. It's not a lot, but it's enough."

I slipped back into my shoes, still damp but dry enough to handle a walk back to the office where a fresh, dry change of clothes awaited me.

"Billi," Miranda said, a note of apprehension in her voice. "You said that these portals were conjured up by those magician types, right?"

"Yeah," I grunted. "Those necromancers were always pulling rabbits out of their hats or lightning bolts out of their asses. I tell you though, if Houdini were still alive, he'd have a fit trying to discredit them! It's always hard to discredit a wizard when you're missing your mouth, dealing with a third arm growing out of your back, or trying to adjust to your transformation into a patch of bog moss."

Miranda simply nodded. That's my girl. So accepting of things beyond the realm of the believable! "Well, okay, so you came through one of these portals along with the Singing Sword, right?"

"Right."

"So...*what else* do you think came with you?"

We just looked at one another. This was one of those times that I really wanted Miranda to have a severe moment of stupidity, but this was not to be one of those moments. I really didn't know what to tell her. My *World Book*. Me. And nine talismans, each infused with the same level of destructive power, and if brought together, possessing the ability to make The Great War look like a court jester's routine gone bad. One of these talismans turned up in Egypt, made its way to my back yard, and was now on permanent display in a Chicago courthouse. Another was stolen from the Smithsonian by some whacked-out European nationalists.

So where were the other seven?

And if that wasn't bad enough...what else, besides the talismans, had come through these random Portals of Oblivion?

Wizards. I just hate them.

I turned back to face Buckingham Fountain and pulled the fool's gold coin out of my pocket. I'd kept it with me since that night at the warehouse as a reminder. The coin, with its glyphs and runes carved into it, couldn't catch the light on account of there was no shine left in it to catch. A dead trinket, now surrendering to decay.

Still, it was a coin. And appropriate as it now shared a bond with one of the nine talismans of Acryonis. I closed my eyes, made a wish, and flipped the coin into the air.

My thumbnail striking it did manage to coax out of the coin a dull "*ting*" that continued to ring in my ear as it flew. I watched the metal disc flip again and again, its speed creating an illusion of a dozen coins all spinning as one in its little space. Then it struck the water with a hard, loud "*per-loup*" and a small spike of water shot upward for a moment, collapsing into a series of rings that extended from the point of the coin's entry. It floated down to the fountain's bottom with a gentle rocking motion, coming to rest among other coins that carried hopes and dreams.

And this realm doesn't believe in magic? Hardly.

"So," Miranda asked as she stood up, "what did you wish for?"

"If I t-t-told you, sweetie, then it w-w-wouldn't c-c-come t-t-true," I said through chattering teeth as a light breeze gave my water-soaked self an unexpected chill. "Trust me, Miranda, you'll want this one t-t-to."

"Okay, boss, we need to warm you up. How about a nice lunch special at Mick's...on me, since it's my fault you might catch your death of a cold?"

I hopped down from the fountain's lip. Nothing outside of a black *mennisha*-skin blanket could warm me up better. "Seeing as I just saved the city from a new age of darkness, I think I've earned it."

We headed over to Mick's. No doubt we'd have to tell the story behind how I got into Buckingham Fountain several times over for Mick and his lunch crew. If that was the penance I had to pay in keeping secrets from my girl, it was a penance I could handle.

So, we were one month ahead on the bills (would've been three if Julie had been able to make that Monday-morning meeting and I hadn't become a silent patron of sculptors), Miranda's salary covered, and I...well, I didn't need any fun for a while. I'd gotten plenty of that on this case one way or another, and all I needed now was a break. In fact, I was starting to find a new appreciation for the calmer, gentler days at Baddings Investigations. Besides, I couldn't help but reflect on what the Dwarven Elders would say to us soldier types when we were all itching for another fight after a war: *"Patience is also a virtue of the soldier. Remember, just because the dragon is slain does not mean its children are dead as well."*

Yeah, I figured I'd revel a bit in the slow time—maybe even catch a game at Wrigley Field—before the next hatchling came knocking on my office door.

About the Author

Referring to himself as "the accidental author," this professional actor's portrayal of Rafe Rafton led to his debut novel, *MOREVI: The Chronicles of Rafe & Askana* (penned with Miss Lisa Lee), a finalist for EPIC's Best Fantasy of 2003. Tee then appeared in Dragon Moon Press' *The Complete Guide to Writing Fantasy*, a finalist for ForeWord Magazine's 2003 Book of the Year award. While writing *Billibub Baddings*, he shared the editor's desk with Valerie Griswold-Ford for *The Complete Guide's* follow-up, *The Fantasy Writer's Companion*. In between chapters, he reviews movies for The Dragon Page Radio Talk Show.

With both *Billibub* and *The Companion* completed, Tee returns to Morevi with *Legacy of Morevi*, scheduled for a Summer 2005 release.